MANTRAP MOUNTAIN

By the same author:

Haginstorm Land, Book Guild Publishing, 2008

MANTRAP MOUNTAIN

Ken Baker

Book Guild Publishing
Sussex, England

First published in Great Britain in 2009 by
The Book Guild Ltd
Pavilion View
19 New Road
Brighton, BN1 1UF

Typesetting in Baskerville by
SetSystems Ltd, Saffron Walden, Essex

Printed in Great Britain by
Athenaeum Press Ltd, Gateshead

A catalogue record for this book is
available from the British Library

ISBN 978 1 84624 356 4

Prologue

Mountain ranges are nowadays visualized as making a slow but distinct encroachment upon the land masses, this characteristic being much too slow to be seen within a man's lifetime simply because such leisurely processes take millennia to witness. Only the young upheavals receive publicity, mainly for their sheer impact and spectacle. Not only are these volcanic eruptions frighteningly immediate and awesome, but they are also repeatable on the most uncertain of timeframes. The one saving grace of such activity is that it occurs only in certain well-defined locations and the interested spectator must travel to see the only natural pyrotechnic display that features a glowing mass of molten rock flung violently from the earth's crust. This aspect is normally less welcome to the humans living nearby, who would far rather have an extinct variety of volcano, and preferably one still viable for cultivating grapes. But only time will achieve their longing for the eventual dormant entity, because the newly formed compacted solid residue must first be subject to the processes of weather and many other kinds of decay.

Such processes allow for these and other immobile heaps of mountainous rock to eventually be riddled with holes for some other generation to explore. These later people might then be expected to reap handsome rewards, simply by scavenging through what remains of the original bulk, or failing that, make money from tourists by exhibiting natural marvels in solid rock. Their rewards are based purely upon chance, and decided well in advance, for the skeletal rock might have chosen diamonds; although equally the prize yielded up might be of excessively low value.

So it is no surprise to discover if there is any chance of valuable commodities being discovered, they will form an irresistible lure to adventurous souls of our community. Such are the ones that are quite prepared to seek their fortune in any old subterranean pore or artery. Avidly they set out to discover priceless gems; but even so are quite willing to plunder anything that nature's vast store-houses of treasure can offer, despite most valuables being protected by a hazardous proliferation of rock or some other danger such as flooding. But however much is sought, and however many there are that seek, there are bound to be both undiscovered rare mineral deposits, and many unique places hidden from our eyes.

Danger lurks along the many eroded highways. The mere tourist, in paying for the experience might fully expect to re-emerge with nothing more than a transient memory of this dark world and will very likely consider risks as non-existent in such time worn caves. Any thoughts beyond this are unlikely, for custom insists on trained guides who would of course avoid every known hazard.

Such beliefs are in the main well founded, in view of the many arrivals and departures of whole coach-loads at numerous caves. But perhaps for any solitary cave enterprise, say for example one in the Pyrenees, there must always remain a risk from human error. And once released into an extensive system of connecting caves, the mere tourist is all set to discover those unique places assuming he or she survives to do so.

1

The Cyclists

The Youth Hostel bed was uncomfortable. Hazel Gray, full of aches and pains from yesterday's cycling, lay awake. It was too early to get up, for today she was only getting up to a hired bike, a bike that would injure her delicate constitution even more than it had already. The early morning light didn't help her much either; she asked herself repeatedly, 'Why don't they use thicker curtains?'

The bed creaked and rocked as she turned over, her mind fully active: 'Maybe,' she told herself, 'I ought to have a plan of action. Yesterday was so bloody awful.' She lay wallowing in self-pity and fully immersed in the sheer misery of their trip. Angrily she turned in the bed as if doing so would detach her from the memory, but then the thoughts came back of how stupid she had been to come at all. Once more she rolled over: other figures in their beds shifted position. The plain fact was she had woken, and to lie here would only disturb them that much more.

Hazel washed and dressed, moving like a shadow that flitted over the creaking boards and then into the transferring of her possessions to the dining room. She could choose whatever she wanted from the Continental breakfast, but for now coffee would do until Terry arrived. Hazel scribbled a postcard for her mother in praise of travelling in such scenery, not that the countryside had grabbed her very much really. A quick dash to the postbox, and she was back spreading her map right across the table, for she was resolved to see where they were going. Terry was too enthusiastic by far and it would do her no good at all if he were allowed to make all of the decisions unchecked. She was not that enamoured of him anyway; he had just become conveniently available when Eileen fell for his mate. Their mutual friends, still in Lourdes, had been the ones with strong religious motivation and a decided

3

affinity was soon evident between them. Both she and Terry found themselves increasingly the odd ones out; left as company to one another and very soon seeking trips out of town.

The break came when they heard you could hire bikes at the station. Terry, she found, enthused about bicycles in much the same way that he enthused about those marvellous eagles, kites, and buzzards up on the mountains. And here of course he had found the right location for both. Once his narrow beam and those long legs were set in motion upon a bike he toiled tirelessly ahead of her – she hated him.

Mother was happy thinking she was with Eileen, but of course it was not Eileen, it was Terry, the fellow who had also been dumped by the romance, and likewise needed to rejoin the pair later in Lourdes. Was their common goal reason enough to drag oneself along on wheels, and seemingly always uphill?

'Is there a plate with butter pats on, under your map?'

The voice broke in upon rebellious thoughts. Hazel turned to see a fair-haired girl smiling at her. She hurriedly groped at a bump under her map and found a plate. Thanking Hazel, the girl reached between the rucksacks that were sitting upon her own table to take it, calling to her friend who was searching the food display, 'Over here, Sophie.' The clear English voice cut through the sparsely inhabited breakfast area. Sophie waved her hand, and started back. The girl at the table smiled at Hazel through the gap. 'I'm Edna, cycling like you are. We saw you arrive with your friend yesterday. It's all hilly, isn't it?' Then excitedly, before Hazel could reply to this, she added, 'We are leaving our bikes to do the Cirque de Gravanie by bus today.'

'I'd like to get Terry on a bus but I think he is wedded to his bike,' complained Hazel. 'It won't matter a bit that I'm raw from the saddle.' True, he had warned her off the wide one, but she wasn't mentioning that.

'Why don't you just cycle towards Lutz-St-Saveur and visit the caves?' The voice came from above Hazel's head. It was Sophie looking down and pointing to the map. 'It's here on the map,' her finger jabbed the paper. Hazel studied the map, feeling the chair behind grating into her back as Sophie sat down. Conversation buzzed, the two girls were exchanging gossip. Hazel kept her mind firmly focused on the map. They still had a long way to go and towards the mountains it would be more uphill. In fact today

4

especially there would be nothing but hills – the more she looked the less keen she felt.

'Hello, beautiful,' Terry's reedy voice intoned over her shoulder. 'Deciding our cycle route are you?'

Hazel roused herself from the map – well he had raised the subject himself, hadn't he! 'Terry, why not do it another way? There is a bus tour; we can do it in comfort.'

His face dropped as he sat down to fix her with his gaze, cup of coffee still poised in mid air, then exasperation gushed out of him as though he were a small boy. 'It will be hot – we will stop everywhere and then be rushed through the best bits just for their schedule! Besides that you won't get fresh air on a bus you know, it is so much better on the road!'

'Yesterday was all smoggy and uphill – I need a rest.' Hazel said it firmly and as finally as she could to underline the things that mattered. Not only was their arrival late last night, but also, still keyed up from road activity, Hazel had barely slept. She took her time explaining how she felt without seeing any sign of sympathy on his face, only a piggy, antagonistic look that suggested he was not going to give in.

'You are coming to the clean air of the mountains, and all that wildlife,' he exclaimed. Throwing back his head he flicked his mop of fair hair, dramatically fixing her with blue eyes as he smiled in preparation for delivering another commercial. Hazel lifted the map high and folded it deliberately the wrong way, the most she knew she could do to upset him; why argue? The face he pulled just as she obscured him, looked the same shape as the saddle he chose yesterday, sort of narrow and mean. No, she couldn't let him pursue the subject of eagles and kites again. 'Don't be surprised if I don't go far then,' she warned him.

'Oh you'll be all right, you see.' He got up and headed for the food table. Hazel made a face behind his back; all of this had been inevitable. She rose to join him as the two girls behind her called goodbye.

'Will we see you tonight?' queried Edna.

'I don't think so,' Hazel shrugged. 'Looks like the beastly bike's won!'

Breakfast completed, they headed for their pushbikes. Already the day had warmed, and the emptiness of both road and countryside near the hostel had Terry raring to go. He very soon fastened the saddlebags to their bicycles and sounded jubilant, 'We can break the back of it today, and have an easy ride tomorrow.' His lean six-foot frame towered over Hazel as she opened her bag again for some last-minute triviality. Terry flicked his hair back, watching idly as she dallied; then failing to hurry her he hunched his shoulders over the sturdy frame of the hire bike, testing the brakes by pushing with them on.

Hazel finished what she was doing and then waited willingly for him. Only too soon he was mounted, and moving off along the level stretch of road near the hostel. She followed, feeling her calf muscles pulling and aching dully within the first hundred yards, then even more so as they hit the first slope, after which most of yesterday's pains returned. The drag of her wide saddle chafed high up under her shorts, despite the skincare cream she had used so lavishly the night before. Terry, by contrast, looked set for the day; already his narrow bottom was bobbing up and down, and his long legs going like pistons. The distance between them increased. No, she was now quite decided – rushing did not feature in her horoscope today.

'I can still go back and join the girls,' she thought, stopping on the grass verge.

Terry was already on his way back, his face as black as thunder. 'What's wrong? We haven't even started yet.' He spoke loudly, still mounted and poised for a sprint start.

Hazel whinged. 'The wheel must be rubbing on the brake, its very heavy going.' She held the bike away from her, managing to look pathetic and even more of a novice than she had been yesterday.

Terry laid his own bike down and picked hers up, running it expertly by him. 'Brakes are all right. Try my bike for now – I'll soon tell you what's wrong!' He spent the next ten minutes adjusting his own saddle and handlebar height for her.

Whilst he was adjusting her bike to his own dimensions, Hazel was quickly upon the flat road, trying out her new steed. 'That's just right, I can reach the pedals,' she sounded enthusiastic, her voice gladdening his heart. But even before Terry had climbed on to the ladies' cycle frame, he felt a sense of despair – it was heavy like a truck. He turned towards the road, noting its performance, whereupon the back end heeled over, for despite having a stout frame it was far too top heavy. Hazel must have stuffed the saddlebag with everything she could get into it, he decided. Once upon the road, he was soon to make another discovery: the gears were set low, he reckoned one and a half turns of the pedal for every one of his own bike. Perhaps that was a good thing, in view of the weight, but no way would he sprint past Hazel as he really should – sort of leader fashion.

Hazel was already up the road, pleased to be in front and waving to her friends passing by inside a bus. She was looking eminently capable now, almost as if the bicycle was her own speciality.

Terry needed to overtake, if only to demonstrate that her bike was quite roadworthy, and so he began making up the lost ground. Hazel's back view was closer now and she was quite curvy, something he hadn't properly noticed before; but then the mousy brown hair flared out behind her, reminding him just how plain she was when viewed from the front. Hairdressers he thought were by and large sort of cute, but surely she wasn't, for none of her clothes were trendy. His sceptical gaze tried to penetrate and visualize the outline of elastic beneath her white fabric shorts, even her knickers had to be old-fashioned. His mate he knew had got the best one – proper bit of red-headed, high-voltage crackling that was.

The need to overtake was beginning to take second place. It was something to do with the leggy exertions in front, which reminded him of a preoccupation among the blokes at work who stood watching girls' legs as they went by – the appeal of a hitherto un-sampled experience fascinated him for several hundred yards. Terry imagined the disposition of everything she had balanced on that narrow saddle, and began to appreciate physical differences that explained her preference for a wide one – excitement throbbed through his veins. Oh crikey! Suddenly he was aware that his own seat was making him tender already. She had been silly over that perishing saddle; his mind returned to yesterday and her determination to choose for herself, which stopped him from inspecting the bike. He couldn't forgive that easily. Now she was reaping all of the benefits of his almost decent bike, whilst he was toting her chosen heavyweight, laden with an entire wardrobe. Conscious of the unnecessary work he was doing on the pedals, hatred simmered and completely erased female imaging from his mind.

Hazel signalled a right turn. 'Good God! Where is she going

now?' Terry looked at the road sign. 'Caves & Café' it declared. He was unable to do anything more decisive, so quickly followed her off the main road, swearing. Ahead there had been a steep hill; the reason for her action was not hard to see.

Hazel pulled up, and called over her shoulder, 'There ought to be a loo here somewhere.'

Terry groaned; any reminder that they had hardly started he knew would be totally unproductive. He followed her slowly, allowing more distance between them during the short ride to the caves, for there the road terminated in an empty car park. Terry decided that she could have her rotten bike back; but that only heralded a succeeding thought. He must offer to swap luggage with her – otherwise they would be going nowhere at all.

The toilets were straight ahead of them. Hazel stopped at a brick building constructed against the rock face and very close to the cave entrance. There was a heavy padlock and chain securing the toilet entrance. 'The shop,' cried Hazel scooting her bike towards the nearby dilapidated wooden building. Terry waited, and soon she emerged with a rough, elderly man who unlocked the chain, and slowly wended his way back to the shop with it. Hazel disappeared only for a very short while indeed, and beckoned to him upon reappearing; she had stopped short at a board displaying the opening times for the caves.

'Terry, now we are here, perhaps we should visit the caves?'

He pulled an agonized face, and threw up his hands. But Hazel was not to be thwarted by this. 'At the very least, we ought to buy something from the shop.'

Gritting his teeth, Terry walked with her, pushing his bike back to the café/shop. Once he passed the shop's unimaginative shed-like exterior, and found himself within, Terry was not a bit surprised to find the within was just as much a shed, apart from being unimaginatively equipped with tables and chairs. At the other end, forming a rear wall beyond the service counter, a stack of bottled spa water towered high over the elderly soul who sat reading a newspaper between the two.

Terry touched a warm, clear plastic box fixed to the counter, noting that inside were meat pies, and to the side of this a few plates of cream pastries buzzing with flies. 'Would you like to risk their botulism, or the salmonella specials?' he asked Hazel sarcastically, following this up with an inane chuckle.

8

'Quiet,' she whispered kicking him on the ankle. 'I'll have two cans of coke,' she said loudly. She had forsaken a prior resolution that she should use her imperfect French whenever confronted by an inhabitant, but she did so simply to point out to Terry that the man was very well up on his English. They emerged from the dark interior into the comparative extremes of heat and brilliant sunlight, holding cans that were anything but cold. Behind the café flourished a wide apron of scrubland, terminating where the grey rock, interspersed with patchy grass, rose to the mountain. They pushed their bikes into a thicket, and fell down upon the ridge of a long oval hollow, where the sand and grass looked soft enough, to drink their cans of tepid liquid.

Hazel unbuttoned her blouse and stretched herself out in the sun, reclining drowsily inside the grassy lip of their small hollow, basking in the warmth and wondering how long she dare prolong the rest. Through near closed eyes she could see Terry looking across the curve in the hollow towards her in an interested manner, one that sent a thrill tingling its way right through to her toes. He was not thinking of his precious raptors, or wanting to move just now, for he was definitely viewing her. Hazel lay without moving a muscle, her mind running over an inventory of how delightful she must look to him and then, convinced that she was a beauty of the first order, changed her pose to something a little more compact, feminine and tasteful. She relaxed there awhile, just relishing the sun before allowing herself to open her eyes. He had not moved one jot; he sat that short distance away staring fixedly at her breasts. The jolt from this realization hit her hard; far from the gentlemanly pursuit of her imagination, he was wallowing in a lust entirely of his own making. Hazel pulled her blouse rapidly together over her bra and buttoned it up. She sat bolt upright and stared at him belligerently – he was a right weirdo. Then, feeling properly attired and offended, her astonishment moved rapidly through derision into a severe expression of disgust.

Hazel's sudden reaction could not pass unnoticed and Terry rapidly became red about the face; not only was he caught out, but lost for words. 'It was just something I wanted . . . was curious about.' His words mumbled disjointedly; saying them being more a cover for his own embarrassment, whilst his face continued on towards beetroot red.

9

Hazel relaxed, but still gave him hostile looks. It was quite obvious whatever he was trying to say was stupid; an apology would be more appropriate. This phase she felt was hers and ought to be handled with severity. 'What are you trying to say?' Hazel's voice was hard and challenging. There was much mileage to be made, as well as point scoring that promised to favour her in any subsequent dialogue.

'It was the bra I was looking at; does it have hard pips built into it? You know, those fabric bobbles in the cloth?' He was regaining composure; but not daring to breathe the word 'nipple'.

From what she knew of him, Hazel estimated he was perhaps a year or two younger than herself, which made him about eighteen – boys of that age could be stupid and dumb. She maintained an indifferent composure; let him have to find an answer more detailed than that.

Terry was struggling with words again; a self-conscious voice that tailed off. 'What I mean is, it's all stiff material, and if they make dents in it to look natural, they need to be in the right place. Or does it just all just fall into the right pl . . . ? Sort of . . . er . . .'

She knew he was beginning to wish he hadn't started – well that was a better tack than the buzzards, and the dubious joys of getting back on the bike. 'Haven't you got a girlfriend,' she asked, realizing that his embarrassment could be prolonged that much more.

'No, I play football for the local club.' Terry was conscious of an instant withering look, but continued, hoping to stay her anger. 'They say I could turn pro if I stick at it. Football and girls don't mix, you know. It's just I'm curious about the way things are designed.'

'You'd better contain your designing, until you start kissing girls. And right now I'd prefer you to be on this side of the hollow.' Hazel was still wary of being subjected to indecent ogling, and did her best to sound cross. Then much to her satisfaction the response was immediate; he came over and lay down close by. Even while they had been talking, the hot sun had been increasing Hazel's desire to drowse. She laid her head back; it was only too easy to nod off after such a rotten night's sleep. A short way off, Terry fidgeted, his wakefulness apparent every time she raised her head. Each look reinforced the last, giving an impression of strained inaction. He was all ready to bounce back and threaten her rest – subconsciously she awaited the words 'let's go'. It was something that must be overdue, and only stopped by him feeling a fool from that last episode.

A shadow crept over her face, she felt his breath coming and going before he kissed her. The kiss had to be the culmination of extreme boredom, and nothing at all flattering to her, that she knew. Hazel contained the protest that was welling up. He kissed again; against lips that simply stayed shut, soft and pliable maybe, but certainly nothing at all that yielded. She just lay there feigning sleep with lips like putty. This was good, he would get tired. She allowed herself to drift and verge upon sleep. Kisses pecked at her face, immature kisses. 'That's what he is, immature,' she entertained a dreamlike thought, tolerating the nuisance. The kisses kept coming, and very soon hands began to stroke the surface of her blouse. He was very gentle, so gentle the pleasant drift extended. Hazel was only just aware of a hand caressing her bare midriff; this she could relax upon and doze. But once up under the blouse the hand gently smoothed its way under the bra and she was surfacing fast. His fingers brushed its material and a forefinger began circling the protuberance, triumphantly tweaking hardening tissue. He had found an answer to his own query. Hazel, moved by the strength of sensation, briefly cuddled into him putting those irritating hands out of distance; but then averse to the shade that this entailed, she roused herself to deliver more tense words. 'Why don't you go and put the bikes to rights again?'

His long frame retreated, and soon she heard the tinkle of metal parts mingling with the feathered songsters, the ones more able to lull her back to sleep. He was just a big schoolboy really. She dismissed him from her mind and let her heavy eyelids droop. The time for a drowse had barely got its act together before Hazel was dreamily aware of his touch. Terry was close again, blowing his breath softly through the material over a breast. She played possum, part wakeful, her body aroused and tuned to every move.

Terry's weight shifted, he started leaning across to balance up the steaming action of his breath upon the other side, and as a hand rested flat upon her abdomen as part support, fingers slowly slipped lower almost by accident, under shorts, under pants, to where they dug into pubic hair.

Hazel slapped his face, only half connecting, as her dormant head rose in protest. 'Keep out – why can't you just behave yourself?'

11

Terry's face moved in very close to hers, pushing her head back with kisses until she was quite flat again, whilst hands reclaimed the midriff region but very gently.

Slipping a button upon her shorts, Hazel compromised, and was soon leading a captive hand back to bear upon the fine weave of her panties. Having made a territorial move that he would understand, she relaxed enjoying the sensations whilst again drowsing in the hot sun. Waves of erotic sensation soon put her beyond sleep, or even a pretend one. Hazel's back curved until it was parting with the sand, and she grabbed him to her, extending his kiss with her tongue and working upon it to excite with consummate skill. His hands retreated as they cuddled close, and thereafter Hazel's 'French kissing' lesson was much blunted by inexperienced responses. Nothing now stopped her sleepy frame from drifting towards sleep in his arms, her comfort temporarily much enhanced.

Hazel awoke to find she was alone in the hollow. Her head turned abruptly to see two bikes in the thicket, and she was much relieved to see he was still around; her spirits rose. She was awake, really awake, perhaps for the first time today. Where was he? Maybe having just a Barbie doll for company all this while had sent him off adventuring, for certainly the tools scattered around showed boredom with the job. She pondered on her responses, finding that he intrigued her, or was she just taken by his sheer naivety? Eileen's man was suave, and had charm: by comparison Terry was very much a juvenile trainee works electrician – oh so tame!

The sun shone well over its zenith, there would be no hope of reaching the next hostel now. But going back meant seeing Edna and Sophie, who would be interested in how they had passed the day. 'The caves, yes, we must visit the caves.' Hazel crossed to the bikes and tripped over the tools; Terry had only serviced his own bike. Her saddlebag was detached and lay upon open ground – how like him! Hazel moved speedily, he could return at any moment, and if it were to be the caves then she would need to dress warmly.

The contents of her saddlebag rained down as she inverted it over a patch of grass. The largest bulk was her Puffa raincoat; this she swooped to retrieve, laying it upon the grassy verge. The Puffa she liked, as its aluminium-based material reflected much sunlight

12

in hot weather, and an expanded lining resisted temperature change, ensuring she stayed cool and dry; but now she would use it in there to stay warm. There were three woollies, one of which she threw over her head. Hazel's foot scraped the pile; no slacks, her economy packing had left them in Lourdes. The nearest heavyweight was a roll-on skirt, short and effective. Pity that where the skirt stopped her shorts carried on, so speedily she swapped them for a good thickness of panties. When it came to shoes, none were as suitable as the ones she had on; Hazel kicked them all to one side. From what remained she separated a small handbag. Pausing with a wallet that was clearly too big before rejecting it, she chose the pot of skin food instead and followed that with a clean handkerchief. Her wallet/passport was tumbled back into the saddlebag with the other discards. She closed the lid and thrust the bag low in the undergrowth near her bike. There, shining up at her, was a small scuffed silver package. He was coming – she picked the shape from the grass and put it into her handbag. Yes, there he was, bearing two ice creams and more coke.

Even before he arrived Terry was eyeing her and looking upwards at the sun, communicating with looks that her warm attire was crazy. 'I can eat them both if you are cold,' he teased, looking down on her from the grassy bank, his hair all awry and perspiration running down his face. Hazel laughed, and took the cornet-shaped ice from him; at last they had something, even if it wasn't strictly solids. He had more food in his pockets, several chocolate-covered biscuit bars and most of these had already melted in his skimpy linings. 'There was a young chap minding the shop, he was a sight more help than his dad.' Terry chuckled to himself at getting in another gibe at the old man. For one who had simply marked time all day, Terry was in very good spirits. It was a relief to eat something, even if it wasn't much. They stuffed their mouths with the sort of things they would not normally consider as a meal.

'We are going to visit the caves,' said Hazel between bites. 'Otherwise we have done nothing'

'I don't mind taking a look,' he agreed at length. 'There's two coaches parked down there, but I think that the people from them have all entered the caves.'

From his tone Hazel deduced that he wasn't keen. It was hot; the unwrapped biscuits were awash with molten chocolate, and having lost much appeal, were washed down with coke – this time

13

it was cold. Terry pushed a face deliberately left smeary with chocolate at her: Hazel giggled, fast retreating, but overbalanced, rolling them both unexpectedly down the slope. They dug into the sand at the bottom, faces pressed together kissing. Sand stuck, waiting to get in, so it had to be a long kiss – this was more Hazel's element. Her choice of clothes, too, had left kissing the only option, confounding his every other intention – kissing went on like some marathon love-in. The sun beat mercilessly down on Hazel inside her warm clothing, but she had worked herself up into an almost hypnotic state, where nothing except emotions counted.

They parted momentarily: Terry spluttered on sand and the spell was broken. Time had passed; the sun was decidedly low. Hazel looked at her watch urgently. 'Terry, I'm going over to see if we can make the last tour – better get some warm clothes on, it can be chilly in those places.' She grabbed her Puffa raincoat and ran over towards the parking apron, where a single coach stood very near the opening, almost butting on to the queue that was protruding from the caves entrance. They must be going in, she thought, because there's not a coach-load standing outside. She hurried into the toilet, and was out very shortly, to find Terry last upon the queue's tail end. He stood there wrapped in cycle cape, head bobbing about in all directions, evidently looking for her; a smile appeared when his eye alighted on her.

'Crikey, it's so slow there must be a cretin on the money,' he chuckled. The woman in front of him turned, winced at him, and turned away again.

'Careful,' said Hazel cuddling up to him. 'Everyone you meet seems to know you already.'

The queue trickled in until they reached the ticket kiosk, where Terry found he had the wrong money and fumbled about in all his pockets.

'You didn't say which side of the counter the cretin was,' Hazel laughed at him. But that was the signal to be smothered, as they reached the cave side of the turnstile. For as soon as Hazel emerged inside, she found herself peering up in extra dark, completely enclosed within the orbit of his cycle cape and wrapped securely there by long arms. Underneath the cape, the consequence of travelling light was abundantly evident to her. Only one of his fluffier shirts kept Hazel off a bare chest.

14

2

Intrusion

In a cosy microcosm of their own, Hazel and Terry stood together amid the party; the first of many stops for the cycle cape. But crowds move on, and their common outer wrap only ensured them further standing places at the rear. Preoccupied with one another, neither found much interest in what the guide had to say, or bothered that the acoustics distorted every word – they were present simply to claim later, 'that's what we did'. Feeling more at ease now, both stood with arms comfortably clasped about the other's waist. Hazel blended inconspicuously, her Puffa fully covered by Terry's traffic-stained yellow cape, and hidden from direct view she cuddled up to his long frame.

Hazel saw very little, and heard even less, but she was aware of the crowd about her and knew when its shadow cleared the floor. Terry, she deduced, had started looking at the well with a view unimpeded, and quite unaware of any curiosity she might feel was apparently ready to move off. Hazel's hand swept up into his shirt, not wanting movement as yet, just the desire to hold him back whilst she looked. No, he couldn't move at all now – not whilst she stood firm and was anyway trekking her fingers ever so lightly across his back. Terry's whole body changed its stance, tuning in to Hazel who knew she had him hooked with her little pleasurable touches; but having pushed out of her cocoon to see what could only be described as an anti-climax, she was back, drawing the yellow waterproof curtains for more amorous stuff. She warmed to making him wait and guess, where and what she might touch next.

The grating of heavy rocks first disturbed and then brought Hazel to a stop. She peeped out to see a heavy giant of a man close by them dismantling the well, and making peculiar cries as he did so. Terry too, was jerked out of a stupor and made a hasty move along the path previously taken by the party.

15

The crowd was close to the other end of a short tunnel, and streaming away from a brightly lit grotto that contained a sculpted 'Madonna and Child'. Hazel veered towards it, attracted simply by the spectacle, but Terry jerked her onwards to catch up with the party as it filtered through into a much larger cave. Set in this great cave was a raised wooden stage, with numerous barrels set about it and each one bearing a white candle; self-evidently for use as tables. Their guide stood on the platform addressing them as an entire group. As latecomers they joined the crowd and listened properly for the first time. Hazel stood in front of Terry with his cape framing her head, and at last they both attended to the guide who was entertaining as well as audible in here. As the party prepared to move on, Hazel's arm circled her tent support to find his rear pocket and with this as sufficient to link them together, they stayed on the tail end following the party over a rough narrow downhill walk among sulphurous smells. They were still hooked up in this way when they arrived at the next cave – it was dark, but UV lights picked out everyone in an odd, almost subdued, brilliance.

The couple instantly reverted, with Hazel pursuing her French kissing in the dark, and such undercover delights meant that the party could go to hell if it wanted. But after a while the realms of sheer pleasure faded, much as did the unnatural tints marking out the position of the lights up above which were now fading. Slowly it dawned upon them that the lights had been switched off, and that they were probably left behind; recognition of this possibility started a panic move towards the entrance. There came very briefly a flash of yellow light as a figure strode past. Hazel was elated at how clever their timing must have been, nobody could have missed them. A disorganized throng was passing and the sound of so many agitated voices was truly alarming; this very soon dispelled Hazel's smugness. There was something wrong going on here, causing her to remain anxious until they had caught the main group. As they tagged on again, her curiosity mounted as to what could possibly be exciting them – surely the guide only carried a brand because the lights so often went on the blink?

The party streamed up the main exit route and into the large cave where the barrels were, with Terry being more competitive now. Georges the guide had hurried on ahead, and mounted the slope that rose to the entrance. The crowd fanned out, impeded by the bottleneck where the tunnel began; all of them intent on

16

staying close to their guide. Hazel was relieved now that they were safe among people, and what's more in a position not too far from the exit. She dragged her feet and slewed around in the spare length of cape, neatly arresting Terry; they were once more at the tail end of the party and positioned for 'just that extra kiss'.

The tunnel in front of them emptied completely and the noises coming through it were vaguely disturbing, especially the ratchet of the turnstiles going hell for leather every so often. Stumbling forwards with their tandem attire doing its best to hinder, they hurried up the empty slope, only to find that the entrance gate was being dragged across. Barring the way just ahead of them, and shouting aggressively out through the gate, was the bulky madman, a man who she knew had brute strength enough to dismantle a stone well – and that was when he was calm! Hazel backpedalled Terry towards the rear end of the entrance hall, where she promptly caught her heel on a step. Overbalancing, she sat down hard on it. The tug almost brought Terry down too, but realizing there were stairs behind her she continued pulling him into its recess.

Terry was strangely reluctant. 'Look, he's hurt.'

'Don't be daft, Terry, why'd you think they shut him in!'

Hazel released the cape, moved in front and began towing Terry up the dark stairway. The stairs continued round in a spiral, rather like an old church tower but terminating in a heavy wooden door. The door opened easily when they pushed at it, and beyond was dark to a greater extent than the stairway. Hazel immediately collided with a sort of bench, but that was before Terry discovered the light switch and turned the lights on. Instantly the room was revealed as a tiny office just wide enough for desk and chair. Hazel grabbed for the door to shut it, but was much surprised when the light went out before she was able to do so. Terry had briefly seen a hurricane lamp on a shelf, but the moment he took it in hand he realized neither of them would have matches. They stood, not at all sure what to do next.

Eyes in the meantime were gradually adjusting to the dark, until they could see several feet of wall above the desk glimmering weakly, this caused a pattern of very diffuse light to be thrown upon the opposite wall. Terry was speedily there, standing on the desk and helping Hazel up, but this manoeuvre also had him stand upon, and tread down, piles of paper, which moved under his feet.

Together they looked out through a large rocky hole in the wall; it was obviously one of the many high-up apertures that perforated both entrance and well caves, allowing through a little natural light. The office was most probably chosen as a convenient site for the purpose, overlooking the cave entrance hall, as well as a place for doing clerical work – work they stood upon.

Down below them, and across the entrance chamber's width, the burly character in a greenish leather jacket stood in the ticket recess, prising open a drawer with a long metal tool – his curses and the sound of money dropping upon the stone floor reached them faintly. The noises ceased, and he emerged from the ticket recess with a hefty backpack on his shoulders. There was a clinking of keys as he headed towards their refuge, kicking at the notes that lay upon the floor. They ducked down, but he was already exiting their limited field of view. Sensing a possible threat, Hazel quietly descended from the desk to the wooden floor, where she urgently wedged the chair against the door. Terry jumped, and landed with a hefty thump beside her; she whirled on him but it was too late for recrimination. They froze, waiting for footsteps on the stair, but not a sound came. Were the acoustics in this cave odd, or was he waiting for them? They allowed a good while to elapse before cautiously creeping downstairs into the entrance chamber.

A long line of zigzag light pattern showed through the heavy ironwork and behind it lay a wide expanse of empty car park. Hazel couldn't believe her eyes; those responsible had just gone off without them. She rattled the gates, feeling like some kind of prisoner.

'Don't worry, they'll be back – something unusual has been happening here,' said Terry grimly, but his words lacked conviction. Together they walked down the slope until they were stopped by sounds of movement ahead, enough to start them on their way back to the small office. Terry had already decided it was the most defensible spot, assuming the man could find it.

Hazel felt much happier once she had the door closed; this was comparative safety, even if the office was too cramped to be comfortable. They sat on the desk and Terry's arm was soon comfortingly crooked about her; but coming after having seen the intruder's size, Terry's arm was about as reassuring as a chicken leg. Dispirited now, she began to feel her way through the desk drawers – something for self-defence, perhaps?

First a packet of cigarettes. More hunting and finally sheer elation as she brought out a box that rattled like matches. Terry looked startled and was taken by surprise as she struck her first match, but grabbed her hand as she struck a second, guiding it towards the lamp where it burned her fingers. He clumsily retracted the glass and the third attempt had the wick alight, only for it to fail on them, leaving an orange line smouldering in the dark. With the smell of burnt-out wick in their nostrils, Terry took charge of the matches himself; it was then she knew he didn't trust her not to waste them.

Some time later they entered the cave of barrels again; this time it was empty. Three candles were still alight with about two-thirds to burn. Terry took one and set off to check that the man had exited all connected caves in their immediate vicinity. He was soon back, reporting that the man in the green jacket had completely vanished. Whilst she waited uneasily for him, Hazel had decided to block the opening that led to all the other caves and make the cave of barrels more secure. Together again, they rolled barrels into the gap, blocking it, until finally both were convinced that no one could enter without them knowing.

Terry wanted another look at the entrance; maybe those gates could be dealt with, because for sure the burly man had not really tried. He took his candle off to find out, leaving Hazel to her own devices. Hazel was feeling more secure, but far less sure of exiting fast, which promoted ideas for staying the night. Sleeping here seemed inevitable. There was time for her to be busy, and prepare some extra pleasure for their overnight wait. Her eyes gleamed, filled with girlish, playful mischief intended for her travelling companion. She poked about behind the stage, finding a great deal in the storage space: first a huge cardboard box of newspapers which she crumpled almost page by page, creating an extensive pile of crinkly paper upon the stage – her amorous intention had devised a bed for two. The wooden recesses in the stage contained candles, hundreds of them. Terry stayed away for good while, and that suited her. For all of that time she was busy. When he did return it was to candles lit upon at least twenty barrels – with Hazel laughing at his incredulous face.

'I thought that the place could do with brightening up,' she said proudly, with brown eyes flashing, her plain face all humped up into a sunshine smile. Terry thought she looked very self-conscious, but tender and silly all at the same time. It might be a plain face, but it was the kind of face that he liked, a robust one with freckles and a mouth that emphasized her lips. The lips had become a strong point, now that he knew how she kissed. What was extra was the smile, it seemed especially warm and welcoming, a special one for him.

But Hazel was conscious that the mirth behind her smile might show through, and pointed about her to the candles on display. 'There are plenty more of these, if you want more light for the gates.'

''Fraid not – there's damn-all opportunity there!' Terry was feeling angry and dejected to have to say so, but then began to notice her other trophies lined up for his inspection. In particular a drum of paraffin that she had heaved, with considerable diffi-culty, up onto the stage. There was a kilo packet of sugar, several bottles of wine and a half-eaten bar of chocolate.

When she felt sure that Terry was fully aware of her cleverness, Hazel led him through to the shrine. If the barrel cave had been well illuminated, then it was nothing compared to this. He could almost feel the heat of the candles as they stood on little mounds of wax everywhere about the floor. Taking him by the hand she led him to the stone figures and pointed at the baby standing upon its mother's knee. 'I thought there was something odd about that one, so I lit candles and took another look.'

Terry shook his head in wonder; it certainly looked a very ordinary statue. 'It's a baby, so what?'

'It's a girl baby, that's what.'

Terry craned his neck. She was right – no Madonna this; the baby had an indentation where the genitals should have been. 'They could have been broken off you know. It only means just one vandal in several hundred years,' he said, still disbelieving.

Hazel pressed her finger to the child's abdomen, where a tiny mark confirmed her assertion; elsewhere the stonework was per-fectly smooth. 'It is a girl,' she said quietly and authoritatively. 'And for little girls like us, it is only the likes of you who need to wear stuff with designer nipples tacked on as an afterthought.' Hazel's smile widened coyly, passing over to him the little silver packet.

She turned away and a step further, chortling at the clever way she had set him up for that remark.

But Terry recognised the pack immediately, and demanded, 'Where did you get this?' His voice sounded so taken aback that Hazel had to struggle with herself not to tease him more.

'Ms Phillips gave us all one in our last term at school; actually there were two, but we all put one on a cucumber in class. The other was given for our personal protection.' She giggled nervously. 'Eileen's brother volunteered himself, and I went home with them to see it done. She did and made it seem so simple that I didn't bother; in fact it was awfully embarrassing!' Hazel pulled a pained face. Terry eyed the silver packet, concentration written upon his face, and one hand passed through his hair in an action that spoke of doubt.

Hazel decided the time was ripe to leave him with the idea. 'I'll go and blow the candles out in our bedroom,' she said. 'The ones in here can stay; there ought to be enough light shining through for our bedroom. Just give me a minute or so.' Hazel had prepared a bed for sleeping, and with minimal changes in apparel carefully arranged the loose papers about her before placing the Puffa on top. Hazel slowly submerged herself into the newspaper mattress which was noisy and awkward beyond anything she might have expected. She was attempting to appear well settled as Terry began to undress behind her on the stage.

The Puffa was on top holding the uppermost newspaper layers in position, and so Terry spread his generous area of cycle cape over it to help stabilize the heap more adequately. The side illumination had produced huge shadows in the cave, causing Terry to look suspiciously about him before entering the heap at the most appropriate level of paper. Worming his way into the paper heap he collided with the firm boards underneath, for these were only slightly cushioned by the paper, and even through the many layers he could still feel gaps between individual boards, each possessing an uncomfortable, cold, sharp edge. These he recognised had to be minor discomforts surmounted for the thrill of impending physical love. He found himself facing a back; there was something unfair about this, it was not at all the warm, loving reception that he had imagined. Terry tried to bolster what was beginning to be a flagging excitement by reaching round her, to find even more disappointment on the hard material of her bra.

21

He moved in closer inadvertently touching a bare bottom. Terry pushed himself close, instantly discovering the necessary lust, but the way ahead still defeated him. Suddenly unsure of himself Terry felt a profuse sweating. He must not fail at this, or his self-esteem might never recover. Was it his angle that was wrong, or was it those big wide hips that caused him to hang mid air, casting around for essential support. Terry was unsure about this, but whatever it was had him alternately propped up by this arm or that limb – strenuously doing something very similar to 'press ups.' It was unsustainable, and with this fear uppermost, he cast about for better purchase on her, only to slip off each loosely papered feminine curve as he did so. Only his thin cycle cape still covered them.

'Turn her with kisses,' he thought; but curled up like a hedgehog, Hazel was not ready for turning. 'It would be a lot easier without her,' his mind told him, as relieving bruised support toes for the umpteenth time he again distributed his body weight elsewhere to alternative sharp wooden edges. Despite all his woes, Terry's persistence paid dividends, with paper rustling and a nearby pedestal ashtray rocking threateningly. Suddenly the upper layers complete with Puffa slid off them to plunge from the stage with a dull thud. Cold air moved in and chill air currents caressed his back.

Hazel was unimpressed. She was going off the idea fast; any thought that this might take her over the moon was totally misplaced. After a teeth grinding hurt, it was all fits and starts. Was he a robot with a cog missing, or one of those jerky chameleons in disguise? She couldn't quite decide but told herself that there must be value in having the experience. And since there was no let-up in sight, she addressed herself to the question, 'What country do I lay back and think of – remembering that I am abroad?' At last she felt sufficiently ready and composed for an orgasm, expecting one might arrive any time now.

Weathering every imperfection Terry kept the effort going, despite failing to find reason why her ideas of love should prove so very uncomfortable? But that being so, he detached his mind from the task and let wayward thoughts turn towards the redhead back in Lourdes. He speedily completed his task very energetically and with intense excitement. Terry flopped back, breathing deep breaths of relief and scraping nearby scraps of loose paper over him; there was only one thing he wanted to do now – sleep it off. But no! Arms encircled his neck and quickly manoeuvred him into providing an arm for her as a pillow against the hard boards.

Hazel lay feeling restless; somewhere in all of this she had been cheated. There were years of sentimental thoughts that had used that little silver pack as a focus, but none of her imaginings had ever given up on her quite as suddenly as he had. Hazel cajoled him, not knowing exactly what she wanted, whispering small encouragements in his ear, but totally failing to elicit a response. All to no avail, her hands delicately touched his chest, and failing to revive him she ventured much further – with him too exhausted to be aware. The stroking moved progressively downwards until the side of her hand hit a floppy penis.

'Why the hell can't you just roll over and go to sleep?' Terry's voice sounded drowsy, whilst her hand meanwhile had traveled its full length.

'Terry! Where has it gone?' Her voice screeched at him and the uncomfortable scrape of her fingernails brought him to life.

He rose befuddled, trying to find his clothing in a sea of crumpled paper. Terry paused as he saw Hazel roll her skirt down and move off the origami bed; it was only then that it began to dawn upon him she had hardly disturbed anything she had on. How bloody unfair; she had been stringing him along all the time, despite him giving everything. A few candles were lit now, and her agitation soon communicated the relevant fact to Terry; there on the bulb of his penis was bare flesh – the condom nipple end was missing!

Hazel was distraught, knowing only of disaster.

Having found his clothes and dressed, Terry wrapped an arm round her; an arm she instantly brushed away, making him wish he were somewhere else. Furious with her and swearing to himself, he decided to go for a pee down the bottomless hole. There being no hurry to come back, Terry detached several lit candles and set off still angry, marvelling at how a woman could be so ungrateful.

There was no change in her when at last he did came back; Hazel was just as fraught as when he'd departed. He turned his attention to the bottles of wine, and producing a large penknife that sported a corkscrew he opened one; two were open before Hazel calmed down. Terry could not take it seriously, for after all it was not his rubber thing that somehow came out of the ark over

23

four years ago. Nevertheless, it would still appear to be entirely his fault, for breaking it in the first place!

Hazel looked sufficiently calm now to be told of his earlier expedition. 'Nothing was moving outside the caves, and so I looked for a tool the madman had been using. To me the bar looked good enough to prise the gates open, but there was no sign of it, or even anything else that would do the job. The upstairs office had several metal oddments, but they all bent under the strain, there was no moving either the gate or its fixing in the wall. I ended up looking through the papers in the office and found plans, as well as that useful big penknife. I brought everything back to show you.'

Hazel had recovered her composure she looked about her. 'I didn't see any plans.'

'You were too full of what you had done,' he said scathingly.

The tears that had never been far off began to flow again. Terry quickly reached for the plans that were laid out on a barrel. 'Look, I can't read the perishing lingo, but they appear to be plans for a cable running through the caves. And its route also indicates some kind of walk to the next hamlet.'

Miraculously, Hazel's tears stopped and she began smoothing down the papers, getting ever more excited as she did so. Reading through with some difficulty and explaining nothing throughout she was soon looking triumphant. 'We don't need to sit here waiting, you were right; it says there's local authority permission for an electricity supply to be routed through these caves – so it must be pretty straight. Let's go!'

Terry was not moving off without some discussion, for if he let her start a rush to the other end then it would end up also being his fault that they hadn't moved off earlier. 'It's no good going in the middle of the night. If there are people at the other end they are not going to like being knocked up, are they? Anyway, I don't think we should just go without some sort of preparation; we might have to wait around a good while before they let us out. I think we should sleep now, and wait at the gate, in case it's opened in the morning.'

'But Terry, tomorrow's Sunday, the caves are not open!'

'The caves will have to be opened sometime because they think they have a madman loose in here. Mind you, he was not so mad as to be unaware where he was going. He made no attempt to get out this end, though with his tools he could easily have done so. And did you see that backpack? He was all ready to go before ever he came in.'

Hazel turned a puzzled face towards him; she had not seen any inconsistency in the madman label. 'But Terry it's so awful in here, I think we ought to get out if we can. If it's too difficult then we can just return again.'

Terry looked at her, more than a little exasperated. 'If that's what you think, I'll get the hurricane lamp and we might find out how he left here.'

Hazel's face brightened. 'He went through that opening,' she said, pointing to the entrance blocked with barrels. 'I know because there is fresh candle wax on the floor.'

A while later, armed with paraffin lamp filled to the brim with paraffin, they rolled the barrels away from the entrance. Not far down the slope beyond, a recess was visible and a heavy door barring the way. Here again candle wax reflected their light. Hazel with both hands free turned the door handle and pushed. It remained tight shut against them. The door was relatively new and helped to confirm their idea of location; added to this on a sidewall cables and metal pipes exited.

'He must have locked it again,' said Terry, quick to re-adopt his wait-and-see proposal. They retraced their steps with Terry fighting himself to stay silent; but aware of Hazel near to tears again. He could not help sharing an observation with her that put the whole matter into doubt again. 'There might be back-up keys to that door in the office drawer: I did come across some keys, and they could be the spares.'

If he had other conversation to jolly her along with instead, it would have been better, but no, he had said words that needed to be lived up to, and so he trudged away up the slope. When the keys were tried out one of them fitted, and the heavy door opened to a blast of dank, mineral-tainted cold air. Even so it was more of a pleasure to breathe in than the acrid oxides of sulphur tang that wafted up from the lower show-caves. With a start Terry realized that he was now committed to following the crazy fellow and hoped that the man had moved well ahead. Perhaps there are good reasons to go now, he thought, as he stood appreciating the draught's finer points. For sure, Hazel's highly strung state would ensure there was little sleep tonight; much better to give her something to do.

'Let's go then,' he commanded, grabbing their hurricane lamp and taking two steps forward.

'Hold on, I don't think we are ready to go.' Hazel waited stubbornly until he had returned and slammed the door shut. 'What if there is a locked door on the other end, or we have to wait?'

Terry was visibly angry, his face contorted with frustration as he said, 'He went that way, didn't he?' A hand passed repeatedly through his hair, Terry's usual stress sign. Furious, he stormed off, ostensibly to put the keys in a safe but accessible place, just in case they needed to return and wanted to lock the door once again. Terry deliberately kept her waiting this time; his visit to the entrance cave turned into a browse through the sales literature relating to the show-cave.

The part-eaten chocolate bar Hazel bothered enough to put in a makeshift waste bin whose metal edges were sharp and ragged enough to cut her finger. The sugar she decided was worth keeping, its granules could fill her shoulder bag and tip out easily when no longer required. An empty wine bottle she rinsed and filled with paraffin, thinking that it ought to be carried besides taking a genuine bottle of wine. Finally she chose lots of paper for sitting on.

When Terry did return, Hazel was cheerful beyond expectation. 'While you have been sulking up there, I've been collecting everything we need,' she said. Accompanying her statement of fact with action, Hazel took up her load, which was as much as could reasonably be carried. She then pointed to a similar heap. 'That's for you.'

Indeed the clouds had lifted from Hazel's world and she was not put out in the slightest when he simply picked up his lantern and stalked off with it in a stroppy mood. He was soon at the door and looking round for her as she struggled gamely along behind him under her bulky possessions. The door creaked open on rusty hinges, and a repeat blast of cold air ripped past them, fluttering several of Hazel's newspapers out of her hands. Arms full, and trying to hold on to her crinkly paper, she stepped hastily aside from the door as it crashed inwards at her. Her sidestep from the door had Terry crying out aghast, for there was nothing to grip on

their side of the door. He cursed, fed up to the back teeth with
her: then even more so, as she cheekily pointed to the wall. There
in full view was a large key behind breakable glass. They pressed
on, but feeling more at odds with one another than ever.

3

Green Jacket

The lantern bobbed along in front of Hazel, casting a tiny circle of light about Terry's lower half; nothing else was visible in the all-pervading dark. The way between them must be clear for he walked along easily, and as a consequence Hazel was quite content to lag behind in the pitch dark at her own pace. She reasoned that Terry had only stalked off feeling cross about the door, and if she held out long enough he would feel sufficiently bad about it to make amends. When he did, then was the time to make him sorry for his failings.

Occasional litter kicked underfoot; very reassuring as it meant they had encountered a public footpath, but apart from that it might as well be another world. On their left there was an irregular wall of dirty grey rock, which reflected Terry's light to a greater or lesser degree. In the other direction it was black enough to prevent any idea of dimension, but it had the feel of spaciousness. The initial great draught that had sprung up between separate pressure systems ceased when the door closed. There was nothing now except stillness, punctuated by the sound of their own footsteps that echoed off places unseen, almost ghostly and certainly unsettling in the darkness. Soon the low line of bricks at Terry's feet rose steadily, protecting the services before evolving into conduit bolted upon rock, and as the services began to rise higher on the wall of rock their path was becoming a gully.

Suddenly there was an ear-splitting bang, and the slither of heavy rock shifting. Terry dramatically threw himself flat against the rock face, whirling his lantern around his head as he did so. Hazel just stood there; he looked so ridiculously dramatic that she felt like laughing. Terry waved his lamp urgently for her to come and hesitantly she moved towards him, finishing off with a rush as stones clattered their way down from far up on the rocks. They stood there waiting until all was silent once more.

'Someone's using explosives,' Terry said unnecessarily. He wrapped his arm round her, but Hazel wriggled free, she hadn't forgiven him yet.

They set off again, but this time side-by-side walking continuously for some twenty minutes before encountering a problem. Rocks lay strewn across a soaking wet path, and the air hung heavy with dust well permeated through with the smell of high explosive. Within a dozen paces they needed to protect their breathing with pocket-handkerchiefs, whilst underfoot the water was still rising and wetting the rubble. The mound became higher under them until it was clear that the incline had taken them out of the flood. Terry's arm soon protectively encircled her.

'Shouldn't we go back?' Hazel gasped, stumbling on the rubble underfoot.

'No, the whole path will soon be deep in water,' he replied. 'Just keep going!'

The incline soon became more difficult, with rocks two or three feet high barring the way. Hazel stuffed her bottles into the Puffa pockets so as to free a hand for climbing the hill of rocks; being the only mule wasn't easy. They cleared the dust cloud, only to be sprinkled with water. Terry stopped to remove his face cloth, and then attended the paraffin lamp, assessing new requirements for the wet area. Their limited field of view was beginning to make sense of what was wrong, for just ahead and not far above them the services spanned a natural gap on an ironwork bridge, a bridge that was sagging unhealthily from a fall of rock, whilst a broken pipe gushed forth water.

Terry pointed upwards. 'The services enter the next cave right there, so our exit must be somewhere underneath the rubble. Let's press on beyond and see if there's any hole we can get through.' What they had with them was beginning to have more value; Terry relieved Hazel of the newspapers and stuffed them into his shirt, quickly buttoning it up. Then he covered himself and most of the lamp with his cycle cape, before clambering into the deluge. The falling water soaked Hazel that much more, as she couldn't help inclining her head to see great shadowy slabs hanging over their heads; it was clear the ironwork was ready to fall. They pushed ahead quickly into relative dryness as the hill reached its summit. Standing there they surveyed what could be seen of the decline. It almost certainly led into deep floodwaters upon the other side. So far they had seen no sign of an exit hole, and none was apparent in front; it would seem that all of their climbing had merely marooned them underneath rock that threatened to fall upon them.

'We may as well go down and find out if there are possibilities there, perhaps another route forwards. I don't want to go back through that lot again as we might have to swim. Even if we assume the water isn't above our heads in the gully, we would never open that door whilst it's holding back so much water on this side.' Terry's voice was emphatic.

A miserable descent started, until Terry who had been keeping their movements clockwise and close to the wall began to realize that they were moving off the rubble. Soon it began to be evident they had moved to a ledge and were wandering slightly uphill, no longer on freshly disturbed stones. Some chance of finding a hole in the cavern wall had yet to be dismissed.

'Stay with the wall, we might find another way forward.' Terry's voice boomed enthusiasm with echo more apparent, the new location giving him hope until the curvature suggested otherwise. They had passed any prospect of a way to the public footpath; the trivial rubbish was absent, just a scramble over and around big rocks in their path. Soon even Hazel realized that they must have outdistanced any connection with routes forward to the known exit. She called Terry back, and they decided to take a rest on what had now become a wide ledge, over seemingly nothing.

The newspapers barely disguised a rough surface, covered by small, sharp, flinty stones, nevertheless it was a big relief to be off one's feet and to swig wine straight from the bottle. 'You might have brought the red,' grumbled Terry, handing Hazel the bottle back, the contents too sharp for him.

'You are lucky to have any at all,' said Hazel. She poured a little sugar from her handbag into the bottle and tasted it after shaking.

From somewhere out in the blackness came an easily recognizable sobbing sound, cries that were unmistakably those of the violent man. A distant rushing sound met their ears. Hazel flattened herself back against a rock. 'Oh,' she said shakily. 'It's him dropping rocks.'

'He may be our best hope,' said Terry reaching for the bottle. 'He's got to get out of here too, you know, I still think he knows what he's . . . my God! What have you done to this?' He spat out some of the precious wine.

Hazel grabbed the bottle and glowered at him in the dark; he should be more appreciative of her ingenuity. 'I shouldn't like to meet up with him,' she said sharply.

'I'm not sure we can,' replied Terry. 'He's almost certainly on a different level, and a route that goes somewhere else. We could be on a new path altogether, for I doubt we could have reached this spot at all without mounting that heap of rubble. The good thing about that is we have been brought closer to the cavern wall, and if the ridge we are on allows us to move forward round this side then it must surely take us over the caves where we started. There's all those galleries high up that we could shout from, even that underground lake must have some connection because it must be fed from streams entering from above.'

Hazel looked at him suspiciously. 'Where did you get a lake from?'

'I read the advertising literature, the English version in the ticket area – it's the one bit we missed!' Terry felt he was being as reassuring as he needed to be.

Hazel felt miserable, damp, and lost; despite their success so far she was neither reassured nor prepared for the exercise involved. This was far worse than cycling, but through it all Terry seemed to know what they should be doing, so she got to her feet and began to trudge behind him.

An hour further on, the nature of the cave walls began to change. Streaks of white appeared and the boulders in their way became less frequent. More disturbing was the edge of the plateau diminishing, exposing a dark void beyond.

'It's a bit like climbing a mountain, inside-out,' said Terry.

His voice cascaded into the blackness. An echo came back clearly, and then a further six times in ever-diminishing intensity. Hazel shuddered; she thought it bad enough that they were walking without a map inside a cave, without the extra complication of imagining mountain climbing inside-out. Terry paused, anxiously looking ahead, and slowly Hazel began to realize what it was that disturbed him – the path tailed off to a wisp of white stuff against the cliff face. How do we know this is going anywhere? Hazel asked herself, deciding they ought to be turning back now.

'Step over, step over . . . over . . . over,' shouted Terry, emphasized by a series of diminishing echoes. His hand reached out for her, motivating an urgent move and Hazel, suddenly aware of a fissure in the ledge between them, stepped towards him, feeling the chalky stuff crumble and give way beneath her feet. Something crunched and depressed deep down under one foot and she stepped even more rapidly towards him, with pieces of path rattling ominously from under her feet to crash noisily somewhere in the gully below. She crowded him as she arrived, and unbalanced he wobbled sideways along the narrow ledge, trying to retract both of them from its dubious area. Still off-balance, Terry had the feeling he was about to topple and making a stop managed to flex his knees a little, leaning back to feel shoulders on rock behind. Thus steadied he was able to firm up more support to give her. With doubts about the ledge they were standing on now paramount, given that pieces of its substance continued rattling downwards on a diminishing scale, Terry was forced to move crabwise holding the lamp, moving just as fast as his legs could take him. Hazel hung upon the hand of his other outstretched arm. She was frightened and hung on well past the danger zone, pestering him for reassurance. 'Shouldn't we be trying to go back?'

'No, we are over the worst bit.' Terry sounded confident enough, but was indeed horrified at any thought of going back.

He can't possibly know, Hazel mused to herself, her sense of panic still uppermost. But there was more breadth to the ledge now, and as if to reassure her in this particular respect it widened abruptly into a vast triangle that supported huge irregular lumps of cream-coloured rock, all quite easily passable. She realized then how he had seen it just ahead when the path was so thin, because of it reflecting the lamplight so well.

'Let's have a rest,' she said, and that was something he was ready for. Moments later they flopped into a space between the rocks.

'It's not chalk, is it?' asked Hazel, not expecting to be answered.

'I think its dolomite,' said Terry. 'And thank goodness that's more substantial.'

Hazel was left mouth open and impressed. Eagles and bikes she could understand – but now minerals? 'Aren't they mountains?' she asked, taking a sickly sweet mouthful from her bottle, not particularly interested in the reply, more relieved that she survived.

'Aw, I think there may be some there too,' said Terry, less sure.

He snatched at the bottle, knowing that to ask for it would only invite a lengthy tease. There was no response at all from her, and moments later, when he had satisfied his thirst, he found Hazel already lying flat and drifting to sleep. He shook her by the shoulder. 'I think we should press on.'

'Why?' Hazel opened one eye.

'Let's reach somewhere that we can be rescued from.'

He was bullying her. Reluctantly Hazel got to her feet and checked her watch. It was 12.30 am as they moved off. The cave wall appeared to be turning them; Terry was keen to stay with it, so they stayed close in to the rock-littered widening space that could easily have provided other routes. Terry, still keen to convince her that he knew what he was doing, pointed out that any caves of interest to them must come off the wall, certainly not the space in the middle.

Obvious or not, Hazel was impressed, and warming to the lanky chap in front.

The rock had switched again to a uniform grey, and was quite as uninteresting as it ever had been. Half an hour after the last rest they arrived in their first cave; the one which Terry considered might be above the show-caves. In any case it fitted the rough rule he was working to, so they part walked, part scrambled clockwise about it.

There was an audible trickle of water. Finding water would be very agreeable, but their hopes were dashed, with nothing tangible found. All of the rock was jagged and not even providing enough flat space to spread out for the night. They were soon right back in the cave mouth again.

'Terry, why did we do that assault course? We are right back at the start!'

'Because we had to. This cave is probably above those high-up galleries over the entrance cave, but there was nowhere to shout from and neither was there a way down.' He sounded a bit short and grumpy, so Hazel did not object when he turned into the next opening off the cavern.

The next cave dripped water on them even as they paused in the long entry hole; it was most unpleasant water to the taste. Chance pockets of sulphurous fumes had them even less at ease, but with their coughing came the realization that the nasty taste at the back of the throat was due to this. They moved in nevertheless, only to find conditions pleasurably different further inside the cave. The cold water raining from the rocks above gave way to a clammy heat, and the humidity penetrated their clothes until they hardly knew they had any on. The tropical climate was an oddity; in fact it was the last place on earth either one of them would have expected to find it. The cave was a small one, small enough to see most of it at one time by holding their lamp high. A tiny pool at the far end caught their attention, and instantly they headed that way. Hazel climbed on to a large flat rock that overlooked it, discarding her Puffa and wriggling down her tight skirt; previously retracted for climbing. She sat there feeling exhausted, legs over the edge, and just catching some light from Terry's lamp; there she swigged away at the wine bottle until it was quite empty. Terry wasn't waiting, or begging for a drink, for he had thrown himself flat and was taking long wet draughts into his mouth; he lay upon a soft silt deposit that stretched a good way from the edge of the pool. The water, once disturbed, soon cleared, and though at first it tasted of bad eggs, this improved with supping, turning out to be the most pleasing water that he could ever remember drinking.

Terry rolled on his back, catching sight of the sleek outline of what was a tight skirt perched above him on a rock; it constricted the protruding legs enough to imagine Hazel as some kind of mermaid. The skirt was currently in use, stretched a little at the knee to catch any spilt sugar as she transferred it from handbag to bottle. He was seen looking, but Hazel only giggled at him; her wine intake had been over usual limits for drink and was clearly taking effect. The remainder of their sugary energy source soon moved back into her handbag, partially clumped by the prevailing humidity. Then freed from the task and feeling self-conscious under his steady gaze, she grabbed a wad of very wet newspaper and threw it into his face – jumping off the rock to rub it in. The struggle was brief, for amid the closeness and temperature of the cave it was a pointless struggle and one that could only end in kisses. The exercise proved to be too much for them, they were both tired. Cuddling together and laughing at the many stupid jokes remembered by an inebriated Hazel, comfort was right there in the pool's beach of soft silt, just above the waterline; an ideal place to recline and drift to sleep.

4

Transformation

Hazel extended her arm, there was a plopping noise; she moved it again more vigorously still asleep, and the splash made her sit up sharply. Her eyes opened to the sight of water gleaming in the lamplight. Terry lay only a yard away, obviously fast asleep with his head and shoulders propped up nicely on the shallows; the lamp and papers rested safely a bit further up upon what she now viewed as a beach. The water was pleasantly warm and covering her like a centrally heated bed, a bed in which Terry was temptingly close. She pushed water forwards so that a tidal wave swept over his face. He sat up spluttering and coughing, looking panic-stricken at the water, which took a moment or two to register. Then he saw her sitting part submerged in the water, laughing at him.

'It came up tonight,' he gasped; it was more of a question than not.

'How do you know it's night?' queried Hazel, looking at her watch. 'I'd say it's about five o'clock on Sunday morning.' She stood up and paddled in the water, looking over to the place where the rest of her possessions were just visible on the rock. Hazel moved the hurricane lamp and soggy papers upwards to join them; the tidal wave she created earlier had washed the base of their one and only lamp, and left her with a strong sense of guilt. Water still streamed out of her clothes, as she stood there assisting the flow by stroking down the material.

Terry approached her, also soaking wet. 'Nothing will dry in here,' he said. 'The humidity must be close to a hundred percent.' He stood clear of the water, and stepping out of his trousers he wrung them out. Off came his shirt, then down to underpants he squeezed water out of the shirt. 'It is quite warm and comfortable in here for us, so I could take our clothes outside the cave where they can dry. We could even sleep some more,' he suggested.

35

Hazel thought that a good idea, at least she couldn't think of a better one. 'Turn your back then,' she instructed.

Terry turned about whilst Hazel divested herself of skirt and jumper, wringing them out as best she could and one pair of pants was relinquished to join them; after all there were still two layers of her extras and a bra to go. Hazel passed her clothes and the lamp to Terry, bidding him goodbye; but no, he wanted to borrow her Puffa. Hazel thought that too much of an imposition and passed him the newspapers that were still sopping wet, wrapped with his own cape. The yellow-clad figure eventually struggled off carrying his load along with their lighting, plunging her into darkness the moment he rounded the entrance hole, in which he ran the full gamut of unpleasant sulphur smells. No movement was possible now for Hazel, who sat there in bra and panties waiting for him.

Terry's light was perceived as returning: she twisted her back towards him as he approached the rock. 'Turn the lamp right down,' she said in her stroppiest voice.

'It's just like ice out there you know!' He cuddled up to the exposed back with a cape still running chill water from the entrance. The shock of cold, wet cycle cape made her flinch, for it did seem impossibly cold. Hazel only partly managed to suppress her cry of annoyance, for now she was being made to regret not lending him the Puffa, and he dwelt there long enough to see she got the message properly.

When Terry did discard the cape there were delightful warm curves available, and these were soon being pressed into service; she had to be his Eskimo wife. As the chill blunted between them, kisses that had been denied a day earlier came easily. No need to indulge in thoughts beyond a soft body that cuddled; there was growing excitement. Hazel was not being a hedgehog today and they met so easily it was like a dream. After sex another sleep but this time high and dry upon a stone.

They awoke with the bitter taste of sulphur compounds in the mouth, and both were aware of a need to depart. Hazel had lost her extra pants, but she didn't feel a pressing need to search for them in the dark; there was a pair drying wasn't there, and right now she wasn't feeling so prudish. They drank from the water that was clearly ebbing away, and taking the opportunity Hazel dipped her sugared bottle in the water until it was full. Next priority for her attention was her hair, it was a mess; but the comb took some finding.

Terry remained with the water. He had expected it to flow in some natural way, but instead it was retreating towards the level where they found it. He looked again and failed to find the connection it ought to have to the subterranean lake. This disposed of any hope that they could either crawl or swim through. Even room to sail a bottle with a message inside was out of question. But here was an intriguing mystery that perhaps he could part solve. Hazel's gauzy pants lay where they had fallen off the flat stone; they were ideal material to see how the currents did move from opposing ends of the pool. Once immersed the flimsy garments moved at much the same rate towards the centre where a number of rocks protruded at the bottom. Swiftly one pair sped up and slipped sideways into a crevice underneath there. The other appeared to be going to the same destination but was suddenly sucked in nearby – his fingers found a substantial hole beneath the rock. Then, following his nose, there was that extra puzzle in the doorway where the air hung so heavily with sulphurous fumes. This one was unresolved, as the encrusted openings he saw must puff fumes only now and then. His success in the part-solving of these mysteries pleased him, although he knew Hazel would not be so keen about her underwear being used. She would get stroppy again that he'd lost them, despite their being ideal for the task; so he determined not to tell her. He concealed an occasional laugh on wondering what if the remaining flimsy bit had blown away outside, for he forgot to put a stone on it.

Hazel had finished her preening and was putting on her Puffa. They set off through the dripping rocks to retrieve their clothes, and found everything thoroughly dry and intact in the prevailing chilly draught. Dressed and carrying a few items of damp under-wear they felt almost comfortable again. Fruitlessly the next cave was examined; but its only attribute was a draught-free, dry atmos-phere, which made it an ideal place for refilling the oil lamp.

The next opening forwards from the latest cave was more aptly an irregular split in the wall. Upon entering, they found themselves right on a bend, which gave them the choice of two possible ways. Terry thought it might well have been some long-dried-up riverbed, for it was smooth and formed a tunnel big enough to take a train. After inspecting the walls Terry asked Hazel for a sheet of her paper and he stood flexing it like a bullfighter in either direction before choosing the one that showed the strongest draught coming towards him. The draught suggested to him quite conclusively that there was not a dead end in either of the alternative ways. He wanted to descend now but both were level. Did they still want to follow the perimeter walls, hoping for an exit, or did they make for centre ground instead, knowing caves over the tourist area were of no help? Why not head towards the one man who must know, or even the place where work on essential facilities must shortly commence? 'Let's move inwards on the right-hand path,' said Terry, having finally made his decision, sugaring the pill for her with an encouraging observation, 'Look, the water's eroded a clear path for us.'

Hazel was eyeing big rocks scattered ahead. 'I don't see how you could possibly call this a clear path, it's worse than where we've been. And why has it all gone white again?'

'I think that's limestone.' Terry didn't sound quite so sure this time and quickened his pace so she couldn't question him further. They continued in silence, able to avoid rather than climb for the most part, and for the next hour they made fast progress as the tunnel continued almost in a straight line. Predominantly white walls were soon streaked in various shades of green, and in some places pink, as if some giant of an artist had daubed them. The light had begun reflecting differently, because white crystalline solids had formed tiny barriers right across their path like some fairyland in miniature. Tiny, frozen, cracked icicles scattered light from their lantern, and these small, fragile structures seemed to be threaded by myriad illuminated filaments. Hazel was reminded of a prized nursery picture of cobwebs shining in the dew. But this was a real wonderland of thick scintillating crystals holding water loosely trapped in their interstices and providing little scenes with an all-over sparkle. Stepping across one beautiful structure in blue only led Hazel to encounter another even more beautiful in pink, and beyond even this seemingly endless array of little pink or blue wonders that was slowing her down, there hung a curtain of thread stalactites which shimmered across the tunnel's entire width.

'We have to go through it,' Terry stressed forcibly. He knew only too well before he got there that Hazel would object to destroying even a fraction of that beauty.

They crept under the far edge of its fringe, carrying off some tiny, wet, lime-laden pipes with them. A further half-hour of walking, and the tunnel began to wind about, narrowing and spawning numerous holes, some huge, which appeared randomly on either side of them. Terry paused so abruptly that Hazel who was just behind, collided with him. She froze before grabbing him as they both teetered on the brink of space where their path ceased to be. Ahead was vacant space and their light touched nothing at all. Terry shouted, and the hollow noise made them realize there was a vast space ahead of them. He dropped a stone, and the length of its fall was sufficient to convince them that here was no simple walk forward.

Hazel had been tolerant up to now, but knowing they had to go all the way back again really angered her: it was no good saying, as Terry did, 'There is no way of knowing' – she knew it was bad luck to break that curtain. He was beginning to fail her, and Hazel felt her opinion was being disregarded.

The way back seemed quicker for knowing what lay ahead, and even before their arrival back at the bend, they had decided to walk along the rest of the tunnel. It was beginning to resemble a big game of snakes and ladders.

Where it did end some two hours later was dramatic. The tunnel wall had been broken across by gigantic rocks that appeared to be multiple fractures of something much bigger, reducing them to a hunt for a way about or over these huge slabs at right angles to their path. One that was more accessible enabled them to mount and walk downwards, a novelty in a place where everything seemingly led to higher ground. Unfortunately as they progressed the lantern's light reflected off water; below was flooded and that entailed turning about. In this crowded place, what was forwards and what was backwards had became nonsensical. In the end what mattered most was finding a giant slab that enabled you to scramble onto other giant slabs, perhaps set at less of an angle.

It was maze of considerable proportions. They managed to reach a steep rock passing the one they were on, which avoided going back to the broken tunnel. This found them heading upwards on a severe incline which soon had Hazel pleading for a rest, but the best they could manage was a stop to drink sugared water, as the slope was too acute for sitting down. Their brief refreshment on the hoof was taken as they viewed some other problems looming. There were more tumbled rocks ahead, coming very near the one they were on, and at their limit of visibility one rock slab leaned sideways across it, a threat to them later. Terry groaned as he saw all their effort could now so easily go into another dead end and maroon them up here.

They climbed higher, noticing the sheer drop opening up to one side of them. Their lamp could reflect on water far below, and in the air a noticeable waft of fried bacon odour enveloped them, salivating their mouths. They hung there looking over the edge, where not far below them a light flickered from a cavity, illuminating the figure of a man, although in the main it was a shadowy outline. The head was more visible and this time encased in a safety helmet from which projected a very bright light. To Hazel it was at first ghostly, but then she saw part image of a familiar leather jacket and the cry stopped short in her throat.

'Our lunatic's wearing an acetylene lamp on his hat. He's got all the right gear.' Terry whispered; but he whispered without reason for the weakness of their light protected them from being seen. In contrast to Hazel, he was heartened by this, because from their current observation the man must be converging, and for sure the stranger was less frightening than the prospect of starvation. Overhead he sensed was a void in which somewhere their rock could turn out to be propped up with nothing at the end of it. The possibility of moving to another rock was apparently still viable, as there were other plates of rock with less inclination ahead and particularly another slab, which appeared to cross under the one they were on. It turned out to be only a matter of climbing down the ragged edge of one massive slab to another at the intersection. They very carefully transferred to this path and pleased to find that its incline hardly taxed them at all. Terry predicted that this huge, flat slab must butt against something pretty soon. He was shortly proved right, for their rock came to an end buried into a softer, brownish-looking overhang, with much-fragmented stone all around it and this very soon became the surface on which they stood.

Their rock had evidently fallen and lodged on much softer material, creating a dent of sufficient depth to enable an easy dismount. Terry hurried off the leaning surface to examine damage similar to that which caused them to abandon their last dried-up river trek. Agitated that he might be on another dead end,

Terry scrambled to dig out broken rock around the dent and finding a small hole blessed with an air current that he could feel. He called to Hazel, who hung back in the dark ready to veto any move; she had exited one very uncertain place only to come to this very claustrophobic one.

'Terry, come back!' Hazel's voice was sharp, and the tone strangely reminiscent of when she reprimanded him over the bra episode. He reluctantly withdrew from the hole with lamp. A bit sullen, she thought, but fancy, plunging me in the dark. I know we need to find a way back, but he is in our path. Her mouth quivered, and with an involuntary shudder she looked towards the opening, as if expecting a man to suddenly pop out.

'Let's rest here and take a break, at least we know he's not behind us, don't we?' Terry soothed her, taking his time to use many quiet reassuring words, at the same time drawing her into a recess between the nearest rocks, softer rocks that had evidently crumbled away from the walls. It was time for rest and to refresh with sugared water once more, but the drink only had their mouths aching for something solid and chewable. Hazel settled down with thoughts uppermost of the part-eaten chocolate bar she had thrown away, her mouth relishing what she might have had. Terry was restless, but seeing Hazel was lying there on cold rock more asleep than awake he relaxed upon a few dog-eared newspapers, eventually reaching out to lower the lamp wick.

Suffering discomfort some hours later, Hazel prised herself out from under the weight of Terry. His body moved limply to recline on the loose rock, leaving her with cramped muscles and feeling chill. The lamp looked as though it was running out of oil so Hazel turned the wick up, and was surprised at how bright the flame flared. She took a sip from the bottle, and looked down on Terry – he was still out cold; yes cold was very apt.

It was a good opportunity to spend a penny before he was about, so she crept round the rock into the next recess, the lamplight bouncing just enough illumination for her surroundings. Her bottom neared the ground and touched fragile sticks, which snapped off as she crouched. Hazel pushed them aside, bringing a section of the offending fragments into the light. Whether she screamed first or dropped the bony limb was unclear, but what was certain was that Terry came at the double, clutching the lamp.

There between the boulders sat a small skeleton. Hazel grabbed at Terry, almost trying to hide behind him, opening and shutting her mouth noiselessly, shaking with fright.

'People don't come this small,' he said easily. 'It's probably a monkey but the skull looks very human. I think you broke his leg off with your pee. What strong stuff it is!' He doubled up with laughter, and kept on laughing until Hazel recovered enough to hit him. She knew she would never live it down, and that glistening patch on the floor made it seem so much worse. Miserably hot and shaky, she tried not to look at it – why, she had actually sat on a skeleton's knee. Desperate to be away from the place, Hazel was quite ready now to enter the hole.

But Terry was in no hurry to go. His watch told him it was 4 am on Monday morning and he was in a mood for laughing, especially if it could be coupled with showing off, so he left to water the remains himself for luck. 'See if I can break the other leg,' he said.

The ritual of the lamp came next, in which the flame was transferred to two candles before they began to refill the lamp. The wine bottle was now only one third full, and each time there were losses due to spillage. Each time another of their precious newspaper sheets had to be sacrificed; but on the good side, ignition gave them a pleasant flash of warmth and light before they started again. Terry moved off in a particularly good humour, which stayed, especially as his broken-through hole connected into a wide tunnel and boasted a high enough roof to allow comfortable walking. But getting Hazel through the tiny hole that was long and arduous was a different matter, as she was someone sporting a little more flesh.

Inching her way behind him in total darkness she struggled and snagged on its rocks. Her heart raced and pounded fast in her ears, she was scared she might not make it through the pressing walls. But suddenly there was a light ahead; he had cleared, holding his light so she could see and saying reassuring words that made all the difference. It was a near thing, she wouldn't want to do that again. And now with only the most minor of setbacks they walked mile after mile on an incline, during which she slowly recovered from her panic attack.

Here in an easy stroll it was wide enough for Hazel to walk alongside the lamp. She caught sight of tears in her Puffa and saw its stuffing protruding; a sorry state for her to emerge from the caves in. Such thoughts could be shelved because the walls were an interesting shade of grey, wildly decorated with cream veins; everything here looked well rounded with age. The roof they noticed soon became decorated too, with spidery white crystals hanging down – Hazel could imagine them as chandeliers. Further on, the floor dipped temporarily and a stream of sufficient depth to cover their ankles ran cold and clear. They removed their trainers and waded for about a hundred yards, to where the stream disappeared into another small opening, leaving the passage ahead dry to walk. Hazel filled her bottle, scraping the last clumped morsels of sugar from her handbag which was insufficient to sweeten the water very much.

Soon afterwards they entered a large chamber. Terry spilt a tiny splash of paraffin on a sheet of paper and lit it. The flare briefly illuminated a huge cave with boulders at its centre and perhaps as many as four openings ahead of them. High above them, just blackness, but from a clicking noise high up there Terry was aware of bats. He made no mention of them to Hazel, for she was bad enough as she was, but to him it was good news.

They walked clockwise all round the boulder strewn centre inspecting the openings as they presented themselves: the first was an obvious dead end, the third one and another at the very end looked promising and even more promising when Terry carried out his newspaper test. They would first give the third one a try, for there were marks on the floor and even more significant at its entrance, a sweet wrapper. With rising hopes of an exit leading to human habitation they pressed on.

The tunnel was smooth and quite unlike anything they had walked so far. There were no obstacles to contend with and that pleased them because they were weary. The walls became glassy, another experience that helped, enabling Terry to see well ahead because the lamplight travelled much further. It revealed a slight curve in tunnel ahead, and reaching there the air warmed as they rounded it, perhaps another warm stream in the offing? As they progressed, the tunnel walls were beginning to look dull and more so all of the time. Terry scraped at a wall which carried a pink tinge, and underneath revealed a more creamy slime, which wiped off to reveal its underlying bright reflective glaze. A thrill went through him; these were living processes, real signs of life, could the outside be that far off? It might actually be edible he thought;

43

but on tasting a bit on his hand, its astringent taste made him spit it out.

'Look at this,' Hazel tapped him on the shoulder and pointed to the wall behind him, one she had given a tap with her newspapers. 'It's a little curvy yellow light,' she enthused. 'What is it? It's yellow back there too,' she pointed behind her to a glow in the tunnel.

'It could be a luminous mineral ore excited by our lamp,' Terry said knowledgeably, holding the lamp near her scrape, and taking it away again. The yellow shape shone on apparently unaffected. Somewhat annoyed that it didn't work he said awkwardly, 'It must be phosphorescence like from those organisms in the sea,' lapsed into silence and walked on, now concentrating on the sweet paper. Did it mean that man was ahead of them? He turned to Hazel and suggested a break, gladdened that she was only too willing to stop. They sat on one of the last bits of paper and drank what remained in the sugar-water bottle, which by now was too weak to be attractive.

This simply had to work out, for their provisions were coming to an end. Terry refilled his lamp; it didn't need doing but he topped it up anyway. Going through the motions he looked objectively at the soft light coming along the tunnel and trying to sum it up. Were they through? And was that the outside world with daylight ahead? It would be nice to think so; only the air quality contradicted such an idea. He ran his hand along the wall; the creamy skin was pimpled now and tore rather than wiped. Yes, it had that 'off odour' tainting the tunnel air; this might explain his remaining reservation. With gathering hope, he set them going again, and the light drew nearer. There were things discarded at the side of the path, the odd rubbish of civilization, a sight that buoyed even Hazel's hopes.

Standing in their path was a huge rock practically filling the tunnel, but towards their left the rock was broken away, and a well-defined path in the dust led the eye onwards to a more subdued light upon the rock face. Strangely enough these were not covered in that all-over skin. Terry wasted no time in entering the bend that passed their monstrous entrance rock; Hazel was a few paces behind and not now needing lamp light to see, which was convenient here as the very narrowness denied their walking abreast. He passed through with the increasing certainty that they had found an exit, and was taken suddenly unawares by a shock wave of pain to his chest which struck forcibly hard like needles up and down his body. The tremor had him shaking uncontrollably and as sharp pains danced through his eyes he was losing balance. Tottering forwards while still heading for a previously perceived opening, he completely lost his footing and fell down upon his lamp. He made a weak attempt at crawling forward impeded by a tangle of loose creepers. There he vomited, struggling just yards further on.

Hazel was right behind him and in stepping over creepers in her path, saw him fall. She ran forward only to be hit by a sudden jolt that caused her to trip over the roots and dive inadvertently down, landing heavily over his prostrate body. Sudden pulsating pains within her frame threatened stability, but with her mind set on dragging him through into the light she drove herself forward quite regardless of pain. Barely conscious and heading towards the open gap she dragged his cape hood with her, crawling now with the narrow corridor behind them. A band of heat she passed had left her hot and now with stabbing pains of light whirling around in her head she had to let up on her mission.

Overbalancing she collapsed forwards, with her arms trying to raise herself but only scraping at the floor and retching. Terry was behind and everything was too distorted to see properly. From overhead walls hung long whip-like fingers stretched out to them, like brambles – that was what put her down? The floor was a wide, uneven space with shaky colour designs on the walls and ahead another vision supervened. She was in fairyland. There were tiny women dressed in gold fabric. Hazel knew that she had to be hallucinating, for closely approaching her was a copper-coloured butterfly. It was quite enormous and shaded her as it homed in. Something pulled at her Puffa and drew her along towards the fairies. Pains radiated from head and abdomen, but with effort almost beyond her she forced her eyes to stay open. She was drifting or at any rate numbly sliding past a naked, sore, red body that reminded her of the mad intruder. Her eyes closed, and her brain ceased to care.

5

The Commissar

The first official to be affected by the explosion was Claude Brie, the acting Commissar for Lutz-St-Saveur, although he didn't know it at the time of the first call. In the early hours, still warm from his bed and with eyes semi-focused from sleep, he flopped into his car cursing out loud, 'She's done it again.' The frequency of these disturbances was disruptive; not so bad in the day, but night-time call-outs when they came always left him weary throughout the following day. This was not a one-off occasion: no, it was worse than that, a veritable certainty that whenever her husband left, which he did for considerable periods, there would be a cry for Claude. She had more troubles for him these days than his entire police station. True her dog had died suddenly and her tears would be wetting the pillows. Was she was missing a man in the bed to comfort her and straightway thought of him? He hoped not, and from her perceived actions of late it was more likely she saw him as her knight in shining armour. This dreamlike thought mixed freely in his latent sleep with the obvious fact that what she really needed was a substitute dog.

The Commissar, with a mind somewhere else, turned the starter key and quickly came down to earth as the car jerked away, his feet for ever unsure on the pedals of his official car; a car intended to suit standard-sized policemen. Among his friends he would defend this shortcoming, 'What I lack in leg is amply compensated for in the mind.' And this last sentiment had an element of truth in it, because his mind was clever enough for the police department to want him: physique quite immaterial. But clever or no, when your chief is away on perpetual police advancement, you cannot avoid being responsible for his domestic front, even if you cannot abide the woman that occupies it.

Claude's car traversed the rear of two sleepy towns divided by a river, and climbed the twisting road that led towards two rather superior houses overlooking the town. The road in that locality was in darkness, every light out. A likely reason for dragging him out of bed? He drove through the open gates, and quietly drew up on the broad sweep of her drive. Soon he was knocking at the front door and waiting; he expected silence in the house knowing that there would not be the usual dog barking. Waiting there, she always kept him waiting, he regretted not bringing his jacket for it was cold. The Commissar's broad face scowled with annoyance, an annoyance occasioned by the frequency of such performances, his frown progressing ever further to dent the narrow fringe of fluff that divided his temples from an otherwise bald scalp.

Julia Masse was surveying him from inside the hall, as the lighting failure had robbed her of a usually clear reflection from her visitor. She paused there, a not unattractive woman in her late thirties driven by circumstances to live alone in a big house. Clutching her dressing gown tight about her throat, she spread its rich embroidery over her cleavage before finding courage enough to open the door. This was her final hesitation, for after all, the vague outline of short figure, big head, could be none other than Claude Brie.

Madame Masse opened the door and in her most decidedly troubled voice invoked his help. 'The alarm bell was ringing over there when I rang, but it has faded away since then!' The voice sounded unhappy, almost as if she blamed him for it. Julia stabbed her fingers several times towards the next house, that's the direction he ought to take, and for clarity of message she held the door tightly against herself as if to deny him entrance. There was a quick final jab with the finger and Madame Masse withdrew, closing the front door with a bang. Claude was stranded on the outside, open-mouthed still without having uttered a word.

Shivering in the night air, Claude set off across the grass to the next house at a quicker pace than he had arrived on her doorstep. The Commissar skirted several outbuildings until he came to the house, which responded not at all to his knock. All around it no light showed through uniformly intact windows. He had seen enough to allow his return to the same place, but gasping a little from his unaccustomed exercise in unsocial hours; the worst time of night for any man to take exercise. His ensuing respiratory distress admitted him without further ado into Julia's hall.

'They are not answering, are you sure they are at home?' he said.

'The house is empty, as well your policemen know,' Julia retorted emphatically to match the emphasis on the question; but then her eyebrows lifted and the hard expression softened visibly, as she was prepared to forgive him such departmental failings. Her dark face beamed. Claude stepped back a pace towards the door. 'The lights are out Madame Masse! When did the electricity fail?'

'Just . . . Oh I suppose it was an hour ago.'

'Ah there you have it, Madame; the alarm would have been triggered then, and the battery, it has expired!' Claude took another a step back.

'Oh, that is good.' She looked longingly at him and the warmth of her features again caught his attention through the dimness of the hall. 'Because it has given me an extra little problem as well; there is a more delicate matter for you to attend. It is in my room upstairs.' Her words penetrated Claude like an arrow and for a moment he stood speechless, watching as she lit another candle from the one that stood in the hall but deciding he must follow her up the stairs as she moved towards them. He felt snared as she glanced back with a face that tenderly softened towards him; she was revealing far more regard than ever he might have felt appropriate. In view of normal matrimonial niceties, her bedroom was the last place he wanted to be.

Madame Masse came to a halt at the door for one of the main bedrooms, the first at a commencement of an extensive upper hall. 'The alarm woke me, and as my bedside lamp did not work, I opened the window wide to see next door properly. A bird flew in, passing me before I could shut it again. The dear little thing seemed to be fleeing the racket,' she added thoughtfully. 'If it is in among my porcelain collection, something may get chipped. I am relying upon you and your skill, to put things right.' She smiled a weasel smile. 'If anyone at all can do it, I'm sure it is you.'

To his immediate sense of relief the compliment gave him reason to move away, except that now he needed to enter the room and perform. The room had seemed silent until then; but the moment he entered a sound of movement caught his attention, to be exact a flutter of wings and the clink of some well-rattled china. He froze, rooted to the spot, listening to the rasp of claws on woodwork. 'A dear little bird': Claude did not believe for one moment that the description was an apt one. The door drifting towards the jamb behind him suddenly banged shut, helped from the other side, leaving him trapped with some mysterious wild animal.

Cautiously Claude inched to the windows looking back into a darkened room as he did so. The light inside was not very good, fitfully changing as clouds drifted across the moon. He strained his eyes to see directly ahead and make out a shadowy bulk bowing the flimsy shelf of trivia. It was a bird that lodged there very awkwardly, crowded against the wall. Its cruel black eyes sparkled with light from the window; a white heart-shaped face watching him intently over a wicked-looking curved beak – definitely an owl, and a most unsettled one at that. The owl rasped its talons again upon the edge of the shelf, each move displacing a row of fragile ornaments that were slipping down the slope and stood like a delicate little train, nestling into the bird's feathers on either side. Even as he watched, a slight movement toppled one of them, leaving it very close to the edge. Claude had no illusions that he ought to leave promptly. But then, with a desire to act that surprised even him, he threw the nearest window wide open. Ducking down and scuttling across the room he squatted underneath the bird's chosen shelf.

It was a sheepdog-like technique, designed in an instant by his fertile brain, one that would surely drive an owl through the open window. Nothing further was needed; the bird took off with powerful wing beat, fanning Claude's balding head as he rose to rescue the delicate porcelain creation and righting it on the shelf. As he did so a heavy crunch sounded behind him, the owl had crashed into the adjacent unopened window. To Claude's startled glance, the bird was now a sorry heap on the window sill, its vicious beak gaping pitifully. Then to his horror, the feathered mass gathered itself up and took off to flap frighteningly large over himself. He was instantly sure that the owl blamed him specifically for its mishap. Claude cowered down under the shelf trying to be more inconspicuous as powerful wings beat the air above him. There was another crash as the owl ran into a large mirror reflecting the window opposite; the unfortunate bird then slithered down the wall back onto the original shelf again, and having arrived it scraped frantically to remain. China started to fall. Claude miraculously caught the delightful piece he had rescued earlier, and ducked yet again.

The moment the bird looked settled Claude ran doubled-up to the windows, opening all that would open. Instantly a dark shadow passed him by, and joyfully he closed both windows behind it. But as he started for the door with job apparently complete, china crashed beside him, a bedside lamp toppled, the alarm clock pinged noisily as it hit the floor – somewhere the assumption was flawed. Feathers, stiff like a brush, hit the Commissar full in the face, and flapped off; not only was the owl still there but its mate had joined it. Two sets of black eyes looked interestedly at a figure bent over double to avoid flying talons. The owls had chosen to perch at either end of the trivia shelf over the supports, and were staring at him in a most aggressive manner as he bobbed up. Their white faces gleamed in the moonlight leaving Claude intimidated by vicious beaks, but even so he stuck to his mission and valiantly trying to achieve something before retreating, pushed both windows wide open. Crouching low in case they made for the window Claude beat an immediate retreat, and came swiftly back into the hall.

'Has it gone?' enquired Mme Masse, hopefully envisaging a return to her bedroom.

'I very much regret Madame; there is a pair of very large owls in there. They are barn owls, birds that are used to entering buildings and so we simply have to wait until they leave for their normal home,' he said, not looking her in the eye. He handed her a Dresden china figurine, its head loose in the palm of his hand and waited impassively whilst she had hysterics over her favourite piece. He stood there in contemplation, remembering the rest as an expensive crunchy feel under his police-issue boots. With an absent mind Claude sought to wipe some excrement off his shoulder with a handkerchief.

'You can't go now!' cried his damsel, with tears running down her face.

'No,' groaned Claude, already resigned to his fate.

A while passed without any further noises coming from the bedroom. Julia Masse had set herself down upon a chair in the hall, whilst Claude busied himself lighting more candles from the one they had. Eventually, Madame grandly rose from her chair,

50

and carefully opened the bedroom door just a crack. The Commissar held his breath, guiltily remembering the well trodden-in china covering the carpet – two mice ran out of the room. Julia slammed the door very fast, and screamed; then lifting her wrap she danced sideways towards the bathroom. Claude followed her there, taking up a defensive rearguard position, but at the same time admiring an unexpected revelation of shapely legs along the way. Madame Masse was not happy until she was standing in the bath, gripping the slack of his shirt and feeling safe from wee rodents. They sat upon the rim of the bath, she inside and Claude outside. Her feet were inside, his were out, a position maintained until Madame saw him as a bridge into her refuge for the unmentionables. The exhortation to lift his feet, combined with a hefty tug on the shirt brought Claude tumbling into her refuge, where he decided to wait and allow the scare to die down. The wait was longer than he guessed, and grew longer by the minute as the frightened, shaky woman hung on to him with all the grip of a bulldog. There came a point when both subsided upon the hard wide bath, and Claude, still tired from his otherwise normal working day, drifted off to sleep.

It was either the dawn chorus or sheer discomfort that woke Claude. Able now to disentangle himself from the arms of Madame Masse he eased himself out of the bath and headed for the door of the master bedroom. Strange noises could be heard, sounds like cloth ripping. The Commissar opened the door a little and saw inside it was raining white feathers. As the feathers cleared he saw the owl; startled, the owl turned an inquisitive head towards him. It was sitting right in the middle of the bed with a strip of pillow still in its curved beak, and at its feet were materials arranged artistically to form the base of a nest, part bracken, part feathers, and nearby lay a dead mouse.

Mme Masse too had awoken, and struggled out of the bath in a totally disorderly state. She pushed past Claude to see for herself the revolting mess her bed had become, and was acutely aware of what was crunching under her feet. The lady's retreat was instant, as a second owl arrived through the open window bringing yet another curly-tailed morsel. Moments later Claude was roughly shoved aside as a raging woman hit out all over the place with a sweeping broom, and in seconds the room was clear with windows tightly closed. Mme Masse was having hysterics again in a room of shambles with nothing ceramic left to break. Julia emerged looking dangerous. Whereupon Claude decided she was primed for something more immediate than poison, and set off hastily for his car.

Before he got halfway there, she called to him, brandishing a telephone at arm's length. 'I doubt if I am doing them a favour in calling you back,' she said nastily, and left him to it. A minor official in the Commissariat of Police had a message for him, but not without making an unappreciated comment. 'Got you first time – Sir.'

The accompaniment of chuckles in the background enraged Claude. Gritting his teeth, and mentally promising to dispense proper retribution for the sally, he took the message. The call was set to extend his night's work considerably, for there were yet further phenomena deriving from the hidden cave explosion – his assistance was most urgently requested at the Montagne Source Minéral Plante.

6

Cherchez la Femme

Claude arrived at the spa offices at almost the same time as the insurance agent, an Englishman called Wigglesworth. He was as ever, a warning sign to the Commissar that money complicated the issue somewhere. Mr Wigglesworth leapt out of his car, hurrying towards the factory office doors. He passed without attempting to acknowledge Claude's hearty '*Bonjour*'. The policeman ignored his rudeness, and reflected on what had caused people to be so active at this early hour of the day, and on a Sunday too. He found an old pullover in the boot of his car to wear over the stain upon his shoulder, and trudged wearily in the wake of the man whose name he had mentally abbreviated to 'Wriggles', in part a response to the snub and partly for the man's reputation for squirming out of things like a snake.

Inside the reception area, Wigglesworth was already talking to a fat, elderly, even rough-looking man, whom Claude recognized as the proprietor of the adjoining tourist caves. Emerging from an inner office and looking unusually agitated the manager of the spa water plant hurried over towards him, totally ignoring the others. Still too preoccupied to talk, Monsieur Vilette the manager escorted Claude into his office. There a surly workman stood with his boots imprinting a square of carpet facing the managerial desk. Claude would normally be an impressive chief of police, dressed in a smart uniform, but the circumstances of his night-time emergency call-out had him unshaven and in clothes he would normally wear at the weekend. His condition did so much to lessen the formality of the occasion that the man on the carpet positively stood easy.

Invited to repeat his story, the operative launched into an account of how the filters had blocked only an hour after they started bottling. On opening up the outer coarse filter screen and removing the obstruction, they were surprised to find two pairs of ladies' knickers. The man pointed to the rear of the office where the offending garments hung – now quite dry. Claude headed towards the spot accompanied by Villette, a close friend of his, who explained further in a low voice.

'When I came in this morning, I found this treacherous chap phoning the local press. If it gets in the papers, our sales will drop out of sight.'

Claude was wary. 'It is hardly a police matter, but you have the grounds to dismiss him surely?'

Friend or not, Claude wanted to distance himself from the matter. He looked at the label and closed his eyes; he had heard the name before. 'Harrods. This lady, she is connected with England!' Vilette was not listening, he had already decided that it was an English tourist and had picked up the telephone. Within minutes of his summons the cave proprietor, Henri Severac, and his insurance man joined them. Vilette was certain that a vandal tourist must have dropped the garments into the water from the high observation platform, and said so in an angry manner. Henri countered with an argument. 'The subterranean lake overflows into other chambers when the plant is idle overnight. The plain fact is that you run the plant on Sunday to avoid dirt from all those upper caves, which means anybody's personal garments could easily be among the rubbish floated in from elsewhere.'

Wigglesworth, much heartened to see Severac holding his own, interrupted. Could he use the telephone? Vilette, who by now was fully occupied with Henri's argument, merely pointed the agent towards an adjoining glass-partitioned side office.

Claude watched Wigglesworth intently through the glass. It was evident the man was earnestly engaged in a difficult conversation. That was enough for Claude; he was out of the room quickly. He slid past the partition, neatly replacing the receptionist cum tele-phonist who was moving towards her other work. He was plugged into the line before she quite realized he had seized her handset, and when she did, a tug of war began between them. But before it occurred to her that she could unplug him he had heard enough; there were substantial inducements being offered to keep the matter out of print. The receptionist, having intercepted him, was difficult to get away from and Claude was moved to identify himself. A mistake because she had found somebody who might have time to listen to all her gripes, and a list of all the everyday incidents that were unfair to her personally began. The Commissar struggled with politeness and empathy as the woman moved into a further highly strung set of complaints.

At that moment another member of the scruffy Severac family rushed by, and immediately entered the manager's office. That ended Claude's empathetic episode. 'I must go,' he shouted, and rushed off after him. It was Georges Severac, keen to see his father and impart urgent news of real vandalism in the caves. When Claude entered he was pressed into accompanying Wigglesworth and the Severac pair to view damage in the show-cave. It was only of incidental interest to him, but having arrived he found an officer from his force, shaken and well out of his depth – so naturally he stayed.

His man, Officer Mullet, was not among the brightest, but had enough brawn to be the one chosen when a violent intruder was reported as locked up in the caves. Mullet and Georges had earlier tried a pincer movement round the cave circuit, and were astonished to find it empty. Mullet almost didn't survive to tell the tale, because he strode unknowingly towards the unfenced bottomless hole, and just managed to leap over it at the last moment. The reckless way he'd covered the ground in his half of the cave had left him quiet and decidedly lacklustre; so much so that when Claude arrived he was in a mood to obey rather than his usual tendency to obstruct senior officers.

Henri could hardly credit the damage that had been done; money was strewn in plenty upon the floor, so it was hardly the work of a thief.

'A madman,' said Georges, basking in thoughts of glory and all ready to take any credit available as he had struggled with the hulking brute – one who could single-handedly heave a protective stone wall into oblivion.

Wigglesworth was pleased he was there, the takings were safe and no one could say they weren't. Neither did he think that the dry stonewall would take much rebuilding; so jolly good on that score too. The shrine cave held more intrigue than anything else as little mounds of paraffin wax covered the floor, but of course it could all be cleaned up.

For the Commissar the mounds of white were painfully reminiscent of bird droppings, and conjured up more guilty thoughts about a certain bedroom. His mind eagerly shut out such a connection, being that this was police evidence, and as police business had to be seen with clear mind there was no sense in confusing one with the other. A shout came from the adjacent cave, and at once he gravitated towards Mullet, who was steadfastly turning others away from a pile of crumpled newspapers. At the very top of the pile was another garment exactly similar to the two recovered earlier: it was stained with a smear of blood, and nesting upon that was a wisp of rubber. His audience stood back respectfully, as the detective of local fame instructed a policeman to carefully lift the garment and read the label.

' 'Arrods,' Mullet said. 'The blood 'as been wiped, it is not as worn.' Mullet stepped smartly back having read it haltingly in English, for the benefit of Wigglesworth who had queried everything so far. There was a certain dignity about the heavy constable interpreting salient facts.

Wigglesworth threw up his hands in exasperation – it was a link with the bottling plant that he could well do without. But recognizing an English girl's impression of 'spilling cockerel blood onto a bed sheet' as a lost virginity rite was quite beyond him, especially as she only had a finger bleed to do it with.

'Was there a woman with your intruder?' Claude asked Georges. The facts were not fitting together; Claude knew that a woman was there and that her presence would have to be explained. He awaited an answer, whilst Wigglesworth shifted his feet uneasily, impatient to be off.

Georges racked his brains to remember that last party. 'There was someone wrapped in a yellow cycle cape. I didn't see her leave – she could have stayed here with him.'

Claude nodded to Mullet, who needed no further prompting to set off up the slope towards the entrance. Georges led Claude, Henri and Wigglesworth further on into the caves, retracing the route taken by his party. They visited the lake, and then a number of empty caves including the ultraviolet cave, none of which yielded anything new. Eventually they arrived at a door separating the show-caves from the others, and there found the floor submerged in at least an inch of water. Again there were wax stumps in evidence; and upon examination the door was found to be unlocked.

'That's what they stole!' cried Georges knowingly, 'they needed my keys!'

Henri looked at him sharply. 'Keys were requested by a big

fellow wanting to go through there the day before yesterday. I said no and off he went. Very polite he was.'

Claude was inquisitive. 'Was he over two metres in height and dressed in a smart city suit – a Walloon?' All present looked at him in confused manner, except Henri.

'No, not dressed in a smart suit and neither was he a local man; but he certainly was a heavily built, tall man, dressed in an expensive pale leather jacket,' Henri added thoughtfully. Georges suddenly left them, urgently striding up the slope, as the cavern door opened causing the group to move. Feet hastily retreated from a tide of water flooding in through the opening door, but not before it had washed over Wigglesworth's expensive shoes, even managing to take a little whiteness off Claude's boots. Henri shone a torch ineffectively into the black void; there was nothing to be seen from the vicinity of the door, just light glinting off ankle-deep water. He slammed the door shut, much to the relief of the others who were shivering in a small gale of chill air that arrived with the water.

For Claude this was a further chill reminder of Madame Masse and her doorstep. He shook off the unwelcome vision by pinning Henri down for a statement accurate enough to identify the big fellow. One man was present in his thoughts and he steadily became more convinced as they talked that it was Marc Casserta, but this man in particular was unlikely to have a female accomplice. It was steadily becoming more important to discover how many remained in the cave the previous evening.

Georges had returned, ushering into their presence someone unrecognized by Claude, a tall heavily built man in waders carrying a heavy-duty lantern. Triumphantly Georges entered the conversation, clinking keys together above his head. 'These keys were still at the entrance,' he said, 'I found them laid on the turnstiles.'

'To burgle a ticket counter, leave the proceeds scattered over the floor and then so very kindly return the keys is astonishing – unless the intruder really is a lunatic.' Claude's comment had his audience aware that he saw contradiction in such a sequence of events. The Commissar fixed Georges with a most penetrating stare. 'Where are those keys normally kept?'

Full realization came to Georges, his brow visibly moved. 'He didn't want our money in the cash box, it was the keys that he wanted, wasn't it?'

Claude's attention strayed to the newcomer, a much tattooed, fleshy individual in a string vest who was trying to attract his attention. 'I can see Monsieur that you have something to say?'

Georges' companion launched his news immediately. 'There was a huge collapse in the cavern last night cutting off the services to the high promenade. If people have strayed into the caves out there, then we ought to start finding them.'

'Who are you?' asked Claude, now half-recognizing the man, but quite determined not to be ensnared in problems other than the current investigation. That was not a constructive reply for the man in a string vest, and for a moment he was lost for words.

Georges was quick to supply the introduction. 'It's Monsieur Kee,' he said respectfully. 'I thought we all knew him; he is the maintenance man for the services and key-holder for the other end of the local caves. It would appear that he has already cut off the water supply this end, as the pipe is broken somewhere in the middle.'

There was no way that Claude was going to view the damage; the string vest had him feeling cold, especially after the draught revealed even worse conditions beyond the door. He realized that he was getting deeper and deeper into some kind of chilly 'tar baby.'

'You two are better equipped to inspect the extent of fall. I must excuse myself, for another matter has arisen that I must attend.' Claude moved well away from the little group.

Wigglesworth hurried to catch him up with his neat shoes squelching water and quite unsuitable for the task of walking; he needed to dry out and borrow footwear from somewhere else. Claude suspected that Wigglesworth was still on the defensive and was staying close to the action for reasons other than wet feet.

Mullet was in the cave of the barrels when Claude arrived with Henri Severac and Wigglesworth. The policeman was sitting on one chair, examining the contents of two cheap fabric saddlebags standing upon others. Mullet pretended not to notice his boss until the Commissar queried what he had there. But Mullet had noticed the others there and made his announcement to all present in his inimitably clumsy way. 'I found two bicycles on the waste land, gentlemen; both were partly hidden in the bushes. The lady's bike, and also the gent's bike were hired in Lourdes, both of which were adjusted for persons of over two metres in height. The lady's saddlebag contains the passport of Hazel Gray, and further indicates that she is the woman of the abandoned underwear.' He pointed to the nearby pile of crumpled newspapers and then, as if matching playing cards, he lifted another two pairs of knickers out of one of the bags and remarked excitedly, '*Voilà deux culottes de femme, 'Arrods.'*

Claude was finding this non-stop investigation of a crime scene a little too much, so he called a halt to it. Other facts could be dealt with in a more regulated way. Un-breakfasted and dry-mouthed he started for home. At the mouth of the caves he saw Wigglesworth, who was stomping along towards the cars in ill-fitting boots borrowed from Henri's shop. Not wishing to interact with him further, Claude followed behind upon the winding path that connected with the spa complex. A faint recollection had entered his mind that his friend Monsieur Vilette would surely be taking morning coffee about now; thoughts of coffee tantalized him. Why go home? Claude continued on to the Montagne Plante offices. He was quickly admitted to Vilette's office, a businessman he knew better as Simon, for they were on first-name terms. Simon already had his morning tray, and Claude had found a convenient oasis. The warmth of the office, and the simple pleasures of coffee with fancy biscuits, had him listening to the many problems that had arisen this morning linked to the finding of foreign materials in drinking water.

The Commissar was soon offering some friendly advice to Simon. 'The disgraced workman, I think you can easily keep him, for it is likely the papers will not publish. And even if they did, the management is quite within their rights to experiment with new filters, for they should try materials readily available, be they knicker-shaped or any other for that matter. Whatever transpires now, the flood in the cavern gives you a good excuse to suspend manufacturing and supplying bottled water for the time being and concentrate on the spa services.' Pursuing the point Claude told him of the fractured mains supply as reported by the man in the string vest. Simon Vilette started when Kee was mentioned. 'That's Jan Kee isn't it? He is a neighbour of mine, who lives in the next street; in fact he's extremely close as our gardens butt on to one another.

'I always think of rats whenever I set eyes on him, and besides the obvious there is a very good reason that rats come to mind. As you probably know as well as me there is a rare rodent, a sort of mouse called Dansk living around here. Jan caused a stir by stating that he knew of a whole colony breeding deep in his part of the caves. I can only guess at his reasons for piloting a zoo in the cave beyond us; but his exhibits were false and eventually shown to be rats. I can tell you that the elderly ladies attending our spa baths didn't like to hear anything of rats, and there was an immediate decline in the numbers of customers attending the spa. That is the background for my mistrust and that has made me always take special note of him. There are other instances; but the latest is a blonde woman who has suddenly popped up at his house, and I am sure she meets the description of a lady who disappeared from the caves about a week ago. Maybe it is only a coincidence, but unless proven otherwise, I shall stay very suspicious.'

Vilette's comment encouraged Claude to air his views on a related subject, namely the fitting of locked doors to the show-caves, which brought with them a whole new dimension ready to creep into police work. 'That disappearance you refer to for instance, it couldn't have been more bogus than the one today. For we now appear to have missing, a pair of exceptionally tall sweethearts who have left their borrowed bicycles on your spare ground. It seems they entered the caves separately, made a costly mess of them, and then had sex before disappearing along the back route. So if Monsieur Kee used the caves for traditional elopement, then that is likely to cause me a lot less trouble, especially as doing so stays sweetly in keeping with the romantic nonsense surrounding these caves. Locked doors are turning it into a nightmare to me; for where the eloping lovers used to stay singly overnight and then disappear through the caves with their lover, with everyone knowing that they can just walk out somewhere or other, they now have doors locked in their path. The locked doors in my mind leave room for all sorts of tragic mistakes to happen because the folklore enjoys wider publicity than the locked doors. These latest two, for instance, have created a big fuss to establish they were here and when the relatives come knocking it will be our access door that makes us responsible. You can be quite sure that those two will not be found under a fall of rock – they will be well away by now, and I for one will not be in a hurry to look for them.'

Their chat had completely exhausted the coffee supply, and

before long a much-refreshed Claude was on his way home for some overdue sleep. He arrived to the morning papers, varied items of mail, and a small cardboard box evidently delivered by hand. Opening the box he found a small egg resting upon nesting material. He examined the egg closely through a magnifying glass, it was a pottery memento not a real owl's egg. It would seem that she had forgiven him, and was sparing him for the next time, probably tonight. He smiled grimly to himself. From what he knew, the electricity would still be off; and doubtless there would be mice – he headed for bed.

At much the same time Georges was putting away keys for the caves' rear exit. He was realizing that they were not the keys he used occasionally, but a separate set of spare keys normally kept in the upstairs office drawer. The significance of finding that two sets of keys had been used last night, a fact that would have radically re-organized Commissar Brie's views had he known, meant little or nothing to Georges. His immediate thoughts were directed towards local ironmongers and where best to get another set made. Unknown to the Commissar, his simple scenario no longer fitted the evidence.

7

Second Birth

Hazel was aware of someone bending over her. She opened her eyes and the shadow resolved itself into a human face – a dark-haired woman smiled down on her.

'My name is Annita, and if I am right, you are Hazel.'

'How did you know that?' croaked Hazel, discovering she had a sore throat. Not only was the throat parched, but also her body was exceptionally weary and this extreme limpness was topped only by a severe headache. Attempting to disregard all of these afflictions, she listened for an answer; her eyes roving past the kindly face towards a bowed, translucent, yellow-tinted wall; it looked distorted somehow. Under her bare back solid supports dug in, rigid and uncomfortable. Hazel felt beneath her and encountered hard metal bars narrowing to a point where she rested. The kneeling woman Annita was dressed very simply in a thick woollen grey-green knitted shift, and that was a whole lot more than she could boast.

'It was all detailed in the bag over your shoulder.' Annita smiled to reassure her.

'Where's Terry? Is he all right?' Some details started to filter back, and Hazel's cracked voice rose as fear took her mind.

'He will be all right – we are accepting everyone who arrives at present. There is soup waiting for you and from the sound of your voice it will do you good; just relax for now and I'll fetch it.'

Annita left by opening a door which appeared to have been simply cut out of the material forming the room; it hung back on a thong, the thong acting as a hinge for connecting both parts together. Annita took care in closing the door as she exited, and this alerted Hazel to the fact there was a second tie made through other eye-holes in it; she was in effect a prisoner. She looked about her, feeling dizzy and listless, but more aware now of her surroundings. The cell was not deformed as she had at first thought, expecting them to be proper walls – it was spherical instead. A sphere bathed in a diffuse, slightly yellow light – light apparently coming in from all directions. Touching the wall that rose at her side beyond the metallic ridges underneath her, she felt a smooth, rigid and plastic-like surface. The wall was one that she could not easily see through; etched perhaps at eye level, but clear above. Looking through the wall higher up there did seem to be neighbouring spheres.

The hard, greenish, powdery metal support she lay upon so uncomfortably was the only other major structure as it formed a floor right across her cell. And beneath its mesh was what looked like water; she touched its surface – yes it wetted her fingers. Annita was back carrying a woolly-backed tray, upon which rested an oddly shaped soup plate. The plate looked rather too long to be a container for soup, and appearing more artistic than functional certainly stood its ground in a level fashion. By contrast the spoon supplied with it was in a class of its own for style and brilliance, rather as if she were to eat expensively. The contents steamed in an enticing manner, and soon Hazel was eating a thick mushroom gruel. The tray stayed in Annita's hands for she turned it over and sat on its soft side, moving in to be close and putting a question to Hazel. 'What do you do for a living?'

'I'm a hairdresser, but not a fully trained one as yet.' Hazel took another sip, she felt hungry, but had to rearrange her legs on the mesh for eating.

'That will make you popular here, but you will be pushed for time to do it. I was a trainee teacher, but even without the children, I find I am busy all of the time.'

Hazel felt the bumps in her peculiar plate. 'How long was I unconscious?'

Annita laughed a laugh that twitched her eyebrows. 'We created a record this morning, you and I. Normally people are there for hours; but you came along when I was all dressed up and doing the job. That and the quick way you entered must be why you have regained consciousness in little over an hour; normally it takes four to eight hours. The other good thing about it is that you are English, and we can talk easily to one another.'

Hazel had finished, and was staring at Annita's reflection in the spoon's brilliant metallic yellow back. 'Isn't it bright,' she remarked, driven by curiosity.

'It's solid gold.' Annita broke into a laugh at Hazel's incredulous look; her bushy eyebrows waved like flags as if in some curious way the laugh had activated them. The infectious laugh soon had Hazel laughing too. 'It's a bit like only having cake,' Annita continued.

'Is this an isolation ward?' Hazel broke free of the laughter.

'You could look at it that way,' burbled Annita. 'For the moment you will have to live here until we can house you in the village.'

'Did we make it? Are we outside the caves?' Hazel was desperate to know.

'Sorry to disappoint you,' Annita held her hand tightly. 'We are cut off here and very deep in the mountains. But in all it is not so bad as you might imagine.'

Hazel rested her head down, it felt heavy; the news had swept through her fatigued frame and left her feeling gutted. All of that walking was to no avail.

The voice continued on and on; but what Annita was saying seemed to be from further and further away. Annita looked kindly down upon a sleeping girl.

The rocking motion persisted, cutting into dreams of her sister Heather tangled in Dad's fishing line; the boat was tilting over and making a reflection on the water. It was her name being called. Annita's face came fuzzily into focus, accompanied by the scent of meaty food, causing a hidden appetite to spring to the fore. Annita proffered the tray, this time together with another unusual soup plate, shaped more like a hollowed-out cabbage. There were meaty solids there, and possibly vegetables floated. Hazel dreamily sat and took it over – was this for real?

'You still look tired.' Annita's voice was sympathetic.

Hazel collected herself as she ate; everything she wanted to know seemed to be eluding her. 'Are there many of you?' she asked at last, even then finding her mind having trouble in concentrating on the answer. She just wanted to lie down right away and drowse but forced an over-weak arm to transport soup.

'There are thirteen of us and you will make it fourteen. Also I can tell you your job is settled; you shall be our new Charon and take over from me.'

'Did you all decide that, or was it you? Hazel had a feeling she should have been consulted over this, for after all her occupation had to suit her personally. But her indignation somehow didn't rise to the occasion as she expected it would; she was feeling weak and it was all a bit hazy.

'No, our Queen visited you yesterday, and she confirmed the matter.'

The effort of talking was getting too much for Hazel, her jaw felt numb and heavy chewing with effort as it closed over the last spoonful. Yesterday, did she say?

Hazel opened her eyes. She was wide awake and the mesh at her back almost tore away from the skin as she sat, and the back of her arm bore a deep imprint of metal mesh. She had puzzles in the mind. Thirteen, and I will be fourteen – what about Terry? – Then there was the other man, were they both included? And then what about her new name, was she being renamed Sharon? Or was it a function as say Charon – the boatman of hell in Greek mythology? The idea didn't appeal to her one little bit.

She rubbed her thigh, it felt wrinkly and the skin was heavy with scurf; how long had she been here? Her mind darted about without solution of any kind. She got up and paced the uneven floor frame, each bar was cut to cross flat in another's groove, rather than being fixed rigidly; in fact the whole floor was not fixed it just rested upon the bottom round of a sphere. More pertinent to her, the floor was even slightly uncomfortable to her bare feet now that she stood. Where were her clothes? Not that she needed them in the comfortable warmth of this place. The half-light intrigued her, where did it come from? Was it tied in with the blinding flash that knocked her down – the same energy source?

The door was fastened from outside, but the gap about its edges enabled a finger to move the door on its fastenings and easily enough feel the edge. This was hard and springy material, more like stainless steel sheet metal than plastic despite its transparent look. She shook the door, it barely rattled, but in the midst of shaking it she saw the outline of a facing rocky wall. The door was misty at her level, but clear higher up, so she could see some but not all of it. There were neighbouring globes, and that fact probably accounted for her confusion, she decided. Perhaps like seeing through a lot of clear balloons. Hazel's wanderings ceased, she sat upon Annita's flat perch and wondered why she was in the altogether? Certainly the aches and pains had departed leaving her with a clear mind, and although thoughts arrived and departed by the score, not a single thing was resolved as the hours passed.

Hazel slept, but lightly enough to awaken when the door was unfastened. Annita entered with two steaming mugs and a plate on a tray; over her shoulder was suspended some grey knitted material. Putting the tray down on the floor mesh, she took one of the two mugs and clutched it, sitting cross-legged upon her flat seat.

'How do you feel?' Annita asked sympathetically.

'Was I drugged?' Hazel felt she ought to know and, before Annita could answer, she had blurted out her several other worries as well.

Annita sat there sorting out what she had to answer before replying, and mentally trying to assess what was the more important, harking back to her own fears at this point. 'Some of the plants here naturally induce sleep; everyone who comes here recovers by sleeping off the side effects, the routine hasn't altered for centuries. It is twenty days since you entered, and you have had the shortest length of time given; that is because you were rather small naturally and met our limits easily, without the treatment you were likely to go on feeling not right for months. Your Terry now, was he the man you pulled past the sentry or was Terry the one who stayed ahead of you?'

Hazel's eyes opened wide in astonishment. 'I didn't see a sentry but I helped Terry in.'

'Sorry,' said Annita, 'we call it the "sentry"; it is a huge stone giving out shocks. You probably saved that man's life by dragging him fully through, because in there he was difficult to reach, usually they crawl out. Tall men who are underweight do tend to be hit a lot more in that sentry passage, more so for men than women, although we are told it's probably because they are in front and release the full force. Others say we have more subcutaneous fat to protect us. But the fact of greatest importance in here is the one that has so many men survive; they outnumber us easily, there are at least fifty of them.'

Hazel pointed to the tray. 'Is it still sleepy stuff?'

'Taste it,' invited Annita. 'I think that you will recognize this.'

Hazel cautiously raised the tray onto her knees, and picking up the same gold-coloured spoon tasted the thick white solids on the plate. 'Its yogurt isn't it?' She did not need her answer; this was a thick creamy Greek-style yogurt, rather like one she had eaten on holiday last year. The dish steadily emptied, as Hazel found it difficult to resist any of the delightful taste – after all, she was ravenously hungry this time round.

Annita confirmed that it was made from fresh sheep milk, watching as Hazel discarded another odd plate, and slid the empty tray under her bottom, sitting all attention with mug in her hand. It was good to see such a recovery, without all the sickness and mess that could easily persist to this stage. Annita grinned happily at seeing reticence blossom into enthusiasm, but then remembered she still had other points to answer.

'Charon is the ferry-man of Greek legend, and that's what I have been doing so far, saving souls for this place. We laughingly call the entrance cave the "Styx cave"; because just like Hades it is a world of no return, our sentry makes certain of that. If you don't like the connection, you could equally think of it as midwifery and you as the midwife, because you assist them to be born into another world. But of course you still will be "Charon" as the name of your official responsibility calls it. Everybody will be pleased to welcome you, because they will all move one up the ladder, including me. I shall introduce you to everyone and do my best to explain the workings of the place, for although it is my pleasure, as Charon it is also my job.'

Hazel looked again at her plate; she turned it thoughtfully, examining its very individual buckles that distinguished it as something new. 'Can I see Terry?' she asked in a plaintive voice, one that doubted her wish would be granted.

'He is not your husband is he?' Annita's voice sounded suddenly concerned.

'No, he's just a good friend but I'd like to put my mind at rest.' Hazel tried to make her voice sound unconcerned, although she was in reality becoming more anxious than before.

'You are so wide awake that I think we could go and have a quick look.' Annita held high a woollen dress, one that was identical with her own, and dropped it over Hazel's head, laughing. Hazel's face registered surprise as the heavy knit dropped to her shoulders, transforming her from pink to grey. She laughed too as her head popped out to face eyebrows that twitched with the laugh, and that particular sign seemed to say Annita was enjoying herself. The transformation enabled feelings of genuine relief to sweep through her.

They emerged without further delay from one of several yellow cell spheres that stood in a row. Her front door opened on to a narrow alley, facing a ridge of rock slabs roughly embedded in mortar, and this crude man-built wall met the roof at some considerable height. Annita said the high wall in front was to protect the village from any Styx cave radiation, and a lower wall behind the cells was intended to partially protect the temporary inmates in like manner. They turned within a dozen or so paces into an alley, which penetrated the low stone wall. Annita moved Hazel into the chamber, her arm steering the newcomer into its centre.

'This will be your territory from now on.'

The chamber was a long one, with the ceiling curve bathed in bright light of phosphorescence sloping down towards the far end where there was an abrupt split, the back wall being just a plain grey wall of rock. On the right hand side this massive rock face was penetrated by huge pile of lighter-coloured rocks, tumbled down to form the alley of her arrival. They approached the centre and Hazel could see further into the split far end where high up a number of rounded shapes shared at least one ledge. Around them coloured patterns moved languidly upon the walls. Annita waved her hand at them saying, 'When there's not much movement, you can be sure that nothing much is happening.' She gave Hazel a piece of slate to ward off the competing phosphorescence and see the root-like appendages hanging down from the gourds, following those bramble-like roots to the ground where a number were evident and were obviously the roots she had tripped over on the entrance walk in.

Annita pointed above to where she had been looking. 'Those gonk-like plants live off meat; they seem to have evolved roots that can be dangled in bodies that used to collect here. It spurs us on to rescue people rather than leave them long enough to find they have become merely fertilizer for the plants. We might not like them, or always beat them, but at least they keep the places we can't reach clear, for even the bones must go.'

More than a little disgusted, Hazel looked about her for the tiny fairy mortals, but none were visible; that part must be sheer hallucination she decided. The space was silent and all eerily empty with an atmosphere of its own. Hazel spoke her thoughts out loud. 'It's a bit like a church.'

Annita nodded appreciatively. 'You're getting warm, the place is at the very least a cemetery. We stand in awe of it, and because we all came in this way it has a profound influence on our lives.' She turned, and led the way back to the junction through the walled alley. Hazel expected a right turn back to her cell, but instead they turned to the left, advancing on other bubble cells. The row differed from her area in that it was longer, and you could see through most of the sparkling clear walls. The third bubble was etched to be opaque and was set lower than its predecessor, which it actually touched. Annita entered this open sphere and walked over the loose aggregate floor, where she stood looking through a cutaway circle in the side wall, peering at the bulge of an adjacent bubble. Hazel was invited to look and was appalled at the sight of Terry; he had been laid on the now familiar mesh, devoid of clothes, his skin looked very red. Perhaps it was distortion, but his body seemed less of a beanpole now although she certainly could not call him tubby. The heap that was Terry was evidently unconscious, with only one sign of care and that was the tube protruding from his nose which gave an air of hospitalization and seriousness. She turned towards Annita, her eyes full of tears and needing to be reassured.

'He will be all right; the men always have a hard time, but he's OK. Look on the other side of you.' Hazel looked into the other adjacent cell, although really she felt too distressed to see any more. It was like looking at a mirror image of Terry, except that the man was just as much a sorry heap. The curve must for sure introduce a distortion she thought, for through the window lay the madman their tracks had so unfortunately crossed; but he did not look the huge brute that she expected either. 'I can accept the men might conceivably have a harder time than me, but even so, they cannot possibly be that much worse, can they?' Hazel's disbelief sparked an answer.

'No, you are right, they are left much longer in the chamber, and then fed for a while via a tube with foods that stunt their growth. It is the only way our food supplies can cope with such a high population, particularly as there are some five times our number of men. Don't worry, you will see how well it works later on.'

69

'Will it make Terry have stumpy legs and a big head?'

'No, I think that you will be perfectly satisfied with him after-wards. He will be about shoulder high on you'

'Am I shorter than I was?

'You were already shorter than average and so you are not much shorter than you were; as far as I am told we tend to be left as we are.'

Annita led Hazel back, but this time into another bubble cell near her own, explaining that it was wise to secure the door herself from the inside. There were several characters she would best meet later, rather than have them as visitors.

'Tomorrow I will fetch you a breakfast to start the day, and later we shall take a walk in the village.'

Hazel knew she had not been up for very long, but tiredness had crept in again, her skin was sore and her muscles ached. She also suffered a headache and it could be that seeing the men had distressed her, but the sum total of what Annita had told her was reassuring, leaving her a lot less anxious after her walk. Hazel entered her new quarters, only to find that they were furnished with a bed of soft fibreboard, which bridged all those hard metal ridges. Soon she had tied the door and lay sweating on the bed in her new thick wool dress, but feeling properly civilized now.

8

The Vanishing Lady

Marc Casserta lay watching the ghost of his reflection in the dome of the yellow bubble; it looked fine up there rather than the red raw reality he glimpsed spread out beneath. Through the hot agony of his skin, a major throb of pain pulsed from head to groin, and beside that everything else was background. The throat tube sticking up so medically restricted him from seeing with ease; a ghostly image in the dome was all that he had. His hands were fixed. Marc soon realized that they were secured at the wrist to the metallic framework underneath him. This place was more a prison than a hospital, although it was medical attention he hoped he was getting. Time passed in an all-embracing silence. The yellow reflections above did nothing to relieve the tedium, they stood out from the translucent material, and were probably a mirror effect of the dark background. Marc turned his head slightly, almost seeing through to the outline of a similar structure close by – the view was not informative. There were no more clues. He tried to cut off the hurts by concentrating on the ceiling until it swam, and with an effort of will kept it swirling and unfocused.

His pain diminished when his head whirled, and that led on to odd feelings of frustration as thoughts of her arrived. The search had been a total failure, but still Marc clung to his impression that he had given of his best in the situation that presented itself, and if it were finally to kill him at least he had tried. Marc could hear the phone ringing even now: he had jumped to it expecting Greta's evening call, only to find his wife's friend Blanche on the line.

'Greta is missing.' Blanche stated it as fact; then rambled on with an account of all the possibilities that she had exhausted – could he come at once?

It was inevitable that he should. But his job was a responsible one as works engineer of a local cable-manufacturing firm, and this decreed Marc's first thoughts would be directed to his work. It was the holiday season, the worst possible time to be away and a matter to bother him on the usual dawn journey; but this time with much trepidation – for he must urgently request compassionate leave. Some hours later the management were being very good about it, understanding his plight to a far greater degree than ever he could have envisaged. His boss in particular, a member on the board of directors, was helpful, wishing him well and offering any support the company could lend; a comforting thought, even if it was just words.

Marc had his suitcase and was ready to go at once, boarding the plane near Brussels before midday. Lutz-St-Saveur he knew could be reached in two hops, because their family friend Blanche often did this trip. She owned shops in a couple of spa towns, giving her the chance of many short vacations, to which they were often invited; but Marc found that his job usually prevented him from accompanying the women. The inescapable fact was that Greta had gone below, visiting caves, and was not present when the party surfaced; Blanche had seen that with her own eyes. She immediately alerted the police but they were decidedly slow in reacting to the emergency; a male relative would probably elicit more success. 'Come quickly' was her advice.

Many were the forms, and several were the minor officials that Marc remembered meeting later that afternoon. Demanding action higher up the official tree, Marc found the Commissar had been called away from the station on an urgent matter. The policewoman who handled the Commissar's appointments explained semi-confidentially that someone called Mitzi had gone missing as well, and this had thrown the great man's day into disorder. Commissar Brie had however worked on Greta's case before he left, and during a mid-morning conference arrangements for an afternoon investigation in the caves had been delegated. Marc passed over photographs of Greta. She was such a shapely blonde that he knew the snapshots would concentrate the minds of policemen wonderfully, or at least perk them up if they were flagging. After his visit he felt more optimistic about things, and returned to Blanche in her holiday chalet.

Blanche had gone to pieces. She was all tears and commiseration. But with or without tears, he blamed her for being the cause

72

of it all and as a result made little conversation. Marc concentrated on looking through his wife's things. The room Greta occupied gave away almost nothing in the way of clues; her clothes were all in there apart from one blue summer dress. She was not wearing expensive jewellery either, just a little charm necklace, his present on her last birthday. He was interrupted in this as Blanche called him to the front door, where a policeman partially blocked the view.

'He is Monsieur Vierne, a police sergeant, who wonders if you would like to be present at the search.'

'I thought that it had taken place this afternoon.' Marc scowled at the man.

'I said that they needed a push,' Blanche said angrily.

'There were too many trippers to do it then.' Vierne sounded apologetic. 'We have asked the guides to stay on after their last circuit.'

It was early evening as they arrived, and the site was quite clear of tourists. The search was a perfunctory affair in slow measure. Marc watched three policemen set off to tramp over all the show-cave routes and finally to check upon the subterranean lake.

M. Vierne, the lithe, peppery, slim-built copper with curly moustaches, took Marc in tow, and together they sought out Henri Severac. He had awaited their arrival and was busily sweeping out his dingy forecourt café. The cave proprietor was in fact the actual guide, who had managed to lose the most stunningly attractive blonde ever to be in one of his parties. So attractive was she that he knew exactly when the disappearance had taken place. Her attention had appeared to be elsewhere and not at all engaged with what he was saying. So later when the party arrived in the fluorescence cave and she was absent, he thought boredom had helped her to the exit.

M. Vierne was standing with notebook at the ready, and looking doubtful. 'Monsieur, did the numbers tally?' he asked tentatively, seeking corroboration.

'No, the exit was one short if you assume the counters are right; we can never be absolutely certain that they are working correctly, but it did make us check through the caves.' Henri sounded mystified, although Marc observed a wary look on his face, which suggested he would not knowingly provide substance for any suggestion of negligence.

73

Vierne asked Henri Severac to accompany them and minutes later all three were inside the caves. Vierne wanted to see the bottomless hole first and examined it closely. He didn't say so, but Marc knew the possibility of suicide was in his mind.

'You should have some kind of grid in here, Monsieur,' Vierne said nicely.

Henri appeared to know what was next required of him, for without a word he led them back into the entrance cave, entered the ticket recess and began unlocking the till. From inside the cash compartments he produced several large keys on a ring. Taking up the keys, Henri shook them right under Vierne's nose, as if to prove he had them safe – seemingly with the idea in mind of obviating more 'after the event' advice. All three headed down the slope to a cave of barrels and entered the sparsely lit section of the caves.

The guide headed for a heavy door just off the main path. Something glittered on the floor. With a gasp of surprise, Marc picked up Greta's necklace of charms, and identified the first positive evidence of her in the cave. Immediately Henri tried the key, which failed to move; this had him open mouthed in surprise, because he had found the door unlocked.

'When did you last have cause to open it?' Vierne snapped, as if he had caught the man out in something criminal.

Henri looked at him blankly. 'I never use it,' he said lamely. 'But I do know that the door was locked.'

Vierne gave him a disbelieving look, wrinkling his face as if the words gave him mental indigestion. He moved towards the open door, a thin, supercilious smile playing around his lips; here was evidence enough for the production of a hard-hitting report. Switching on a portable electric lamp, Vierne stepped into a small gale as the door swung wide. Immediately outside he held the light high, looking for the emergency key in its glass-fronted case, but the key was there in its wooden window, with glass so dirty that it was evident no one had touched it from the other side. Vierne faced Henri accusingly.

'You should routinely check that door, and know for sure that your caves are secure. In any case you have a duty to the local authority.'

Henri shrugged his shoulders, his face fixed in a mask of disgust. He turned about and retreated into his own area, the huff very evident to Marc. Vierne probed about with the light outside the door until Marc interrupted him.

'Will there now be a police search of the caves out there?' He held up his wife's necklace.

Vierne shook his head vehemently. '*Non, non, non.*' He waved his hands, dismissing the necklace. 'Inside you found it – inside we search.'

'But she's obviously gone through this door!'

'Tell that to the Commissar, he is the man to authorize.' Vierne lifted eyes that had a helpless look, but still went on ignoring the raging features of the hefty engineer.

'He will be in the station, ready to see you at 10 am tomorrow. That I can promise, and by then he should have the results of our enquiries to hand – Commissar Brie is the man who can help you, Monsieur.'

Vierne's tone had become very firm and polite, but from that moment on Marc was aware that the man had shut off. Vierne's prime concern was to see him off the premises, and that extended to transporting Marc back to the holiday chalet.

Blanche had a message for him when he returned. 'A Monsieur Jan Kee rang whilst you were out. He said your secretary asked him to make contact with you. He will be present at the Vidal caravan site tomorrow at noon, so if you want to meet him you can.'

Marc thanked her. Support from his firm surprised him, but then of course his secretary Stella would not be very busy now. Jan he knew as a customer for second-quality cable and would be known as such to her; he would almost certainly be one of a number who chatted her up periodically on the phone. He remembered the caravan site too from a time when he was quite junior in the firm, and happy travelling the length of France for a vacant lot on the edge of nowhere. He had been overfull of sales information, squandering the 'know how' and his expensive company time on an equally young Jan. As such he had then enthused at unnecessary length about their recent advances – why he had even stayed to help fit one. Jan had entertained him very sociably, for the man was fond of quality beer and had a gift for knowing the best taverns in the district. Yes, Marc approved of Stella's idea of involving someone he knew, particularly as the man also knew his way around the locality. But for now he was stuck with Blanche. Marc did what he felt was expected and took her out to dinner, finding hers was a sizable appetite; he began to understand more fully the woman's addiction to the spa towns.

At 10 am promptly, Marc was waiting for Commissar Brie to arrive at the police station, a wait which was relieved by the sound of voices penetrating the thin partition wall. The name Mitzi cropped up, and he was almost holding his breath to not miss anything – the one who had diverted the top brass yesterday had been nothing more than a bitch. A dead poodle had been taking up valuable police time; the idea was so foolish that it well justified the laughs penetrating the partition. What sort of values were these that had policemen hunting for lost dogs to the detriment of lost humans?

Marc was still furious when minutes later the Commissar's secretary collected him from the waiting room and ushered him up stairs into Claude Brie's plush office. The Commissar extended a hand, but found its reach ignored by Marc who was barely holding his temper and clearly felt aggressive. He towered his bulk over the little chap, clearly more emotional than your average visitor. Claude Brie gestured to his visitor to take a seat, putting the widest space possible between him and his visitor.

'You have a problem with your wife?' He spoke with some deliberation. The figure on the other side of the desk said nothing, so Claude moved on to facts. 'I regret our search revealed no trace of your wife.'

'There was an unlocked door into the cavern, where Greta dropped her necklace,' said Marc. 'Her life could be at risk – I want that cavern searched.'

'A task of that magnitude would take an army; that cave system goes on for several kilometres, much of it unknown and dangerous. We would need to call in expert people to do it, and much as I would like to assist you, I regret I cannot justify that.'

Marc found this statement beyond belief. He got to his feet. 'But you managed to find a missing dog though, didn't you; and personally found it, at that!'

The Commissar moved his desk chair even further back, his face beginning to look scared; summoning assistance was not far away. 'The dog misleads you my friend, but even that contains an element of mystery, whereas none surrounds your wife. She has most certainly gone off with someone.' Marc felt surprised by this pronouncement, and took half a step back before resuming his aggressive pose.

Claude Brie shuffled some papers and selected two handwritten forms. 'Here are the statements of two witnesses who identified the photographs of yours as a lady seen leaving by another exit – clasping the arm of a portly gentleman.'

Marc was suddenly returned to his senses as a surge of pain coursed through his body, whilst the vault of yellow rang with his yell of agony. He swore with vigour at a grotesque dwarf almost directly in line with his field of view, gabbling in another language.

'He's awake, Leon.' The dwarf switched languages to match Marc's expletives. 'It's one of those with a big scar. He's intended as one of their specials, and not to mix with workers like us.' A foot applied itself to Marc's groin whilst the face grinned at him, ghoulishly appreciating the reactions of sheer agony and bewilderment.

'Leave the poor sod alone can't you, Arthur.' The second voice he heard spoke in a genuine French dialect, unlike the person in view. 'Come on, we must finish.' A spray of cold water struck Marc's naked body and there were scrubbing noises close to.

A malevolent grin split the dwarf's face. 'Take a look Leon, there's two more tin ones in here; I think the bitches have hacked out his balls. How can they now expect a stallion?

The foot levered, and with hurts multiplying way beyond everything else that ailed him Marc shrieked. The toe remained and a face inclined over him, the heavy laugh wafting foul breath. 'They watch you my muscle-bound friend – for you are their new fancy man.'

A second dwarf came into view, tugging the first away with his free hand. In the other the dwarf held something that looked like a hose. 'He cannot help it you know. Take no notice of him – eh?' The earnest face of what was presumably Leon peered at him in a friendly manner. 'When you get down to his size, many lose their marbles. I will be back later and we shall talk.' Leon's voice was receding and the noises in the yellow capsule of a prison suggested they were departing.

Who the hell were they? And who was watching him? He went over the words in his mind, but had no way of putting a meaning to them. Marc wished his hands were free to check over what he still possessed, but the shock episode was beginning to fade and his previous malaise to return. He stared urgently into the glassy yellow reflection, with mind battling to reclaim that comforting, unending, and unfocused blur. He had to steer his memory in again; and unlike returning to a dream that you had, this was a little more controlled – best think of Jan.

Jan had been there in the pub with a litre of beer to welcome him, and within the hour he had told him the full story. It was marvellous how a fellow engineer, all hale and hearty, brought back the sense of reality he had lacked up until now. He found himself laughing at other topics, for here was an individual able to enjoy the round of bars as well as he did. They soon had the town's chief cop identified as a nonentity.

Jan knew of the Commissar as well. His comment on Mark's experience at the Commissariat he said typified the man. 'I think dog finding is the right sort of work for Claude Brie, knowing how hit and miss he is – neither do I believe the "portly man" story.' Jan was personally inclined towards Marc's scenario of 'Greta lost in the caves', and picked up on the deep holes aspect; these he said were not uncommon in the caves. But they were not the only danger for a novice, there should also be an attempt at search; the police were wrong in that.

It was in this atmosphere that Marc decided not to accept the Commissar's advice and go home, for she might just as easily be found by him alone. Jan could offer him a caravan and make access via his own officially recognised door. He gratefully accepted Jan's offer and within days relocated, allowing Blanche to move off home. Jan announced he was willing to accompany him. Why not start with the upper promenade set of caves that were his territory? They were all set to find her!

The upper promenade caves opened onto the main cave system through a single heavy-duty municipal door that was identical to the one in the show-caves. The difference lay in this one being external, and set into the rock at a road junction some two kilometres from town. Jan took him deep into a complex of caves at the promenade end. Together they explored the many well-worn pathways, which extended into the cavern that also embraced the show-caves. It was soon after they began they came upon one of the extremely deep holes, and Marc experienced a most peculiar form of distress, which immediately threatened the mission with a dilemma. Neither dropping a pebble, shining a light or yelling down the hole brought any kind of response. Marc was unprepared for this and consequently found he was unable to leave, not knowing if Greta was lying down there insensible or just out of earshot. A tug of war began with his emotions, for his common sense told him that any distance too great for communication was also too great to initiate a rescue. Horrifying though it was, the only way he could search anywhere else was to put a merciful end to anything below. Accordingly, heavy rocks were dropped into the hole – a humane act, however traumatic.

Three days and some provisioning later, it was evident that he must extend his search to the furthermost caves; she could be wandering in the unmapped regions. Jan was doubtful: it was a far bigger task than he had intended, the caves could go on into infinity. As they explored the nearby cavern another deep hole was found but the place was barren, not a rock in sight. Jan said they needed dynamite with a long fuse, he knew where he might get it and Marc shopped for provisions in the meantime. At last the explosive was available, but then Jan found problems in his business and apologised for not coming.

Already uncertain as to whether or not he should stay; or take the Commissar's advice and go home, his decision was decided for him on reading the local paper. A woman with a blonde head of hair looking tolerably like his wife was displayed on the front page clutching the arm of a short, stout man. The pair seen near the caves were apparently investigating the reports of a rare rodent called 'Dansk' said to live in this region.

The naturalists had failed to find them in the Lutz-St-Saveur caves, and they had emerged to say so on the exact date that Greta disappeared. Marc lost no time in getting to the newspaper office and acquiring a colour print of the lead picture. He was sure that the woman's superficial resemblance to his wife had tricked the witnesses into thinking they had seen Greta – a copy of the photograph was soon on its way to Commissar Brie.

The discovery strengthened his belief that he could not rely on the local police. He must get involved himself. As an engineer he had experience of many things, and those strengths must suffice, for unlike Jan he was not at home in caves. Having already done away with his city clothes and provisioned for two in food, he now sought equipment for one in the many shops which catered for local climbing schools. Carefully he bought the necessary sleeping bag, rucksack and cooking utensils. Lighting he knew was essential, although perhaps not all three separate systems that ended up in his rucksack would be used. Marc soon found himself struggling uphill under his heavy load, heading for the show-caves.

First priority had to be the place where Greta had gone missing; the most vital hole would be the one in the show-caves with its attendant rocks. From there he could access the central cavern area where he knew of another such hole. It was then that a ridiculous train of misfortunes dogged him. At first it was easy, for once over the turnstiles he found a slow party just ahead. This was useful as he had another traumatic moment coming up when probing their bottomless hole; fortunately he knew the heavy rocks needed were conveniently to hand.

It was when he came to the ticket office where he had seen the keys with the inspector that his troubles really began in earnest; the ticket office door was easily dealt with but the light was out. Rather than search his backpack, he followed the surface wiring along the wall to just switch it on. It had seemed natural enough at the time; but the double-throw switch they had used for operating the small lightbulb had a double function of switching everything else off. Gaining a light in there had a secondary response, one that brought an avenging caves-man up from the depths to flatten his nose. But some cave men are even thicker than engineers: Marc could hardly believe his luck when he was locked in, and everyone who could be in his way moved outside. A leisurely time ensued, enough to put on safety hat and find a plaster for his bloody nose.

The first upset was in due course followed by an even more disastrous second. It was the use of dynamite, a mistake he would like to forget. The hole for his next task was the last deep hole he had accessed from Jan's side, which lacked an adjacent rockery. It was on the central ridge of high ground in the cavern and close to the bridge that joined both sets of caves, the high point overlooked a now defunct public footpath. Not easy for Greta to have stumbled into this one, but rather like the hole in the show-caves, did he start to make exceptions for ones that were less likely? He pondered for a while, eating a meal with his legs dangling over the hole's brink. It was still total silence below him; explosives he knew would be needed. 'The slow fuse job,' Jan had called it. He lit the fuse and hurried away; but did not get far enough before an immense bang split the ridge from top to bottom, occurring before he had moved more than twenty paces. Deafened, Marc ran whilst the black atmosphere rained rocks of all sizes about him.

Lucky to still be in one piece he limped off, massaging all the knocks received and hoping that none were serious: thank goodness he had worn a safety hat. Stumbling about in a dust cloud trying to find his things he vowed to himself there would be no more explosions. And finding his rucksack he urgently vacated the dangerous area of loose rock that he had created. Soon there was a chance to stop in the uncharted region where his pen could scratch paper; perhaps it was just these maps which would be all he could dedicate to the memory of Greta. Even if his mission proved unsuccessful he would at least have drawings enough to map out some of it, and hopefully prevent further personal tragedies like his own. He was clear that his parameters would include only the feasible routes she could have taken, and those he would map. But the series of caves that began there took him many kilometres. He pressed on tirelessly circling each area he chanced upon. Caves and tunnels there were in profusion, connected by a web of routes; the only holes were the ones he found early on. All was recorded upon his map and nothing ignored. The more he progressed, the more he doubted whether Greta could really have wandered this far without equipment or food.

There were now and then ways out of the caves, but besides filling his lungs with fresh air, he always returned to continue the mapping. Pressing on, there were fewer alternative routes, and he then moved faster, culminating in a huge cavern with several offshoots, and this he saw as the top limit of Greta's capability. Always there seemed to be other noises echoing through the tunnels, keeping him alert lest it be her, but they were to stay out of reach and remain a puzzle as he stuck rigidly to the combinations available to someone on foot leaving the show-caves. In this far-flung cavern he laid his bed in one offshoot tunnel and left the heavier equipment there; by doing so he rapidly visited all the many tunnel offshoots available from its lower floor space.

Of the tunnels around him one stood out from the others; as it sparkled with vitrified rock, for it was evidently the one blown through with earth's exhaust gases, but when, he had no idea. It was cold now but impressive all the same, so he marked it out for special note upon his map. This more interesting-looking tunnel attracted him, and so he chose it first for mapping. Quite early on his senses detected further differences, and an ever-growing curiosity drove him forward. The atmosphere had soon become warmer; there were odd odours, and even daylight ahead. Yes, the incidental light was strengthening now, yet he saw in it a flickering quality reminiscent of lights that kill insects – a thought that made him wary. The way ahead was blocked with a large mass of rock, and to the side of it was a rocky corridor in which all the common signs of an entrance were displayed, particularly the rubbish deposited. There Marc felt the influence of a strong field similar to a cathode ray apparatus working nearby only stronger. But Greta might have wandered this far, and although his long experience as an electrical engineer told him to beware, he stubbornly stuck to his task; life without her was simply not worth a light.

Having entered the corridor a really strong radiation caused him to feel strong undulations throughout his body as though he were at sea, and with this internal upheaval he felt sick. There was no easy way he could turn about with a bramble of sorts tripping him below and his projecting rucksack above conflicting with the walls; much better to power his way through as he badly wanted to see this destination. Ducking and hurrying he powered his way forwards tripping successively as he stepped out, dragging the brambles that wrapped round his feet and pushing his way towards that lighted gap. But now quite unable to steer round the curve he had some nasty collisions with the rock-face. Sweating profusely he was bathed in pain that seemed to have a definite pulse of its own, and even affected his eyes, causing mounting interference as lights in his vision. He was further in and pitched forwards as a sudden stab of pain paralyzed him, but leaving enough momentum behind for the fall to carry his body on beyond the alley and into open space.

The lights still blurred his eyes and vibrations filled his head as he subsided on the floor, the lights merging into fleeting yellow reflections, which smothered all the other sources and gathered again confusingly upon his ceiling dome.

9

The Village

Hazel opened her eyes. It could be morning, but it was hard to tell in a place of constant light and without clocks. Her fingers sought the place her wristwatch would have been, they touched skin as wrinkled as a rhino's; the flesh underneath didn't feel too good either, sort of stiff and stringy. Had she passed the pearly gates after all and this was some kind of decomposition? Things were so different here she wouldn't know, but if she had done so then their beds could be criticized as being far below top quality – the straw board was surely not of heaven. Neither was the temperature. To have kept the dress on had been a mistake; one she was pleased to think was rectified early in the night.

The floor rattled to her regime as Hazel moved to tone it all up, and to her delight much of the stiffness departed. Success begat success in other things, because before very long she had found the reason for bars placed over water in her capsule; or more exactly her bodily needs had determined the reason for wider bars towards the rear end of the floor. Why was it that she had been unaware for so long, without ever a thought of toilets here? The notion bothered her little, for of course that had been somebody else's concern. All those things need attention, she told herself. 'It's a place where people arrive unconscious; but even knowing and appreciating the fact shows I have the right kind of insight to fit me for my new job. The satisfaction of making all these deductions had her smiling at her own cleverness. And having made such an important connection, she was suddenly enthused to take over from Annita.

But taking over from Annita was not going to happen just like that, for Annita when she arrived was in a hurry and brusquely told her it would take at least a month. The change between them might not take very long, but further up the ladder the Queen's activities would be anything but instant. Besides the shying away from trivia Annita was being objective in bringing a pair of sandals with her, and very soon Hazel was being hurried into them.

'Shall I be Queen too?' Hazel was quite ready to envisage times well beyond the status of nurse.

'In about twenty years' time maybe.' Annita was hardly listening as she fobbed her new recruit off, almost without thinking. Tolerance was not her strong point this morning after pleading for a rarely granted release from duty as tuition time, and then seeing it wasted through the difficulty in getting Hazel to the breakfast, rather than the breakfast to Hazel. It was so easy to make such a mistake because everything decidedly routine to her was brand new and stimulating Hazel's inbuilt curiosity, ensuring that there were far too many questions to answer properly at almost every step of the way. They turned to their right as they left the bubble cell, heading into an opening which took them only a few further steps before dividing into two well-trodden routes. The tunnels were similar to the walls about Hazel's cell, seemingly constructed rather than natural, and of these they took the left branch. Light from the Styx cave did not persist here, instead illumination was taken over by luminous plants that stood in a couple of shallow recesses, and despite a minor lighting deficiency the tunnel was easily negotiated.

'They are "Fonz", we change them every month.' Annita made a quick 'on the march' response to the inevitable question. Dead ahead, and fitting into the tunnel exactly, was an illuminated sphere of translucent material – it looked rather like her cell with its thin door standing ajar. It was only on entering that the sight of heavier metal fastenings suggested a secure structure to her.

'This is the small gate-house.' Annita's voice was pitched and continuous like a travelogue, pursuing the vain hope that she could drown all further questions, and spouting a barrage of information she marched Hazel across another prime example of an aggregate-type floor inside a bubble. They emerged into lofty space, a space lit with such sun-like brilliance that Hazel's spirits rose, and then more so as she realized it was a dome-shaped hall that might easily compare with an exhibition centre near home. Such was the expanse of it, all bathed in plentiful light, that she felt freed from the close walls that had dogged her ever since entering the show-cave; it seemed almost as good as being outside. As her eyes adjusted more to the unaccustomed intensity of light, she discerned a ceiling dome worthy of a church, with its many recessed circles of semi-opaque material. The circles were suspiciously like her cell wall, but pleasingly shaped, and held rigid by a continuous metal frame, which stretched across the chamber's full width. Below it sparkled two huge misshapen heaps, each towering like a pile of soap bubbles freshly dropped from some gigantic washtub. These struck her eye forcibly as Annita urged her towards the nearest one. Hazel deliberately dropped behind as they passed a number of amber translucent globes, all rather like her cell only larger and connected somehow as a string of igloos might be. If dwellings they were, then each terminated at the boundary wall behind.

Then almost before she knew it, Annita had stepped into one of the two huge sparkling mounds of bubbles except that here none were uniform in shape. They were in an anteroom, and ahead a further marvel stopped Hazel in her tracks. Immediately she was swayed by the beauty and the artistic cleverness of two bright metal spiral walkways, which swung round each other as opposed spirals, arriving a small distance apart at the top splayed out in the shape of an earwig's pincers. A huge area of cellular material appeared to have been cut away in order to construct a hall of sufficient size to contain the walkway.

Still on the ground floor Annita conducted her into the space behind the spiral walkways and pointed to the outer bubble cells, explaining that these were the best loos for routine use in the village. Hazel peeped inside one to check on whether the seating was familiar. Annita called, having reached the halfway point of the ascent spiral, intent upon breakfast, only then realizing the new recruit no longer followed. Hazel was drifting into the slope-way and noticing how the other sweep connected to all the floors, whilst the one she trod went directly to the top. Annita led on more slowly now as they gained enough height and position for a stunning view of the village, getting busy with her travelogue voice again. Hazel by now was doubly distracted after looking down at her feet, where underfoot she pounded a smooth white floor which first reminded her of chalk and then in train Terry.

Annita looked down on Hazel puffing along behind to catch up, the girl was starting to peer at the houses; she was so very out of condition on such a minor slope. 'Those are our houses you can see; can you imagine where they might have come from? Or something similar to what you have seen?' To neither question could Hazel even begin to answer. This was a thoroughly alien world to her, so she just shook her head.

'Do you remember the gourd like plants at the sentry rock? They are enormous and we believe their fossilized shells are what we are using to live in. Our thinking suggests these shells are discarded and have passed through oven-like tunnels before emerging from the furnace-like caves around the sentry. That is not counting the multiple ones responsible for the food house and church; which could be another related plant either budding off the discards or even welding those gourds together in our pre-history. They certainly made good houses when we found ways to open them up.'

The spiral walk had flattened on reaching the summit and as Hazel neared her, the explanation cut off as Annita backed through a pair of spring doors that flipped shut after her like beetle wings closing. Hazel followed hurriedly, and then was relieved to see straight through the next three circular rooms ahead, for all were cut away without doors. Each room had another room off on either side.

So in the first she passed a couple of tables with chairs on her left, duplicated there in the right-hand room as well, but she followed Annita nearly to the middle one where a food counter protruded on either side. There at last Annita stopped. Hazel dallied, looking with interest in the last partition at the table's coppery metal legs, for seeing such familiar things meant to her that they had the essentials for civilized living. It was not until Annita passed by with a loaded plate that Hazel headed for the food, pondering over the many items, still not feeling hungry and not knowing what to take from the impressive spread of dishes covered with metal lids. These were strung out along a hygienic-looking metal counter stretching for much of its full compart-mental width. The chilled yogurt was easily found, but much of the rest was warm vegetation, coloured green, brown or yellow; these items appeared in a variety of shapes, tendrils, mushroom-like piles of thick fleshy stems, or a pulpy mash like melon. Having too much choice, she put tiny helpings of everything high on the rim of her plate, but filled its centre with yogurt. Hazel returned to sit facing

Annita, who was eating as if starved. The hotplates Hazel had seen had wires, so they must be electric; most things here must run on electricity. Her mind ran amok, making deductions about everything before spotting Annita's steaming hot mug and realizing that she had missed out an essential in the breakfast routine.

Hazel hurried over to choose a mug and fill it with the hot dark-brown liquid. The mug, like all the others there, had a degree of buckle that was disconcerting but even so remained upright on the counter; the liquid itself had a strange taste and was possessed of a texture like a thick cocoa drink. Seeing Hazel's hesitation and questioning expression across the room, Annita called to her, 'You'll get used to it! You will have to try what we have for there's no tea or coffee here.'

Hazel returned with the mug and in doing so her gaze diverted, sticking to the spectacular view through an expanse of curved window, that was the outer wall – in short, it was hard to eat anything at all. The strings of spheres that she saw below sparkled like huge amber plastic caterpillars reflecting the light. It looked much like part of a theatre set, so unreal and yet so curiously attractive. Her eyes feasted on it. If the bubbles had little raised pieces on top, they could be decorated like some eastern palace, or expensive jewellery.

'Why is there a six bubble house over there, when all the rest are five?' Hazel stabbed her fingers on an impulse towards the tinted transparency at her side.

'That's the palace.' Annita spoke, momentarily disengaging from food. She looked searchingly at Hazel's full plate and then back to her own almost empty one.

Hazel reluctantly took the hint, and forced herself away from the sights to tackle the odd food in front of her. Nothing was familiar, but each item had a distinct flavour, and in many cases a flavour able to challenge all her previous eating experiences. Thankfully, she finished the oddities, and began eating the yogurt.

Annita sat looking at her with empty plate, but now inclined to talk. 'This is the food house, we all relax here, and it is open all the time if you are looking for a handy rest room.' She paused in her explaining, as a small, stout woman with dark hair and a wide friendly face moved across her view in the background. Hazel's head turned at once, intercepting the prime reason for hesitation. The newcomer was talking noisily from the counter to someone in a rear recess – it was an excited voice with a Spanish accent. Hazel, in turning to look, first viewed the woman's hair as it was arranged in plaits that coiled up neatly in a bun. Her clothes were the standard wool knit dress and so hardly counted.

Annita, having quite lost her train of thought, hastened to identify the image. 'Oh, that's Maria standing over there, she runs the food house. Maria will be surprised to see me this late, as I usually eat breakfast earlier with the patrol. She is talking to Freda, who is our current Queen, although from the sound of it that priest woman Patricia is also there. They are both top brass, and have to stay in the village when the four ride off to organize the day's work.'

This was beginning to go over Hazel's head. 'Ride off?' she exclaimed, suddenly aware of an ever-expanding horizon.

'Yes, they go on horses, it's a longish way.' Annita looked at her as if she were some kind of dimwit. For the moment Hazel did not care what Annita thought; with a view like that, she could sit here for hours just drinking it in – why waste energy in conversation? It was so very visual up here, with that brilliantly lit scene outside. She again focused her eyes on the spectacle just beyond her window seat – but she was destined to be disturbed in this.

'You are up and about quickly.' The voice with a trace of German accent broke in on her absent mind. Freda stood there, a shapely blonde woman with a polite expression and smiling face. Hazel stood up, not knowing if there was some measure of respect to be shown to the woman who after all was Queen.

'Yer needen git up fer me,' rasped Patricia in a loud voice that drowned out any other, leaving Hazel to wonder if she were joking; or whether the church did rank higher than the Queen. Certainly the woman did wear a very important-looking medallion – Hazel's bottom hovered halfway to the seat.

'Oo are yer,' the cockney voice rasped again.

Hazel quickly found herself tied to introductions with a barrel of a woman, the one she least wanted to meet, whilst behind her she could hear a calm quiet voice asking Annita what Hazel did for a living. She struggled to bring Pat's talk more into line with the topic, 'hair', noticing only then and choking back a laugh for the prelate's hair had been hacked off very close to the scalp, monk-like.

'You like our breakfast, yes?' Maria had noticed Hazel's predicament and rescued her. Even her English was arguably better than the cockney's speech, despite being laced with a distinct Spanish flavour. Hazel said a dubious 'Yes.' This response had the chubby woman seize her hand, and lead on towards some other delicacies, not evident in the row she had inspected. To the hot reddish meat she could say positively 'Yes.' It was as near to the taste of bacon as to be one and the same. Maria now took on an exuberant mood, triumphantly showing her fried mushrooms, then eggs standing beside a vessel of boiling water all ready to be dipped.

They trickled back to the others; but the conversations were over and the women all ready to set off. Hazel was annoyed that she had not managed to get a direct word in with Freda. The beautiful woman seemed so warm and approachable that Hazel had a distinct feeling of having missed something, and even though the contact was so indirect she still had a feeling of being welcome in the village. Hazel almost floated towards the exit of the food house.

'Do you know what it was Maria had you tasting?' Annita asked.

'Don't say it's horrid,' Hazel said, knowing instinctively from her tone that there had to be something wrong with it.

'It was bat,' laughed Annita, not wishing to spare her and relishing every moment of Hazel's disgust. 'Maria cures it and serves it up fried – just like bacon.'

The living house spheres stood in a wide circle where they walked. Hazel's gaze fixed on them knowing she had one too and found them totally absorbing. 'That's your place to be,' cried Annita. She pointed to a bubble that was blank where it ought to have had a front door. 'Look, they have drilled a line of holes, that's the first stage; then it has to be ground off with a power tool. You have a new house, most of us don't; you can thank Cora and Tanya for that, because they haven't expired quite as early as they might have.'

Hazel pushed at the rounded bottom to the house with her sandal; like all the others it was part-submerged in the grey, springy mineral which covered the entire cave floor. 'What is it set in, it isn't natural is it?'

'When the village was constructed they had huge heaps of chippings from the mining operations everywhere. So it was an opportunity to blend that with the extracted ore sludge from processing metals, then use both as a waste filling. To bind it together, the work caves were stripped of thousands of bats and their carcasses cooked at high temperatures to make a sort of collagen glue – the glue bound it tight together.'

Hazel absorbed the explanation with only a part of her mind engaged, for there was a greater fascination in the smooth exterior on her first ever dwelling. Her hand stroked and the mind stayed right there with it. 'Aren't they doing this today?'

'Yes, but it is always after lunch, the four patrol have to come back first.'

Hazel's brow furrowed in perplexity, something was eluding her in all of this. 'Why? Is it for security? Is there some kind of danger here?'

'You could say that, but it is a danger that is well handled, the main object is management.' Annita pointed to the church that she was very nearly touching, a multi-bubble structure that towered above them, similar to the food house. 'Shall we go there next, because the church is the very centre of our security measures? The dangers have been with us always. Historically, danger has invariably concentrated on this particular place, because it is by far the most habitable spot. Even when there was nothing here at all it alone received some heat and light from the Styx cave.

'In the early days the cave system was open on the Spanish side, and copper was mined in the nearby caves. The people were characteristically small, but rich comparatively. By Roman times they were mining gold and stamping the coins, which made them even richer. The caves attracted craftsman, who produced stunning objects in gold, silver and copper to trade with the whole civilized world, the trade made them richer by far than anywhere locally. But it was not to last; late in the fifteenth century Pope Innocent the eighth began to harass witches and magicians. He opened the way for rich nobility with private armies to storm any place harbouring them. The people who lived in the caves were small in stature and had a combined wealth beyond any individual rich man's dreams, a fact that made them vulnerable. Local envy and prejudice was manipulated by their rich lords, who said these strange small people were practising black art in the caves and then using such stories as a pretext for direct action.

'The military were shortly set on occupying the caves; but they were facing miners and craftsmen who were all intelligent men of the world, resisting, and hiding their valuables even at the earliest signs of occupation.

'It was a war against Satan, and so the military did not need to do their own dirty work, they could call on priests who would systematically torture the miners' families to pressurize a release of treasure. From among the many large anvils used for working metal they chose a huge one, the largest, setting iron rings in the floor around it, and with this set-up they were equipped to stretch the unwilling recipient tightly over its length. This was a recognised way of dealing with women in that century and the ordeals were made worse by filling the victim's stomach with water and manipulating it until they choked. Many so-called witches were tortured until they or their spouse confessed, resulting in certain death and bodies burnt in the caves – with hidden treasure usually a bonus along the way.

'But it was not to be all one way; a depleted band of miners struck back with gunpowder, blowing up the entrance shaft and causing a massive landslip that isolated the caves completely. The revenge must have been marvellous for the residents, with troops and clerics panicking in a dark hellhole and now completely at their mercy. The people who lived there had previously brought cattle into the caves, and in addition cultivated the mushroom; but having won the hostilities there was now a battle on with starvation. No doubt the previously neglected hazardous far end of the caves exercised ingenuity to make an escape, however it is unlikely that many got away.'

Rounding the wide exterior of the church, Annita stepped into its anteroom through a doorway cut in the outer bubble shell. They entered and turned sharp left where the anvil had been exposed in the next bubble; it was a massive-looking piece of ironwork, and self-evidently connected to the stout-looking metal rings set into the rough stone floor a short distance from each corner. The floor was the original site, and to preserve it accurately the base of the multi bubble had to be holed and cover it. 'To remind ourselves,' said Annita solemnly, 'we have preserved the whole barbaric thing just as it was; but more recently it has been put to another function, that of keeping order among ourselves.' She paused for Hazel to take its sharp unyielding edges and heavy metal bulk into her imagination, before stepping back on to the anteroom floor once more. Moments later they were in the church itself.

The holy chamber was a lofty spacious place of cut-away bubbles, heightening over the altar to use the entire height of available bubble material; elsewhere the cell-like structure had been cut away to make an ample nave.

They walked upon a floor that featured surface tiles of mottled rock, drinking in the penetrating and musty odour that they could associate best with a church. In their immediate path were three benches sculpted out of the same rock as the floor and beyond these rose the flat stone of an elevated altar. All of this blended together in matching rock, and led the eye on to a white marble statue. The statue was exquisitely sculpted in the form of a woman holding her baby forth. Their features had been exactingly fashioned by an artist of some considerable talent. Hazel's heart leapt to see the original of the grotto statue. She marvelled at a much more impressive representation of the familiar face – her senses were swamped in the rediscovery of its tender smile. The original had far more warmth than the one she had adored in the Green Nun's cave, but of course the artist in the grotto must have been working from a copy.

Hazel occupied the seat next to Annita in the pew: her immediate prayer led on to thoughts of her own mother, and how by now she ought to be on the return journey. Mother would be waiting at the airport, and the seat booked would be empty. She could visualize her mum's alarm, her plump face full of despair; and her dad lending a supporting, if slender, shoulder to cry upon. Hazel's eyes filled with tears, a trickle came readily and then a stream, as she found she could cry. Warmth and wetness lifted her frame into a succession of heavy sobs. The lid was off, and emotion released itself fully; until at length her sobbing subsided. It was then that she became aware of Annita's face, just as wet as her own – they sat not speaking; Hazel put out her arm to clutch and both fell together in a heap full of tears, abjectly miserable. But it could not last, one red-eyed smile kindled another and there was movement; weakly they stumbled through a door out into the rear of the church.

Beyond the door, a long circular corridor arose at base level, but to Hazel's pleasure and surprise they moved only yards along it before entering a small bubble refreshment area. Shutting the door Annita filled an electric jug with water, then dipping into some dried herbs kept for infusion she offered them up to Hazel's nose. 'We all cry there sometime or other,' she said unsteadily. 'And afterwards, this service room with a warm drink helps a lot.' On the metal floor lay several yellow balls, approximately two feet in diameter. Annita sat on one and invited Hazel to use another. The sphere was most uncomfortable for it didn't give much at all, but it was better than standing or sitting on an uncomfortable floor so Hazel sat there. The brew, when it came, was aromatic, wafting it seemed the most delicate trace of menthol on some grassy background flavour; it was by far the best thing to drink that Hazel had tried.

Annita turned a sympathetic face. 'I don't want to bore you with all of this early history, but it does help to explain how we look at things, and the basic history gets more involved later as we move towards events we know more of. It is those things I have a duty to explain so you can see our background, and if you want to go deeper into the past you will have to save such questions for Freda our historian. Not that any of us can properly know it all; even the people there at the time probably didn't, so we have to depend on the little that's written. But it will take our minds off more personal troubles and woes, if I tell you about the lady of the statue, St Lucinia.' Hazel nodded approvingly as it was her chance to almost relax on her hard seat, clutching the mug of hot brew.

Annita took a big gulp and, when her eyebrows finished their gyrations, began. 'It must have been hell for anyone trying to live here after the land slip. The wall we built to screen the village from the Styx cave has cut the light off now, but in that day this spot was dimly lit, relatively warm, and already site of their original houses. So it is reasonable to surmise, that after the collapse anyone left would move to here and subsist off the remaining stock, bats and fungi. Clearing the rotting bodies of mainly soldiers and priests from the cave complex must have been a necessity after the battles, and luckily for them there are suitable cremation sites nearby.

'Whether many of the original residents survived we don't know but they would have been saddled with the duty of rescuing those who inadvertently wander in past the sentry. As time passed it is likely that any resident woman tending new arrivals here would regret doing so, as the wanderers of the caves were mainly ruffians, their women would blend in although they were few in number.

The males saved were both fitter and heftier than the men in the caves, so they quickly took over, making the residents pay heavily for starting their humanitarian work. In this punishing location people were already small which meant that the miner who was "top dog" today found himself dispossessed by a hale and hearty, full-sized newcomer on the morrow. All would have to fight for existence and the miners' widows, after watching their man slaughtered, would then experience a victorious master enjoying his acquisition to the full. None of these interlopers would of course be able to avoid the need to forage for bats and help out the poor diet that was fungi, however much they acted the tyrant. Collection of fungi was woman's work which involved travel right to the other end of the caves for most of the edible varieties still growing where they were first cultivated. Mushroom cooking put chemistry in the hands of women and many poisonings arose from their cooking which soon made men wary and matricide common.

'The arrival of Lucy was an event which caused her contemporaries such joy that they recorded it. She didn't come past the sentry in the usual manner; in fact she wasn't even heading this way. Lucy had been waylaid upon the mountain, and raped in some distant cave. The cave was close to a fast-flowing river and that carried her body until it crashed over the falls in our sheep cavern. Lucy was pulled from the river by the mushroom trekkers more dead than alive; lots of fractures, but despite all injuries she survived to give birth to a child.'

There was a noise outside their room: Annita moved off her ball seat and peered into the corridor. She returned immediately, to a questioning stare from Hazel. 'That was Pat being inquisitive about us; she gives me the creeps. Sorry, I was distracted. Now where had I got to? Oh yes; Lucy was something special and later arrivals called her St Lucinia the goddess of childbirth, for her baby was the last one to be born here.

'At that time there were a small number of women doggedly surviving the mayhem all around them. Lucy was too broken to be of interest to their men and so the women contrived to keep her alive; the child when it came was a girl. Lucy's daughter was doomed to live in this hell hole of a place, a fact that made her mother resolve to sort things out for the better. Her influence increased markedly on finding that the women were decidedly a downtrodden lot. Working with them she targeted new arrivals and stopped the resuscitation of any male who managed to pass the sentry. Their bodies were stripped of anything useful and left within easy reach of the gourd roots. This alone was not good enough for Lucy. She began investigating odd fungi near the Styx chamber, which appeared to have pronounced lethal or soporific qualities. It was a surprise when she discovered a variety that stunted human growth, and the discovery promoted its use as a dry powder disguised as seasoning for dosing food. Eventually the size differential between men and women was made more favourable and the dosage was adjusted more easily. The worst of the tyrants having lost their command of a place in society were duly poisoned off, and a virtual nunnery began. They stayed poor, because they were too few to properly manage the resources, but even so they were able to use the few remaining men to assist food acquisition and give them much more to eat. Into this world and from a mother crippled with severe injuries, St Itzla was born. She was soon to become a force to be reckoned with . . .'

Annita broke off as a fanciful idea took her mind. 'I have the day off so let's not waste it,' she cried. 'Let's go for a swim: everybody is working and I'm excused duty, so we can have the pool to ourselves. I shall tell you the rest later.'

'I didn't know you had a pool,' cried Hazel astonished; but then she had to chase because she was addressing Annita's back.

10

Surprise Invitation

Hazel realized that they were heading back the way they had come, for she recognised the gatehouse route; but then all became confused afterwards because they turned sharp left into another tunnel. Again a tunnel lit by fonz, but this time there were several hundred yards of it. Splashing noises, together with the wetness on the walls, heralded the women's pool.

The pool lay in a neatly rounded cave of its own, a natural rock hollow faced off with a cement compound to form a series of white flutes intersecting artistically in its far reaches. From this eye-appealing background the water twinkled at them, enhanced by soft lighting beneath its surface – in fact over fifty yards sparkled clean and bright. Pouring artistically through the ceiling decoration water fell upon an illuminated, transparent yellow sphere floating in the water; bouncing off at its apex it fell as a curtain of bubbles that caught the light before plunging vigorously into the pool. Hazel noticed that the sphere was identical with her cell, but had lights inside and this formed the only light source in the cave. This internal illumination caused the sphere to glow above water, and underwater its omnidirectional light reflected from pale sides to surface all along the air interface, making the water appear luminous, and causing ceiling reflections above that lit up the place even to the flat stones bordering the pool.

'Like it?' shouted Annita dashing over to the far side and throwing off her dress, which was apparently the only thing she had on, then stepping out of her sandals to dive into the water. The dive erupted as a huge splash behind her. Hazel hesitated, she had never swum before without a costume, and needed to accustom herself to the notion; but soon she followed suit knowing in advance that her dive would be the better of the two. She was accustomed to staying down for a swim underwater first, and was immediately impressed with the smooth vertical sides of the pool, which would have gained little from being tiled. Lights shone out all ways from the cascade bubble, making the pool extremely well lit with light trapped from within, but at the other end a third of the width was just one big black hole. As if to contrast with it, Annita's bottom half showed pink at the cascade, and using all her remaining breath Hazel swam there underwater.

'It's marvellous,' she enthused on breaking the surface. 'Temperature's just right too.'

Annita's head streaming with the cascade water, displaced even more of it as she laughed. 'You're as bad as Jackie, creeping up underwater, but it's good you are not of her ilk.'

'Who's Jackie?' queried Hazel 'I have yet to meet her.'

Annita's face became serious as she dodged the cascade flow. 'I'm sure that you will soon come to know her, either with or without introduction – she's gay.'

Something other than people she had yet to meet was intriguing Hazel; she was driven to ask, 'What's that big black hole doing halfway down the pool?'

Annita tried hard to recapture the guide-like voice she had been attempting to develop especially for Hazel, but it was being lost in the noise of falling water. 'You are standing in a mix of two streams.' She raised her voice, finding a few more decibels. 'This is a place where if either of two streams are about to flood they can be allowed to overflow harmlessly into an old watercourse. And since that phenomenon rarely happens we have adapted the duct for swimming. The great thing about using it is that one stream is warm and that allows us to set the temperature. Further downstream the men have a similar pool, but it's about another half a mile along our overflow watercourse. As you might expect there are a number of grids between the two.'

They swam up and down, but Annita didn't seem that keen on exercise in the water. She soon stopped, preferring to let the cascade run over her and wait for Hazel to finish. That was not long either, because out-of-condition Hazel had decidedly lost her usual push.

'Let's get dry now, and I'll tell you a story.' Annita was mounting some steps near to the cascade, but these remained undiscovered by Hazel as she had already tumbled herself over the side. Annita promptly handed her a chunk of pumice, very nicely rounded, but still pumice. Annita met her look of astonishment by apologizing. 'There's a square sort of wipe over there, but we don't use the towels because they are not cotton and don't do the job very well; the air flow and a bit of pumice are ideal. Annita ran the pumice expertly about her as she moved into the far corner and lay flat on the rocky floor, beckoning Hazel to join her. Hazel arrived to find a stream of heated air warmed the rounded overhang. 'It is just a fan blowing over the copper duct that carries the warm stream onwards,' said Annita airily. Then adopting an odd schoolmistress-like voice she began her story. 'Now, if you are all sitting comfortably, I'll tell you about St Itzla.'

'Yes, Miss,' giggled Hazel in schoolgirl mode and lay down on the porous slabs in a most decidedly comfortable warm air stream.

Annita noisily cleared her throat. 'We are not sure what name she was given, but the one that came down to us was the name that people called her later; you might even hear the name Itzla shouted in the village on occasion, for she is the goddess of the flint knife and a liberator to us. If you remember: Itzla was all set to inherit a population crisis from her mother, who had ended the chaos by simply arranging for all new men to perish.'

'Yes, Miss.' Hazel took her cue, piping up in a tiny voice before settling her aching limbs to a more comfortable position upon the stones.

'The colony was deeply religious, and so she was taught to read the only book they possessed – an early Bible. Genesis she liked, particularly she appreciated Jonah's fate inside the fish monster for surely they had much in common with him. It was inevitable then she would discover quite soon that his prayers hinted at the right philosophy for them to follow. Not as you might think "save me lord from this horrid place" but rather giving thanks for saving him as far as this place. It demanded also some other kind of ending for them, as the cave could not spit them out. It was their final destination, which must be modified if it were to be enjoyable.

'Lucinia still was not well, and by the time her little girl was fourteen only two extra women had arrived to join the few ageing survivors. She speedily made her daughter Queen, retiring to tend her various chronic conditions in the background; remaining simply as an adviser to her daughter. Inevitably ability drops with advancing age and the long trek for fungi was beginning to weigh heavily upon the few women who did it. At the same time their tiny men produced fewer and fewer bats. The colony's future was beginning to look black. Even so their problems had not long to wait, because Itzla solved the population crisis very early in her reign. She used the Bible as a textbook, but still managed to shock everyone else. One morning her subjects awoke to find that she had created Eve by simply removing the genitalia from the latest man to arrive; a practical version of Adam's rib, with no more than a flake of flint for the surgery.'

'Was his name Adam?' Hazel interrupted, cheekily as any schoolgirl. 'And in the dark did she mistakenly read nib instead of rib?'

Annita was too intent on her narrative to fall prey to any childish bantering, and answered solemnly, 'In the early days Adam just meant man – he could even have a name like Bill. Now stop interrupting me or you will go to the bottom of the class.' The eyebrows flagged the fact that Annita was quietly enjoying herself.

'The man survived despite a near fatal loss of blood and soon he was part useful putting life into the business of bat collecting. But even before he had begun work in earnest, Itzla positioned herself once more to watch the sentry stone, and after a relatively short time had created a further two "new women". Heated words began to be said, but Itzla heeded only her Jonah philosophy, and much as he tamed the violence of the Ninevites by his prophesy, she knew she had an answer to both the incoming barbarians and their population crisis with just one cut.

'The real women were getting mutinous, as they realized the castrates were now a significant part of the population, even in small number they could take over. "Your latest eunuchs are stronger and bigger than us; if you save any more they will surely kill us," the women were fast complaining.' Annita paused, as Hazel rose on elbows to interrupt.

'These flint knives were they heavy with sharp bits like yours?'

Annita barely paused. 'No, they were thin like a comb; Freda has a few in her collection. But let me finish the tale before you discuss it. Itzla knew of her mother's experiments with fungi and asked if she could use them to waste away the newcomer's additional bulk. Some of these specific fungi actually reduce height as well as weight and gratefully she made use of them. Using the new food additive in moderation the eunuchs were manipulated until their size fitted them to their work and no more. The women still complained, wanting to preserve some physical differences, knowing before long there would be many more arriving. This was easily accomplished and all further male entrants were simply castrated. The women's complaints declined, but Lucinia, also sensing an influx, considered their proportion in the population, and further decreed that numbers of castrates must never rise above the ratio of four to one.

'No longer was it necessary to expend every effort in collecting food; materials could be fashioned to make life more tolerable in the caves. It was inevitable that they would sooner or later reach the limits, and when they did the additional male bodies had to be discarded in the Styx arrival zone. The colony was then poised to be a success and these principles have persisted to the present day, except that we now favour part castration.'

Hazel sat up with her mind aflame, without the need of further cognitive thought. 'Is that what you are doing to Terry?' she snapped angrily with a sharp intake of breath, and rising threateningly on straightened arms. Hazel's shadow projected blackly across Annita's delicate pink back. A storm raged inside her almost beyond control, threatening to explode and launch at this advocate of mutilation. But there was no response whatsoever. Annita's eyes were full of tears and not reacting in the least to an aggrieved Hazel – instead it was her particularly traumatic memory of what that four to one ratio had meant for her.

Annita raised herself on one elbow. 'Don't blame me, you still have the lad you met; but I lost my husband – they saved him, but only just to incinerate his body in the destructor major!' Annita shed more bitter tears; the subject of her cry in church was still wringing her heart. But this time there was added emotion, as it was additionally an undeserved reproach. No she was not like Jackie and her villain accomplice – deliberately destroying someone's spouse on an archaic premise that was no longer strictly adhered to, so it simply was not on. 'I think the person who is your partner in life is important, because you have chosen him out of a world rich in choice; no one wants alternatives when someone dear can be saved. I also think that both Jackie and Maureen were being deliberately wicked, as the connection to them was seen as a heterosexual one.' Annita said it with emotion and emphasized how strongly she felt about this with a flood of tears.

Far from staying angry, Hazel found very soon that she was

100

comforting Annita, quelling the uncontrollable sobs that shook her friend's frame: her true friend she decided, although how far that held for the rest sounded less certain. From out of her sorrow Annita emerged, papering it over with something else she had ready to impart. 'We have been invited to lunch with Freda. She can tell you a whole lot better than I can about Terry.'

Hazel was impressed – to dine with the Queen! Maybe she had reacted badly, for it was true that Terry was still in the land of the living; at least he was here. She felt sorry, and wanted to apologize to Annita, preferring to hear her friend's version if she still could. 'Is it still the same – the same thing being done now?' she asked very casually.

Annita had begun touching her damp face with the pumice; she was dry apart from that and with a much more composed voice answered, 'It is only the decision to save that is part of the Charon job; we hand the men over to Maureen who carries out the operation for all of us. She removes a testicle whilst they are still unconscious and exposes them to the Styx chamber radiations, which we find counter infection. Finally she takes a fortnight feeding them a diet of fungi that doesn't nourish at all. The bones shrink most – it's what Freda calls osteoclast activity – and that leaves them rather plump. They soon become normal because we all shrink slowly, and none of us are sure whether it is some of the things we have eaten, or just due to the environment in this region of the caves. As the men are fed for rapid bone shrinkage rather than the flesh, they actually look more attractive; almost boyish you might say. We choose one to be the village stud and if you are not lovesick over Terry, you can join in too. As people can't help becoming sterile on entering the caves there are no drawbacks for us – no reproduction – our ovaries are only any good for supplying hormones. In the case of men nowadays, we believe one testicle is all that's necessary for normal behaviour, and find that the technique produces work with an acceptable level of aggression. They are told it is necessary because the skin wrinkles up to be tight on their balls, and they do seem to accept this, although to me it's doubtful.'

Hazel interrupted as specific words struck home, quite ignoring the tone of disbelief surrounding Annita's last words. 'Is the skin on everyone affected that way when they arrive? Mine has all sorts of furrows, and feels hard.'

101

Annita paused, and commented only after looking critically at the coarse skin on Hazel's arms. 'You came in so quickly I didn't think you would have the problem that I did; leave it to me.' Annita passed by the rear of the cascade, and slipped into what she laughingly called her smock.

Hazel felt clean, fresh and loosened quite a bit by her swim. She took a last appreciative look at the pool; the word grotto came into her mind as a good name, but she could not make up her mind whether it would qualify as such in the real world. As together they entered the village Hazel heard a vociferous group of women laughing. It would seem 'the four' were back, but Hazel was not destined to see them, as she was shepherded towards the Queen's apartments.

11

Boron

Freda was near to the door waiting for them, a door that hung upon proper metal fittings and not a thong like the other houses. Hazel stepped through into the comfort of carpets, where the extra-size rooms were hung with tapestries to strip away any suggestion of austerity from the royal bubble, besides disguising the roundness of the rooms.

Freda stepped forward to hug Hazel's shoulders, making her feel welcome, her oval rather delicate face maintaining a semblance of formality throughout, but behind a friendly smile. 'We are all pleased to have you here Hazel and everyone I know wants to make your acquaintance.' Freda steered her into the next segment of her abode, where an elegant-looking table with ornate silver legs stood, its highly polished centre a gleaming shiny black. Seating Hazel at one of six matching chairs, Freda chatted to make her feel more at home. 'That's right you can sit there next to Annita. Franz has gone for the dishes, so we should not be kept waiting long.' Freda gestured with her head towards Annita, speaking humorously. 'You can see that Annita has been here before.' Annita was already seated and pouring liquid from a bottle into her wine glass, one that would have passed muster anywhere. 'Help yourself to the wine. Yes, we ferment sweet things for it,' said Freda interpreting the surprise so evident on Hazel's face. Then as there was still more time to spare she decided to bring Hazel into conversation. 'You must tell us all about yourself, and how you arrived here.'

Hazel started a swift history of her misadventures, but did not get far before the main dishes began to arrive. The food was carried in by a diminutive man dressed in a tight-fitting, bright green outfit, who then deftly arranged it along the centre of the table. When the task was complete the serving man moved between the guests to supply hot plates and Freda introduced him as Franz. He stood close to Hazel's eye level, a tiny man whose face looked brightly at them, his chin adorned with a fair goatee beard. The pale complexion and small eyes took on a nervous worried look, shifting feet uneasily as he fell under Hazel's gaze. The cutlery gleamed, its brightness deflecting Hazel's eye from him for a moment, and as their exchange of words ceased she realized the implements had the lustre of silver. However, her eye still followed the little man as he moved towards Annita, noting how he shied away from her immediate vicinity. Hazel realized that it was Annita making him nervous.

'It is leg of lamb,' announced Freda. 'You might think it very grand after your first breakfast selection, Hazel, but make the most of enjoying it, because the range of foods you are used to has shrunk considerably.'

The lamb gave the room a pleasant aroma of roast meat. Hazel judiciously helped herself to minute proportions of everything else, but a mega helping of the lamb which was there in plenty, and some green beans. By contrast, the others favoured the alternative white meat, and took much vegetation well-steeped in sauces. Between courses Hazel continued speaking, much encouraged by occasional appreciative glances from Freda. By the time the sweet had been eaten and what passed for coffee stood upon the table she had told them all, blaming her misfortune squarely upon the madman who had arrived here. They ought to take special note of the kind of man he was.

Freda totally ignored any grievance in her voice, for whatever the cause that brought her, another woman to Hades was always welcome. And so without any kind of commiseration she was ready to change the subject with a more general question. 'You have just undergone a dramatic change to your lifestyle, and not only that; you have been grappling with our customs and history. It is complicated and I would not be at all surprised if there were real problems in getting to understand us. So it is perhaps a good time to ask whether there is anything that could be helped along with more explanation.'

Hazel was by now acclimatized to the friendly atmosphere, and being in Freda's warm presence she had relaxed fully, helped along with a liberal glass or two of wine. She answered more frankly than afterwards she would like to recall. 'I find it hard to believe that I am alive, because there is something not fully down to earth about this place. Maybe with time everything will fall into some kind of reality but at the moment it's more like being in a dream than something live.' Annita nodded her head as if she agreed with this, causing Hazel to press on, encouraged. 'The things that you have here seem so different from everywhere else, that to me it borders on the impossible.' She broke off abruptly, aware that she was on the brink of criticism, and fast becoming discourteous to her host.

Freda was smiling at her – seemingly not in the least put out. 'That is only a natural reaction, we all feel the same when we arrive. But when you reflect on the fact that this land has been cut off for hundreds of years it is not surprising. Modern travel has made everywhere else so alike that even places with spectacular differences and customs become visited sufficiently as to make them appear familiar and thoroughly normal. But we are not in that position, we have to live with what we have here and wait for the inevitable breakthrough from outside.

'I have heard that in South America there are a whole series of tropical lakes with narrow channels connecting them to the sea; but unlike the sea, some swarm with jellyfish, some have none and others have jellyfish that actually swim upside down. The lakes in those regions are probably part fresh water, and part sea water, so it is only the mineral salt content which is affecting the life and balance of creatures there. Our tiny environment is likewise influenced by exceptional mineral wealth, which can unbalance things. You, yourself, are swimming in a different pool here, but soon you will adjust, and every month your hormones will tell you that you have not changed from the woman who entered.'

Annita interrupted with her own doubts. 'It is all those strange fungi and radiations that make it hard, even for me, to believe that I am still on the same planet.'

Freda's quick glance was disapproval. 'You arrived whilst Jackie was Charon and our chat was limited by the animosity between you, so we didn't get round to it.' Freda looked from one to the other and put a question. 'What do you know about boron?'

'It is an element,' said Hazel – quickly enough to leave Annita behind.

'That's right. It's very similar to carbon, yet strangely uncommon. It does not react at all easily although the atom is much the same size as carbon and sits next door in the table of elements, yet it is strangely lacking in ability for combining and often needs an atomic pile to make it happen. Yet in this place we sit on a very rich variety of boron compounds and that appears to be the root cause of all differences. Just as diamonds are pure carbon, so boron makes its own diamond, a yellow one, not as yet discovered naturally. But knowing this, none of us would need to look hard to find something very similar to a yellow diamond around here, would we? This high reactivity we think is due to a catalyst present in the rocks of the Styx chamber, and that makes sense if we consider the sentry rock as a rather unique kind of electrical cell based on boron. The fact that it delivers a life-threatening random discharge is what keeps us imprisoned here, but the products remaining from that discharge certainly make for interesting forms of life surrounding it.

'In earlier times the copper from here was much in demand because it was harder than from anywhere else, and this again indicates the influence of boron traces. No one realized what marvels we possessed, until just before the second world war, when two German geologists and a chemist arrived here complete with portable testing kits. Then as now, all technical men are carefully treated, in the hope that they might be of use to the community. The Queen of the day was inquisitive, and after retrieving their backpacks from the scavengers, the men were asked to run their tests on our many oddities.

'After incineration, significant boron levels were found in certain of the fungi, our house material, and scrapings of Styx chamber wall micro-organisms. They reckoned that both the fungi and the wall bacteria were metabolizing boron compounds straight from the rock, and that's why we have a number of totally unknown species and odd medicines. To them it suggested that our dwarfing is due to complex boron compounds contaminating things we cannot avoid eating. These substances, they believed, alter the carbon complexes that travel in normal human metabolic pathways, and it is this that can lead to stunting of growth.

'The men wanted more resources to investigate the remarkable plant life, in particular the ones that had evolved to dangle roots in corpses. They also wanted to investigate the abnormally rich assortment of rocks here and the metals in them. However, the Queen realized they were only prospecting for a foreign government and they could be dangerous if they found anything. Such a judgement consigned them to the hunt cave. Today we have their results, which I at least can read, even though it may not make much sense to either of you. For me is inspiring to find out why our location is especially gifted and could give rise to ways we can use our resources more intelligently.' Freda was finished, and her audience sat quiet, assimilating the new thoughts.

'Annita, have you told Hazel about her responsibility towards the men who arrived with her?'

Hazel looked on blankly, as Annita replied defensively, 'Sorry, Freda, we have not discussed the matter. One is her boyfriend Terry and she will need to make adjustment for her new role.'

'Then I will simply point out to both of you that when Terry is ready for work in about a week's time, he will become a labourer in the sheep cavern. For you, Hazel, it means that you will see him occasionally. The other man we expect to be a successor to Franz and he also will be part of the individual responsibility.' Freda smiled benignly at Hazel, and then stood as if to usher them out. Instead she said, 'I wonder if Hazel would like to see the treasure that the miners hid in the caves.'

Freda led them through two doors, and Hazel guessed, rightly, that this was the extra bubble on the palace suite. The difficult shape of the room was ingeniously arranged with shelves, stacked with ornaments of bright golden metal worked into rounded but intricate shapes that could only be gold. The sight reminded Hazel of seeing the Tutankhamen treasure in the cinema. Gold flashed in the tinted yellow light of the bubble, accentuating its own colour and then imposing a reflected yellow tint on to the relatively few silver items. Largest of all, but lacking the craftsmanship of other pieces, was a throne.

This outdid everything else, but only for sheer size. The throne's seat recess contained two cushions, one of which was horizontal and bearing a crown; the crown was almost as roughly made as the throne, despite gem-like stones that flashed from it. 'The throne is just something the girls "lashed up" years ago.' Freda explained modestly, conscious of Hazel's eyes making critical comparisons. She moved over to the extensive shelving, the section lined with that odd black wood, and picked up a pair of dancers – putting them to rest in Hazel's hands. They were wonderfully crafted, the figures were crisp lifelike mirror images and poised as if frozen in action. Such was the perfection, Hazel had never seen the like; she stood there transfixed until Freda moved along the shelves, tempting her to examine more of the wonderfully worked pieces that would have graced any high-class jeweller's display. There were many equally compelling works, but taken all at once it was too stunning to be fully comprehended. Hazel, still dazzled, stood with the dancers clasped in her hands, the feel of them emphasizing what she was being shown. What wealth there was here! Freda replaced the dancers on the shelf, the show was at an end and she was ushering them out – casually enquiring, but at the same time directing Annita.

'Have you introduced Hazel to her staff yet?'

'Sorry, Freda, I'll do so on the way back.'

Freda was soon saying her goodbyes, but invited Hazel to call again if she wanted any help or advice. Annita retreated almost gratefully, as if she was expecting some other omission to be remarked upon.

Their feet trod the now familiar path until they passed Hazel's cell, in fact all of the other cells as well until they were looking into the mouth of a large cave. A machine stood between them and the cave; its heavy frame of greenish metal was enmeshed with and part hidden among threads of material. With some surprise Hazel saw at the machine's lower end the fairies of her entrance memory, but dressed differently and quarrelling. Close up she could see them as tiny wizened figures in ordinary grey-green woollen dresses. One of the two had a huge hook nose and hair that had obviously been dyed, perhaps with henna, Annita tried to introduce this one as Tanya, but without eliciting a response of any kind. Indeed, from the vituperative multilingual exchange in progress, it was probable that she would have to wait for the English reply. Less colourful was Hazel's other entrance fairy, boasting a snub nose and silvery hair; but she had a voice that penetrated like knives on a grindstone. Annita said she was called Cora and came from south London.

The indifference shown by both of the tiny ones was total, emphasizing the fact that Annita had little control. In truth they were quarrelling so bitterly over a rucksack that stood between them, that their quarrel would have totally excluded any other consideration. But the position abruptly changed when one of the pair perceived Annita was there to use.

'Tell 'er, this 'arf's mine,' Cora whined in English, instantly reinstating her supervisor, whilst standing protectively over an array comprising many pieces: a razor, a torch, a leather jacket and several candles. With one accord both Hazel and Annita shied away, and left them to it.

'Those things belong to the madman,' Hazel exclaimed, recognizing the jacket.

'Not any more,' said Annita. 'That's the inducement for them to do the job, an inducement that makes them very keen on their work. "Finders keepers", that's the motto of the tiny women, but to divide anything up brings into play another watchword and that one says "fight for your dues". The pair of them first fell out when Marc arrived, and are only shelving it until now because Freda confiscated some of his stuff. They were mad about that; but it seems he drew detailed plans of our locality. That's why we believe he is not mad, and that your view arises from seeing him in different circumstances; the women here are quite taken with him. Come, let us walk by – we will not get much that's sense out of these two.'

'I can understand why they may have possession of most things,' said Hazel. 'But why do they have to have my watch or underwear? Both would be handy in my hot cell.'

'That's one I'll check with Freda,' said Annita, not wanting more involvement. She moved them a few paces forward.

'Is that the "hunt cave"?' Hazel asked, her mind jumping into the gloom of the large cave just beyond the quarrelling women.

'The whole system is loosely called that . . .' Annita's voice sounded hollow and the end of her words tended to get lost as she moved on through the opening ahead of Hazel. Nearby another cave budded off and heat welled out of it in uncomfortable eddies that hung upon the still air. Annita pointed into its mouth, towards a descending rocky expanse. 'Only the miners of old have ever entered that cave; but if you can stand the heat and it's worth it you might find more of their hidden treasure.' There was another bout of heat some hundred yards further along, where a side opening in the cave wall gave off a flickering light, and such intense warmth that they were obliged to curve their path around it.

109

'That's the "great destructor" that is,' said Annita reverently. She pointed to a wall facing it, a wall covered by stringy white growth clearly dusting a powdery white stain on the wall and floor. That suggested spores to Hazel, and so she gave the dust on the floor a wide berth.

Annita continued talking over an increased space between them. 'Extracts of these spores cause the body to destroy bone, or rather, to scale it down. It is natural for your metabolism to remake bones over seven years, but that stuff can speed the process enormously and do it in just weeks.'

The wall facing them had an opening on either side both leading separately into the penultimate chamber, the home of 'destructor minor'. This was another but less regular hole in the wall, giving this chamber a warm glow rather than the heat as seen in preceding caves, making it immediately comfortable. Against the far wall, which boasted openings at either end, were a series of stands. On closer inspection these proved to be various kinds of stocks, all fashioned in a well-corroded copper. Here the wall that faced the heat source was clear of vegetation, but stacked against it were targets, woven rather like those used in archery practice.

'You people have some pretty horrid furniture about the place,' remarked Hazel, looking at the stocks, mentally associating them with the anvil in church. Annita lifted the heavy top section of stocks high upon the posts, and playfully let go of the upper part so that it clapped down with a heavy clunk. Close by there were two seats, each with a movable wooden-looking tray in front; Annita swivelled one idly to show how easily it moved before passing by. The structure was evidently well lubricated and looking extremely well maintained. 'It is a rather grim place this cave, but every society has to keep law and order. Here what you see is all to do with the men, rather as the church anvil and all its surroundings relates to us. But in our case the anvil is a relic and a reminder of past happenings, invented and diverted by men into pain for us. It is an icon that says to us, you cannot trust men to coexist upon equal terms.'

Then dismissing dark thoughts with a shrug of her shoulders, Annita moved on, pointing out another weird fungus sprouting in one recess showing dark blue growths. 'These are the fungi that could have us all sleepy, so beware of anything quite that shade of blue. There exist some half-dozen varieties in these caves and you can regard them all as poisonous.' Annita passed into one of the two entrances to the last of the caves. Inside a dull orange light revealed a wide expense of cave with much of the central space taken up with an outcrop of pointed rocks or small stalagmites at its centre, making it look rather like a hedgehog's back. Over the top of them gleamed a line of holes in the wall showing perhaps the tail end of the warm glow from the previous cave. This light was restricted to two relatively small holes, and the resulting limitation conferred a menacing appearance to the cave. As they passed the heat holes, Hazel saw a well-defined path circling round the otherwise treacherous needle-shaped rocks.

'This is the "hunt cave" and the one that gives its name to them all.' Annita put on her best travelogue voice so far, and then almost triumphantly added, 'This is still a place where an individual can be set free and hunted to the death; assuming it is the will of the community of course.' Hazel shivered and asked if they could go back.

As Annita emerged into the cave of stocks, she suddenly ducked down and jumped to one side, grabbing a rod from somewhere beside the wall; shouts rang out and there was noise of metal on metal. Hazel jerked back, frightened, then peered out cautiously to see two women exchanging blows, each caught up in some strategic defensive movement or other. It reminded her of judo or karate exchanges, but as efforts surged this way or that, it soon became clear that this was some kind of good-humoured fight. A young girl with reddish hair and freckles fought a cat and mouse game with Annita, who seemed to be in her element. Their lithe movements and quick reactions had Hazel watching the bout in a state of perplexed fascination, for she couldn't imagine herself moving at any such speed. At length their efforts subsided in a sort of stalemate, whereupon Annita moved to introduce them.

'This is Bernadette, we call her Bernie: it's our normal afternoon custom to do a training session, and because I wasn't expecting to do it she almost caught me out today. We have to keep it up for our job with the four.' Annita was keeping a wary eye on Bernadette as if she were unpredictable.

Bernadette came across the floor and shook hands. ''Tis a pleasure to be meeting you.' Her voice, overlaid with a strong Irish brogue, sounded pleasingly musical, and she smiled imp-like at Hazel before standing her weapon down. Smaller than either

Annita or Hazel, who were of much the same stature, she was thin and possessing a wiry strength which easily compensated for both small size and immaturity; but after meeting her Hazel had no doubts about her being friendly.

'Now if you want to survive this afternoon,' said Annita, 'I would suggest that you return to your bubble, whilst I wipe the floor with this upstart – see you after dinner tomorrow.'

Hazel left them and was very soon securing her door from the inside. She felt tired after her first busy day, but at the same time pleased with her lot. All that had seemed so frightening at first had now become familiar and acceptably real; not that she could relax her guard in this strange place, for there must be more to come.

It was considerably later, and at a time when she was drowsing almost to the point of sleep, when she heard a tapping on her door. Throwing her dress on speedily, she hurried there to investigate. Facing her was a woman dressed simply in jeans and a chequered shirt; she was supporting a fleecy heap, much of which dragged along the floor and due most evidently to its bulky length.

'Hello, I'm Jackie. I bring creature comforts to welcome you here. There's something to lie on, and a little something for the tight skin.' She was so alive, so vibrant, that Hazel felt positively dowdy; but there was no retreating, and Hazel was reduced to helping Jackie drag the bulky duvet-like thing in. 'Put it on top of the base.' Jackie's voice was pitched low and husky, so authoritative it was obvious she was used to giving directions. Hazel dragged one over the other; realizing as she bent over the bed to push that Jackie had taken a pace back and was assessing her every movement – a prickly feeling ran right through her. Jackie's voice continued, sonorous, pleasing and self-assured, but still at a distance.

'I thought it high time I met the new Charon for myself, and besides to make you aware of an invite for joining our crowd. We meet in the club house most evenings – there is no reason to sit at home you know.'

Hazel could not think properly. She was overawed; just stammering her thanks and feeling obligated by the other woman's gift. Jackie produced a small bottle from her pocket. 'Arriving leaves the skin so strained and rough, it helps to know what puts it back in good condition – here, try a little'. Jackie took hold of Hazel's hand and rubbed some into its surface, looking up into her face with eyes of sparkling blue. 'There, you see, it works like a dream – smell it, there, isn't that nice?' Her smile widened. Transfixed – almost hypnotized by the beauty caring for her – Hazel felt akin to putty in the other's hands.

'Let's try a little on the face.' Jackie gently patted Hazel's cheek with the fragrant oil on one hand, the other easing Hazel backwards to sit upon her bed. 'Go on lay back – and relax.' The voice that came in almost a whisper was soothing and persuasive; Hazel lay back, cosseted in the soft, warm, woolly fleece. And as she did so, Jackie sat close by on Annita's usual perch, with hands performing long circular movements encompassing forehead, neck and face. 'Your poor feet, you must have been going barefoot,' whispered Jackie, reaching out towards the other extreme and slowly winding oil into the soles of Hazel's feet. Nimble hands engulfed her ankles as the action climbed to Hazel's legs, enriching the skin and making a multitude of enjoyable tactile sensations. Each move started with a tickle for which Jackie made encouraging noises, almost as if Hazel were some little girl. It was only when these tactile, sensuous moves encountered thighs that Hazel's head twisted and caught a fleeting glimpse of her grey woollen dress neatly rolled back, a barrier obscuring her view.

Distraction was only momentary, for then Jackie's face filled her view and their lips met. Hazel was stunned. She had never kissed a woman like that before, or even thought that a woman might want to. Jackie spoke softly in her ear. 'We can't just leave out the bits that don't show you know.' Her mouth kissed again, whilst gentle hands moved on firmly indenting flesh to set her pelvis afire. The sensation was intensive but brief; Jackie straightened up and allowed her imprint to fade, before the oily touch moved on. The dress began to snag about oily fingers, and aware of a hindrance Hazel adjusted it upwards to a point just beneath her chin, and from that moment another lingering kiss began. The oily hands, having been everywhere else, travelled behind her shoulders, and caught between dress and shoulder pressed Hazel upward – only to emphasize the last kisses. A strong elevating thrust pushed the yielding body very firmly into contact with one predatory female. 'You need me,' said Jackie. 'Just say when you are ready, because that's only for starters.'

Hazel looked at her dazed, was she was really going? But having conquered, Jackie knew when to go. To Hazel the streamlined

113

figure looked so positive, especially the longing in that last lingering look; the distinctive clothes contrasted briefly against the yellow of her gold-fish bowl and then Jackie was gone.

Hazel lay still with the impression of that last kiss stamped upon her face, not to mention her mind. Annita must have sent the woman, probably trying her out. She lay, gathering her wits, and putting the whole day's pieces together. She was more comfortable than ever here and so completely at ease, as she lay upon that new soft nest of a bed – an unavoidable permanent reminder of Jackie. She was not unlike a senior girl that Hazel had admired in her school days. Yes, anything could happen here, in this place where everyone was sterile and reproduction quite immaterial. That put gender out the window – love could equally be man or woman. She would have to be careful now, and decide who was to be her friend by using plain common sense, for any fraternization with Jackie would certainly aggravate Annita.

12

'The Little Ones'

The huge, multi-bubble, restaurant floor followed its routine break-fast pattern, efficiently seeing off the 'patrol four' by 7 am, and was well clear of the early breakfasters when Rose emerged from the kitchen area. Now was the time for her usual quick repast well before the 8.30 rush. Quick breakfast took Rose most of an hour, as it was her nature to be slow, even getting up in the early hours rather than hurry her work along. Rose was one of the smaller women of Hades, in fact the next to arrive after Tanya but rejected as a potential Queen. Her pleasant disposition was not well known among the women, partly because hardly anyone spared the time to await her responses, and partly because she worked long hours out of sight in the kitchen. Rose had been different from the moment she entered, insisting that she lay on the hard entry cell mesh until she herself felt ready to move. Today Rose drifted towards the food and had barely collected her breakfast items some ten minutes later when Poppy, her usual breakfast-time com-panion, arrived, skimming through the dishes and beating her to the first mouthful.

They looked at one another across the table. It was a friendly look but strangely silent; there was not even a 'good morning'. Poppy had arrived immediately after Rose in the entry stakes, and had somehow managed to be even more of a disappointment; indeed she was by far the biggest disturbance the indigenous population had needed to weather. She was saved against all the odds by the entrance 'tinies' who were quick-minded enough to realize fungi would be digesting the new recruit before ever Rose got herself into the retrieval suit. So it was with hook and line that Poppy was hauled to safety across the Styx chamber. The tinies immediately possessed her identification, and coming from a long line of inveterate gossips, they couldn't resist passing on the fact that she was British, knowing full well that it would cause a major upset. The majority language spoken then was French, but the balance had been changing for some time, due to the advent of more and more post-war English-speaking tourists. Rose was the first to tilt the balance firmly towards the English; but Poppy's arrival made the change impossible to ignore. Prompted by Cora, Queen Tanya decreed that English would be spoken. The French were horrified; but from existing law were driven to comply.

Before long it was Cora's turn to be horrified, as she learned that the English girl from the centre of London spoke only Chinese, as Poppy had been reared in Chinatown until the day her boyfriend took her on holiday. The delay in such news becoming commonplace was such that it filtered through Rose like a time capsule. An ever-resourceful Cora gratefully manipulated the news gestation period, and began to give Poppy a crash course in English. In the time available enough words of good cockney lingo were instilled, leaving Poppy like some unexploded verbal bomb – triggered at your peril.

And so this day, as any other day, the two misfits could comfortably sit looking across the breakfast table at one another in a state of repose, which brooked no interruption. Into the midst of this another early riser chose her food and blithely sat at their table. She had passed without pausing through the first section, which held a woman bearing an ugly scar on her face. The injury was not offputting, but the area was, because in the outer bubble niche sat the newly acquired, quarrelsome staff Cora and Tanya.

'Hello, I am Hazel,' she announced herself to the strangers, much to their evident surprise. Poppy seemed pleased, a smile lit up her small but delicate well-wrinkled face.

'Che's Sloe's, mee ahrre Pop-pee.' The fact that Poppy pointed her finger as she spoke did not assist Hazel's understanding one bit.

Hazel introduced her own silence as she sat considering, but then looked at Poppy before answering triumphantly. 'You are called Poppy.' Poppy's face beamed silent praise.

'And I am Rose,' said Rose, quite unexpectedly. Her voice animated the long, blank face and neat pigtails, which swung, confirming the fact it was she who had moved.

Her comment completely floored Hazel, who thought that she had decoded the thing completely. There was another prolonged

116

silence, as Hazel began to realize that any other corner of the place would have been more conducive to breakfasting than here. She ate in silence as she groped for the next pleasantry.

'I never know the time here,' she said at last for something to fill the silence.

Poppy pointed vertically through the ceiling and laughed, a bubbling laugh, quite delightful to hear. The oriental features that hinted a lemon tint, took on a round orangey smile.

Hazel looked up through the transparent roof into the brilliant lighting illuminating the village. There, projected somehow in large numerals, was the time, day, month, and year. She joined in with Poppy, laughing against herself and feeling a bit foolish – it had been there all the time. To see the rounded ceiling was one thing, but to look beyond its confines simply because it was transparent, was quite another.

'Yes it is, up there,' Rose summarized, not wishing to be excluded.

Poppy produced a series of strangled sounds, and lifting her cleared plate vertically from the table accompanied the action with such a surge of verbal effusion that this time Hazel did not grasp a single word of the outburst – intricately encoded as it was in Cockney-Chinese.

But all was well, Rose had tuned into the presence of a newcomer. 'She says, she makes the plates with three bumps so they will always stand level.'

Hazel turned an astonished pair of thankful eyes towards her interpreter, but instantly there was a fresh outburst, as further strangulated diphthongs hit the air. Poppy had fetched a solitary plate surviving from her predecessor. It had survived because she had preserved it, and then only because it would justify her theories about pottery, rather than any genuine liking for it.

There was a pause, and Rose once again came to the rescue by mouthing the words very deliberately. 'The plate is flat, but it rocks.' Hazel followed the pantomime closely, which involved seeing the only true plate since her arrival, trim and white, rock minutely on the table under Poppy's slender hands. Poppy homed in on a pile of her own plates, and was soon indicating all of the bumps and hollows to show that none were alike, yet all stood level.

'Look, they all have different designs.' Rose's voice, blended

117

into the shrill oriental, incomprehensible sounds, revealing that she was so well-versed in Poppy's argument that she could simplify the speech even faster than it was being delivered.

Hazel nodded her head in agreement, which seemed to fill Poppy with all the oxygen necessary for more verbiage.

'She is inviting you to her workroom,' said Rose awkwardly, fitting together a fragment that even she had been unable to anticipate. Rose hesitated, and would have said more but at that moment a voice behind the scenes called 'Rose.' With obvious reluctance Rose moved her angular frame towards a door at the end of their compartment, and rather like a film in slow motion she looked back with a decidedly pleased expression. Poppy also decided to depart, and Hazel followed, doubtfully aware that she now lacked an interpreter. But that only lasted until she reached the table she had avoided on her arrival. Cora and Tanya gesticulated urgently for her to stop.

'I'll find you later,' Hazel called out after the little woman. But her rate of progress had continued undiminished out of the bubble, leaving Hazel with the tiniest of the tinies.

Cora looked at her over an open bottle, clumsily pawing her plate with humour in her eyes. 'A right pare o frens yer 'ave,' she cracked. 'Poppy makes'um: Rose brakes'um.'

Tanya laughed so much over this that Hazel wondered if they all reached senility early here; but then something else on the table caught her eye.

'Is that a birthday cake?' Asking the obvious really, because written on top was 'Happy Birthday Cora'; the only unlikely thing about it she thought was the middle being real cake.

'Rose made it,' said Cora.

'Come to party,' said Tanya her tiny face upturned in some kind of rapture. These were the last words that Hazel ever heard either of them say.

Hazel patted the little woman on the back. 'Happy birthday,' she said before passing out of the club, and taking the wrong gate in her search for Poppy's workshop.

Back in the club, Cora gathered up her cake and bottle. They departed to the sounds of 'Happy birthday to you' sung by Maureen, the woman with a scar. The two scavengers headed for Cora's dwelling, where the cake was placed reverently upon the table. It was a glory hole, stuffed full of booty: piles of clothing littered the floor, heaps of shoes, strings of watches, lanterns, the portable bric-a-brac filling every conceivable space. A tiny cassette player was flipped on, and music played.

'Where's Arfer?' Cora looked about for her husband, but he was not in the dwelling at all and destined for a wallop when she saw him. She knew for fact that he would arrive with Leon when he surfaced, because the two were inseparable – rather like Tanya and herself. They were all in the same boat really, all exceptions to the conventions of today. When she had reigned as Queen, Cora had decreed that husbands could remain with their wives, Tanya having the distinction of being the only other person benefiting from this ruling. It had soon been made null and void by Maureen, the feminist who succeeded Tanya because neither Rose nor Poppy was considered able to do the job.

The dance music had them jigging about as they watched the clock, for Cora had an appointment with the Queen shortly. Nevertheless she determined to await her husband, dancing to the tunes as she waited, but then twirling about, a bit tipsy, her whirling perpendicular foot caught on a strap hanging from a pile of rucksacks and sent her crashing to the floor.

When he entered Arthur noticed the spill of rucksacks, and effortlessly locating the portion emitting hiccups, performed a brilliant rescue. Reaching below the fallen bags, he took hold of the form underneath and lifted. Kicking away the remaining straps, Arthur raised her up in his arms like some giant meatball from spaghetti. And then, rather like the hero he was, he topped this noble performance by presenting her with a bunch of coloured fungi shoots. Leon also bore fragrant leaves of some associated plant they had gathered.

Cora clutched at both in turn, giving each a big showy kiss. Inevitably it had to be a glass all round, and then filled to the brim from her bottle, a gesture which put everybody in celebratory mood and feeling pleased they had remembered her birthday. She was happy now and all ready to do battle with the 'frump', her name for Freda. This one she disliked even more than she disliked Maureen; confiscation of the heavy man's maps was unjust, because it ushered in a whole new concept – one that threatened their salvage rights in the entrance chamber.

Freda was waiting for her, sipping a coffee substitute and even pouring some for her; at least this was all right for a start. Cora sat slightly mollified, and accepting the liquid peace offering. She settled, watched narrowly by Freda who decided to start with the merest of trifles.

'I was talking to Hazel, your new companion of the Styx chamber a short while ago. She has been asking what had happened to her underclothes – mightn't it be friendly to hand them back now, as she is one of us?'

Cora was not ruffled she had heard this request many times before.

'Er tits wone fit 'er bra, nah she's shrunk.'

'Well then, she might appreciate her pants.' Freda's tone was icy.

'We save 'er life, not 'er bleeding cloves, ungrateful cow.'

Freda fully expected this reaction. She had merely set a ball in motion. She cajoled. 'It would be a nice gesture, you know. Hazel was a short girl when she entered and she has not needed much adjustment; her bust is still suited by a shallow bra.' And before Cora could react to this, she popped her surprise question. 'Why did you get the workmen to open up another bubble in addition to the one that they were opening for Hazel?'

Cora's wrinkled face looked at her unbelievingly – the guilt self-evident. 'It's fer me box, ain' it,' she said sheepishly, without mentioning Tanya's coffin.

'Do I understand you right? With all our shortages in that particular resource, you have a whole coffin made from it?'

'A box wiv brass knobs an 'andles, like me Dad – Cor 'is was a righ' posh do.'

'You are not having a right posh do here,' Freda scolded the little woman. 'You are not having brass knobs, and what is more, you will not move a single coffin into that bubble.'

'Everyfing's got posher fer 'em nahdays – awl soon'll git boxes wiv brass knobs on! It's bleedin' well not fair!' Cora protested vehemently, looking close to tears; signs which made Freda less severe – this was a member of the elders' inner circle whose support could be lost, especially since the damage could not be rectified.

'What do you want of us, for your, er ... "box"?' Freda attempted understanding.

120

'A funeral – befitt'n the Queen I wos.'

'Let me see what can be done.' Freda reached for the bottle she kept handy for such occasions, and they both savoured one of her better liqueurs.

Tanya, swaying slightly, looked down the Styx chamber, but there was nothing of note happening in there, the swirls of colour were moving very slowly. Soon she was entering an observation sphere in the cell row; she would see how the men looked today. Tanya peeped, pleased to see the unhealthy red colouration was departing and they were beginning to look pink again; even their size was part way there. The muscular man looked even more muscular now. The girls would all go for him, and she would too; Leon was past it and she wanted this man's thing. The tempting dreams lingered on as her steps took her to the usual place of work. A loom stood waiting where they wove the dress material, but she didn't feel in tune with the task. No, but to exercise her fingers on the suit the new man in her life would dress in was far more titillating.

Tanya hurried into the hunt cave, to where their cache of specials lay, and dipping into it she extracted the mackintosh fabric chosen for him. The blue material was already cut to size, for they knew his eventual measurements with only the need to move the studs over at some later stage. She sat there dreaming and sewing on press studs, waiting for Cora, but all of the time eyeing the two brown paper cylinders remaining from their quarrel of yesterday. A good way to end the dispute, she would give them as a present. Cora was later than she had anticipated, and now with the last stud sewn she would go and look for her work-mate. But Cora was already home, and supping the bottle again. Finding Cora was but to run into a stream of abuse directed against the Queen. Tanya took no notice, and Cora was reduced to mumbling all to herself, with a stiff, white face and glazed look about the eye. 'Me box, frumpy wants me box, outer storidge.'

Tanya held up the cake, to take her out of depression. Almost in reply Cora held up a pair of ladies' knickers.

'Nah, we start's givin' it all back – well, I ain't bleedin' well gonna!'

Tanya put the cake down, placed her two presents right at its centre and started lighting the candles all round the rim.

'P'raps I ough'er wear it as a veil.' Cora peered half humorously through the flimsy material, then froze, as Tanya's match caught the fuses she had trimmed to match the candles – surely they were sticks of dynamite? Nothing extraordinary to Tanya, just a fizz, as the sparkler didn't light properly and then vanished inside the paper: Cora's heart thumped a brief moment as she watched helplessly. The explosion happened in an instant, but contained by such enormously tough material as the bubble's fabric it made a resounding din, like a cannon firing in the enclosed space of the village.

Freda and Patricia rushed out immediately, to find the door blown off Cora's bubble, and a tear extended from doorway to the ventilation holes in its roof. In front of the bubble was a long column of shredded material, the proceeds of many years' scavenging spewed through the door; and among the extrusion, gory evidence of the tinies who had collected it. Above, a couple of panels had blown out the dome but in the main things were as before.

Arthur and Leon arrived, to stand appalled, not really knowing what to do.

'Christ, I s'pose they were both in there?' gasped Arthur, to a suddenly mute, white-faced friend.

'You had better find out then,' commanded Freda, without a shred of feeling.

'Me ol' girl could be in the back.' Arthur scrambled over the stained debris, clawing his way inside, only to re-emerge later, sadly shaking his head.

'Use coffins, when you clear up.' Freda was not leaving them in any doubt about what to do, and having at last seen much more merit in a 'box' returned to her house.

There were not many remains left with which to identify the two women, who must have been more intimate now than ever they had been in life. Moreover, what was left of them was scattered through Cora's possessions, making it difficult to know what part was mostly human, and what part was mainly collectables. Arthur and Leon made the best selection that they could, and filled the coffins to the brim, labelling the one that seemed to hold mostly Cora, as 'Cora': and the one which seemed to contain predominantly more Tanya, as 'Tanya'. Their wives had disappeared as if by magic and throughout their work the low-ranking spouses had a strong feeling that they might hear a stentorian voice bellow at them from behind, 'What yer doing with me coffin?'

A small group attended the funeral in the hunt cave: few there remembered them as great Queens in their heyday, but most remembered them as nothing more than a couple of unprincipled scroungers, backed by a unique wealth collection harvested in the Styx cave. Jackie in particular stood in sombre silence, for she had gained immeasurably from them. Her clothes were testimony to such an association, the jeans and shirt strikingly at odds with so many grey-green woolly dresses about her. Everybody present was dressed in some kind of input material from the deceased, but the majority dressed without trade-offs – just the normal production from their loom.

Arthur and Leon were the only men, the necessary muscle for pushing heavy boxes into 'great destructor'. Its mouth yawned open wide, flickering heat and light upon the bottom of the coffins, which themselves additionally glittered and glinted from coppery knobs and carrying handles. Arthur looked around the silent gathering; he could not just heave the boxes into an almighty furnace and walk off without saying something.

He gathered his breath and spoke. 'The Missus allus wann'ed a posh funeral an' she got it. She allus wann'ed to take it all wiv 'er – an I guess she 'as.' With those profound words he pushed his wife's coffin, assisted by Leon, until it fully entered the gaping hole in the cave wall. Then, solemnly as a pair of undertakers, they cleared the other in like manner. The ends tilted, fleetingly showing light upon the polished black surfaces as they reflected back an incandescent rock mass to the eye, the coffins moving smoothly onwards into their falling mode. Where they fell, no one knew, but certainly it would be a lot hotter than any other cremation on earth.

Freda had to be logical about the position as it stood; she gathered Hazel, Poppy and Rose together before the group dispersed. 'Hazel, meet your new reception staff for the Styx.'

Hazel stared at the two, utterly appalled at who the replacements were, and having suffered this blow even before she started work in her new capacity, she was aghast. 'What about their other work?' she gasped, noticing the pair looking pleased, as if promoted.

'Leon can take over the canteen work, at least he's the clean one of the sewer men. That leaves Arthur to carry on alone, until we have the help of a new man. But neither Poppy nor Rose must move house,' Freda warned. 'Tanya's dwelling will be closed until we can examine its contents.'

From the expressions on the faces of her new staff, Hazel realized that this latest stipulation had completely squashed much of the euphoria.

Suddenly Poppy's face lit up. 'Ah know-se, sum clev vur clows fash-ons.'

Freda turned a stern face towards her, having comprehended the full import, whilst Hazel still grappled with what was relatively straightforward Poppy language.

'Do nothing else besides watching the entrance – unless Hazel says so. You will check frequently every evening until supper.'

Freda turned her attention to Rose, her speech firm and slow. 'You will get up early – just as now – and watch the entrance; tell Hazel at once if anything at all happens.'

Rose nodded her head almost sadly as the message trickled through. Freda hurried away. There were now other urgent things to arrange with Maria. Hazel watched her go; the cave seemed barren now without its crowd. She was drawn to the outer lofty entrance where she stood awhile to consider the implications. What a sorry trio they made: herself not knowing, Poppy not communicating, and Rose not reacting. This was surely the most incompetent team that could have been put together.

13

The Dog Lead

Claude Brie opened his office door, and on entering began to back out once again; his desktop was brimming over, even his seat was piled high with evidence. For over a week now he had been fully occupied outside, and this was what he'd got for a homecoming. He knew that it was all of his own making really, simply allowing the case of the drowning dog to merge with other investigations into the cave explosion made the work more interesting to him but lengthened it all considerably. There would be little sympathy from his superiors for his idea of priorities had they known. The explosion was paramount in their estimation, but to Claude retaining one case of novelty had a double benefit of keeping Madame Masse at bay, and supplying some left over enthusiasm for seriously chronic stuff that had little hope of resolution.

Delegation was the answer to accumulations of evidence and paperwork, but Claude knew from bitter experience that his subordinates were not up to it. They were little more than local bobbies, and anything remotely connected with the slippery or evasive customers that undeniably existed, that was not for them. The best he could do during his absence was to use them in a teamwork exercise to probe the explosives angle, knowing that the dynamite almost certainly came from a local quarry; but beyond that he was on his own. Mainstream enquiries such as this ought to be given to the workforce, but precious little progress had resulted – it was he alone who had cracked it. He was elated, no need for more than a quick look in at the office today, he would just show an element of management function and then be off – it was nice that feeling of time to relax.

However his secretary, the girl Sylvia, had recognised the symptoms, and discerned spare capacity even as he backed his way out.

'You can't leave those disappearances for ever,' she nagged, 'the evidence is clogging us up and the relatives keep ringing me!' Then ducking smartly behind her desk she showed mock fright as his fierce gaze of exasperation fell on her. In his bout of defensive uncertainty, the Commissar vacated his own patch to tour the Commissariat. Staff from everywhere seemed very pleased to see him and unload some knotty problem or other. Sensing there was even more of this in the building he very quickly retreated to his office. Ahead of him Sgt Vierne stood tapping at his door accompanied by a character wearing a clerical collar. Mistake or no, he ushered them in, and immediately found that there was nowhere for them to sit. Fortunately Sylvia was watching the situation and opened the door of his superior's empty office that lay upon the other side of her.

Gratefully he trooped them in and closed the door, whereupon Sgt Vierne introduced Charles Chapman. Charles was Terry's friend, returning to France determined to put some action into the matter of the disappearance, above and beyond normal correspondence. Implored by both family and girlfriend to represent them, he had chosen to wear a token of his role as a local lay preacher, hoping to carry more impact on the authorities concerned. He easily passed his first test by convincing Sgt Vierne; but on realizing there might be someone more demanding upon the next step of the ladder, he began to copy the mannerisms of his local vicar.

'I have a particular interest in the disappearance of a young couple that I took to Lourdes, for communal religious instruction,' he intoned. 'Recent copies I have received of your local press report that my thin, lanky and even puny fellow parishioner is reported to be a heavyweight bull of a man who left a trail of destruction, dismantling masonry and carrying off a woman into the depths of nearby caves. The article goes on to mention a local custom of using this well-known route when eloping. Here again I can well testify that those two people barely knew one another, and would be quite ignorant of the districts peculiar customs on the day they disappeared.'

'Why then did members of your religious group decide to tour the countryside on bicycles rather than attend the various festivities in Lourdes?' Claude Brie sounded unconvinced.

Charles drew a postcard from his pocket and handed it over.

126

'The girl wanted to see something of your countryside as well as Christian institutions, as you can see from this card to her mother. The young man is both a keen amateur cyclist and an enthusiast in ornithology; he decided to use part of our excursion cycling into the mountains and observing wildlife.'

The card Claude noted was typical of a tourist praising the countryside. 'The girl of the card left behind striking residues from a sex orgy in the caves,' he said. 'And as if that wasn't enough, she went on to choke up our spa bottling plant with her knickers.' Charles staged a clergyman's look of shock at the suggestion, and mastering the situation with a competence of his own he chose to question the whole notion.

'The girl quoted is reportedly over six feet in height, wheras in fact the lady is both demure and petite, so I begin to wonder whether you have confused my parishioners with two other quite unrelated people, and if that is so would you please start looking for them?'

There was an uncomfortable pause, before Claude replied that the press reports were inaccurate and that he was pursuing as many as five in connection with the reported cave incident. Handing back the postcard he sympathized with the parents of both youths and said he would certainly do his utmost. 'If you will now accompany Sergeant Vierne, he will enable you to make a statement to that effect. The sergeant will take also take you, if you wish, to see the place where your party members vanished; but for the moment there is little we can do for you beyond this.'

The two men left, leaving Claude reclining in the soft upholstery of a plush office. Sylvia was summoned and duly brought him coffee. This was a good time to reappraise the direction of the case. It had been easy to lose sight of this young couple innocently caught up in something beyond their control, a feeling he was often having, and despite this had done very little for them. Certainly the prospect of having young innocent victims added that much more interest to the boring work arising from damage to property. He decided to leave the office and perhaps see Vierne at the caves.

The rear entrance of the caves was wide open and dumper trucks ferrying broken rock issued from the official door. Picking his way he moved warily through what looked to be a dangerous approach, but soon revised his ideas as their bright lighting and a segregated walk-line enabled a problem-free stroll into space where previously there had only been a block of rubble. Ahead of him he could see the foreman talking to Wigglesworth, who moved off as he approached. The man melted furtively into the crowd of men working further on. He asked the same question that he always asked of the foreman, and then received exactly the same answer he always did, noting that every time the man was finding it easier to say he thought there was nobody underneath. It was now becoming obvious, besides the fact that it would also smell badly by now. Coming towards him was Vierne and the cleric, the policeman jangling keys as he walked. Before he left, Claude stopped him to ask if he had noticed how bright and shiny the keys were; they were not at all like the ones he had seen.

Parking in front of the caves the Commissar first visited the shop, and found the elder Severac minding it. Henry was able to explain the keys; it would seem Georges discovered that they were using their reserve keys and had bought a complete set to replace the ones that were missing, namely the entrance kiosk. As there was no point in venting his annoyance on Henry that Georges had not bothered to tell him, Claude left the premises.

Only a short walk from the shop was the spot where the bicycles had been left; this was the most opportune moment to revisit the site. Here the ground was still riddled with scrape marks, which suggested angled metal had dug into the surface during a possible mechanical readjustment of bicycle seat and handlebar. There were even a few washers and one valve replacement rubber evidently spilled from a tool bag. He could easily imagine that last cave tour approaching and there being no time to finish the adjustment. This to him fitted the facts, because if both cyclists were equally tall as the bike evidence suggested, then there would be no reason to change anything for either person. Considering this point further he had to be right in his assumptions. The burly fellow he had already met, a Walloon called Marc Casserta who was understandably distraught over his wife's disappearance and likely to pursue a lonely course destroying hazards. All of this added up to a pair of youngsters lost in the caves. Much of what the Anglican cleric said he could accept, even though the character seemed particularly thin: considering the demeanour of the man with Sgt Vierne in the cave, who seemed devoid of the mannerisms present earlier in the office.

The Commissar had lunch and returned to the police station knowing he must at least see the full extent of chaos in his office. Clearing his chair, he sat uncaringly at the desk, almost unable to see over the mound of evidence that covered it, but meditating on the relative merits of the short morning excursion which yielded actual clues; comparing it with this bulk of paper which probably contained very little. There was no enthusiasm to begin sorting through it all; a job bound for Sylvia. His mind wandered over the other unconnected excursions recently, the ones that had brought matter facing him so much nearer resolution. The action had started with doggy events on that overwhelming day when a neighbour of Madame Masse rang in to report the lady as very nearly drowned. His staff knew it had all the hallmarks of a message for top brass, and called their chief back. Unfortunately, it was just as he was getting enmeshed in an engaging cave hunt for a missing blonde beauty. Because of this Claude was on the scene within half an hour, so there could be no complaining about lack of response.

Evidently Madame's dog Mitzi had gone swimming in the lake, and just sank: Julia Masse had literally thrown herself into the lake for the rescue, when she saw her dog's little front paws go up in the air and its tiny muzzle slide beneath the surface. Mitzi was destined for the lake's bottom, and so would the non-swimming Julia have been, if it were not for her neighbour who chanced to be out walking. Julia was still there at the lakeside, the water dripping off her wet clothes, when Claude arrived. She was still insisting, through the shivers, that she should wait and see if by some miracle Mitzi had dodged death.

Claude shuddered in memory of his reply. 'All dogs can swim. Let's go back to the house, she may well have returned and even now be waiting for you to let her in.' Relief had showed upon Julia's face on hearing these sensible words; but the homecoming was not to be greeted by a bark, and their return turned into a trek of penance about the house for Claude. He was soon gathering the necessary towels and dressing gown, that she might change her clothes – which presently dripped water over the kitchen floor – whilst pacing there in extreme agitation. Going was not an option, she was insistent that he stayed. 'Just turn your back,' Julia instructed. Claude, always the gentleman, did turn his back, only to be confronted by exactly the same view reflected in the kitchen window, set off against the dark of a nearby shed with mirror-like

129

brilliance. Making due allowance for the double glazing and its extra reflection, Claude judged the woman to be extremely bed-worthy. But a little later as she spent so much time dallying in her birthday suit, it was evident that she was well aware of the reflection. Claude tried to pretend that nothing at all had happened, but had more than a suspicion that she also used the reflection to observe him and any masculine reactions it set in train. Of course, the little dog was not home as promised, and once dressed the weepy woman was soon reminding him of his words and looking for a comforting arm; but not getting it, as he promptly left.

The body was found next day: Claude arrived to see the dog collected by its wet-eyed owner. Mitzi had surfaced late in the afternoon, slightly distended from the effects of decomposition – gas sufficient to float a dog wearing concrete. The long white fur was hard like armour, so hard you could knock upon it. Claude brought his soothing manner into play, and Julia, succumbing to personal interest and professional manner, was soon telling him the tale of her poodle's day. She had taken Mitzi to the poodle parlour first thing: Mitzi always objected to the perfume they put on her, and on the way back after doing her duty she indulged in rolling the wet grass around it flat; the roll concluded with a short paddle near the lake to retrieve her ball. Hours later, smelling slightly from dog dirt hidden in the long grass, she still looked a treat with her coat and pom-poms all fluffed up, in fact to all appearances the dog was ready for a non-fatal afternoon walk.

Claude, having rapped the dog's shell and surmised its weight, reckoned Mitzi was just too heavy and restricted about her breath-ing to go swimming. He was curious enough to stop off and pay a visit to the poodle parlour the very next morning. There the manageress succumbed to his pleasantries, and they took coffee together in a nearby restaurant. He insisted on treating her, and among much chatter she was incautious enough to say he could come again sometime if he wanted to watch the complete job. Her memorable comment, 'We have nothing to hide' was one which would come back and haunt her afterwards.

That afternoon Claude took up her offer and was back watching intently, enough that when the handler used a very liberal dressing of dusting powder he swooped on the material. The powder was soon mixed with water at a nearby sink; however the resulting liquid remained thin and finely divided. But he was not to be beaten and soon challenged all of the other powders available, until there was one that set well enough to repair a kitchen wall. The test result gave rise to a further bout of questions for the poodle parlour.

Alarmed and confused at this turn of events, the manageress said the powder was an experimental one; a man sent it from St-Saveur when he discovered the powder worked wonders upon his own dog. Yes, they had tried it out many times. And yes, Mitzi had the benefit of these advances, so that when she was all fluffed out with it she looked wonderful. The reason they were not using it at the moment was that the assistant who had dealt with Mitzi was off sick today. She was incapacitated through dermatitis – a factor that seemed relevant to Claude because it was clearly pertinent to the case. A further explanation was attempted but seethed with damaging admissions. Claude took possession of the pack, quite convinced that Julia would insist on a court case afterwards. All of the evidence needed to be saved, dog included.

The dog, he reflected, had served him well; his chair now backpedalled and backpedalled almost to the wall away from the well-piled desk. He did not notice as the door opened, until the respectful voice of Sylvia interrupted his train of thought.

'Will you want your afternoon tray, Monsieur?'

'Yes, Sylvia, I am staying here for the moment, but I will take it in the other office.'

'I did think you would be sorting all this out,' she remarked as a mild rebuke.

'No, it is all yours, order a new filing cabinet and sort all this in some kind of order for me. I will look at the evidence when I have more time.' The new office beckoned and Claude relocated for coffee. Sylvia noticed a look of satisfaction about him this afternoon which seemed to denote nothing more than his beloved thinking time, and so when she brought in his tray not one further word passed between them. The decidedly distant look remained, and on being lubricated with coffee his mind ticked over in contemplation of the recent past.

Emil Simon was in his mind, the man who had supplied the powder turned out to be an elderly, red-faced, shotgun-toting fellow in braces. Emil welcomed him into his home as he would a friend, and adding to all these aforementioned attributes, his manner was very open about the powder. The white powder had come from the quarry conveyorbelt rollers; it fell as fines at every transfer point after the kiln. His dog had made the discovery, for the dog's favourite place to lie down was under the conveyor, always emerging with a white back that needed brushing before entering the house. The dog had a naturally grey, uninteresting coat but Emil thought the powder did much improve the dog's coat when he brushed it out, so much so that eventually the idea of selling it occurred to him. Claude asked about water, but the man scoffed, his dog was much too intelligent to take a bath.

Emil took him to see the works, and the conveyor belt where it all happened. It was there the Commissar made a discovery which started off another train of investigation. Viewing the conveyor Claude noticed the wiring was new, and stretched away to the distant quarry hut housing a kiln. Was there an influx of money from Emil's sideline?

'Surely all of this wiring is new?'

Emil, who had become very chatty, immediately told him, 'Yes, all my friends are getting electrics done very cheaply, there's a local chap called Kee who gives an exceptionally good quote.'

In the following week the Commissar revisited quarries that used explosives locally, and found that Jan Kee was known everywhere for his low prices. The man's customers told him that Jan bought up material that failed to meet standard specifications from a Belgium cable-works, and that he did so at very low prices. Remembering his conversation with M. Vilette, manager of the Montagne Source Minéral Plante, Claude was ready to see Kee as an unscrupulous rogue. In fact enough to have him chase around, trying to connect dates between cable laid at any one of his listed quarries and the explosion.

At one of the quarries, not only did the dates overlap, but also his notes dating from the audit showed a loss of four dynamite sticks – sufficient reason for arresting Kee. But first he had to be located: Claude contacted the company clearing debris from the cave system and discovered that they had two addresses for him. One meant a short detour from his way back; it was the St-Saveur Vidal caravan site.

Not expecting things to work out, the Commissar decided to take a look at the caravan park. As he drove in, a familiar figure drove out; it was Kee on his regular evening tour of beer houses.

The short distance to a beer garden was soon covered, and Claude was able to follow without overmuch precaution. The big man seemed overtly nervous when they met face to face at the bar, and it was not long before the quarry name arose in conversation. Claude saw enough reaction to this to make bringing the man in for questioning a necessity. Their respective cars headed for the nearest interrogation point – the police wing of the St-Saveur courthouse.

Barely an hour later he obtained an admission of theft that arose from knowledge of dates that Jan had signed in for doing work in the storehouse, the keys he had borrowed and the data concerning dynamite sticks. Jan was impressed that his signatures were on record and by the accuracy of figures in the stock-book, which were damning. Claude realized with some surprise that the staff at one quarry on his list could count. The fact that all the other quarries stocks did not add up was of course omitted, for Jan was confessing.

Jan's admission was enlightening. 'I took the explosive for my friend Marc Casserta, but I had no part in using it. It has given me all sorts of trouble, that explosion, so you can't say it was beneficial to me.'

'Is that the same Marc Casserta, a Walloon, who came looking for his wife?'

'Yes, that's the man. You know about him then.' Jan looked appreciative and ready to rise, obviously concluding they were coming to the end of the interview.

The Commissar waited until the man regained eye contact. 'That's the man whose wife you stole!' Claude slapped the table so hard with his hand that the magistrate sitting in jumped; but Jan merely looked unhappy, preferring to say nothing. That alone was a good pointer for Claude who was by this time getting onto thin ground. 'You hoped that he would kill himself with that explosion in a confined space, and he would not be aware you were living with his wife.'

Jan's face drained of colour, but he said nothing more. Claude was sure enough now to put him in a cell; the evidence he would use could easily be found.

14

Parsnip

The rattle became a knock, and increased in volume as Hazel vacated the realms of sleep, to lie there awake with her heart thumping. 'Surely it's the middle of the night,' she told herself. The thump, thump on her door sounded flat-handed as she stumbled over to it; releasing the tie, which now always faced her way. Rose stood there, her lips moving, as if holding a private rehearsal before she spoke.

'Where do I go now?' She put her question at last with great deliberation.

It was a relief to realize that Rose was reporting for duty in the entrance chamber, and then Hazel remembered being told Rose was a particularly early riser who started work in the early hours. A minor panic confused Hazel's mind, she was in charge already – what did they have to do? Her first muddled thoughts could only imagine knocking on Annita's door, but it was far too early for that. Rose must simply sit there and watch the space – ideal work for such as Rose.

'Come with me Rose,' Hazel said, trying to sound authoritative. She put her hand on the little woman's shoulder, which was surprisingly bony for one who was ex-canteen, and guided her towards the loom. Taking one of the loom stools she did a demonstration walk for Rose's future guidance, setting the seat in the aisle between cells with the Styx chamber in front; from here Rose would have a clear view right through to the sentry. All that was required now was the very minimum of instruction.

'Find me, if you see anything move.'

Rose looked towards Hazel, her face full of indecision. She had been all keyed up to ask a question which had petered out on her lips before it could be uttered. The last thing Hazel wanted this early was questions. Rather than appear to retreat immediately, she wandered back to the loom, trying at length to understand its action but without the benefit of seeing it working. Poppy would arrive some hours from now, and there would be unintelligible questions, along with much confusion, of that she could be certain. How the loom worked was a mystery. Hazel pushed and pulled the wooden levers attached to its frame which clonked back and forth apparently doing nothing at all, so she gave up in disgust. A garment lying on the worktop caught her eye; this she picked up authoritatively for the benefit of Rose and took it back to her cell on the pretext that it was her main reason for leaving the scene. Sleep would be quite impossible after this. She sat down feeling very tense and disturbed.

Twice afterwards her feet trod the path to the village, a route that was by now familiar, just to look at the clock, and on the second occasion she decided it was not too early to disturb Annita. Hazel approached Annita's bubble house and knocked timidly at the door. There was a babble of voices within, her knock had not been audible. Hazel pushed at the door and it creaked open, directly ahead was Annita with her back to her; she was yelling at Franz, her arm in the air clutching the flail. Hazel watched in astonishment as his tunic was already open from the neck down and the flail struck heavily on his bare back, a back already crisscrossed with a surprising number of dark lines. Hazel backed out and shut the door; whilst a 'domestic' was in progress it was decidedly not the time to arrive.

The nearby club beckoned. She could have breakfast early – yes, why not? The place did seem empty, she was still early, and just as well too because there didn't seem to be over much food available. Hazel's own favourite yogurt was there in plenty and a few other things too. Water boiled nearby, all so handy for self-serving the hot herb beverage she liked the best, and further along the counter a boiled egg intrigued her. Without so many alternatives ready to confuse her, Hazel saw in addition mushrooms just like those at home, civilized mushrooms that had been fried in a pan; her mouth watered and she added some to her plate. She sat in the first partition, and with the entire area empty ate breakfast. She was still tired; today even the spectacular view did nothing much for her and disregarding the chair's straight back she reclined at an angle, feeling much like a piece of chewed string.

Her mind simply would not quit going over what she had seen. Franz had such a plaintive face with the brightest of blue eyes peeking out from under a mop of unruly blond hair; a face of woe she thought. The plight of Franz had moved her more than a little. Hazel sat dreaming depressed thoughts before emerging from gloom with an uplifting resolution. She would save this heathen world that fate had thrust her into.

A noise intervened, and in vain she brushed it aside mentally clinging to her Utopian thoughts; but all to no avail as discordant clashing dragged her back to reality. The metal covers clanged again angrily and then a red-headed girl entered her field of view. It was Bernadette, surely far too young to be using the swear words that were issuing from her lips. She winced as more dishes clashed, with covers lifting and clanging shut in quick succession. It was noise much too early for Hazel.

'It's a disgrace; to be sure it is – they'll be starving me if I let 'em.' The youngster showed her recognition now and headed for Hazel's table. Bernie gave her a quizzical look as she slid into the seat facing her. In her hand was a plate that looked very similar to her own choices, the yogurt would run out pretty quickly at that rate. Hazel now had a better view and looked critically at her; girl was an apt description, for Bernie was very young. Her small, thin face was topped by long, straight auburn hair, hair that was tied with fibre where it reached into her back. Obviously not in good heart, the thin features looked fierce and continued searching Hazel's face, silently questioning her interest. Bernadette, who had not answered the initial greeting given as Hazel jerked upright in her seat to see, now broke the silence.

' 'Tis stupid, letting us starve, it's going to sleep that they are.'

'Today's probably a bit short of staff; did you know Rose has a new job?'

Hazel felt she could handle some conversation, now that she had returned to earth from her musing. But the explanation did nothing to engage the youngster in conversation. Instead she was looking towards others who had just finished serving food. Bernadette, decidedly distracted, part rose, then remarked, 'My friends. D'you mind if I go?' She looked hesitantly at Hazel, still rising uncertainly to join Jackie, and what was presumably Frances, both of whom had chosen the other table recess. Of course she was now eating with 'the four', albeit on another table; although in fact hers was probably the table they normally occupied, a thought which was almost as uneasy as the youngster leaving it.

Hazel sat listening to the complaining voices talking about the skimpy breakfast – with the Irish girl proffering the explanation that Hazel had just given regarding Rose.

A familiar voice behind her suddenly lifted her spirits, for Annita had arrived to sit with her. 'I won't be offended if you want to sit with the foursome,' Hazel said, quite resigned to losing another. 'Or are you preparing to take Bernie by surprise later?'

But Annita it seemed really wanted to sit here, and settled down to eat the smallest amount Hazel had previously seen on her plate. 'No there has to be a truce between us now, for this early we combine forces to peck at the worms.' As she spoke Annita was doing semaphore with her eyebrows again, heralding a return to being her normal self and acquiring the cheerful, carefree expression she recognized.

'Did Bernadette have a job before she came?' Hazel was curious now, having seen her in the light as opposed to depths of a cave.

'No, Bernie has always been a problem. She arrived just after me. Seems her dad was keen on caves, but stopped for a smoke somewhere off route and she just wandered off. At thirteen she couldn't be Charon, so we started her right in as one of the four. A proper little madam she is too with her childish ways. I am especially annoyed with her this morning, so much so that I will not be sparring with our young wasp for some considerable time. In fact it's a relief to be able to sit somewhere else. But that's my troubles, what brings you here so bright and early?'

'It's not early to me now. Rose arrived for work so prematurely that I got up in the night and couldn't go back to sleep. Can you come and show me what it is they are supposed to do, before you set off?'

Annita glanced at the other table, they were still chatting, and without saying a word she moved across close to Jackie, whispering something in a rather low voice, then beckoned to Hazel. They set off at fast pace making for the cells, Annita apologizing first in one respect and then another for not having already done so, this she followed with an admission of how little she knew about it anyway. 'I am not going to be much help because Cora and Tanya ran their own show. They had been top people here and it would not have seemed right for such a junior to direct them. By contrast

Rose and Poppy have never ever managed anything at all, so I think that you have a golden opportunity to do things entirely your own way.'

She finished as they arrived at the mouth of the hunt cave, where Annita darted inside and emerged dragging a spinning wheel mounted on a foot treadle; this she butted against the loom. Hazel moved to examine it, but only managing to be in the way when Annita returned with two waist-high halves from a small bubble; one was full of loose wool and the other with mostly empty bobbins. Annita jammed the half-section bubbles to nestle neatly against the loom, grinning as though seeing its funny side. 'You can have the pleasure of explaining this to Poppy, but if all else fails leave them to discover how. Luckily there's no backlog – it's only you that's due for another smock.'

Then, seizing Hazel's hand, she pulled her into the cave. 'But look at all the stuff those two old codgers had stashed away.' Hazel's eyes widened, as Annita with squeals of revelation, dragged over a dozen things out of deep hollows in the rock.

'Put them all in your cell before the other two arrive,' directed Annita. Otherwise you are making them a present, even before they start scavenging. But I must go now; just play it by ear for the time being. Remember you are the boss and can do it your own way – but keep this afternoon free for me, for I am introducing you to Parsnip.'

Annita departed at the double, running the length of the cells and leaving Hazel to guess who Parsnip might be; but for now there were more immediate things to do. She concentrated on the several bundles of men's clothing, a coil of sturdy-looking rope, a bright red torch combination, and nearly a dozen batteries. All of these Hazel dutifully carried back to her cell, able to do little beyond piling them up in an almost bare interior. As the morning wore on, Hazel weathered the many tribulations of setting her staff to productive work. In particular it took much explaining to get Poppy started. It seemed the oriental mind was set on working with silks, which must surely exist in Cora's abode – wool will be so boring. At length they were as settled as ever could be, and by then it was almost lunchtime.

Annita met Hazel after lunch, and their tour of the village commenced by visiting the other two gatehouses. Substantially these were very like the one she knew; they all had narrow doors on the outside and wider ones on the inside leading to the village. The other two, however, deserved special mention because they connected with the caverns and in respect of their greater strategic importance the gatehouse doors were better equipped with heavy-duty metal fittings on the side that allowed village access.

'Once those doors are properly shut they could defy an army,' Annita told her proudly. She was referring to the nearest gatehouse to the houses, which opened on to what Annita called the 'agricultural area'. Beyond this gate she warned labouring men might be expected to roam loose, bringing foodstuffs or taking them away. Once outside the gate it was colder and the gate area itself was not very well lit externally. They passed through an arch and the village lights disappeared behind them; here Hazel found herself again depending upon fonz plants to see the way. A major route swept round to the left, but Annita cut across slightly to the right of them, where a lesser opening was dimly visible.

The smell was a familiar one and not at all mysterious now, for out of the darkness a brown mare approached Annita and nuzzled her shoulder. The horse was not disappointed, for Annita carried some sweet titbits from breakfast secreted in a fold of material tied to her waist. 'Its Cauliflower,' she enthused. 'The horses' names are all names we once used, and will never use again for the proper thing.'

Hazel was silent. Parsnip then was probably a horse, but she would have to wait for it to be called. There were three other horses in there from today's patrol. Annita led her back, enthusiastically talking about horses and only in passing mentioned another stable. 'We stable them this side because the air is fresher and this is the main stable; but if things become uncertain here, they can equally go to the other place.'

They headed towards the other main gate, going behind the food house to reach it, and standing there the small gatehouse for the pool could just be seen. Annita said that this gate was the engineers' small gate leading to two caverns, which they would actually visit. Once through into the cave it became much cooler, in fact noticeably more so than outside the agricultural gate. The cave was as black as night, causing Hazel to step uneasily forwards, having to trust the surfaces were more or less level; but then as her eyes adjusted she could see space ahead inadequately served by fonz plants. The space flared into a wide bulge where a number of half-sized bubbles were dotted and the air became foul, tainted with the unmistakable smell of sewage. Annita turned on some lights and Hazel saw that these small bubbles were sunk into the ground, equipped with some external mechanism to break them open in the middle. Annita opened a metal-rimmed dome of a lid, which unlike the rest had not been secured by a latching device; as it lifted Hazel saw within a part-filled pit of black sludge that smelt appallingly. Annita was not sparing her the niceties; instead she seemed to revel in keeping her close to them and taking a pause to explain.

'Arthur works an anaerobic fermentation for us; he exhausts all of the waste collected, bulking his daily work until it's like this, adding in kitchen waste and guano from the bats. After fermentation he bulks them with soil to make compost. Methane gas is produced in the fermentation and originally it was piped to the eating house, but Maria objected, and now it mostly goes to the engineers' workshop.' She closed the vessel, and leaving the lights on led towards the blackness ahead. 'Here is the first cavern; you see its upper walls are crawling with bats. Most bat species are not very big and suit soup making best of all, but there are a larger variety up there to make the bacon you tasted the other day.' Annita reached for another switch, and numbers of lights twinkled into the distance, as if she was working the stars of some captive night sky. 'These are not all the lights given to this place but we are short of power at the moment.'

Hazel's heart sank, was this it, her new world of caves? Damp, dark and above all cold: how could Annita remain so cheerful in such a miserable place? The space had an 'off' smell all of its own, and the climate could be summed up in one word: depressing. She could see their wild life now; they were high up on the rock face, grey-black blobs clinging there in their masses, a few moving restlessly in the weak light. Against one wall of the cave stood a rickety scaffold, almost tall enough to reach the lowest of the creatures. Despite being aware of Annita watching her for reaction, she could not suppress a shiver.

Annita indicated a barrow standing near the walls. 'All the guano you see on the floor is very rich fertilizer, so after infusing the fresh stuff in our fermentation, the older stuff is collected manually to mix with the recycled soil. The septic tanks output wets it and then Arthur stands the mix in the heaps over there against the wall waiting to become compost. Further on you can see what has been growing on the guano for centuries.' Annita pointed out some huge black toadstools looking much like cart-wheels, one she slapped so hard the noise disturbed bats high above her. 'These are petrified and getting like wood, but they are very scarce now and indeed they are all we have in that direction: you have seen it as tabletops in the club, shelves in the gold room, and more recently Cora and Tanya's coffins. That's what they plundered from us illegally.'

Annita carried on into the dismal bat dirt accumulations of the cavern, eventually arriving at a corridor of splattered stones that she referred to as shale. These led her to a long gash in the cavern wall and within very few strides they had entered it, splashing through a long puddle to do so. The lighting inside helped bring Hazel willingly into the opening; although she still hung back, thinking that it might be another elaborate joke of Annita's rather like the sewage smell. But Annita was turning valves on a huge flexible hose, and getting very wet in doing so; cold water flushed over the rocks and Annita appeared to be dancing upon them. The wet spray had Hazel giving it plenty of room, nevertheless curiosity held her spellbound. Soon Annita turned the water off, and stood peering into little depressions where the water had overflowed. Hazel drew near, only to be told that she would need to be 'more hardy' than she was – the joke in the voice told Hazel that Annita was teasing her again. With eyebrows dancing from the sheer fun of it, Annita pressed a small piece of yellow metal into Hazel's hand.

'People have started giving you presents, so here is one from me. A gold nugget from our very own gold mine, and when we liberate the stuff in Tanya's bubble, I'll fit a chain to it.'

'It's gold, not fool's gold?' Hazel did not entirely trust her friend.

'The Romans invented our extraction process, and left lots of it here; the only disadvantage is that we want hard metals, not ornaments. Come on – let's find Parsnip.'

Annita hastened away, it seemed the wet spray and the cold of the cavern had told on even her.

After turning out the cavern lights, they moved almost immedi-ately through a misshapen part-brick arch, which had apparently been the subject of repair many times. This led on to a slightly warmer engineers' cavern.' Here sulphurous fumes tickled the throat enough to cause an occasional cough, and Hazel's nose could not miss the quenched metal-like smells additionally lurking in this atmosphere. Annita pointed into the distance where some shadowy figures moved. 'That's Red and his helpers, they are situated at the other end of this cavern, but already they appear to be aware of us.' She waved, acknowledging them. Then turning Hazel sharply her voice rose excitedly. 'Look over there, it's Parsnip.' Their steps hastened towards a shadowy enclosure.

With head tossing over the fence of the large paddock, a horse impatiently awaited their arrival; it was a peculiar colour, but this at least did help Hazel to be sure of his identity as 'Parsnip'. The horse moved towards them expectantly and, as seemed routine, Annita produced a reward from the tied-on pocket about her waist, still well prepared to cope. There was something comic about the relish with which the heavy horse consumed the delicacy. It raised its head and flipped its lips. Annita laughed even more now, obviously appreciating the horse as an equestrian type might. Hazel however did see the horse as a magnificent steed; but was not distracted so much as to spoil her observation that there was enough coarse, dry vegetable litter on the floor to bed down several horses, not just Parsnip.

'You are going for a ride, Hazel.' Annita made the point firmly, disguised among much sweet talk intended for the horse.

'I don't ride,' said Hazel, knowing all too well that her infrequent visits to a stable, in order to accompany someone else who did, wouldn't qualify.

'You do now,' laughed her friend. 'From now on you are a spare for the patrol foursome. Here we have both a saddle and a whole afternoon to lunge, and lunge until you are proficient.'

Annita was determined not to let her off anything at all, even insisting that Hazel put the saddle on for herself. Parsnip was very good about it, tolerating the inexpert attention well, not to mention the mounting which alone threatened to take a good slice off the afternoon. It was a wearing session, but after she had circled Annita some dozens of times, Hazel was sitting erect.

Then of course there was an attempt to trot which extended the whole thing into a weary nightmare, indeed by the time she got off, Hazel found difficulty in putting her steps into a straight line, and left Annita to clear the saddle herself. Annita was quite happy to do so because the process of moving Hazel on had started in earnest, so she contented herself with merely handing the saddle to her trainee for carrying. The saddle had seemed small and hard, but even so it was heavy to carry and Hazel couldn't help thinking that it made bikes compare very favourably.

'Right, there's just one more place to visit, and we are finished.' Annita's enthusiastic voice penetrated Hazel's tired and weary mind, hoping to bolster her with an encouragement, before adding more. 'We shall take a break now and come back to do the same tomorrow, in fact every day, until you can ride with the four; but even that's not the nicest bit! With Bernadette out of my good books, you can do your combat training with me as well.'

Hazel was too weary to question this, just groaning inwardly to herself, hoping the combat training stayed where she hoped it was, in the future. The next stop was the tiny refreshment room in the church, and there Annita boiled a friendly brew. Hazel found herself keen, for the cavern's sulphurous atmosphere had left her with a nasty taste in her mouth. She was wary of the hardball seats and stood there wearily toting her saddle. Annita hastened to take the saddle from her and put it down; she was eager to impart more on the combat subject, for it would seem that the church was where weapons were secreted.

'To start with there is plenty of spare capacity in the church bubbles and so it's convenient to use them this way, and hidden too because so many of the bubbles are deformed. The best place to site the entrance is of course in this refreshment room because it is a place people would have another reason to go or congregate. From this room we constructed a second exit, and from there on begins a succession of bubble rooms, each one having several exit holes. Even these are not particularly visible in the transparent material, making what in effect is a maze. Knowing all of the combinations will get you through to reach the armoury,' but having explained this, Annita waited until the brew brought colour back into Hazel's face before attempting anything else.

Then they moved into the next cell and began to follow the tortuous route – most of it covered on hands and knees. The innermost chamber when they reached it was piled with offensive and defensive equipment, some very ancient, some very new; there were guns even. Annita said that a lance or crossbow was the usual thing; only in exceptional circumstances would a concealed handgun be used as back-up.

'All this is because none of you make friends of the men? There's only one result – a big risk of their retaliating!' retorted Hazel. 'It seems to me that your ancient women's customs are outdated, and everything in the code you inherit and follow so blindly makes us all guilty – we are the oppressors.' Hazel could barely cover her aggravation, she shook with indignation; this morning's snoop took charge of her emotions. She was quite sure that this common failing had accumulated like poison in her friend's make-up.

Annita looked at her intently. 'Everyone who comes here wants to bring along the rules they live by, and when you let a determined objector in sufficiently far as to have her way, then you are asking for trouble. You'll soon find that out that both sides here are balanced evenly and if ever you give the other lot an inch, an inch is enough to negotiate with and besides make a fool of you. The rules we have go back to 1850, because one particular lady arrived when the anti-slaving movement was the rage of civilized society. In fact that craze had so incensed Charlotte that when she became Queen prematurely, she expressed the view that our men-folk are slaves. Then she made a decree declaring men to be our equals and free to refuse what's asked. Rebellion flared the moment the men heard they were free to negotiate. "To be free now" also suggested that the women were to blame for them not being free before. If they were free then there was no reason to labour as before, and until that was understood, they would retain what they had for themselves.'

Annita pressed a pike into Hazel's hands and rummaged among the newer-looking crossbows, ones that evidently depended much upon the toughness of bubble material when cut like a carriage spring. She thrust the brightest of them at Hazel who found it surprisingly light; but hardly was this accomplished before Annita resumed her narrative.

'Production of food instantly ceased, and everything available went into a bout of feasting and tumult, whilst those running the place became involved in frantic negotiations to stave off a backlash. Sweeping changes were demanded to give the men not only

144

equivalent lifestyles, but also a right to take a wife as they all did in their civilized countries of origin.

'Queen Charlotte, who had thought her proposals through very sensibly in other respects, argued from her own philosophy. "If you cannot reproduce there is no point to marriage – in here you are all individuals. And as individuals, we all need teamwork for success in harvesting our food: the men have the muscle for labouring, and the few women available are ideally suited to both manage the effort and cater for everyone. Put these qualities together and you have a future; if you don't then you haven't one." In effect she hardly wanted change at all. The men were not impressed, as a zero birthrate meant nothing at all to them; surely it was conjugal rights that mattered. Babies are what gets in the way.

'In those days another thing the men knew for certain was the names of several women who would move in and join them. Those soon moved in where the food was, and worsened the position for the others. The women who fraternized were valuable as mates, but the solving of one man's problem did nothing for the others. The men soon settled whose woman was whose; these were the top dogs, and with that achievement under their belt they desired to settle their women in the warm, habitable region where the village now stands. Charlotte attempted to put things right by meeting the would-be settlers en route. "Do it by making agreements with us," she said. But her words sounded weak, as nobody was backing her up. The men were not going to negotiate now; merry on beer, and only her standing in their path they passed by leaving a corpse with a cut throat.'

Hazel fidgeted. She was tired, and complained that the atmosphere was close. Annita, carried away with her narrative, stared at walls streaming with breath condensation, and becoming silent retraced her route back into the refreshment room. Quite evidently the armory was substandard in ventilation holes, and it was no fit place to remain gossiping.

Their move back was prompt, bringing Hazel's arms to join the saddle as her vital equipment. Annita chose to make mugs of fresh herb tea before returning to their history lesson, seated on the hard balls. Hazel cleverly took up the discarded saddle and turning it the wrong way up, made herself a better seat.

Annita began where she had finished, for there were important

145

conclusions that Hazel needed to know. 'Heavily outnumbered, the remaining women retreated to the hunt cave, where they couldn't be outflanked and where the armoury was in those days. There they survived for a few days off the few bats which somehow manage to enter the rear cave. Tactics changed to guerilla-style raids that very soon solved their food shortage. One for one, the women of course had at least half a head advantage in height, and a skill with weapons that couldn't be matched by the men. Further to this the men were fully neutered in those days.

'Elsewhere, the entrance cave was neglected and all who entered perished. Chaos reigned in all productive areas, with food stocks spiralling down, as none of the surviving settlers were prepared to be the only ones working until the urgency was upon them. For still there remained sufficient livestock for slaughter, removing the need to bother whilst they were busy fighting. Men are like dogs; they need the leader for action such as repelling the armed forays from those in the hunt cave. The women concentrated on this fact by picking off whatever man had a woman. Soon the lifestyle was hardly worth defending any more, and the survivors began making peace with the armed women in the hunt cave. The residue of men left alive were hardly representative examples of a resilient masculine society. They were soon all battle scarred and keen to forget any aspirations to an equal society, quietly returned to their labours.

'The two groups of women got together, and sorted out their own differences in what was nothing less than a civil war; at least they were united again. Wary that there may be others like Queen Charlotte arriving any time now and all ready to repeat her folly, they debated rules which would allow people to exist in better harmony with one another. The "Queenly prerogative" in future would have to be agreed by representatives of the elite posts in society before being acted upon. Secondly, the division within their own ranks needed to be addressed, for it was only the lesbians who wanted life that way. The heterosexual women, pre-conditioned to civilized life before they arrived, had little worth fighting for in earlier cave administrations, and so it was that this particular aspect had to be rectified first. This gave strength to the idea of having a single concubine; one who takes on the job voluntarily. Incidentally this is the bit that affects you directly, as you are next in line to house him. For this reason alone you ought to join in our evening activities because you will soon be a central part of it. The other decision of importance was that every new arrival eligible to be absorbed must be offered a role in society. This is virtually a contract of employment, entitling the new arrival to be fed. Non-acceptance would mean expulsion, which is of course virtually the same thing as a death sentence – but none then can be slaves. In addition to the new guidelines, everything had to be righted once again; food grown and fresh livestock brought in.'

Hazel was intrigued despite being so weary; she positively jumped when she heard the words 'fresh livestock'. 'How do you get fresh livestock?' she asked incredulously. 'And come to think of it, however did it happen in the first place?'

'Hazel, did you ever hear the story of the Green Nun? It's a local tale of one who escaped.'

Hazel looked blank and shook her head: she had been in the caves and seen the carving, but the story had passed her by. She couldn't remember why, but it had.

'Every so often someone enters the caves, and recovers pretty quickly; such a person is thought to have a better chance on the way out. All our risks are minimized from having had the experience of entering, for instance we know that if the sentry is passed speedily, moving near to the floor, the chances are good. But if you take the risk and lose consciousness in that alley, then there are those awful gourd things' roots which can trap you close to the sentry and which will slowly but certainly devour you. Even if you get past them you are probably lost in the caves and might starve. The Green Nun obviously made it out and brought back baby animals, which were dragged through into the caves quite low on the floor. Only animals able to thrive on our fodder were brought, such as goats, sheep, poultry, or horses. These would be transferred to the far caves where livestock were originally kept. It is a fact that if we knew everything about the sentry before we entered, all our lives could be nearly normal.'

'How are the animals obtained, does whoever gets out steal them?' Hazel thoughtfully put herself in that position, half realizing she was a prime candidate for the task.

'No, that's something we don't suffer from; whoever goes out is quite rich because everybody arriving here always has money – money that cannot be used. That local tale I mentioned has the nun quite poor, but that's not our experience at all.'

147

'Maybe she had left her purse at home,' Hazel interjected. It was silly enough to have them both laughing.

Annita had not quite finished, she had a few things to say before they parted.

'Tomorrow afternoon I'll have Parsnip ready for you.'

Hazel nodded, her face more relaxed now; accepting it had been the hard bit.

'Freda has decided that your Terry is going to work in the food house kitchen,' said Annita as an afterthought hit her. 'It seems to me as if Maria objected to Leon working with food; so both your men will be working in the village when they are in circulation.'

'What's wrong with that?' Hazel asked, detecting from her tone that Annita did see something wrong with it.

'It is best for you, and best for them, if they could just be ordinary labourers in the far caves. In the village there's all sorts of trouble they can get into, and it is you as the responsible person who has to control it.'

Hazel had an inkling that Annita was in some way referring to her upset with Franz that morning, but to prolong their talk just now was far too tiring. She only had one question. 'Is there anything at all I can do about it?

'No! Nothing.' Annita was quite emphatic.

15

'The Green Man'

The fugitive ran full tilt into the hunt cave system, passing the great destructor and on towards 'destructor minor', and there he had reached his limit of previous knowledge. Collapsing over the still familiar structures in there he gasped for air, and paused a moment. Sheer pace had cut off the insistent chorus behind him yelling, 'Itzla, Itzla,' repeatedly. A brief moment allowed a bout of deep abrasive breaths to convulse him, painful enough for him to be unaware of the other injuries done, or even that every limb trembled. The lack of sound was beginning to tell him that they were holding back to allow their stragglers to catch up, for here he must be trapped. The harrying had started in the village when the priest's uncalled for blessing was bestowed; starting from that moment ferocious blows rained in from all sides until he was running for his life. And once running, he saw each and every alternative avenue of escape deliberately blocked off. He could well understand that some of the chasing mob had their reasons to dislike him, but the whole population of the village seemed to be involved. Wiping aside blood that smeared his vision, streaming from some minor cut upon the temple, he cast about anxiously for a hiding place. No, there was nothing in here sufficient to conceal him, even their furniture structures stood out from white empty walls. Soon surely they would burst in upon him with their flails and lumps of flint, accessories that stung and bruised, he had seen them as mainly childish ornaments before – but never this.

Tentatively the quarry hesitated in front of a hot luminous hole, the one that faced the stocks: there was nothing to come now but death, that he was certain. An alternative stared him in the face; he could dive into God's furnace with all its ruddy brightness and avoid them – could he dare? To be in the stocks and have flints thrown was a horrifying thought, but even so the necessary impetus to leap was not forthcoming. Ahead there were two more openings, unfamiliar passages through the rock. These he would try now as a last resort, but doubted that either would give him more of a chance for that was where he was being pressured to go; all the same he might have more scope than here. With seconds only to remain on the horns of this dilemma, he stepped down through the nearest opening: the cave went deep without further passages, there were small holes in the wall at about head height which lit it marginally well, although the light from there appeared to be derived from reflections rather than true fire.

The holes were too small to pass, even if there were a chance of passages beyond. He stumbled along the rocks, trying to go into the rough that was off the path, but that became treacherous in only a few strides with knife-like rocks burgeoning towards the cave's centre. He returned, to near fall over in the fear-driven haste that was on him, frantically following the level path running around the cave's circumference; it circled right round to the other opening bordered by high cave walls, walls that were without any sign of grip or handhold. True there were fissures as well, but smooth and no help for climbing. If only he had wings to fly there might be chances further up. He was right to expect that the chamber would be a trap of this kind, leaving him no chance but to meet them head on; for already the narrow circular path was bringing him back to the other cave opening. His legs felt more and more unsteady as he glanced back to where he had started, viewing the whole frightening scene. Lit by two fiery holes like eyes, the centre rocks glinted as if they were a mouth full of teeth; this he felt made a frightening stage dedicated to death. 'Itzla, Itzla,' came the shouts, and shadows slipped in close by. He ran away as their shouts rang round the cave, to stand motionless between the light holes hoping they'd miss him. There were many, perhaps all of them whooping and yelling in a burst of frenzy as they streamed in. Terrified as the first random missile struck, Franz made for the nearest place of entry, stumbling up a step and out into the light.

A figure stood quietly across the floor, where the space connected with the outer cave, knowing all, and waiting. She had watched grey figures dance into the adjacent 'destructor minor' cave; jumping, dancing, and shouting out the frenzied emotions that rent the air and rang round its stuffy space. A stout figure, holding a large flint in her hand, bent double, scanning the footprint marks in sand spread before the hot hole, then hopped forwards with outstretched arm pointing the flint towards the rear outer opening. A ragged line of trim grey skirts swirled into it, chased after by the stout one – all whooping and yelling in a frenzy of push and shove to get in. Muffled now the Itzla cries became, as she wound the crossbow mechanism and inserted a bolt: her hand moved to check a nearby stand on which another stood that could be grasped in an instant. She levelled the weapon.

A man in torn green tunic suddenly emerged, running from the cave just in front of her, his terrified face pale like the beard, contrasted sharply with patches of blood that oozed from minor abrasions. The first bolt hit him full square, straight through the chest wall, causing an involuntary shriek as forward impetus faltered; the frame momentarily righting itself to coincide with yet another bolt. In the instant of releasing a second, the crossbow jerked upwards by reflex action as a thin figure emerged right behind the victim stabbing amidst the protruding bolts with a long knife.

'He's mine, it's fer sure I got him!' Bernadette yelled, wresting a knife from the figure that her arrival had knocked to the floor. Annita launched herself across the cave and began battering Bernadette with tightly clenched fists.

'Stop that at once.' The voice of Freda boomed from one of the savages emerging through the outer arch. Annita reeled backwards, and finding a suitable rock there, fell across it sobbing.

Bernadette smirked as she faced the little group. 'I was t'real Charon, t'at I was.'

'Go back to the village Bernadette, and stay there. You knew very well that particular exit was dangerous.' Freda turned to address the little gathering clustered about the other opening. 'Can someone clear the floor?'

Her voice commanded the attention of a few raised heads, and having spoken, Freda imperiously stalked off. The heavy figure of Patricia, accompanied by Maureen, detached from the crowd and, recovering the hardware from the body to decorate the sand, they tossed the small man rather as a sack of potatoes into the fiery opening. From behind those who stood there, Hazel emerged, looking quite out of touch with the flail and stone she carried –

for her props belonged to Annita. It was Annita she wanted to comfort; having to slay your own man must be traumatic, even without some clown getting in the way. Annita clasped Hazel, the tears glistening on her face. 'It was such a shock when she popped out like that – I could easily have killed her.'

Maureen set the cave to her liking, for it was all hers now and she took pleasure in doing the housekeeping thoroughly, mostly by removing all traces of spilled blood before she took over. The cave was hers for a whole week, and in that time it would be used intensively. It was a big relief to have the manning out of the way and the cave quiet; she had it all to herself now with every aspect of harvest carnival gone. The departing crowd must take a break from their sexual predilections and await her vital moves – at least the heterosexual ones must and that thought cheered her. Freda was the one who had taken most interest in the latest arrival; she more than anyone else would be pushing for her to finish. And despite all her other advantages, it was especially satisfying that the Queen would have to take second place to that latest prig – for she would certainly be housing the Belgian. Maureen's face twisted, relishing the problems of a fading Queen, problems she knew only too well from her own direct experience – a scar twinkled in the light, her trademark. The trademark was there, fresh in the minds of two semi-conscious individuals who had seen it hanging above them; a shadowy disfigurement poised against the pale yellow curvature. It was a sight that seemed to connect with pain in the throat and fluids tipping into a tube, followed by severe indigestion. Today, however, the movements she made failed to summon up either a tight throat obstruction or a sickening acidity – it had stopped.

Neither man was properly conscious, but both subject to a systems recovery soon after the stomach tube withdrew. Marc returned to consciousness first, his hands free to lever himself up; ghost memories stirred in his head of an unpleasant dwarf gibbering at him and toeing sensitive places. His hands traversed the site with gentle palpation, finding much to his horror unconnected hard shapes that reminded him of ping-pong balls, and close by a partly healed scar. Marc swallowed; the raw tissues of his throat hurt, and perplexed by this he spoke out a loud. 'I am still here, at least most of me is.' He heard it clearly, and was gladdened to have his voice confirmed before flopping back with his thoughts jumbled: Oh, for an aspirin. Driving weak limbs into vertical movement seemed difficult as if there was too much slack about his bones. The muscles seemed to hang from them; his reeling mind was appalled. Marc craved water, but his condition precluded further movement, the floor frame pressed against his back; he would just have to relax for a while.

Through the cell wall Marc could be seen as upright, examining the structure that held him, for unlike the women's resuscitation bubbles it was not sandblasted on the outside. Maureen entered Marc's cell, accompanied by Pat, for it was not wise to take chances, despite her having a pretty good idea of the man's debilitated condition. He stared at them amazed, much as she knew he would. Such a huge man must have looked down upon most of the population given the naturally high vantage point, but now his perspective had altered radically. Maureen would prefer him below this, but she was approaching the tinies in size herself, and he must conform to Hazel's shoulder height to meet the requirement. But of course there was one attribute Maureen could use more than size, and that was a fluency in French – her second language. Maureen's first words were commanding to counter his inevitable rash of questions. 'Silence,' she ordered. 'Look down when I speak, for you are not a dog's worth here.'

Marc murmured apologetic words, for he could see she was sensitive about her horrific-looking face. His eyes lowered, catching the pink of her breasts pushing shape into the coarse, open-weave knit, but feeling unsure about even this he looked uncomfortably at the floor, and then slyly to the side, observing the other woman. She was a real Friar Tuck, wearing the most extraordinary short haircut that he had ever seen.

'Come with me.' Maureen took him under the shoulder, helping him to his feet and then as a stumbling man out past other spheres exactly similar to his own; they moved from there straight into the wide mouth of a cave. Moving past a belt of hot air in one cave then through the roasting heat of another, he was acutely aware that his present state was an indecently naked one. Marc determined to ask for his clothes at the next possible juncture.

They entered the next cave where a much-reduced opening emitted both heat and light. Ahead were a series of metal structures like clumsy furniture. Maureen sat him in the first, which was a bench-like seat, and unexpectedly brought a lever across the front of his legs, there was a click, and he was held fast in its shape. Moments later a desk top swivelled about his chest and locked itself there in position; at its sides he could see further channels perhaps to lock wrists, a locking that was unlikely, because she produced a tray on which there was food and drink. Both women departed leaving him to the meal, which was uninspiring to say the least. The food was awful and only the emptiness of his digestive tract provided him with the need to fill it, although hunger was strangely lacking. The meal consisted of mainly amorphous vegetation, topped by a few pieces of imitation bacon. The water that swilled down with it was for him top cuisine, he sat there unable to do much else but be aware of someone approaching.

From out of the entrance gap came another dressed naturally like him; the lad was demanding the help of both women because he looked in an even worse state. The end result was the same, given that there was a similar chair arrangement about two metres away. Soon his companion was seated there and also eating the food supplied. The one with odd hair moved off, but the other approached briefly, introducing herself as Maureen. Next she asked all about him and cut in to make his answers brief. Marc almost relaxed, realizing he must allay any fears, and explained his mission, asking after Greta. Maureen looked blank and gave him an honest civilized answer. And before he could put his next question, she moved on to the limitations of a food supply that could only support some who enter here. He must be prepared to accept the work offered, or be left to starve. Marc was quick witted enough to realize she was in earnest and said work did not bother him. Even so he was taken aback by the first qualifying question she asked. 'Are you gay?'

'No.' He sounded very sure about it, and for her mind that clinched his future occupation. Maureen took hold of one arm, moving it gently towards the side channel. Marc resisted: there had to be a point where he drew the line, and he thought this was it. Where she took it from he had no idea, but taking a stride or two behind him, Maureen struck his back with something that hurt; she continued to beat until he gave up and slotted his wrists into the grooves. Immediately she desisted, and locked the fittings.

Maureen moved over to tend the lad, talking to him and pointing out the stark choices that were available. After Marc's experience, his companion knew the problems associated with being bold, and permitted his wrists to be secured. She moved off with the trays, and there they sat unattended for perhaps six hours. Marc's shoulders, besides being sore all over, seemed wet, he might be bleeding, but there was no way of telling – the dampness eventually subsided, helped along by an interplay of draughts, a cold one behind and a warm one from the front. He made conscious efforts to talk to his companion, but as he spoke French and the lad only English, there was a long silence after the first attempt.

Maureen approached carrying a thin collapsible metal chair. This she placed beside him, and sat talking about his future role. 'You are the preferred candidate chosen by the women,' she said informatively. 'It is a rather a special occupation, and even though there are no alternatives I think that it will be pleasurable. Most men would think themselves lucky to have a harem of wives, this could be said to be the inverse of that, and there are probably many who would rather jump into the furnace than be so endowed. You have stumbled upon a place where the women are segregated from the men and have chosen you as a common sexual outlet; it is the preferred solution for stability in our society. If you haven't already guessed, the title on offer is Concubine, and the women here believe you are masculine enough to carry it off.'

One thought immediately jumped into Marc's mind. 'How sure are you that my equipment will still remain adequate, if it isn't then I may be forced to jump very shortly.'

Maureen looked surprised. 'I can assure you that the offer is not based on anything so superficial. Love is more complex. Think it over – tomorrow I shall release you to choose between us, or the fires of hell beyond that hole. If you choose us, then you have the intriguing prospect of love and passion that must surely await you. If you should prefer to jump, you might just conceivably be lucky, as no one knows accurately where the heat source is down there. Think about it, and make your decision.' Maureen had said her piece, and exited without a word to Terry.

The night passed slowly, with both men restrained in a sitting posture where odd pains sprang up from misaligned muscles given too little room for movement. Sleep was not easy to come by, and remained an ever-receding prospect. Terry began their discourse, saying the few words he knew of French and their English counter-

155

parts. Marc, improving the pronunciation and doing likewise in English, seized upon his French: soon they were carried away in a pronunciation-improving period. The yes/no, *oui/non* dialogue led on to Marc summing up his English. Soon exceeding what either knew, they attempted other comparisons, where fingers first helped to count and then to point. The game held their interest, and tested intellect until, with heads resting uneasily upon the surfaces in front of them, sheer weariness brought even this to a close. The inset table surface supporting his head intrigued Marc for it seemed to have all the wrong properties for wood, but what it was eluded him.

Marc had already made his decision to stay; it followed on easily after coming through all the agony of the yellow ceiling, any sort of quick jump into total release now was ridiculously late. Afterwards if he did not like doing the job offered, he should be in better physical trim to depart. He watched as Maureen attended to Terry, the first to be released from his chair; she pointed towards a mound of sand where he basked in the warmth of destructor minor. Quickly she moved over to release Marc also, warily threatening him away from the several exits with a plaited leather strap. He joined Terry upon the sand, sand that was obviously there for relieving themselves. Making the most of the opportunity Marc strove to do a number of simple exercises also, and carried them out so imperfectly he couldn't credit it; falling over on to sand did however sugar the pill. Too soon did she call him back to the chair, a point at which he was again intending to rebel.

Maureen wrestled him towards the chair, easily overwhelming what little strength he still possessed, but then Pat emerged unexpectedly from the inner cave behind him and struck with her heavy flint, a move that left Marc just a limp heap. Maureen thought the blow over-enthusiastic and totally unnecessary, but there it was, she couldn't control their unpredictable priest. If he didn't recover, then it would be much the same as if he had jumped, and then the puppy going obediently to his high chair might be considered as an emergency candidate for a different job. Terry was clicked in and then neglected, as the two women combined to plant Marc in his chair before leaving. A lesson had been learned when Marc rejoined the conscious world; in his state cooperation was a necessity if he wished to be around for making an escape later on.

Towards the end of Maureen's week, both men were dressed and obediently doing tasks that would soon become part of their routine. Marc's smart tunic in blue mackintosh material seemed a bit tight, but Maureen said he would soon slim into it. She laughed, 'You truly are dressed as befits our green man.' This remark seemed to have deeper meaning, but then he decided she might just be colour-blind.

Maureen dressed Terry in sheepskins, which could be tied on with either surface uppermost; one piece rounded his shoulders as a jacket and another at the waist served as a loincloth. Next day, Terry and Marc were introduced to the village, but not wishing to have them immediately familiar with it Maureen deliberately hurried them through all of the marvels that might inform. Soon the fast pace of her walk concluded at an upper level of the food house, where they passed over the staff ramp and penetrated the many internal sets of doors that led to Maria.

She had jobs in plenty awaiting them and Terry soon found himself cutting up the many bats that extended rations, his clothes being turned to have the fleecy side inwards for the task. Marc by contrast was inducted as a waiter into the distribution of food; the waiter's job extended, and before he had quite grasped the full extent of this function he found himself tending the Queen's table. There was so very much to do for Maria who had to train them whilst continuing to manage singlehandedly providing food for everyone. Not only were there meals for women who arrived with great regularity and must be catered for, there were also the men's rations, which in quantity far exceeded them. Most meals were packed into tricycle boxes to be collected by other men calling from different areas. The outside receiving of foodstuffs Marc found was another major part of his job. Maureen was at last proud of them, receiving glances of approval from passers by as she daily led her duo between multi-bubble and the cells.

The last evening of Maureen's responsibility arrived when she led the sedated stupefied Marc into the food house. Terry had preceded him and been passed to Maria who found accommodation for him in a below stairs part of it. Maureen, content that she had completed another tricky part of her job, settled down to celebrate with a complimentary carafe of wine in a food house recess. She soon relaxed and became so deeply immersed in her own thoughts that the usual background of laughter and noise did not impinge at all. She had done it often enough before, but her days of doing the job were numbered and on this she brooded. Before long her diminishing height would relegate her to the tinies. Pat's inept assistance was required these days as back-up, but it was her assistance that had very nearly brained the women's latest prize acquisition. They would have been extremely put out had she failed them, and it was a near enough thing to envisage talk in the community consigning her to the tinies. Now, before it happened for real, she must get herself used to the idea of relinquishing one of the more vital jobs in the community.

Her place was arguably third in importance to the Queen, and as the old 'war-horse' of the community she was justly proud of her record. There was a long history of being first to leap into the fray when insurrection threatened – how would they replace her? For sure it would not be the noblewoman on horseback that sported a wound across the face, almost like a badge of office. In her next job the scar would just be something ugly, something that detracted. Strange to reflect that it was one of her own men that had come at her with a flailing hoe during one of those occasional dissatisfactions, one long forgotten by everybody else. The quarrel she remembered was to do with the inequality of rations, some-thing she would have been sympathetic with. Unavoidably it had come from one of her men and for whom she represented authority.

It was in fact the women of the village who expected a soft life and greedily always wanted more than their share. The young ones who would never know the hardships experienced by her gener-ation, like that new girl Hazel for instance. But putting bitter thoughts aside, there were still many who would want to know her and even relish her company, such as Poppy for whom she had a soft spot. Brief thoughts of love flickered, and for some minutes her mind flirted with amorous thoughts – the scar was even an asset. A gash below the eye, nicking a nostril before meeting the lip, gave her a dominant attribute, one that she believed made her uniquely irresistible.

The mugs rattled and Hazel arrived carrying one. She perched herself on a chair looking distracted as voices nearby rose in a crescendo of shrieks and catcalls.

'You are late, they started a while ago,' observed Maureen.

'If you have no objection, I'd much prefer to join you and wait,' said Hazel. 'That man gives me the creeps – he's quite mad you know.' Hazel shivered involuntarily, before meeting the astonished Maureen's gaze. She put her most abject query yet. 'Do I take him back to my place?' Annita was not there to ask, and Hazel very timidly decided to ask the one who should know.

'Yes, he's all yours, if they leave anything of him that is.' Maureen was caustic, her faint Irish accent was there but hardly showed, coming as it did from sheer attainment in linguistic skills; she smiled at the thought, still managing to look pleased under the scar.

'What are they doing, it all sounds very noisy in there; will they hurt him?'

'Well, they went in with their individual flails and flints, but it's really all part of a planting ceremony, every so often we turn one into a major event. They will only tease him, and ultimately when their amorous wiles are exhausted he will sit upon laps and be cuddled, as they whisper the delights they each have to offer. By the time they are finished inciting him and one another, they will have decided when and with whom his time will be spent. But in truth he is but a pale imitation of the man they chose in the Styx cave, in fact totally out of any proportion that might resemble him.'

Maureen relaxed in her seat and swilled some more wine before adding her advice. 'And although you will find him a weakling with nothing to fear from him at all, do not be surprised if he is a liability, as every petty jealousy and squabble will come your way. Freda might be a useful ally if you do have problems, for I am sure she is sweet on him – but I haven't told you so, have I?' After this confidence Maureen winked, and offered Hazel wine; wine that was gratefully accepted.

Maureen felt herself warming to the girl who had been so aloof, pausing to let her appreciate the wine before continuing. 'You are unlucky in having two men in the village, and sooner or later you will regret both, because you will be held responsible for any of their follies.' This echoed Annita's remarks, but before Hazel could follow this up, a door opened and a number of slightly inebriated women spilled out of it. 'You had better go and find him,' laughed Maureen, and so warmly that Hazel realized the Irish woman was yet another friend.

When Hazel entered the room Marc was looking dazed and his face heavily flushed. He stood unsteadily alongside Bernadette who sat upon a chair alternately snapping press studs together and hugging his bottom half. She let go as Hazel approached, giggled and made off. The man was not recognizable as her madman; his hefty bulk had been reduced so considerably that his head just reached her shoulder. Marc was barely aware of her presence and did not respond to English; so rather like a big child she led him away. Today had been her best day yet, the first one in her new house she called the 'igloo'. She called it that despite the fact that it was five connected hemispheres – to call it 'the igloos' would be a step too upmarket for her. At least she knew that the one bubble only half sandblasted on her sphere was for Marc, and that's where she shut him in. Anger boiled within her as she did so, for he, and he alone, was directly responsible for her predicament.

It was late and Hazel was entertaining thoughts of bed, when the outer door was thumped. She opened up to find Annita holding out a bottle of the local brew: 'I almost missed the housewarming,' she spouted regally. Annita's apologies flowed as if she were visiting aristocracy, and the words alone suggested she was tipsy.

'Come in and help me drink it,' said Hazel, all ready to put off bed, especially as earlier she had been looking for her friend.

'Is he in there?' Annita moved across from the entrance to the door Hazel had tied off. 'I must just take a peep.' She giggled, untying the tight double bowknot; her look inside the room included leaving the door loose behind her and then wandering through into the reception area as if she owned the place. Hazel dallied just long enough to re-tie the cord before rejoining Annita who had by then opened the bottle; together they toasted the new habitation. Annita was unsettled and looking behind her, almost as if she expected Marc to join them. Probably there wouldn't be a better time to question her on the seemingly unnecessary complexity surrounding concubines.

'You are lonely now that Franz has gone?' Hazel said it more as a statement of fact rather than one requiring an answer. She was all ready to commiserate if her tentative words gave rise to grief. But Annita responded with no emotion at all.

'No, he's just the one big problem that has departed, just flown away.' She fluttered her hands upwards, spilling her drink. 'I am not missing him at all. It is my reason for such a long celebration.' Annita sounded very sure about it, nodding her head and making a humorous toast to 'absent concubines' but seemed to twist her tongue on the word.

'Did you sleep with him? I'm not being nosy, it's just I don't know what's expected.' Hazel said it with emphasis, summing up all of the apprehension that she felt; apprehension that had largely stemmed from Annita in the first place.

Annita looked her way a mite more objectively, for even in her stupor she realized the raft of problems an inexperienced girl like Hazel had to face and the many things she had failed to say. 'I never took him to my bed, but it was nice to be cuddled on his, especially early on when I had him for the evening rotation, and that often led on to late sex.' She wrapped her arms about her chest dwelling on the cuddle. 'But after a time, the spare flesh on them goes and they lose that nice soft puppy fat they start out with. You even have to move their press-studs in often enough to get sick of doing it!

'Franz deteriorated even faster than most, helped along by Jackie who got at him early in his career and left his sex organ like a corkscrew. The others were mad at me for not keeping a proper check on him, not that it was something I could have foreseen. The complaints went to a special meeting where Jackie was called to account for her action and banned from going anywhere near him. As the person responsible for him I was found guilty of a far more serious crime, the ruining of our communal sex life. They said I should have foreseen trouble and been monitoring on the days that her love Frances had a routine date with him.'

Annita stared blankly into the drink she had just poured with a hand that visibly shook. 'They sentenced me to be tied "in the altogether" over the anvil for two hours every evening as a punishment for a whole week. It hurts worse than any stocks possibly could. I know that we have lost a lot of our size here, but that anvil is still damnably narrow, and a hard shape to have on the flesh, just imagine being stretched out over a block of cold metal. It doesn't give at all, just hurts and leaves furrows in your hide as you wait for the time to slowly pass. Then to make it worse there is Patricia snooping around, and all the others who come to gawp; it is so very upsetting being tied down like that and in public.'

'When you say public, you don't mean the men?' Hazel was

alarmed but needed to wait whilst Annita came out of her drift to engage with her question.

'No only women are allowed in the church, for you know that's our high-security place. What's more it's well etched on the outside so no one can see the interior, in fact like all of the women's quarters. And after that ordeal, I watched who was going with him every night apart from mine so I could better understand the dangers. There's Maureen who's no trouble, even though she's forever unsure about Poppy, so I stayed nearby mainly for her. Of all people Bernie proved to be my big problem. On her night she took him back to her place and kept him until morning. I stretched the rules because she was my special friend who claimed she ought to have been Charon anyway. That's OK if you can trust someone, just as even more special friends like us can trust,' Annita said with special stress on the words and then stopped hinting heavily to pour herself another glass. 'But Bernie is very unpredictable and failed to shut him in well enough, allowing Franz to run off to a lover in the men's agricultural section. And all because that childish little girl had no control over him he was never there in the morning, whatever she said. Just think what the women would say about that homosexual interlude if it got out. The only mitigating thing is physically he's useless. That's why I am so pleased to be shot of him and her as well.'

Hazel spotted Annita's speech was becoming more lucid if a little hazy, and decided to probe the dangers of her new role. 'Why ever should Jackie do such a horrid thing?'

'Oh, I think it was because Frances had claimed her turn in the club to be with Franz. It was all right for Jackie to flirt, but the moment Frances did likewise, she was jealous.'

'Was his injury the reason why he had to go?' Hazel put it as delicately as she could.

'Goodness me no, everybody liked him, but you can't have two concubines, there's only one permitted. If you allowed any number we really would be unsafe; this way there is only one in above average condition. Didn't you know? When the next new man is preferred by all, yours must pop his clogs.'

'What about Terry?' Hazel was suddenly alarmed.

'Oh don't worry about him; he's not concubine, he's got a nice little number in the food house. Have you been to see him yet?'

'I didn't know I could.'

'He's your man, you have every right. More than that, a need; for he's in a sensitive place and you have a duty to keep your tabs on him.'

'Is he really a problem?' Hazel had no inkling of what could be sensitive about it. 'But surely he is in Maria's hands?'

Annita raised her eyebrows and stared vacuously at her. 'The village is poised at the crossroads with about fifteen craftsmen and engineers on one side, and nearly thirty labourers on the other. Both your men are bang in the middle, delivering food and receiving the empties. Because of that they might be used to carry messages from one lot to the other, or indeed be put upon to do any thing else, which undermines us – so you watch them for subversion. Get Maria on your side!' Annita lapsed into a mellow silence again, and they sat drinking until the bottle was through. When Annita finally rose to go to her abode it was very late. She dallied in the anteroom.

'I must just see my muscle man again.' Once more the knot was unfastened and Annita peered in. 'Isn't he lovely,' she chuckled, her eyebrows doing semaphore.

She would have entered, if Hazel had not helped her on her way. But apart from musing over Annita's attraction, the visit had put question marks as well as clouds into an otherwise blue sky over the new house. Hazel was beginning to feel harassed as she felt the extent of responsibilities entailed. They were starting to weigh heavily upon her.

16

'Prelude'

Time flew by as Hazel got to grips with her working life. Each day started early, well before the soft lighting of night was stepped up to daytime levels. The early start proved unavoidable because Rose, in keeping to her early hours, always knocked on Hazel's door reporting for work as she passed. This left her boss unsettled, and part wondering what Rose might find in the chamber today. The one thought singularly able to arouse Hazel to action was that of being responsible for Rose, the one she understood to be unreliable as Charon; on that basis there could be little to commend her as a fairy either. And so before very long she would be up dressing, just to make sure Rose was not having problems. But even as she asked, Hazel's eyes would be scouring the Styx chamber to check that there really were no new arrivals. Her rough scan would finally confirm the matter, merely by noting the absence of any movement in the gourds, as flagged up by the wall microbes which were supposed to get very busy with their light patterns if they moved. Always she viewed the same languid movement of coloured light patterns, which suggested that there were no bodies about or even hidden round the corner. Always it seemed clear and she could go for an early morning swim. As an early bird, with time a plenty to indulge herself she always came back feeling so refreshed that the rest of the world just ought to be on the move. Marc took the brunt of this, because his dull duties in the food house demanded he be there ahead of the breakfast preparations. And also as a result of her recently found vigour she was there early for breakfast as well, even before the foursome.

So when it happened, Poppy reporting for work was easier to deal with, because it came relatively late in the order of things, and rather like a tooth that has to be pulled, it is best done when you are good and ready. Poppy had moved on from the spinning of thread to the weaving of it, and there was no need to instruct her, for the transfer to another piece of equipment was as smooth as if she had designed it all herself. But it was the fast competent clatter of the loom which disturbed Hazel so much more, for she could imagine all sorts of herringbone patterns sliding out of its other end. Not that she was far wrong in this, because the first dress made was the right side of smallness to fit either one of the two loom hands, and when she looked more closely Hazel found pockets cleverly let in at the hip. Her worst fears were realized; not that the pockets were unreasonable, but she could be quite certain that this was only the start of another Poppy-led artistic boom.

Hazel was adamant that the weaving must be kept simple, but in no time at all the thread came down to a thickness more suitable for nylon tights. The two of them conspired to anything and everything other than what was basically required, laughing at how clever they were. Annita too laughed when Hazel told her, dismissing the problem as trivial. 'You are next in line for a dress, so they can't harm your reputation yet can they?'

Late into every evening, Hazel began to wait in the food house for Marc. Annita's words had resulted in her being in place for the whole of the first week, scrutinizing each nominated mistress as unobtrusively as she could. During that period Hazel sat comfortably in one of the partition niches, tasting samples of the various alcoholic brews when available. In this she was encouraged by Maria, who felt kindly disposed towards the one who provided workers for the food house. Maria herself believed in having a drink of some kind occasionally, and began joining Hazel every so often to enjoy a sip of whatever was on offer with her. At some point in the evening, freshly cooked bread rolls joined the drink, a delicacy Hazel hardly believed to be real.

'It's late before I have time to bake,' explained Maria. 'Everybody stops by for a bite in the evening, and the rolls when available are all gone by breakfast time.' Maria chatted at length, explaining she was limited by the small amount of grain production and the hold-ups in grinding the flour. In with the chat was an idea all ready to check out with Hazel. 'Suppose I set aside a room in the club for you to do your hairdressing? The price of the room could be doing my hair on some regular basis.'

This fitted in well for Hazel, and she jumped at the chance to say yes. Having said so, she sat for quite a while afterwards viewing the complicated works in the bun that sat atop the woman's head. Then realizing Maria's questioning gaze had settled on her, Hazel self-consciously countered it with another thought that was never far away in the food house, and asked if she might visit Terry. Maria hardly considered it, for this she had been expecting to happen, and certainly didn't know of the many days Hazel had been bolstering herself up to ask. But now, with the permission granted, Hazel wasted little time beyond that needed for politeness, before seeking the cell he was kept in. It was with some surprise she found it hidden away on the ground floor butting on to the toilets; it was only later that she realized it was access for the sewage men that had grounded it. She identified his bubble easily by the ribbon which tied the door, for it was tied up rather like she did for Marc.

Terry looked very alarmed, and stared at her full of disbelief, for she was relatively tall; his more than a whole head advantage in height had been replaced by what was now a whole head disadvantage. He was naked and groping for his loin fleece; obviously he was confused about looking directly at her, something to do with the conditioning that had markedly altered his behaviour. Hazel clasped him lovingly in her arms, smitten by all of the changes in him, for he was plump where he had always been thin and way down now with his face buried into her breasts. All of this helped to intensify her overwhelming emotional thoughts, muddled and yearning to protect him from this harsh place. But that was before the feel of a real cuddle took over; she cast about for somewhere to sit, and saw only his bed at floor level. They flattened towards it, and losing control crashed down to the bed, which was every bit as hard as any straw mattress can be.

It was only later that they found time to recount their experiences, tucked somewhere among the wealth of reassuring kisses and cuddles. Time passed, and Hazel was further fascinated to hear him propound confused ideas of the society they had fallen into. She was wary of these suppositions that were largely nonsense; was he proposing them for her to factually correct? Listening to him talking her eye caught the open flooring, a familiar but almost forgotten sight to her and reinforcing the ideas she had about its placement. The mere knowledge that it was a cell like Marc had in her bubble reminded Hazel not to add overmuch to his knowledge, or at least beyond what he would eventually see for himself. Full understanding of this subterranean world was not for the men; already she was finding it expedient to accept the women's philosophy, for if the enlightenment only led to subversion, why make problems that were specifically hers? Consciously or not, she was aligning herself with the women, just as she had done with the heterosexuals.

But his talk was thinning as he became conscious she was no longer interacting, and he switched to a more affectionate role, for talking was not over-important to Terry right now. Despite seeing more child-like behaviour from him than she had before, the imp in him recognized her as the girl he knew in the sand pit, and Hazel emerged much later the same evening feeling far more self-conscious than ever she went in. Besides committing herself to visiting frequently, she decided to take him a hot drink on each visit and perhaps she would cut his unkempt hair. When she rejoined Maria for a hot roll she was already thinking of the long hours he must be bottled up in his cell after a full day's work, and how the wearing of those sheepskins must get uncomfortably hot in that warm stuffy cell. Human rights, didn't they have any? And then she shrugged it away with a resolve not to be another Queen Charlotte.

Freda visited 'the igloo' next morning with a request to interview Marc after lunch. Hazel thought that this confirmed Freda's attraction to Marc, but the thought was virtually dismissed when she did appear at the igloo's door. Freda had arrived carrying several large rough maps on skins, ones showing the external approaches to the caves, and upon entering the igloo she immediately explained the necessity of Marc's involvement.

'Marc it seems was surveying the caves and has brought sketches of the cave system butting on to here. What we have to do now, is to combine his more accurate notes with the rough plans that are already in existence.' Hazel still was not entirely convinced, and was glad she had her combat training to take her elsewhere; she left them outwardly engaged in work.

The riding was now part of her day's labour, and Annita was riding along with her, rather than shout directions from afar. They rode through the bat cavern followed by the engineer's cavern, both of which stretched for over a mile in length and almost a quarter mile across; but in neither was the atmosphere very pleasant. The cave with bats had Hazel feeling unsettled and squeamish imagining all those hundreds of tiny eyes watching her as they clung to the cavern walls. The shiver for them merged with a shiver for the cold that always struck most here, and right through the dress.

The engineers' cave, although warmer and better lit, had other eyes watching. The surveillance they felt in there Annita dismissed as mainly suspicion, a normal factor whenever women rode through the working men's areas. Someone called Red controlled the area with an iron fist, apparently because he was the only properly qualified engineer. Annita called him difficult, and always out of favour. Most engineers did not even get selected to work there, for it was Frances's team and she preferred homosexuals, especially French-speaking ones, working for her. This Annita said prejudiced any successful outcome. She went on to say that the area was hard to penetrate, for only Jackie seemed to make headway through all the yes-men.

As they progressed through the workings Hazel saw great holes sunk in the wall. 'Many of these are mines,' said Annita, pointing out the heaps of green or pink tinted rocks piled up outside which of course they carefully skirted. In between these irregular heaps of mineral there were other heaps like steaming soil. These Annita said were a continuation of the compost heaps, like some she had seen earlier in the bat cavern. There were worse obstacles yet as they moved on, block-built structures with metalwork hanging out of them. Annita said they were furnaces of one sort or another operated by the few expert men who lived in their own enclave behind the engineers' shantytown. There was much dumping, which may be due to either but seemed unnecessarily deliberate, making the vicinity less accessible.

Once the horses were put away it was time for target practice, and after this there was hand-to-hand conflict that called on aching muscles for agility. Archery was new to Hazel. Though delighted at first to discover how lightweight the crossbows were, she very soon found out how cumbersome the detachable mechanism that clawed back the bowstring was. Hazel would have avoided every-thing if she could, but Annita impressed upon her that it was all a necessity – just like the riding – her life may one day depend upon it. So yet again she was diverted into long hours, with skills quite alien to her. Annita did not regret losing her afternoon duel with

Bernadette one bit, and was quite happy to spar with a raw beginner, especially as she was soon rewarded by seeing her pupil making the grade – not that she would say so.

One day she said, 'I haven't shown you the retrieval suit yet, have I?' Hazel, who was as always keen to shorten training if she was able, delayed not at all in her acceptance. 'Can we go now? Will it fit me?'

Her questions were soon answered; because it was housed only a few hundred yards away from the hunt cave. There they found the suit in the first of the men's cells. It was a bit like yellow armour: a loose extended fitment of backplate hinged over the shoulders to a breastplate, and both of them ending with a short hook for an abdominal skirt, behind which was an adjustable chain able to touch the ground. Further to this there was tie-on protection for the backs of the legs, and an elongated fin for each of the upper arms. On the head, the design shouted fireman, as it had such good neck coverage

'It's all solid gold.' Annita's voice was modest, knowing of old that Hazel was particularly impressed by gold, and so the look of astonishment when it came was its own reward.

'If it's not locked up, someone could steal it!' Hazel's voice rose excitedly, half disbelieving that they would squander so much of that metal on a suit. Annita, she felt, might be having her on, that is until it occurred to her that the quality was much like the gold throne.

'It's quite valueless here,' Annita crowed. 'But we lack lead, and it's the nearest heavy metal available; besides which it stays bright, and reflects a lot of the sentry's radiation – those are all valid reasons for using it.' Annita helped Hazel into each separate piece, and Hazel began to know she was supporting a considerable weight.

'You must keep broadside on to the walls, and go sideways like a crab. The wings are supposed to shield whatever you are handling,' instructed Annita, who was relishing someone else bottled up in its heavy shell.

Hazel's movements were cumbersome. She could easily imagine herself as a ballet dancer trapped in a diver's suit; knowing all of the time that Annita was bursting to laugh at her ineptness. So she put on quite a show for her. 'They lie on the floor, sort of dead and I just pull them in? You did this for me.' Hazel puffed her way forward and then back, hamming up the actions, with a view to moving Annita's eyebrows – and when she succeeded the laugh followed not far behind. 'At the time, I thought you were some big, exotic, gold-coloured butterfly,' Hazel added truthfully, whilst Annita still laughed at her; but then obviously gratified with the description her eyebrows stopped in their dance.

'Well then, that's exactly what you are now – a big beautiful butterfly. And if you can also be a brave horsewoman as well, you can join us on the patrol tomorrow.'

Hearing these unexpected words lifted Hazel's spirits over the moon; her face lit with joy. 'Fancy me being invited to ride with the four.' Discarded metal clanged its way to the mesh floor as she dropped it; its status in her estimation had already fallen likewise.

Upon returning to 'the igloo', Hazel found Freda still within and openly occupied with maps, so she waited in her living space, reflecting upon the increased pace of life – it was becoming hectic. At length Freda extracted herself from the concubine bubble, and re-tied the door. Hazel hastened over to intercept Freda, drawing her away from resident ears.

'I hope you don't mind me asking you for advice; but you did say I could?' Freda nodded her head and waited, for the pause was lengthy. 'Do you remember when I came to dinner, you told me that everyone who comes here keeps their normal monthly cycle?' Freda continued to nod, and Hazel pressed ahead, part encouraged to say what she had to say. 'Well, I should have had a period a week ago, and it hasn't happened – you see I have always been so regular in the past.'

Freda looked thoughtful and paused awhile. 'Too early to be bothered about that; but because you did break all our existing records when you arrived, we cannot neglect the slender chance that you might be pregnant. If that is so, then we shall all rejoice; but for the moment it's nobody else's business, just keep clear of the arrival zone. Carry on as usual, and if there are any "retrievals" to be done, call Annita.'

Hazel felt relieved a load had been taken from her shoulders by simply sharing the problem, and further on if things did come to a head it was comforting to know that the event would be welcome. Her mind was unwilling to stay on baby things, for the euphoria that filled her after Annita's news floated the evening by like a lovely dream. Neither bringing home Marc, nor ending Poppy's evening vigil disturbed the dreaming about her newly acquired prowess.

She was beginning to feel equivalent to everybody else here, and seeing the latest material upon the loom whirled her into fantasies of dressing everybody in new styles of clothing. She would start by making cool evening wears for Terry and Marc, then go on to do great things for everybody else. Cut their hair and bring them up to date with clothing; savages to civilized beings and only she could do it. Her head whirled, dreaming of the acclaim, egged on by a particularly soothing display of lights upon the walls of the Styx cave.

17

Donor Dog

Jan Kee had hardly got used to his cell before Claude was investigating the second address he had acquired for his prisoner's residence. The sun was just clearing the horizon when his knocking at the given door produced a startlingly beautiful if sleepy blonde woman, who on opening the door stared down much as if he were some odd species of delivery man. Claude quickly identified himself before she could say 'not today thank you'.

'Are you Mme Greta Kee?' She hesitated before affirming.

The bullseye he scored was her Christian name. His second question was that much more certain. 'Mme Greta Casserta as well – are you not?'

The woman opened the door further. 'You had better come in.'

Claude entered the house, only to hear a tale of woe about a husband workaholic back home, and eventually much more unhappiness with the man she had joined here. It would seem Jan had spent so much time diverting her husband that he had apparently mislaid the reason for doing it; her life was in tatters and reduced to a pointless existence. Claude listened sympathetically, although he was principally concerned with hearing facts about their background disappearance story.

'It all started long ago. Jan used to call my husband on the phone, he was always so nice to talk to. If Marc were still at work then we would chat, for he practically lived there. Holidays too were never popular with Marc, he always wanted to stay for work reasons and never arranged that many; that's my reason for taking a break with my friend Blanche. She was quite happy to go any place I liked provided I kept her company, and of course when offered the choice I chose somewhere to be also in Jan's vicinity. Quite early on we found the spa baths suited both of us; Blanche

172

enjoyed a massage and other expensive pampering, whilst I was content to be found there by Jan.'

Greta sounded hoarse. She moved about the room preparing drinks, and on offering the bottle to Claude, had it immediately refused. Having lubricated her throat Greta continued. 'Some time early this year Jan met a couple who were out walking; it was near one of those quarries where Jan spends his time doing things. The man was a keen naturalist, an authority on the subject of natural history and his wife bore an uncanny resemblance to me. They had failed to find a species of mouse they were looking for, and Jan, as ever looking for extra business, pointed out that he was quite often in the area and would call them back if he saw anything. That incident gave him an idea, and the next time I arrived on holiday Jan arranged they would also come to Lutz on some pretext or other. All I had to do was visit the caves; Jan had earlier unlocked the connecting door for me as he often had before and so the walk to Jan's part of the caves was easy. At the other end I waited in his car, because Jan was having the naturalists photographed for the local newspaper. The woman looked a bit old and tweedy to pass off for me, but as Jan said, it was only to convince the locals enough to throw Marc off my trail. He thought that people would then be quite sure I was eloping with a gent from goodness knows where. But in this Jan simply underestimated the tenacity of Marc, for it took a good week to pack him off.'

Greta became tearful on hearing Jan was in jail on an explosives theft charge, and was disposed to go to his side, if only she could. Claude warned her off, advising her to go home, for that's where he'd advised Marc to be on hearing that she was lost. 'If you stay in Monsieur Kee's house you will almost certainly be called upon to give evidence.' These were his last and most telling words as she so quickly opted to go home. Claude was on hand to ferry her to the station and see her properly under way.

During the next few days his evidence was collated and deliberated upon before agreeing to a preliminary hearing in the courthouse. Jan Kee's plea of guilty for illegally procuring explosives could only be considered on its own at this stage; the rubble had still to be cleared before determining whether the case involved a corpse or not. Much as Claude expected, the man was bailed to return some months later when further charges might have come into being.

Sylvia greeted him with feigned surprise, much as she always did when he was away for more than a day, a habit that was intended to suggest he'd had another holiday. His attention diverted from her as he opened the door, not immediately recognizing the office for all of the changes. Quite simply the clutter had been cleared and now all the homely stuff he lined his office with was contained in a decidedly new office cabinet. So now like a fish out of water he sat at his desk, which shone with a glassy sheen and smelt of some ghastly polish full of floral fragrance.

Upon the desk in front of him was a single neat parcel tied with string, which at first glance had to be a joke. But no, the handwriting gave it away as Sgt Vierne, and inside there was more. Releasing a bow on the enticingly exact package he began to scan the writing. At that point Sylvia looked through the connecting door.

'Madame Masse is on the line for you, sir. Will you speak to her?'

On the point of saying no, Claude's eyes were traversing the package that he had absently opened, for there, neat and flat, were the famous knickers that had stopped the bottling of water. The attached note said 'Recovered Five Only'. As it is the custom in England to sell in half dozens, the one that was lost may help when it came to identifying her. It was sheer exasperation with the text that made him pick up the telephone for something else to do, and instantly wish he hadn't.

'Is that you Claude? Come on, I know you are listening – if you are, why not say so? That dog must be buried. What you are doing is not fair to me, and if you go on insisting Mitzi is evidence, I shall withdraw my original complaint!' Claude well recognised Madame Masse's voice, but still said nothing. Julia's voice took on a more ominous tone for she was serious. 'I have arranged a van from the Pets Graveyard and will be coming personally to collect my darling Mitzi. You have an hour, so no more procrastination – just do something!' The phone clicked, and instantly all became quiet and peaceful again. Claude scraped his chair back, it was time to leave; there were urgent police matters somewhere else, all he had to do was find them.

As he left he encountered Vierne about to knock upon his office door, and what's more Vierne was insistent upon seeing him; matters couldn't always wait indefinitely until he came back. During the investigation Vierne had been following up each of the Commissar's visits with an audit of explosives at each quarry visited. Of the seven quarries using explosives, not one had passed the given criteria – the stock was either over or under the ledger total. To Vierne this had put a very big question mark over them all, since only a single item was responsible for the explosion. Now he wanted each and every quarry prosecuted, because their sheer inefficiency had completely invalidated the whole police investigation. Before Claude knew it he had dug himself deeper by pointing out the damage was done, and the shutting of any number of empty stable doors would not affect the issue; this could be accomplished at leisure. To hurry it along would not help to solve the crime and so saying he attempted desperately to bring the interview to a conclusion.

'But Commissar, officialdom will expect action on this, and as we have failed so far, they might at least see we have tried.'

Claude was loath to say that he had cracked it, so they talked of litigation. Because of the man's nature Vierne's visit took time, and although Claude kept looking at his watch and heading for the door, he never actually passed its verticals. The hour of grace soon elapsed, and before he could make the one exit that counted, reception rang to say Madame Masse had arrived to see him personally. There would be no dodging her now, so Claude decided to take the brave course. A dog pickled for weeks in formaldehyde, would by now be more preservative than dog, and given all those lethal fumes Julia really ought not to have it.

'Send her up,' he told the girl in reception, and turning he busied himself clearing the ladies' underwear from his desk along with Sgt Vierne's notes into the nearest filing cabinet. He glanced over all those newly labelled files, making a good attempt at looking overwhelmed as the door opened.

To his astonishment Mme Masse appeared, almost dancing into the room. 'Oh you dear man, I really thought you wouldn't have Mitzi ready.' Sheer enthusiasm took her round his desk and she kissed him upon both cheeks.

Claude pushed her into the nearest seat and hurried towards the door. 'Er excuse me whilst I look into what has happened.' He couldn't shake off the memory of a whole dog swirling about in a jar of yellowish fluid; it was far too vivid in his mind to conceive a dog in that condition being described as 'ready'.

'Sylvia, Madame thinks that we are getting her dog, did you say something?' Sylvia looked blankly at him. Claude dashed downstairs and towards the enquiries counter, where he pulled up short on seeing two policemen bending over a small white sheet; underneath was a very dead poodle, a white one. Officer Mullet turned about, stood smartly standing to attention and reported. 'The patrol car ran over him sir. The dog was just loose in the road.'

Claude felt the driver deserved a bonus, if not a medal. 'If nobody claims it, have the dog ready to be loaded; there's a funeral van due.'

'That's quick action sir, I didn't know you knew.' Officer Mullet's face showed his astonishment, and he started to apologize for giving his original explanation, but Claude was already moving away. Breaking off in mid-sentence, Mullet turned to his companion. 'The Commissar must be psychic, it has only just happened.' Together the two officers moved the dead dog in the general direction of a loading bay to the rear of the Commissariat.

Claude made his way back to the offices, hardly believing his luck and deciding to grudgingly give up the road victim, but without once referring to Mitzi. He managed to be charmingly officious about it; and she felt too happy to be called Madame Masse.

'Call me Julia,' she spouted, before kissing him again. Claude pawed at the papers on his desk, relieved that she was departing. Pleased that he had warded her off successfully he was nevertheless left with a feeling that his stroke of luck might have left him vulnerable in some way; it ranked in his mind alongside the owl incident. But if he could not celebrate over this, there was a further reason in progress. Earlier that day he had approved the bail conditions for Jan Kee, fully knowing rocks must be cleared before bodies could be ruled out. This afternoon he hoped would take the investigation one step further.

His telephone rang, heralding the long-awaited call from Greta. Her voice was angry, rising in decibels to say, 'Marc is not at home, and my neighbour said he has not been here at all! You said he would be here and he isn't, my journey was pointless! Clearly you are not aware of what is going on.' There was no hint of loss or sadness in the voice, just aggression.

Claude groaned and sighed as if the news disappointed him. 'I much regret, my dear lady, that he did not heed my advice and act

176

upon it as you did.' Many were the consolation phrases that Claude used then, honed to perfection in a place where loss of spouse was the commonality. He promised to make every effort to find him before replacing the receiver, but all the same quite well aware that the lady didn't want Marc back.

He began upon his fresh coffee, which had arrived during the conversation, with Sylvia smiling down on him as she heard those well-worn platitudes. He began to feel like he could celebrate, Marc was not there, for if anyone could find Marc in Brussels the wife ought to be able to. Now he could be reasonably sure Marc was this end and without doubt somewhere in the caves. But there was even more to be had from knowing she had returned home in full expectation of finding her husband alive, and that in turn suggested that she had not been in a conspiracy to kill him. At least this conclusion put a good distance between the accused and a potential witness.

His brow furrowed into the wisps of fluff above – the ones his sister-in-law called his second eyebrows. If he were honest, he could allot himself a goodly share of the blame for the loss of Marc; despite being factually correct in observing, 'Greta absconded with a lover.' Perhaps it was unnecessary to flout evidence he did not believe himself just to get the man off his back. That could have been an unnecessary spur causing Marc's decision to find her, so doing the job that would have been otherwise been left with the police. A local paper sent through the post had shown that the man, having exposed faults in that particularly dubious evidence, was about to return to his original tack. Claude knew he had missed his chance to prevent this, and he must now wait until the caves were clear of rubble before the official investigations could enter a new phase.

18

A Queendom Traversed

The day to day business of 'the four' was an hour away, but this fact only served to have Hazel hurry for the horses early. She was still feeling elated at being chosen, and saw it as the start of some big adventure. Parsnip saw her coming and cantered about the yard demonstrating his pleasure at seeing her, and Hazel now quite accustomed to being the cause of such excitement rewarded him with a few titbits from breakfast, Annita-style.

A while later crunching noises sounded behind her as the firm characteristic tread of Annita arrived in the stable cave, bringing forth the long neck of Cauliflower, one that was patted as it wrapped itself around a variety of tasty morsels. However, in addition to fussing over her animal, Annita was also aware of Hazel and shouted across to her, 'Bernie and Frances are coming, so you are Jackie's relief, and she will stay with the engineers today.'

Within ten minutes the other two had arrived and mounted with minimal delay. Soon all four horses were trotting through the cave aperture and heading for the agricultural areas. Recesses beyond the village arch housed a collection of tricycles, with carrier boxes that Hazel in all her ignorance could imagine ice cream being sold from. This was the first time that Hazel had seen anything of the food house transportation system, a fleeting and confused glimpse to puzzle over before properly leaving the village bounds. But almost immediately her attention was taken over by the cavern of fungi, which was rather warm and not very well lit. The way ahead widened, and the path moved them against the left-hand wall. Hazel found herself approving of this warmer cavern, with its cleaner air and the neat layout of individual plots containing the several kinds of fungi growing there. Smooth walls of the cavern bordering the path showed its importance as compared with the engineering services cavern, which must lie parallel to it.

Here and there irregular patches had even been bricked up in a workmanlike manner, suggesting to her that the burrowing of miners had been tidied. Parsnip seemed familiar with the route and followed the other horses, which maintained single file, a fact that left her to comprehend alone the marvels of small-scale horticulture, straining to ask, but all without being able to pose a single question. Soon the plots were succeeded by a wide expanse of white caps and she was able to identify the common mushroom all on her own, for once not needing to ask.

There were huge numbers present in the several terraces of dry stone wall that stretched right away towards the far cavern wall. She could easily see why it was that the common mushroom maintained its place here as a food; for most other kinds of fungi she had seen in the food house had an insubstantial look about them, enough at any rate for her to reject them. But there were just a few, she now admitted to herself that had tickled her taste buds.

They progressed further and moved on to other fungi, divided now mainly by a good many walkways. These small paths she saw all came together at a split-like opening in the rock wall, and here it was marginally better lit than other areas, leaving her wondering whatever was so important around here. But with no one to ask her attention moved on to a whole series of terraces where several wildly coloured and stringy varieties grew. One clump was recognizably translucent with bean-like tendrils, and that caused Hazel to exclaim, 'That's the mycelium dish, surely!' Then they rode past a forest of tall, black, striped mushroom shapes, to one with a black top that looked tough enough to be a relative of the ancient hard tops.

Her loud exclamations and questions died in the space between Frances and herself. She wanted to move over alongside her for there was plenty of path, but there must be a point to this single file riding so Hazel reluctantly maintained her distance. She passed a sprinkling of tiny old men who fitted the network of small paths like garden gnomes on someone's colourful allotment, all holding wide baskets and self-evidently collecting produce. She realized that this kind of horticulture had an important place here; despite her own preferences that caused her to eat these kinds of fungi more for the sake of variety than anything else.

The party had arrived at a small clearing which was better lit, and where a group of five men chatted outside some low stone-built cottages; all small people, with predominantly white straggling beards, reminiscent of Arthur. Bernie dismounted, and gave one little fellow with a bald head so much 'agro' that Hazel felt the display was put on just for her benefit; except that the small man set off in the direction of her arm afterwards. The stop was brief and with Bernie back in the saddle they moved on. Soon the hooves were engaged in a noisy hill of rock chippings.

Bernie began riding parallel to Annita, giving Hazel the excuse to move up alongside Frances; here at least she could ask her questions. Towards the end of the chippings they were on higher ground, where a low wall ran alongside the path. Beyond it a lake stretched to the far wall; Parsnip slowed as Hazel's attention wandered. Frances was soon bombarded by questions and replied in a fluent torrent of French, for in this respect Frances was unique. However she had witnessed the newcomer's wonderment and felt impelled to elaborate, even to doing little swimming movements with her hands imitating fins.

Thanking Frances politely in her rudimentary French caused an abrupt cessation of an incomprehensible stream that was still coming. There was now a dark inkling that it might have something to do with fish, for a word here and there had brought menus into mind, which suggested fish. Hazel looked into the water from her vantage point on the horse and saw the bottom very clearly, quite without a sign of movement, tail or fin.

The path started to descend, and hooves were again sinking in noisy chippings, but only a return now to the cavern's natural rock floor. Additionally they were nearing the end of the cavern where the roof elevated and all was better lit, showing cart tracks in the spilled dirt between an opening in the rock face to her right and a huge, rather important-looking gate set in the wall on their side of the path. Almost filling the blind rocky corner to her left, poultry were squabbling over mash in a purpose-built metal mesh enclosure.

As they hit the corner the horses spread out and lost their single-file characteristic. Hazel chose this moment to break ranks with the other riders and catch up with Annita to put questions, but before she had quite caught up the party turned to follow the cart tracks into an open tunnel. Much to Hazel's frustration, the well-drilled order of procession had carried on and entered in front of her. Frustration turned to embarrassment as she waited there, realizing the others would see it as pushy behaviour from an upstart junior. She watched them pass and ended up right back as the rearguard where she started.

The horses, evidently familiar with the route, carried on along the main tunnel ignoring a small, well-used off-shoot, and not even requiring a touch on the reins to do so. This shortly brought them out into a distinctively different cavern. But there were other things to think about now as the new atmosphere was decidedly fresh and a light breeze hit her in the face. The lighting was slightly better than in the fungi cultivation areas, helped on by a background that appeared to be part chalk. Her next observation was of green streaks tingeing the whiteness through with colour, and this had her look about the walls for mine workings. Sure enough there were a number of those bricked-up areas that gave these caverns such a well cared-for look.

This cavern further differed in that she heard the sound of sheep bleating which gave it an inhabited feel; this helped along by having soft soil under hoof and losing the echo formerly always with them. But having attracted her attention with their bleating, the brown woolly shapes moved away from the riders to be against the far wall. There they merged with a mud-smeared background and lost any resemblance to sheep. In fact Hazel could feel herself dampening, it was all much too wet and muddy. Even their course was tainted by a strengthening smell, soon to become a penetrating reek and one that she was quite unable to identify. Thankfully fresh breezes on the face moistly wafted the odour away, and reduced its worst impact. Soon there were sheep in clusters, all looking very dirty and with fleece hanging thick with mud. Growing from the ground about them, and squashed into a mush at the margins of the path, was a ragged brown sort of toadstool interspersed with fern-like shapes; neither variety being recognised by Hazel, who had seen nothing of them in the food house. Enough then to make a better attempt at catching up, and catch Annita's eye by waving her hands to query the sight.

'That's chale, it is full of weed underneath, but it grows too fast for that to matter. The sheep are keen to pick it out, so we just leave the fields with a sprinkle of compost to make effective pasture once again.' Annita smiled, as if she had said everything.

'I would have thought sheep would have needed some grass, it's a wonder they grow?' Hazel said it without thinking, she did not know much about sheep; her afterthought told her it could be a silly question. But it wasn't, for Annita answered her seriously.

'They are hill sheep really, so they are good survivors and do not need rich pasture. It is because sheep are ruminants, with several stomachs, that fungi can be stewed up in the first one to grow bacteria, which are then passed forwards to the next stomach as a more accessible food for a sheep. Taken together with our background fibrous vegetation they do very well without grass. The toadstool, said to be rich in nitrogen, has taken over and the sheep love eating it even if we do not like eating them quite so much. Their droppings spread the spores everywhere, so it would be hard to stop chale now in the interests of quality. Before slaughter we bed them down in hay or straw discarded from the stables, and that helps to remove most of the taint derived from chale.'

Annita broke off, and Cauliflower spurted forwards towards a small group of men who were slightly larger than the previous folk and wore darker beards. Frances was quickly ahead also, and both women dismounted. Not sure what to do now, but espying Bernadette sitting very erect and alert in the saddle, Hazel followed her example and did likewise. There was a pronounced haggle going on and raised voices. Shortly after the women tramped off for some minutes, and returned just when Hazel was beginning to tire of inactivity. Things were being written on a yellowed sheet that might well be parchment. Both parties looked far more amicable now, and she saw Bernadette relax.

Annita returned holding a woolly sheepskin that she draped upon the horse's neck before climbing into the saddle. Moments later the horses moved off to the accompaniment of friendly waves; it was only then that Annita was free to ride alongside Parsnip explaining what had happened. 'Every sheep is numbered shortly after birth, to make sure we get our due; but if the herd weighs in heavier than expected at slaughter, the shepherds are rewarded for their efficiency. This time we have assigned a whole sheep to the men, who can slaughter or barter with it, just as they choose.'

They moved on and the sheep-lands continued to show occasional glimpses of woolly beasts all looking well nourished. To Hazel they seemed big, but without knowing anything about sheep or even her own size now, how could she expect to judge? The cavern had been gaining height ever since she entered it and first heard the far-off sound of falling water, but now the mists from this had become a wet blanket obscuring the whole cavern. The fall now sparkled high over the backs of sheep grazing alongside a placid river taking the water away, and eddies of cold air brushed her face. As they approached the fall, noise volume increased to a roar from somewhere high above them, the water looked indistinct and still like a misty haze raining out on them. They were now being closely hemmed into an alley, with a wall on one side and the cavern's rock face on the other. The water spray fell relentlessly as a light rain, and the thunder of a river drummed the ear; for nothing less than that was funnelling through the hole above. It was being repelled simply by the masonry to the side of them, hearing only the water hiss almost pipe-like as it crashed against a rigid partition, a wall that took away both majesty and view at one time. As they moved further behind it Hazel was elevated enough to see the side view of the fall, a torrent of foaming water plunging in from the roof. Their progressive elevation brought with it backward views of masonry weirs descending behind them, although nowhere could you see the total extent of water falling. As they moved beyond only the rear of deflecting masonry could be seen.

A limited experience but enough to impress itself on Hazel's mind how rough that short but violent stretch of water was, as she tried to envisage the arrival of the original Queen. The concept was little short of miraculous, perhaps doubly so in that the woman's progress had stopped right here at an inhabited level. Further to that more thoughts to scare her arrived; flooding was quite possible if it failed to exit properly. What if erosion caused a collapse? The resulting torrent could easily drown them all. It's a bit like living on top of a volcano, she thought. The thought fevered her mind even though they had passed it by, and Annita's voice was grabbing her attention. 'Every year or so, the engineers remove more of the view, soon we won't see it at all. There are a series of little dams which put the water through turbines, most of them generating electricity. It is our one big power source that runs everything.'

They were coming to another hamlet, this time where the white-beards actually lived, and where several stood in front of their huts waiting for them. Their huts were set low down, and looking more like mud igloos than Hazel liked to see. The men wore sheepskins with the wool surface being used more decoratively than she had seen worn anywhere else. Annita called for Hazel to dismount, and once upon the muddy ground together they approached the group. Annita greeted each by name, and then announced Hazel's name for the benefit of everybody there, bothering only to introduce her personally to the chief man called Sam. Sam sported in addition an element of dignity, for he was dressed more artistically in coloured skins, which distinguished him from the others gathered there. Hazel was quick to notice that everybody dressed in the same sort of style as if it were the in fashion. Sam's beard was trim, short and pointed which picked him out to her. His greying beard set off a wide jovial face, and Hazel liked him instantly, for by now she was getting acclimatized to meeting chest-high people. Annita rattled on about numbers and targets, and moved off down the tiny street going in and out of the squat houses as if she owned them.

Hazel decided to copy her example and showing off a little of her impending managerial status, decided to look inside one for herself. A little fellow followed her inside the one she chose, a nervous creature with a thin pale face that reminded her of a shrew, so much so that she felt like a predator with a victim. He appeared to be in a mild panic that she had chosen his house, standing very unsettled in the door arch. It was warm inside, and the height demanded that she should stoop a little. The anticipated blackness was absent, but even so, she felt the thrill of a challenging exploration for her to be doing all on her own. Circular dwellings she was accustomed to, but this house was not formed from a sphere, and she regretted to see more of an igloo than her own house. This one was obviously a mud-based structure, lined on the inside with a chalk facing; the facing improved the reflection of light entering from about ten portholes in the roof. Hazel ran her hand up to find the glass marshalling light in from outside, discovering it projected light through glass studs wide as her hand. She looked down at the floor, and sure enough there were stones set in it as if to burn something. But the warmth she felt did not come from there and so she cast about until her touch encountered a circle of hot pipe going round the wall area.

That brought her to his bed; Hazel pushed at its bulk, feeling a softness and comfort that well outdid her own. She glanced towards him before taking liberties with his bed; his face looked very apprehensive almost guilty in fact. Hazel slowly counted the many layers of fleece, until her eye alighted upon a dagger-shaped knife. She left it undisturbed, letting the layers just fall back into place. Suddenly everything did not seem so safe here any more; she smiled at the little man pleasantly and exited.

Outside a presentation ceremony was waiting, Annita stood with Sam, holding a pair of cockerels by their necks. Sam immediately headed towards Hazel holding a long bag shape draped over one arm, and presented it to her almost formally. 'You will always find a welcome here, as it's been such a pleasure having you visit.' Sam spoke with a strong Mersey accent, which was very reminiscent of ordinary people back home.

Hazel was quick to thank him and graciously accepted the gift without the faintest clue of what it was. But as she did so she caught sight of one dejected bystander whose face bore a decidedly disturbed look. Hazel returned to him a special smile intended as reassurance – the receiving of which smoothed his face remarkably. Her eye then caught sight of tops to wine bottles sticking up from the roof of his house, and she realized what his port holes were. Hazel could barely repress a laugh that bubbled up her frame as they moved towards the horses. She was intrigued with the bag, which reminded her of a sleeping bag, but despite much looking, she failed to find the opening as they began to ride. Annita had noticed her moves and put her right by saying it was a duvet stuffed naturally with wool and feathers. 'People work at crafts here to pass the time, and often make gifts of that sort.'

As they moved off, Hazel queried the house detail, but omitted to mention the dagger, which she now wished she had not seen. Annita, as always, had an answer, for she was anxious that Hazel should know the details. 'The engineers have lagged pipes coming from the hot stream, and these keep all of the men's houses warm; brought originally for the artificially heated growing areas. In these particular huts, they cut away circles in the roof to allow fires for roasting of poultry – the ones we allow them extra. Or they may want to fumigate with smoke, for they have beetles in this part of the caves, so the vents are made so they can easily be closed with wine bottles if they want.' Annita turned in her saddle and pointed. 'Look over there.' Hazel looked where she indicated, and saw a

185

random mesh of white fronds sticking up from the mud, appearing as a large volume of seriously tangled shoots, which stretched as far as she could see to the end cavern walls.

'Trees don't grow here, but some roots were still growing in the earth the miners left, probably because when they were starving people cut them to chew. This is the best root system and the lads get material to make their huts, or the occasional fire from it.' Annita's voice tailed off as they moved into single file; the leading horse was about to enter a fairly wide tunnel taking them to the last territory of their world, a cavern that was even more odd than all the ones before it.

19

Fishy Vision

A mild draught of warm air played upon Hazel's face as Parsnip entered the last as yet unseen cavern. The horse tilted as if on a slope to reach the new soil level on the other side. Yes, it was earth, not the veneer over rock like elsewhere; hooves were well muffled when she deliberately rode off the path. Of course, this was the cavern where the early miners kept their cattle and even miners' cattle would require a depth of earth to be brought in. A flash of bright yellow took both eyes and mind off such things: there were flowers growing from creepers up the cavern walls, flourishing in lighting angled over them, here it was almost as good as the village. Her ears discerned the buzzing of bees among the plants, and saw below a stone-flagged space that surrounded two hives. Where they had entered strange plants grew on that wall also, bearing dry-looking spore heads, almost a miniature sunflower, she thought, turning her head to see them better.

Annita noticed of course, and called her attention to the things they were all rightly proud of. 'There's all this before you, and you still have eyes fixed on our chicken feed!' Hazel straightened abruptly to face the way she was going, and saw the cavern had a space being used very intensively indeed. After the hives they had begun passing an avenue of square pots, standing packed close together, seemingly holding vines at an early stage of growth. 'These are my favourite plants,' Annita continued, the warmth of her voice confirming the connection with alcohol. 'The men move them for pollination in the light and later find spaces in our sunshine alley when they have fruited,' she laughed. 'The next close-packed pots along here contain potatoes – they are a long way off ready too. They get taken up almost entirely in feeding the men.' It was a necessary thing to say, as Hazel had never seen a potato served in the food house.

She caught sight of men among the pots either with a barrow or tools for weeding and these she could have missed in the confusion of light and shade, had they not waved as the horses passed by. Hazel noticed that some were stripped to the waist and wore a fleecy loincloth, which often was a very good match for the man's lengthy grey beard. They were progressing to a well-lit half of the cavern, the extra light being mainly stray reflections from the lamps hung low over a bright yellow crop of wheat. Above streaming from a hole in the cavern wall were dozens and dozens of black strands, each one leading to a row of lamps.

Annita was anticipating Hazel's look of bewilderment and had seen it immediately, for this place was begging to be explained. Reining in her horse she raised her arm and pointed high against the far wall. 'It's not some big spider run amok; the waterfall is on the other side of that wall and wires for our lamps are simply brought through the hole. There is an extensive chalk layer high in the rock, and bats get to everywhere through the many faults in such holes, but for us it saves an awful lot of wire. Not that we are short of wire for copper we have in plenty; the lacquer to cover it too is plentiful from the stems of that seedy plant you were looking at back there. The glass in the discharge tubes is almost as easy, because we have the materials for making boron-silicate glasses, and a long time ago engineers built a furnace for working it. Do you notice the warmth just here past the beans? The pipes carrying hot water along the wall go on and off to make all the crops here respond to an almost tropical climate.'

What was taking Hazel's attention was not all that boring stuff about wire and other hardware, but rows of golden wheat, all a bright golden yellow, standing stiffly to attention as if infusing their character into the way ahead. The cereal grew in large, roughly square, shallow trays, from which at one end protruded a couple of wheels. Annita droned on, trying to present more understanding to Hazel of at least a hundred years trial and error to attain this high degree of complicated development. 'This is our single most important advance because the waterfall keeps on going night and day, speeding up our agriculture no end; even if these days we are driven to take power off for elsewhere occasionally. When it is daytime in the village and the engineers are using it as well, it has to be night-time for parts of this place. There are no seasons to bother us, so we gather crop after crop from such well-fertilized land. We prepare specific compost for each crop: part recycled soil, part bat droppings and part digested sewage, and in such a way that all our plants receive rich soil. Elsewhere farmers are bothered with pests of one sort or another, but our recycling and location means that little bothers us.'

A couple of long-haired individuals with dark beards stood close to a 'pump it up' mechanical contrivance with wheels. Hazel wondered whether it was intended to move those trays with two wheels, but of course never found out. Annita swung herself off Cauliflower, and grabbed at the chickens, which she proffered to the taller of the two. 'Jeff, I want you to meet Hazel; you too Tim.' Hazel swung out of the saddle to take up the introduction, noticing that the smaller of the two watched her dismount very closely, and was ogling her up and down. As the pleasantries continued, Hazel felt more and more uneasy, folding her arms to cover the angle where the coarse woollen weave of her dress stretched over her bust – he was undressing her with his eyes. Looking daggers at the man made no difference at all, and meanwhile she was missing the full import of the conversation. This second encounter that involved her personally was all it took to shatter the enthusiasm she had begun the day with. Hazel climbed back in the saddle managing to look unconcerned, but at the same time shaken and apprehensive at what might happen next. Soon they rode on and left the men way behind, their attention focused forward to the stone-built hamlet ahead, roofed with proper thatching. Bernadette jumped from her stirrup and was soon talking to half a dozen of the men. Annita beckoned to Hazel, for she had business to do here as well, and they parted with Frances who was sitting quietly in the saddle minding the horses – but watching everything closely.

'Tom, meet Hazel.' This time it was a blond good-looking fellow, full of pleasant humour; but Hazel saw his words as directed towards the pleasing of Annita, who basked in his many compliments. Were they here to simply to impress one another, or to chat about farming? Hazel didn't know. Still restless and full of unease, she wandered not very far this time to look at the outsides of houses, appreciating they were more professionally built here. But now much too shaken to attempt exploration, she was realizing how little the open-weave woollen dress hid from the eyes of men. She had wandered further than intended to the very end of the

189

short dirt road. Ahead she could see concentrated activity going on around one of those long trays. Some hundreds of yards further on she saw a huge tray being lifted by one of those mechanical lifter mechanisms and drawn out of line. Congratulating herself for having got its function right, she watched. First the tray's side was removed, and then a line of ripe wheat was grasped by an overhead mechanism and lifted whilst the soil was raked away from the roots by hand. These more virile men carrying knives would be more dangerous, she thought, feeling shaky again, and that put her on the way back.

Annita's call when it came had her there instantly, and all three set off for the main building which was not far off, standing out as larger than the cluster of dwellings about it. The building they entered was liberally coated internally with an adherent layer of creamy white flour, and underneath showed the dirt where it had peeled off. And that was no surprise after seeing the windows from outside, for each was outlined by flour-stained exterior stones. They headed for the centre of things where a large circular stone grinding wheel lay recessed in the floor; but to get there it was necessary to skirt several wide-open part-rooms, all of which had perforated metal floors but no ceiling. One was stacked with potatoes, and another with bundles of wheat stalks quite devoid of grain but still with root; drying she guessed. Nearer the centre space equipped with stone grinding wheel they passed several rough churn-sized bins of grain, and slightly removed from these were two bins of fine flour. The other two trickled the contents knowingly through their fingers, but it was all very grey and uninteresting stuff to Hazel.

When they returned to the horses there were others standing about them, including the two they had met earlier. Hazel averted her eyes from the man who had viewed her so lewdly on the previous encounter and feeling vulnerable hurried to mount Parsnip, carrying the frightening thought that such a man might well carry a knife. Her sense of unease was not helped by seeing both Bernadette and Frances sitting up very soldierly in the saddle, and both resting their hands inside the pannier-like structures that contained their crossbows. In her unnerved state she was becoming increasingly aware of the fact that she was very much their passenger.

Annita mounted alongside her, quite at ease and totally relaxed, launching into an explanation of her reasons for the introductions. 'All of the people I introduced to you are my men, and when you substitute for me, they are the ones you do business with.' Hazel still looked blank to her, preoccupied, she was obviously not taking it in, and so Annita directed her next words towards rousing her into a more receptive state. 'Get used to the idea that what we are doing here is vital! It's our food supply that's at stake; you will have to make yourself more outgoing, as you are not doing just a soft job in the village. Here we are at the sharp end, and that leaves no margin for error. Whatever weaknesses you show to that lot you will soon regret!' The emphatic words penetrated deeply into a shivery Hazel's consciousness, making contact but not restoring confidence. Parsnip must have been aware of her quaking unabated upon his back.

They were on bare rock now and approaching the tumbled rocks that ended this last cavern. Ahead there were a number of huge single rocks laid upon the surface. Ambush country, thought Hazel, petrified. But fortunately on rounding the monster stones there were few capable of obscuring her vision as they headed up a hill of stones. Here a gang of four muscular men was visible, all stripped to the waist and loading amazingly lightweight black stuff into a large container on wheels – watched absently by an elderly horse. Frances sought out the largest of the workers, a man with tattoos and one earring, who Annita said answered to the name of Harold; the discussions were lengthy. Annita remained in her saddle, taking the opportunity to point out the huge scale of collapse to Hazel, visible as a distinct outline well beyond the place they stood.

'What are they digging out?' questioned Hazel. 'It looks light work for that crowd?'

'They normally dig the composts in or out which is more of a job; but as we found charcoal under the rocks they are the ones to do it,' said Annita. 'The original miners would have used it, and must have stored it here.'

That did not add up to Hazel, conscious of people needing fuel for hundreds of years, whilst having it handy on their doorstep so to speak. 'Why is there still fuel here?'

Annita, as usual, was well supplied with answers. 'This is the best place to take rock from for our construction work about the caves – for in so doing we are also digging our way out. The charcoal has remained hidden through centuries of these occasional excavations, so it was inevitable that we should chance upon it sometime.'

Frances finished talking loudly to the heavy gang en route to her mount, and Hazel was fascinated to hear her last words were in French. She realized that the woman probably conducted all her business that way. Almost immediately they were off, returning so they told her, but despite that statement everyone was still heading forwards towards a blank cavern wall. Hazel wouldn't have been surprised had someone said 'open sesame' and the wall opened. But no, it was nothing to get excited about, because passing a large rock they turned about a tight path downwards, arriving at the entrance of a little tunnel. A tunnel just wide enough to merit the cart tracks it bore, but so low in places she was forced to dismount and lead Parsnip over ground that was deeply scored by the hoof marks of horses. She walked and slipped to the end of it, a place where the small tunnel intersected with a much larger one. This churned-up side branch she then recognised as the same small opening they had passed on the way in; and as if the short cut was not gift enough, she mounted in better-lit space altogether. They had emerged with the large double gates almost in view. 'So this must be the end of the first cavern again,' she mused, well aware that the cut had saved two cavern lengths of the journey back. Wide-open gates of the engineers formed a frame for the figures of Arthur and Leon, high on a horse-drawn cartload of manure; departure looking imminent. Jackie stood there, well placed to supervise the tinies' egress and she waved to the four; Frances immediately turned her horse to join her.

The procession hesitated there, until Bernadette spoke up loudly. 'Begorra! She's found another dyke at "poofters gate"! I won't stay, if that's all we wait for. Come on, it's the straight path we are taking!' Annita waved to Frances and turned her horse so Bernie couldn't see her laugh.

The girl's innate crudity she well appreciated, but knew it was partly aimed at making peace with her own self, and using their shared hatred of the homosexuals to do it. It was a lull which gave Hazel the opportunity to repeat her questions about the lake and without Frances being present to embarrass the questioner. 'It's newly constructed,' shouted Annita. 'There's no fish, but there will be.'

'Its ducks, I want to see here,' giggled Bernadette lifting her crossbow as if she could see them flying already.

'There's going to be some poaching problems, when we get that lot up and running, so don't complicate it more than it is Bernie,' laughed Annita.

The short cut meant that they arrived back at the village much more quickly than the outward journey, and very soon they were entering the permanent stable cave to which Parsnip seemed very well adjusted. All moved promptly into the food house for their late morning hot drink, waiting at ease for Jackie and Frances to catch up. When the couple did arrive they needed to hurry their morning snack, as everyone else was eager to move off to the pool before lunch. All five chattered incessantly as they made for the swimming cave. Probably it's sheer relief, thought Hazel, finding herself buoyed up and talkative also, relieved that it was all over.

For her, the pool was overcrowded with four others splashing about in it, but soon the splashing culminated in a cluster about the illuminated cascade. Once the threshing legs departed, and became mere decorations on that gleaming bubble, she had a clear path to do her customary underwater circuit. Hazel swam, very conscious of the pink bodies clinging to that one corner. Did Jackie behave herself? she wondered. Or did hands wander? A strange reflection caught her eye as Hazel passed the black hole; the one that ducted water downstream, for here was something she had not seen before. The sight took her aback, they were eyes, weren't they? Two large, square eyes moved, gleaming in the dark. The third scare today hit her in the pit of her stomach, was it some monster big fish ready to snap her up? No, the square eyes glinted too much and were joined to recognisable pink appendages that moved independently among the shadows in between, now she could be sure. Hazel swam directly towards the group and broke surface in the middle of some inane chatter; there was a stunned silence as she gasped urgently.

'There are eyes watching us from that black tunnel over there.' She pointed to where it was. The exodus from the pool was immediate; pink bodies dragged themselves out and ran mere paces for dresses that were pulled over wet skin. Hazel was last and still climbing out of the pool as the first one tore into the entrance tunnel; by the time she climbed wet into her dress the whole area was deserted. It was late to bother with running, but still she ran all the way up the tunnel and into the village. Ahead of her, Frances was knocking frantically upon Freda's door and so Hazel ran on frantically following the splashes and wet footprints, which took her out through the agricultural gate. There she encountered a loose horse, which she mounted bareback; the horse, besides being the slowest by nature, was also very tolerant in allowing Hazel to do so.

Hazel was hoping that it would follow the others, for now having got up, she couldn't quite understand how she had managed to do so in the first place, and beyond even that what did she do now? The horse ambled into the fishpond cavern at a pace that was quite fast enough for her; the obvious damage to neat rows of fungi had her urging her horse into a sharp right-hand turn following the trail of damaged herbage. Doubts assailed her. Had she got all this started because she was un-nerved earlier, a nervous premonition perhaps; for then everyone would be so mad at her. Clustered around that well-lit break in the rock wall were the other horses. She swung carelessly down and hurried into the opening, bracing her frame to penetrate its attendant blackness. There were just a few pieces of fonz to light her way among the rocks, before she chanced upon Bernadette.

Bernie saw her coming, and hugged a woolly bundle to her breast. 'I got their four skins,' she shrieked. 'Annita's gone for the rest of them.' Bernie laughed raucously, evidently enjoying a pun devised by her alone.

'Is anyone watching the horses?' Annita's cool voice came up from where she was wading in the water near the opening of the duct. 'I'll go!' cried Hazel and set off at once. She climbed the path knowing there was something positive in what she had said, and wishing there were not, as contrary thoughts of consequences left her feeling just as sick as before.

Little men of the first hamlet were standing nearby and looking at her as she emerged; so many curious eyes among those delicate white whiskers. She gathered the horses into one place, and relieved to find Parsnip, mounted him with plenty of time to do it. Hazel felt far more confident despite still being bareback. The old men murmured among themselves, and when two wet, naked individuals were dragged from the opening, their voices cried out in an agitated kind of way. Hazel was surprised to recognize one of the culprits as Tim, the one with intrusive eyes. Without delay, the captives were roped between horses in the middle, weathering more verbal affronts to their skinny dignity by Bernie. She accompanied them, with their wearing apparel draped over her shoulders and two boxes strung over them.

Hazel led the way, and looking back something stirred in her mind; why, it was just like 'Peter & the Wolf'. She would be Peter leading the way in triumph from the woods, and behind strung between two hunters was her own special wolf; then bringing up the rear came Granddad, or to be precise, a host of Granddads showing off their white beards. Jackie sat upon the last horse waving her truncheon in warning at the white whiskers, until they dropped back to a respectful distance.

The horses were brought through into the village, and the gatehouse bubble secured. Hazel took a deep breath of relief as Freda appeared with the village seniors behind her. 'There will be a council meeting, before you go any further!' she cried. The party of four gathered behind her, whilst Maureen took charge of the prisoners. 'Hazel, your staff will not be safe outside. Go, bring them into the village and secure the pool gatehouse after you. Maria, evacuate the men in the food house, they can stay with Leon for the time being – make secure the gate behind them. Pat, have ready some emergency lighting, and attend to our needs in the armoury.'

Everyone was talking, the noise level swelling, until ultimately Freda held up her hand to halt the voices. 'It is important that we meet quickly – a meeting in the church will be held in twenty minutes – so be there!' With her final command uttered, Freda turned her back, and entered the church.

20

Gone for a Soldier

Leon and Arthur's dwelling was not easily found. The tiny widowers had moved away from the village because of a law that made tenure of any house there strictly for the women. Upon the death of their spouses, the qualification had ceased to include them. It made no difference that one house was still existent, or that nobody else would want to live in the other, they simply did not fit the criteria for residence. So it was then that the little men had been consigned to the engineers' huts, and journeyed to their work in the village. Their daily walk now had to be done in reverse by Terry and Marc, trekking through the engineers' cavern looking for the settlement. Floundering on in the ill-lit, chill, fume-ridden cavern, they were soon having reservations about this; and even impressed with their own previous good fortune in being chosen for food house work. Terry was the first to spot an engineer's hut, the first of many such ramshackle dwellings huddled together with little or no regard for architectural fineness or mere external appearance. In these first huts they saw much in common with the collection of jumbo machinery that had previously littered their path, which at first sight could well have been mistaken for bigger versions of the same thing. Marc observed the buildings with a more practised eye, seeing them as a cluster of ten positioned near the huge gates opening out onto other caverns. There were five better-looking huts at the extreme end, which Marc was eventually told the 'artisans' occupied.

The engineers' buildings were built solidly from stone blocks; the doors and roofs were made of metal. Although the settlement had no architectural merit whatsoever, it was sturdy and straight-forward, and in fact akin to the kind of people who lived there. Upon making contact the temporary exiles were directed with certainty, for here everyone knew everybody else. Having pen-

196

etrated the tinies' door they found the cabin comfortably warm with under-floor heating, completely offsetting the amount of metal in the construction; unsightly heavy plates of sheet copper, covered in a dirty green layer of oxide. The shared hut was easily big enough for Leon and Arthur, but only because they were very small people – normally such a hut would suit a solitary engineer. Their living quarters might be short on space, but this was an oasis in a chilly, inhospitable land, and consequently both of the new arrivals made a determined attempt to fit into what little space remained within the hut.

To assist their moving in with the two remaining village tinies, Maria had provided her staff with four newly fried potato fritters packed in two of the pannier arrangements usually carried down to the tricycles; she was already aware that tonight was one meal that would become unavailable. The fritters were popular favourites with the men, made with added sheep milk, herbs and salt. The food indeed produced smiles on the faces of their friends who shortly after scurried around their neighbours acquiring two chairs, which almost filled the area between the beds. The urgency of the move had left them interpreting 'the hiccup', as Maria called it, to be a temporary affair – and that of course was entirely their own expectation. To them it was but a stay with friends, for after all they were with their workmates, and hence Terry and Marc fully expected to enjoy their stay – a sort of holiday rest for the deserving. Unbeknown to them, but known to all others, theirs was more an evacuation of undesirables in a time of conflict. Their over-crowded friends, being protagonists in that conflict, said little and certainly did nothing that contributed towards the holiday mood. Having seen them settle in, Arthur soon made excuses and beetled off to reconnoitre, for he knew that you could peer through the semi-transparent gate-house that butted on to the engineers door and listen to the sounds that came through the village.

For a while now Marc had been learning English in every moment that was available, and not only through Terry, the women pushed this aim along too so that real communication was beginning to happen for him. Apart from this, any private views or opinions had passed between them in an almost furtive fashion, and were often delivered on the move such as while collecting bats, or that rare moment when Maria was not actually behind them promoting activity. With this as a background they found real luxury here in being able to talk freely to one another, and this unique opportunity to talk openly tended to mask the sabre rattling going on all around them.

Leon, reclining upon his bed without Arthur to distract him, slowly began to realize that the pair had no idea that anything deserving their attention had happened. Vainly at first he pointed out that the women's actions strongly indicated that they were at war with them. Both friends looked astonished; it was necessary to continue expounding the men's discontent to make any headway at all, and he was doing so with the pleasant aftertaste of Maria's potato fritter, tangy and succulent in his mouth. Neither ignored him altogether, for he advocated with particular gusto the worth that was to be extracted from exploiting each of many periodic clashes with the women. Their occasional gripe was traditionally a way of wringing concessions; by arguing over trivia they need not be friendly and so counter frequent attempts to tighten the screw. There was even the possibility that one day the ruling class would get it wrong and the place could be taken over to run more sensibly. Leon grinned at them through sparse white whiskers, owl-like. 'Once we get them all ready to fight, we look for ways to outwit or split them. Why! If we won, young Marc – you would be shagging them, instead of them you.'

'Young Marc' was not the way Marc saw himself. 'I am too old for a guerilla war; and tired of the other – so I shall stay out of it, if I can.' His face brightened. 'Although I must admit it would be a real treat to spank the one they call Bernie over my knee. What I want to do is to get out of here completely, and winning battles in caves would only remove one barrier.'

'No one ever gets out of here.' Leon's emphatic remark smacked of certainty.

Marc was not so sure, and was provoked enough to explain. 'There's rivers of water moving through this place, and where there's rivers there's erosion – to me erosion means head-space. I merely need to choose a time of low rainfall.' Leon looked at him doubtfully, then swivelled to face Terry who, finding a topic close to his heart being vented, almost exploded into the conversation with his own particular idea. His excited voice cut across Marc's more lengthy technical thoughts.

'I am going out the way the bats fly in! On the way here, I heard bats clicking in the cavern before the last approach tunnel; their routes probably connect and not far in distance either. The hole I've seen is quite big and if I can get that high it's a way out without passing anything lethal. If that weren't so, even the bats wouldn't come back.' Marc couldn't imagine how Terry would get up there, though it was certainly a good idea because he remembered the hole too. Before he could say so, Arthur scuttled into the room. 'They're bashing on the gate'ouse over there. They mean bisness awlrite. Gonna tell Red nah.' He turned about and moved off at speed.

'You will need to make your mind up now just whose side you are on!' Leon almost shouted at them, turning to bring up a wicked-looking metal club from the side of his bed. Terry and Marc exchanged startled looks. Their pet projects were being overtaken.

The door frame filled with a ginger-haired, sturdily built fellow, whose grim-set, craggy face had them know instinctively he was the chief man here; it had to be Red himself. Red hesitated, seeing Leon had company. 'You have friends here?' His accent sounded challenging and north of England, but Terry couldn't say exactly where.

Leon was quick to vouch for them. 'They are with us,' he said.

Red looked quizzically from one to the other, and evidently decided that it was safe to speak. His harsh voice hit them as full of indignation. 'Those bloody cows have captured two of the grain men, and all the labourers are banging on the gate-house door. What say you – join the party – eh Leon?'

Leon sat more erect upon his bed. 'There will be recriminations if we show our hand, and still the others get beaten.' The caution in his voice, and the debating style of delivery had them realize that their friend exerted considerable influence.

'They don't know about our ram.' The red beard switched direction towards the newcomers, and hard eyes swept over them again. 'There's no problem if we keep a low profile, and retreat the instant the bitches move in any effective way.' He laughed, the cunning shining in his eyes. 'How about it – are all of you with me?'

To Terry's surprise, Marc not only said yes, but also shook Red's hand enthusiastically afterwards, a decision that made any lack of fight on his part conspicuous. He would have to join in and be one of them. A thought occurred to him that he ought to be there anyway, protecting Hazel were she in danger; he stepped forward all ready to go.

Red looked pleased, and set off with them to the engineers waiting outside the door. Soon as everyone fell in behind him he strode ahead, talking earnestly with Marc. They were still talking as Red unlocked the huge double gates that closed the engineers' cavern. The gates stood at the crossroads of a junction accessing all three agricultural caverns. The men who passed through were carrying what could only be called a battering ram: it was a casting of four-inch diameter copper, some five feet long and with short crossbars at intervals along its length. Terry dropped further back, noticing several men were being armed as they passed Red. The arms were wicked-looking square-section bars; they were some one inch thick and came to a chisel point at one end. All was of mere interest to Terry until Red passed a gleaming copper bar into his hands also. The man behind him was chosen to mind the gate, and Red passed over the key along with terse instructions before he left.

A bunch of engineers, with Red and Marc at their head, crunched their way along the fishpond path and continued on until they entered the arch which accessed the village. There they merged with a crowd from the farming areas. The crowd was shouting aggressive slogans laced with much individual cursing. Most of the noisy crowd were actively slapping and pushing vainly at the yellow globe; recognised instantly by Terry as the village agricultural gatehouse.

The battering ram was cheered as it arrived among them. Then, wielded by four brawny engineers, it was soon making a series of heavy assaults upon the sides of the gatehouse. Almost immediately the engineer team succeeded in making a huge dent, one that popped out again whenever the globe was hit somewhere else. Shaped bars were quickly passed forwards, and driven between the flexible door and its surrounding shell, near to the metal hinges. Forcing bars bent its fabric right back, but the moment the tool relaxed it snapped back to look much the same. The men driving the battering ram made a second dent in the side and the sphere no longer fitted snugly into its embracing masonry. Attention to the door was forgotten and blows rained in at the sphere using all available tools, even Terry's, by one spectator keen to loan the equipment. Denting and distortion showed upon the gatehouse surfaces until finally the sphere showed every sign of collapse, and now was looking more like a crumpled ball of celluloid. Men put their shoulders to its bump-ridden curves and heaved; the sphere eased slightly towards the village. The line of white beards at its base crouched low and pushed hard upwards from its bottom edge; taller farmers reached over them to it; and all the time the engineers kept up an incessant pounding with weighty copper implements.

Spectacularly the sphere failed, squeezing through its retaining walls and bouncing away from the assault. The men pushing it were instantly teetering upon unexpected space, as a pit of some three yards wide by two deep opened at their feet. Grey beards clawed at thin air as they overbalanced and then fell into the hole, especially the tinies levering with their backs who all tipped in head-first. The engineers, taken by surprise mid-swing, released grip on the ram and promptly stepped aside, all feeling relieved to have avoided disaster. The retreat was instant; to lose men in achieving your object might be understandable, but to find an unexpected and insurmountable obstacle when you have just won access spelled disaster to everyone there. Terry stood watching, with a good view just before the arch, but then stood by helplessly as the participating engineers thronged into the bottleneck, followed by a host of grey beards, pushing with surprising vigour towards the exit. Feeling more the spectator and less part of the action, Terry at first allowed them all to stream by, only collecting his bar from the thankful borrower as he passed also. The huge yellow ball was moving again, this time being thrust to one side by a horse. Hazel was in the saddle, armed with lance and shield, her eyes surveying the pit. Instantly Terry waded through the remaining dwarves into the tunnel, fearing that she might see him and misconstrue.

The melée headed elsewhere to find their leader, a man who was already causing a second diversion. Intent upon continuing the battle, a line of frustrated men streamed across terraces of fungal plants heading towards a mineshaft. Terry followed them, suffering much from divided loyalties, but on entering with the others found a distraction in the bright luminosity of plants along the path. His downhill path terminated in a rough cave, barely lit with several of these lights; the place had a passing resemblance to a tube platform, with water running between the tunnels. It was a cave that housed a stream running through its entire length which one of his companions called 'the long pool'. Grey beards moved over the stones, squeezing their diminutive selves up on to a rocky narrow shoulder that avoided the water. He himself would need to go through the water.

Why? He asked himself. I don't want to be part of their war.

The wet revelation had him returning right back to the huge doors, where the doorman eyed him suspiciously before letting him in. Back in his uncomfortable metal chair viewing an empty cabin, he sat looking into empty space. Not for long, for there were thoughts buzzing through his mind and he left the hut for a wander through the engineering locality. He was attracted to the neater dwellings that snuggled in the cavern end beyond the double doors.

On the way there were the workbenches constructed entirely in metal and appearing connected to numerous activities. One had a line of generators that stood in a long queue from the bench, what a waste to have so many out of action? He was looking for ladders, which he discovered, but it was not easy to see that any had the length necessary for his task. Conveniently one such fault used by bats was in sight, but visibly well above the height of any ladder here.

He had reached a place where more complex machines and equipment littered benches. With a start he realized that an elderly fellow was only feet away and working at a potter's wheel. The man greeted him without taking his eye off the clay being moulded and which was evidently at a critical stage. Not everyone here was rebelling it would seem and the chap did seem thoroughly engrossed in what he was doing, oddly mirroring the behaviour of Maria. Beyond him there were at least three furnaces with heavy-duty electrical connections. One piece of plant seemed devoted to the production of copper wire and he looked with interest at metal spools all carrying different diameters. This wire must have been drawn upon these machines, which despite their less than modern appearance evidently worked. The people who arrived here from the outside world must bring with them an insight into all manner of trades and technology, so why should he be surprised craftsmen existed here, he already knew of rations for such a specially treated group from his experience in the food house. The engineers themselves were different again, and not treated well by contrast, seemingly not having any care about this or the wish to do even the small things that might make life in their community any easier.

He walked round an oven stacked with plates, only to see another gleaming with sheets of glass on its rollers. Then as he reached the front row of those much neater dwellings he encountered a stable occupied by a single horse, elderly enough to number among the engineers' workhorses. Diverted into patting the neck of a creature obviously pleased to see him, Terry returned his attention once more to his search for ladders. Not far from the horse, he found the mouth of trunking blowing what he decided was fresh air via a fan. Yes this did seem to be a more fortunate locality, and he did find reason to stay long enough for a good few breaths in the marvellous mechanical wind. Having thought about what he wanted next, he set off in the other direction to the plant machinery characterizing the other side he was more associated with – the common engineer.

The plant on this side of the dwellings he had seen coming, and very evidently had a strong connection with extraction of metals. One furnace had an air extraction hood above it and this furnace he supposed produced the sulphurous odour characterizing the whole cavern. If his assumption was correct, the exhaust pipe that continued on upwards to the now defunct internal bat route was intended to draw off the choking gases. Trunking that high suggested a means of reaching it in the first place, so he only needed to find their ladders or utilize their solution, except that the need to go that high was probably accomplished a century or so ago. Terry took his time and looked for hours among the junk, of which there was plenty, hoping to find some unspecified object or objects which might make his escape plan more feasible. There was no point in worrying about the outcome of the revolution; certainly Hazel didn't need him to protect her – she looked supremely dangerous.

21

Heroics

The village resounded to the noise of heavy blows upon the farm access gate. Externally a semicircle of men beat at it with shovels and hands, causing the sphere to flex under each heavy blow, but the hard bubble material always bounced back without leaving a trace to encourage further energy wastage. This did not deter the men involved, as it was more a way of showing disapproval rather than a serious attempt to enter. Many were the gross swear words that could be expended at such an unyielding surface; the net result more intended to frizzle the ears of women inside. But the commotion failed to turn a single head in the village, for they all knew the gatehouse was impregnable and the noise could be no more than disobedience expected from a protest.

As the noise radiated through the village, individuals hurried to snatch a bite before making the latest possible dash towards the church. The hurry was something the women had in common, haste sufficient to make them all disregard the external racket and use what remained of the twenty minutes to arm and attend bodily needs. The room set aside for conferences filled in a last-minute rush, with individuals dropping their personal armaments in untidy piles about the floor. As a space inside the church it was one of the largest rooms, comprising a solid floor carpeted in tight, woven, root-like material; bubble-thin walls that were deadened with draped sheepskins – the skin side faced the room and adorned the place with maps and drawings. Each delegate as she settled chose her own particular metal chair, and pushed it in to the round table situated at the centre of the room. The table's metal frame glinted gold, as did the ornate legs, which together supported a weighty expanse of polished marble.

The women still arriving singly hurried through the church anteroom, passing Maureen who was self-evidently guarding prisoners well secured to stretchers. Both men lay in the curvature of the bubble and away from the direct path between the doors. Upon the stretchers the prisoners were strongly bound and scarcely able to breathe in the wealth of rope that tied them to the support bars, but aware their plight was known to their friends outside by the drumming of their colleagues across the village. Although it must be said that neither man found much succour in this, or that it raised spirits beyond the infinitesimal. Offsetting anything heartening that might arise from the noise was the grim view of an anvil over them in the adjoining room, neither man knowing whether it was part of their treatment. From her more mobile choice of views Maureen looked questioningly from time to time at the village gatehouse, a remote threat, but one she was prepared to shut the church doors for if the position in any way deteriorated.

Freda called the meeting to order, and the babble of voices tailed away. She awaited silence, glowering at a late tongue. 'Thank you all for managing to appear so very promptly,' she said. 'Maureen will not be joining us, but as I have taken her opinion beforehand we may consider her view. As you all know the pool today attracted the attention of Peeping Toms. One of the men taken, I might add, was a man of mine and as I am still not sure how it happened, I shall listen with interest to what Jackie can tell us about it.'

Jackie spent a moment or two checking the items she had on the table in front of her, then she rose up holding a slightly bent and extremely well-corroded screw. 'It is a long swim from the men's pool to ours, and there are supposed to be barriers in between; but all of the protective grids are now missing from the walls of the canal. The damage is not recent and in part is due to old age, so we can only blame the men for assisting a natural process in order to do their viewing. This activity of theirs did not happen on the spur of the moment either, because they fashioned an apparatus specifically to do it.' She held up an open-ended metal box to aid explanation. 'The construction contains two mirrors and a sheet of glass. It is a simple periscope that uses mirrors positioned to view underwater whilst standing in the exit duct. But today when the usual four came to rest, there was a fifth still swimming and not being aware of this they were found out. Even so we are indebted to Hazel's keen eyesight as they must have been near invisible. So I think we all ought to say a profound thank you, to Hazel.' Jackie pointed, before lapsing into silence, and there was a little clap during which Hazel's face turned a bright red.

Freda resumed control of the meeting, pointing out the relevant considerations. 'On this occasion we have the culprits and we must use this fact to send a very clear message to the men generally; that this kind of behaviour will not be tolerated. If we fail to be sufficiently severe, then you can be sure there will be more intrusion; but alternatively, if we go over the top there will be rioting. It is a fine line because we always risk major trouble when dispensing justice following a gross misdemeanour. Do not think that it does not concern all of you personally, because if ever we are driven to the ultimate recourse of reducing the male population, then each of you will soon feel the adverse effects upon your lifestyle – something like that could easily put our society back twenty years or more. So let's hear your views now; and bearing what I have said in mind perhaps we could hear Bernadette first?'

Bernadette's face had indicated she held strong views on the subject, but not being accustomed to speaking at meetings she hesitated, and at first stood there looking uncertainly across an expanse of table at a circle of faces watching her intently.

''Tis thinking I am – you protect t'em with words! Thay intruded – thay watched us. Surely we have t'place an reason for hunting t'em. Let's get thare!'

Annita's expression had become one of intense exasperation; Freda next turned to her.

'Cannot they be whipped and transferred into the engineers, who don't use the pool downstream? After all, it is nice to know there are still heterosexual men here, who are normal enough to have been attracted to beautiful us, and come back for more.'

Instantly Bernadette was on her feet, her eyes flaming. 'He'd be stepped up on a soap box, and showing off the marks – so that's pure blarney!'

Annita leaned back comfortably in her chair. 'You are only outraged 'cos you haven't any tits to show them.'

The noise at the table swelled. Freda was on her feet calling for order, then holding her hand palm forwards towards the girl, hoping to stem Bernadette's fury, as her howl of anger must easily have penetrated the thickly covered walls. It was lucky she sat opposite Annita or she would have attacked her.

'Jackie, what do you think?' Freda hurriedly moved on.

'For a start, Annita owns one of them and is not keen to do anything at all if she can; but there is no deterrent quite as good as chopping off their balls.'

A hush settled on the assembly. Rose hesitatingly put up a hand. Everyone waited.

'Poppy thinks we ought to put them back to sleep and feed them a reducing diet, before we send them back very small indeed.'

Freda smiled at her. 'It is a very good possibility you have raised, but small eyes are still eyes. Listen to that clamour out there; do you really think we could hold them off that long?'

Maria indicated that she wanted to speak, and was immediately chosen by Freda. 'Let's expel them from the caves. It is a deed that can be seen to be done by our would-be enemies, but we know well that the sentry will see they do not get away from here. Seeing those worthless men in the entrance just now makes me wonder whether they would not be missed if we decided to feed our carnivorous plants right now.'

Freda waited for the laughter to die down before commending her suggestion. 'That's just what this meeting is all about, for we have just heard a new and constructive solution. Moreover it comes from an expert on appetites and very tempting too; but doing so means we will lose two from useful work. However, let us keep it in mind, for there are drawbacks to saving everyone we can. Our gate guardians get so few of them that they may be becoming unnecessarily fierce or ravenous. Is there anyone else to speak?'

Patricia raised a hand some inches above the table. 'I fink's we ough'er, do wot Itzla did, an take their bits orf 'em.' There was much laughter, and a small cheer went up as Pat accompanied her words with a hand action that chopped at the table.

Freda beamed. 'That is almost the view of both Maureen and me, for like Jackie we both believe it should be the simple Itzla castration. It is, after all, essentially a sexual matter that they will expect us to correct, and once done this minor rebellion should subside. We can only accept so much from them and if this problem does not resolve itself in the near future we may be driven to consider a cull of ringleaders. But for the moment I do not see

207

them threatening the survival of our society and as a consequence I recommend castration. The men will accept it as just, and the resulting lack of hormones is perhaps the simple cure that we should be seeking. If you all agree, please show hands because we haven't much time, it's got to be done now.'

Hands waved in the air, and the motion was carried. Rapidly the chamber emptied into the main body of the church.

Seats began to be chosen on the hard stone pews of the chapel, where nothing need be reserved as the women were so few. If it were to be done at all tradition demanded an appropriate place, and in this case it was under the eyes of St Lucinia herself. Patricia was at once in her element as officiating priest behind the altar, insisting that ancient ritual must be observed fully, and pursuing very officiously her earlier view that the men had got off far too lightly. It was a complication that Freda could have done without, but Patricia was the religious authority, and in the church she was on sure ground for insisting on how the task was to be carried out.

The prelate melted away into the background with a smile creasing her face, evidently relishing her victory, whilst others in the church winced knowing that a 'stone-age' operation would entail unnecessary suffering and besides assail their ears unnecessarily.

Freda appeared in front of the congregation. 'Hazel, and you too Bernadette, would you please stand guard at the door.' The seats were vacated rather reluctantly; Hazel thinking it the lot of the newcomer, but knowing for Bernadette it would be because she was too volatile to trust – especially watching Annita do something rather delicate. Without any vestige of hurry, the two retrieved their weapons from the rear of the church and moved towards the door. They found Maureen and Maria waiting very impatiently for them, supporting either end of the first stretcher, all ready to place it upon the altar.

The racket outside seemed to increase five-fold as Hazel moved into the anteroom situated in the outermost skin. She looked outside to where the gatehouse was rocking from side to side under the combined assault. Everybody had said that it was secure enough, but this was now her responsibility and her doubts were multiplying several-fold as she watched. Hazel brought Parsnip to the anteroom door, then dallied for she could see Bernadette was

208

verging upon tears. Anger filled every part of a disagreeable face as Bernie braced her frame to launch the vitriolic emotion that was all wound up and certain to fly once it was packaged in words.

'I hate her, she didn't have need to say sitch a cruel t'ing. I, I can't help having me flat chest, can I?' She smote the inner doorway, then catching sight of the stretcher with a man on it, her mouth tightened and shut, at last aware there were ears other than Hazel's. Hazel put an arm round her shoulders, and stood in the doorway with her.

'You are young, give yourself time, soon enough you will have a figure for them to envy.' A scream rent the air, cutting into her last words.

Bernadette stood on tiptoe trying to see down the aisle, her whole demeanour changing as she homed in to what was afoot. 'Nita's not so much as cut him yet, 'tis jus a sprinklin o' spirit.' Bernadette's voice was charged with intrigue and gathering momentum. A further scream moved Hazel out of the anteroom, realizing full well that Bernadette was intent upon delivering a commentary, and that was likely to include the tantalizing of ears on the stretcher with blood-curdling comment. As for herself, Annita had told her all she needed to know; it sounded grotty enough without the screams. For a new arrival the original incision was always made before the subject came to his senses, using a razor blade taken from one of the many that turned up in shaving kits. With an insensible subject the cutting into testicle would be painless, but what was proposed would be flint knife surgery that totally disregarded the patient – even the sewing up with prepared sheep gut was bound to make huge demands upon the men.

The noises outside commanded Hazel's attention, as the gate-house heaved in a strange fashion; she could see it grinding and growing in size against the wall as it slipped its moorings. The bounce when it came took her by surprise; such a huge but light structure, and then there were men behind it. Hazel immediately mounted and although close by on the horse, hesitated with lance in hand, conscious that calling the others was just as important. Parsnip collided with the thin envelope, barging it out the way until she could see there was nothing visible to attack, just backs making a quick exit.

Was there a whole row crouched in the depression? Hazel approached the pit cautiously, her eyes diverted momentarily by a familiar figure fleeing the scene. Instantly the internal shaft of emotion smote and devastated her soul, whilst her eyes still scanned the ridge for activity. The area ahead of the gatehouse pit had evacuated; there was nobody there. Parsnip stopped when he came to the edge of the trench, and she saw that it was still a good temporary defensive barrier nevertheless. They cantered round the village space, finding nobody there to challenge, until at last she was back knocking with her lance upon the anteroom; its noise brought out the startled face of Bernadette, a face which very quickly disappeared.

Shortly afterwards Annita was in view, mounting; but not before Hazel was chasing off again upon hearing suspicious noises coming from the pool gatehouse. The men had obviously skirted the village via the pool in order to mount a surprise attack on a softer target. Both horses were soon ranged alongside the bubble ready to meet the danger, for even Hazel knew that this gatehouse was not robust like the other one. The men were evidently aware that pool barriers were absent, for it was not a route they had ever used. They were not vociferous this time, but going quietly about dismantling the second gatehouse – just a shuddering of the gatehouse frame revealed a presence inside.

Jackie and Frances were evident now at the other end of the village, both mounted and pushing the buckled main gatehouse back to where it nestled close to but behind its normal position. The friends stood there guarding, equally quiet and all ready to spring a surprise counterattack on that congested space inside. They listened to metallic noise and watched the figures moving inside the pool gatehouse. It was clear to Hazel and Annita that the men were now viewing a gatehouse rather as a bridge across any further pit barrier. The intruders had probably used a saw on the outside latch, which if used again would have no difficulty in cutting the flimsy latch to the village side. Even as they watched, a narrow strip of metal flickered in and out of the space between door and sphere; the door's fastening shed metal filings at a fast rate and was within seconds of failure. Hazel manoeuvred Parsnip to block the door, waving wildly for Jackie.

Annita, from her high position on Cauliflower, watched the saw as if mesmerized, but was also aware of hanging electric connections near her which spanned the gap from roof to gatehouse. She stretched out towards the nearby terminal block and pulled, yanking on the wires until they parted company with whatever held them. The wires came loose in her hand, and she thrust bare ends forwards to the door metalwork. There was a cry, then a silence in which she dropped the line allowing it to swing away, sparking and buzzing. As the lights high above them flickered on and off repeatedly she quickly dismounted. The gatehouse structure heaved and danced about, as the crush inside stampeded out through the external door.

Annita threw back the remnants of the securing lever and entered. Upon the floor lay one little body flat and still. Another man kneeling had toppled sideways, but was now stirring, a much larger individual. Hazel recognised Harold as the labourer with an earring who dug charcoal, and grabbing an arm dragged him towards the door with Annita adding her weight on the other arm. Instantly Maureen took hold and the bewildered labourer, still suffering from shock, was dragged away to be fastened with rope.

As they moved him away Jackie passed them by, dismounting as she went, to run off with lance in hand through the gatehouse. Once outside with the lights above flickering and barely touching the dark space areas she could barely see, but shadowy figures were retreating into the tunnel ahead. There was no way of knowing just where the men were going, so she stayed to guard the tunnel, waiting for those behind her to clear the gatehouse. It could be that the intruders were just around the next corner all ready to sweep back.

Annita, still inside, looked at the white beard lying propped up in the wall curve where she had put him, deciding his head had probably taken a knock from Harold's galvanized reaction to shock. He was breathing easily, so she grabbed him up and carried him to the village side of the gatehouse. Annita knew that a threat still remained and rushed back into the gatehouse to join forces with Jackie; the couple immediately retrieved a heavy bar of copper with a chisel-like end, which had been left behind. It proved invaluable along with extra rope to jam the outer door shut, enough to feel safe, but its mere presence left them both looking thoughtful. Hazel had remained in the doorway on her return, intending to remain as back-up. And here she trembled as she relived her dilemma-packed action slowly winding down that buoyed up feeling. It was remembering the sight of another similar copper bar that quickly took away the euphoria, and left her completely gutted. Until the women cleared the area Jackie stayed on with her, whilst Frances remained guarding the main gatehouse.

White beard had a bump on his head, vacantly blinking his eyes and still looking frail. The other fellow, now more himself, stayed defiant and his looks proclaimed contempt for everybody there. That was the position when Freda arrived fresh from her surgery, wiping still-wet hands down her dress, quite certain in the knowledge that it was she who would have to sort out the aftermath. Her hurried arrival suggested that the church operation was over, this fact confirmed by the number of heads poking out of the anteroom door.

Without hesitation and in the shortest possible time Freda took charge; she stood beside the horses listening to individual accounts of recent events. 'We have no need to discuss this at all,' Freda said quietly to Annita and Hazel. 'Maria's suggestion has put me in mind of our pet plants; she is right about their appetite, it does need to be kept sharp. The old man, I agree is no more than a bystander – he can witness Harold's departure and take the news to the other men.'

Freda stooped to address the tattooed man sitting on the ground with his hands tied; arrogantly he looked straight past her as she pronounced sentence. 'You are to be expelled, do you understand?' The man that they called Harold remained impassive, and the ghost of smile lingered on his defiant face – did he know?'

The consequences following on this decision entailed a marshalling of the women bystanders, who first scoured the locality from hunt cave to pool, and only then moved their prisoners into the entrance chamber. Harold was quickly released from his bounds and still rubbing wrists was shoved in the right direction, walking rapidly forwards across the chamber, as he must have been acutely aware he was targeted by no less than three crossbows. Whether he recognised this as an execution walk or not, nobody knew, but as Annita said afterwards, nobody cared. 'He deserves his fate, because he came within an ace of penetrating the village fortifications, with goodness knows how many would be murderous specimens behind him. That makes him the kind of gang leader with initiative that we could well do without.' White beard had stood watching him go and so there would be no rescue attempt for Harold, he was gone and seen to go. What was in the old man's mind was unknown, he looked perplexed as he turned and was marched back to join the other two. Even as the last of the women left, the excited swirl of colour upon the chamber walls and creepers stretching at the sentry base were simple indications for those versed in the secrets of the Styx chamber that the giant gourds were busy.

Not possessing the main gatehouse meant that the release route had to be through the engineers' cavern. The church captives were now parted from their stretchers, and with hands retied behind their backs they moved along at slow pace. Their white, drawn complexions were preoccupied, with movement not top priority, but they had to be moved before there were further aggressive moves intended to free them. The whole engineer population shortly watched the procession en route as it passed through the huts. No one in the procession thought that the men watching did not know what was happening, and to reinforce that impression no one asked. Carrying their weapons conspicuously the women moved towards the big double gates; gates that quickly swung wide open and discharged the captives – their ordeal was over. Immediately the gates banged shut behind them – almost on the heels of white beard.

Freda was waiting as the women returned. Speedily she addressed them, knowing they wanted to do little now but disperse and eat. 'Tonight we shall all use the dormitory area in the church, for it is not safe yet. Let me say from all of us, a great big thank you to Annita and Hazel, for they have done very well today! Arrange between yourselves to keep watch during the night, and for those resting, sleep well for we shall have a busy day tomorrow whether or not we are still at war.'

22

Morte d'Arthur

A thin line of engineers watched the huge double gates close with a thud; the jingle of keys mingled with harness, but rang loud in their hostile silence. Horses with women on their backs all engaged in an about-turn, their interest in spectators purely tactical. It was a rare display of their armoury to the engineers, employing sufficient weaponry to perhaps deter them from openly siding with the other men. The earlier abortive attack evidently had support from engineers, so there was an element of warning here. The pageant was not inclined to dally after discharging the captives, it moved off at pace leaving the men downhearted and still smarting from the setbacks of their offensive.

The men had barely returned to camp when news of approaching horsewomen broke. The gates had not been closed as yet and there was a rush to close them, for to be found with them open would irreparably show that they had keys. Barely winning the race had left them full of tension, and this was only part dispelled by being able to make an ironical slow handclap as the horses turned about. Red pointed after them. 'That's what we have to work on next,' he said enthusiastically to Marc. 'New weapons can make what they have obsolete; and as it's only us that have the brains and means to make them, we have all the advantages for that sort of battle. Not that a few bright ideas now wouldn't be out of place before the next clash with them commences.'

Terry, standing with them, groaned, he wanted nothing to do with their internal war, for his mind was still concentrating on the ladders. Still he juggled the different widths, and from what he knew of their tread sizes he was slowly realizing how unlikely it was that any pair would come together. He walked back to the hut containing a chair for him, dreaming of tying misfit ladders together and juggling them upon the high mobile platform he now often visited to collect bats. He was still absent in mind and staring into space when Leon passed him a mug of steaming drink. They chatted, and Terry learned of the second reverse in a day – the pool gatehouse rout. Leon was much filled with admiration of Harold, telling of his gallant attempt to enter the village, and sadly of failure also – not that Terry knew the man.

'And come to that, where's Arthur? I haven't seen him since. I wonder if he was still out there when they closed the gates. I had better tell Red.' Leon rose and left his own steaming hot mug, heading for the door. With some relief Terry returned to his dreaming. Things always seem so much more possible immediately after you conjure them up; but continuing on with available material makes for boring complications, enough soon to make the eyelids droop.

'Come on, young fellow, no sleeping now, we have things to do!'

Terry opened bleary eyes to see Red standing there jovial and loud, behind him stood Marc. 'Come on, let's be having you!'

He struggled to his feet, falling in behind the group of some half dozen who were set on course for the big gates. Immediately behind him came the sound of wheels grating as a small cart rolled along pulled by two of the men. Terry could see Marc dropping back from the leading group towards him and accordingly set a faster pace. For Marc there had been no catnap to ease things along, but he just sounded keen as ever.

'It's night in the village, and they have only posted a few internal guards, so during the night we have a good opportunity to erase all signs of our involvement. I have had a long chat with Red. It seems he's a marine engineer, and there is a lot he and I have in common. If we help him I'm sure he will help us, for how easily we get out will probably depend on the continuing goodwill of these men.'

Relief swept through Terry's mind, as for a little while now he had been thinking that his engineer friend had lost sight of their aims, given that he was mixing so purposefully with the opposition's top man. Once again they left the big double gates behind. Terry appreciated another chance to breathe relatively fresh air, and see in much better light. His mind soared, the new boundaries being much appreciated by him after his recent but long time in close confinement. On the lengthy incline bordering an artificial

215

pond the cart slowed markedly and men laboured to move it on, so that both he and Marc were soon helping to push. Terry noticed as he did so a sprinkling of fine sand was dropping from the cart and getting lost into the gravel.

As soon as the hill was behind them, Marc continued. 'We lost a man. He ran the heavy works team and did a bloody good job on it too, that was until those bitches expelled him from the caves. No one knew it could be done, and that's why we are all thinking of making a mass exodus later tonight whilst the pool route is still open.'

Terry's mind ran amok. If it was that simple why hadn't he thought of it first? Marc's voice continued over the top of much confused thought flashing through his head as he wondered why he had dismissed something so basic. Marc's voice was beginning to resolve again, he was enumerating various engineer accounts. 'No one seems to agree on exactly how they entered this place, but a loss of consciousness followed by imprisonment by the women is everybody's common experience. We only have their word on almost anything we know because they simply don't tell us anything beyond how to work for them. They are not short of luxuries in that citadel of theirs; it is us who keep them in place with our daily work. Like superior predators they are not beyond setting traps for innocent travellers; which in my mind puts them on a level with spiders. The women say there is no way out of here alive; but can we believe them? I remember being told to jump into a furnace reflection and chance making an exit, even though it was not the place I entered. There's just one old gaffer not going, because some time ago he wanted a small pulley and Jackie obtained something he recognised as his own belt. He said it was so large on him that he knew he would be an oddity if ever he left here. So discounting any others like him, I reckon there will be no more than half a dozen of us left tomorrow. As I know extremely well the routes through the caves, I think I can help by leading the way; anyway that was the offer I made to Red.'

The cart skirted the bend and was all set to enter the village arch; they fell back to help swivel it round. Sand began to be pushed out over the cart front to quieten the wheels and they eased quietly through the arch. Here Terry tried to offset his sighting of Hazel, using the memory of little men falling into the hole, and wondering only now if they had all climbed out. The

216

cart stopped before a circular pit, perhaps six feet deep and barely lit from the now dimmed village night illumination. Marc pointed diagonally across the hole where part of the ram was visible, standing up on end. 'I would say they've used it as a ladder.'

Red signalled for silence, then without hesitation, two small ladders were taken off the cart and smoothly slid down into the trench. Moments later a wall of dense white smoke lazily drifted upwards. Terry could see that it was coming from ignited material they had deliberately placed on the village side of the trench. Several other lamps were lit on the floor of the hole and following the ladders down he saw the body of an unfortunate soul, his head crushed and broken open. 'It's Arthur,' he gasped, appalled that someone he knew had perished. Red took it all in his stride, methodically dealing with the problem below. Two men descended and elevated the battering ram, smeared with what could only be Arthur's blood, and until it cleared the pit both ladders were heavily put to good use. The ram was recovered and laid close to the cart, leaving a ladder free to convey Arthur. Deferentially his remains were elevated out of the hole, and only then did the cart approach the pit to tip its load. With a rush, sand slid from the cart, controlled and added to by the single sweeper who had formerly been clearing up spillages behind the cart. His broom remained busy feeding ever more sand to those below working in the pit, as they rapidly put it to good use erasing all footprints. Finally the men underneath added some more powder to their still-burning smokescreen upon the pit edge, after which they climbed out to pull up their remaining ladder.

Terry looked down. The bloody scene had been wiped away as if it had never happened, but right in front of him was the grisly evidence of Arthur's body laid very dead upon the ladder. Everyone set to work making sure there was nothing left to see, even sweeping the remaining grains of spilt sand into the hole with their hands. They left the perimeter quite clean and, hearing no reaction from the village to their smokescreen, they relaxed precautions on noise. Terry imagined that even if a guard did look towards this darkened corner from the village, the hazy appearance beyond their beloved gatehouse might well not be noticed. It was only his guilty feelings that half expected the figure of Hazel to be investigating them, and to loom up out of that smoky wall.

The men stowed the ram inside the cart, then balanced the

spare ladder lengthwise over it, lashing Arthur's ladder to the top. It was all over, the cart rattled off back the way it had come. But there was no intention to return to base, the wheels bumped along crushing plants and breaking down terraces, as they headed with very little care towards the men's swimming pool. Arthur's ladder was unloaded and carried below, passing to and fro between them as awkward bends were rounded. At length they arrived at the pool, where Terry saw sticks being lit which produced much smoke along with the light, accompanied by a strong smell of tallow. The first two men clambered into the water, where they stood chest high to take the ladder. Terry reluctantly got in as well, and was surprised by the water; it was so warm. Arms supported an awkward load, which swayed in and out of balance above their heads, whilst underfoot the uneven bottom had them sway even more; the net result made waves that wetted everybody up to the chin. Soon they were entering a tunnel where the water dropped to waist high, but therein dwelt large, awkward stones that slipped and wobbled about underfoot. The funereal tread slowed even more as they progressed.

After what seemed an age, the smoky illumination abruptly faded on those behind, as the burning sticks in front were raised to view a much larger chamber – the women's swimming pool. The bearer party came to a dead stop at its edge for here the water increased in depth sharply. Terry released his hold to push beyond the front men, there he swam a few strokes and trod water ready to fend the ladder off to the bank. Marc joined him, and together they provided support until the ladder's forepart rested upon level ground. As it grounded, they hauled themselves up on the bank and retrieved what was now their end, assisting the ladder in its forward progress. But despite their individual action, the whole operation had become bogged down with those who could not swim, and two needed to be rescued from the mouth of the overflow duct.

With the biggest obstacle overcome, the small party made its way through yet another fonz-lit tunnel leading from the pool, and here the torch-bearing men extinguished their smoky brands. Soon they passed the rows of bubble cells; a memory only too recent and unpleasant for Terry and Marc, who both could still remember the one in particular that had held them. Terry was even uneasier as they reached the hunt cave's entrance, remembering the ruthless

218

way they had been co-opted; perhaps they had good reason for distrusting the women just like Marc had said. Soon the pall party had entered, and arrived to stand in the warmth of the 'great destructor', for it was here that Leon stopped them. He reasoned that if it were fit enough for the incineration of Cora, then it was good enough for her husband also. Leon, not being one for public oration, bent his head in respect and sorrow, before cutting through the creeper holding his friend to the ladder. Solemnly the ladder was tilted until Arthur joined his wife in an inferno, a place where his ashes would mix with hers – impure though they were known to be.

The cremation was accomplished in so short a time that the bearers still dripped water from the swimming pool, but having accomplished their intended task, the party ventured no further into the hunt cave. Instead they reversed the ladder out of the cave and the column moved off still clutching its light frame, and that held good until they reached the narrow corridor between bubble cells. Red held up his hand and they all halted, for here was where they intended an escape on a major scale; their party should at least investigate the route out. They wandered into the cave, walking there with so little care compared to the women, to whom it was sacred. Even without a full knowledge of the place, the chamber's warmth, and the odd moving lights expanding and contracting rapidly upon its walls, soon filled them all with a sense of unease. Their movements became less rash as they progressed: Terry in particular, felt the fine hairs upon his arms standing on end in the charged atmosphere.

Without the inhibitions felt by a small number, the remainder pushed towards the centre, heading for a scattering of objects that were seemingly abandoned near the cave's far wall. Some saw it as fruit dropped from an overhanging tree, for overhead hung many creepers and these questionably were part of the dark masses standing in high crevices of the recessed cliff that they had come forward enough to see. The men stared at their fruit in growing horror, for on close approach the first object resolved itself into a sheepskin mound that was stained a wet red and presumably was a very bloody jacket, one that was common wear for them all. Just beyond it they encountered a substantial rounded blob of offal, which was bloodstained enough to be allied with the sheepskin jacket. Sickeningly the organ appeared to be human, shimmering red brown in the light; raw meaty veins and sinews hung out at either end. Less obvious to those just behind the firstcomers, the meaty blob was gripped at these far points and was ensnared between two sets of fibrous coils, the coils gripped sunk deep in furrows pulling whatever it was taunt. Somewhere in the middle of these another root contracted about it with a bramble-like strand sinking a ligature into and around the surface; this hairy fibrous filament went deep, causing a bulb on either side. Suddenly the organ split in two, squirting a fluid into the air that splattered the watchers and caused them to draw back in horror and then rush back again, assembling in the cell alley. The first to arrive at the cells dashed headlong into their own ladder, so incensed with fright were they.

Marc's attention was elsewhere, being caught up by an odour he recognised from his own expertise, and which diverted him towards the extreme right-hand corner of the chamber. Here he felt the standing wave that suggested electrical interaction of some magnitude relatively close. This helped him shy away from the corridor he recognised as his entry point. Where the gully opened there glinted something metallic on the floor and so falling upon his knees he cautiously reached around the corner, then braving the storm of electrical emission grabbed it. He was looking at a ring, rather too small to be worn on the finger. It was then that he realized something behind his back had caused the party to retreat, and that the others were calling his name. He dropped the ring and looked towards shocked faces spattered with blood, before joining in their retreat. He completely failed to get answers to his obvious questions.

Pangs of hunger, coupled with the shock, had Terry feeling sick, but he soldiered on amid companions who followed the route towards the pool, thinking to himself that soon there was heaven sent water to wash this foul stuff off. But having arrived at the junction, Red turned away, and Terry soon found himself heading towards a second if slightly smaller gatehouse. The lights here were dead, and the pool gatehouse was simply outlined against the diffuse light of the village. Red signalled a stop. He felt pretty queasy himself and knew everybody must be feeling likewise, but this must be attempted at least, as there were no doubts now they would all stay. Quietly, Red approached the gatehouse door, and producing a knife cut through the strands of a cord presenting itself at the door's edge; the door was then worked back and forth. This puzzled Terry until he saw the misty outline of a lever jammed against the door inside. Very carefully, the men inserted one leg of a ladder through the door's pliable upper part, causing its fabric to bend back and forth. The ladder was then wriggled until a noisy thump indicated that the lever had fallen inside.

Unfortunately, this noise was instantly followed by a crash, as the unrestrained ladder hit something. There was a shout from inside the village: Marc dashed in and grabbed the copper bar wrestling it through the door. Terry leant a hand, heaving a sigh of relief on spotting the purpose in all of this; they were not raiding the village as he had supposed but just removing any evidence of their involvement. The whole party moved away smartly with mission accomplished, the sounds of alarm petering away as they hurried down the tunnel slope towards the women's swimming pool. Shortly afterwards they were relieved to be splashing about in the welcoming water, washing particles of Harold's guts from their bodies.

Once the ladders, ram and cart arrived back home inside the double gates, the engineers were enthusiastically moving off again. Terry decided to stay with them, for this time they seemed happy in almost a triumphant way and headed off in a quite different direction. It was all exuberance now, and the engineers sang songs of doubtful moral worth with gusto as they tramped. The tunnel opposite soon contained their noise surrounding them with air that was laced with more than a trace of something savory, an aroma that itself caused a quickening in pace. With spirits rising, they entered a twisted, deeply rutted tunnel lit by a couple of bulbs about halfway through. The smoky smell of cooking was now pungent, steering Terry much as it steered the others. With saliva stirring he hurried round heaps of stones, towards a row of strong, purpose-built houses that were close ahead now. On a wide area before the cottages there burned a bonfire and about it were many small men eating roasted meat. Heaped upon a pile of stones over the hot embers of fire were whole chickens and all about the fire stretched a wide circle of blackened straw ash. Engineers grabbed at meat cooked and ready to eat. Terry was quick to get himself a decent carcass. After the first bites came the discovery that there were other goodies, a fermented beer and some flat unleavened bread that tasted just like heaven.

Terry sat just slightly away from them all, enjoying the plenty around him – noticing that in the background Red was talking earnestly to a group of men. Marc had been seemingly lecturing them earlier, but was now uninvolved. Soon he caught Terry's eye and came over.

'Are you ready for seconds?' Marc asked, hardly able to contain himself with good humour.

Terry looked at him as if he were cracked. 'I've eaten my fill,' he cried. 'There's nothing left.' He turned his head to see any delicacy he might have missed. 'Didn't you see them all slink off?' queried Marc. 'The others have gone for a helping of lamb – come on let's go.' With a quick look at Red still talking, they set off, passing rows upon rows of sun lamps above a crop.

Terry thought this confusing. 'How come all this feasting, we lost on every front didn't we?'

Marc laughed, for he already had put the same question. 'It seems whenever the two sides fall out with one another, deficiencies in stock can be blamed upon the rioting, but nobody ever knows who the rioters are. Even without that as a background there were big meals being prepared around here anyway, because nearly everyone was leaving. They are likely to stay put now and that's what Red is organizing at the moment.'

'You seemed to be lecturing them all.' Terry's full condition had left him receptive.'

'I told them that I could faintly smell ozone, and noticed that there were signs of electrical discharge in that same avenue the women allowed poor Harold to take. That route was good for nothing but murder; it was as well we inspected it first.'

Again there was the smell of roast meat in the air, which at least overwhelmed Marc's desire to talk and he headed for the fire dispersing the extra meaty odour of lamb. Even Terry was drawn that way despite his blown condition. They strode ankle deep through some obnoxious smelly toadstool towards the nearby hamlet of mud-daubed huts. Right in the middle of a central clearing burned a huge open fire, but lacking burnt straw stub-ends this time. Here in much the same manner hunks of lamb were spread out on hot stones surrounding the fire. Several of the engineers were there, and being treated as heroes by the residents who surrounded them.

The songs were getting cruder and taken up less positively now, probably due to the distinctly different nature of the fermented liquor which was more abundant here than their previous stop; sheer volume saw to it that everybody was drunk. Marc nudged Terry, as their teeth engaged in juicy meat running with mutton fat.

'They are grateful that we gave them the means to more than dent those gatehouses. I think when we next do battle the women will get quite a few extra surprises.'

'You sound as if you have decided to stay. Terry said. 'Why ever do we need to take sides?'

'There are at least three reasons: the foremost one being, I have found out that the men preceding me in the job have not lived very long. For a second, it is evident we have to be in one camp or the other, and the women have already decided that we are not in theirs. Third, they are unlikely to help us escape; but the men are.' Marc's voice had a hint of resignation in it as if he knew that the future was loaded against him, but he was shortly passed another jug of the local brew and that was the last sensible thing that he said. The night passed in a sort of fiesta, one that Terry wouldn't have believed possible here, especially if someone had told him about it yesterday. Among a rowdy group of engineers some hours later, they arrived back at the hut to fall on Arthur's bed giggling, and did not wake until next morning, each flat out upon half a bed.

23

Bump in the Night

Maria had been up since the early hours preparing a meal. She was not in her favourite surroundings, nor would she be for the duration of hostilities, but the church kitchen was a good substitute, and one that she personally kept well primed for emergencies. Here were maintained all of the stores necessary to sustain a warrior's appetite, and provide the right background for victory. It happened often enough for Maria to know the importance of her job as being a vital factor in any struggle. When the women occupied their 'wasps nest' as the former village men termed it, they were quite certain to be well fed throughout any conflict.

Upstairs there was a whole room of non-perishable victuals and to balance this one of the roof bubble cells was maintained full of water. Yet another cell contained methane gas, piped so as to be held under water pressure. These were her vital supplies because everything else could be sabotaged. She was thankful that the electricity had not failed this time, and saw that as giving a clear indication that the engineers had not yet openly sided with the rebels.

As the smell of fresh bread baking wafted through the building, sleepy people began to hurry through their morning ablutions, for such an incentive was absent in normal times. Once there however, the selection would not match what the food house usually delivered, for their wealth in stored rations could not compete with the usual freshness.

Breakfast was served, or rather delivered to the conference room, as this was the custom. The hubbub of chatter about the table steadily mounted, as they gathered to discuss the disturbance during the night. An abortive attempt to enter yet again from the poolside of the village caused an emergency turnout and loss of a good hour of sleeping. Everyone thirsted for news – of which there was none. Instead there was news of what they would be doing today, as breakfast time was Freda's delegation time; she had her flock gathered in one place all ready for detail, and detail she did.

With typical efficiency, Maureen had chosen the 'four' from yesterday to do the first watch, hopefully keeping them fresh for the morning expedition. If there were still hostility, then the best group to take action would be there facing it. But even before they started, there were things to be certain about elsewhere. Not only Maria but both Freda and Jackie had serious doubts about the engineers, suspecting that recent action from the agricultural workers was uncharacteristically efficient. Wearing swords the pair headed for the engineers, whilst Maureen tailed them, as a necessary insurance armed with something more telling.

The signs were good as Red listened to his instructions and detailed the men. Freda was deliberately 'pushy', but Red did not even look as if it bothered him. 'I want at least two of the pool grids secured today, and you will see that the fixing is accessible from our side only. Secondly, the main gatehouse must be reinstalled where it was, plus some additional fastening in the rock. By early afternoon we shall have horses available to help squeeze it back; then it is yours to bang out the dents. Thirdly, the pool gatehouse needs new hinges and its bolt on the front door replaced; that I expect to be started at the very least today.'

Red looked at her and smiled. 'We shall do our best, your majesty.'

There was a distinct hint of sarcasm in the way he said it. Freda was quick to respond with a terse response. 'You will complete that as an absolute minimum before the main meal of the evening is served. I shall be watching you closely.'

If Red had any doubts beforehand that Freda did not trust him, he could tell from the tone of her voice that they were justified. Jackie meanwhile had lined the engineers up, and counted them all present. The extras, Terry and Marc, she singled out to return with Freda. Task complete, Jackie moved over to the gate intending to stay in the most strategic position here until the job was complete.

Already the 'four' had checked out nearby surroundings such as the hunt cave and women's pool. Pausing at the engineers' gatehouse, mounted and expecting shortly to pass Jackie on their way out, they waited to collect the most modern weapon in their armoury from Freda and Maureen who were on their way back

In the village normality was returning, with Maria deciding she had a choice of workplace, and promptly returning to her old kitchen with a few provisions for catering, anticipating at least some shortages in supply. She was ready and keen to drive her staff hard the moment they appeared, but their holiday had not left them full of energy and verve; neither of them looked very fresh or keen for everyday work when they arrived. It was a discrepancy that caused the eagle-eyed cook to ply them with questions. A curiously reluctant explanation emerged concerning a shortage of beds, or even space enough to lie on the floor in the place where they had been sent, but luckily there was not really time for an inquisition. Maria was not wasting time on prying into their hang-over and many other tag ends that might shed light on what they had been doing. There were meals to prepare rapidly, giving priority of output to the agricultural men's tricycles, despite her workforce being aware no one would be in a hurry to collect. From her standpoint, Maria knew well she must not leave the indigenous population free to carry on using their own initiative.

Freda was busy out and around the village, in particular she went to see the main gatehouse from the other side, and by the time Red arrived she was probing in the pit sand using a long rod. 'I cannot understand why sand that has always been in short supply should have been dumped down this hole. Do you imagine it is covering something up?'

'They installed this using cement, Ma'am, and would have needed sand to make it.'

Freda shook her head doubtfully. 'I thought that sand might be used to cover bodies down there, and they would eventually smell. At least my check will have saved you taking it out another day.' She smiled sweetly and moved on.

In the entrance of the hunt cave a restlessly wandering Freda encountered Rose and Poppy working the loom. When they saw her they stopped and brought out something small and shining, which Poppy held up for her to inspect. Rose struggled with her inherent hesitation, and spoke for the two of them. 'Poppy found this in the middle of the Styx cave this morning, and we think it was from the man who was expelled yesterday.' Freda took the piece and turned it over, it looked like a gold ring, which could have been shaped for wearing through an ear lobe; this was the first hard evidence that Harold was no more.

The patrol headed out of the engineers' gates, making for a nearby division in the inter-cavern tunnel. They were soon doing yesterday's trip in reverse by taking the tortuous low route. In the place where they emerged there should have been men handling rock; instead they found just the few who remained reclining on the flatter rocks looking mutinous and with menacing looks directed towards them. Frances dismounted and approached them. Hazel did not need prompting to reach for her crossbow, which like the others' had already been primed, but lacked a bolt.

Hazel felt uneasy again like she had last time in this place, raising her bow from the pannier, and feeling a wave of panic with heart pounding in her breast as they waited. She copied her companions, who with weapons loaded pointed them downwards. Frances found no problems with this, and unlike Hazel recognized dejection when she saw it. Other men materialized from around the stones as she checked them off. There remained only a need to choose a successor who could lead the team in Harold's place, and her arms were soon waving the workers together to learn who was boss. The men turned and moved off to fetch their tools, at which sign Hazel felt truly grateful; the others merely relaxed and tucked crossbow into pannier. One team at least had been properly accounted for and could be left to resume work under new management. The heavy team soon passed out of sight as the morning patrol wound its way through the many large rocks about them; they were now heading towards the grain hamlet of stone and thatch cottages.

Arriving at their destination the horses had to traverse a large blackened patch that lay across the pathway near to the first cottage. There were none of the usual signs of morning bustle, not a sign of the men who normally thronged the place. This looked rather more menacing to Annita who decided she would investigate on foot with Bernadette. The two dismounted, covered by Hazel and Frances who contained their friends' horses between their own, standing sentry back to back, each with a bolt in the crossbow. This suited Hazel who had at last decided she was equal to any enemy they could throw at her.

For Annita and Bernadette things were not so straightforward, and so first they took a look at the burned-out fire. The tiny cereal ends were of burnt straw, and the large circle of greasy stones about a blackened centre told of feasting and plenty. There was nobody there at all, and so they entered the nearest house intending to progress along the row; but their effort was much slowed by caution and the possibility of booby-traps. Moving quietly and well prepared for hostilities, Bernadette hung back in each cottage covering Annita with a loaded pistol hidden inside a fold of material about her middle; the back-up passed over at the stable was needed here. But people were absent from their houses, and absent also from the granary workplace. There, grain stood ready for milling, but the flour bins seen yesterday were not visible.

Exhaustively the pair moved through the final cottages of the search, drawing blank until to the very last one where there was a murmuring of voices coming from the interior. Making a quick signal to the party on the fringes of the village to close in, they moved through the house. In a back room they discovered a gathering, and entered abruptly. There, two men lay on beds surrounded by some ten others with voices raised in heated discussion. Slowly the backs became faces as the door slammed back.

'Stay just where you are,' ordered Annita nervously. 'Tom, come here and explain what is happening.'

Tom ambled across the room, his fair complexion creased into a worried frown. 'Sorry, we didn't see you arrive. We have our patients to look after.' He waved his hand toward beds occupied by the castrates.

'You should all be at your tasks, including those two,' Annita said glowering at the men in bed. The group about the beds took a pace away, looking more like scolded pets than the enemy. The truth was clear; they were locked in a rebellious discussion where time did not matter. All looked uneasy, Tom especially, so Bernadette neatly rearranged a fold of material to carry the gun more inconspicuously and wandered further away from the room.

Within a short space of time the group had been counted, and allowed to disperse. Tom was further in difficulty over the agreed production when they reached the granary, for he could only find one bin containing flour, and even that had found its way out of the door. He was soon making promises to grind more, and after his promises were made he began to crave her understanding for his own position. 'When order breaks down and there is no food

228

provided, people will sneak off and disobey rules.' He pleaded for leniency in regard to his men. 'They are good workers, but when left to their own devices they can get up to mischief. But I was tending to my own people quite unaware of what might then be stolen from here; I was far too busy last night nursing those poor souls who arrived back mutilated.'

Annita remained visibly unimpressed. They had once again reached a familiar position, one of part apology and part plea. Such factors always featured in precedents from the past, and from this Annita sensed hostilities were over. Relieved, they moved on to Sam's area, finding yet another even more sizable blackened patch upon his land, and judging by the inroads made into an adjacent thicket of aerial roots it had been some blaze. Any check upon the still roaming flocks was impractical now, but Annita knew that a later party would assess the full extent of deficiency. The sheep she had signed over to the man the other day was obviously first in line to be reclaimed. She lined the men up who worked for Sam and soon everybody was accounted for, which was all that interested her just now. Sam's face did not beam quite so magnan-imously during the farewells, and in this respect it contrasted sharply with yesterday.

It would seem that the main reasons for their expedition were satisfied. They now could be reasonably sure the men had reverted to normal. The rest should have been easy, but it was not to be so when they came to the elders who had been first ones to object. The ones who tended fungi were surprisingly hostile. Nobody seemed to be at work, and wherever they went, scolding words had to be said before a count could take place. Even then insults were hurled at the women about torturing their captives and killing the bravest of them. Not knowing many had hurt themselves falling into the hole, none of the women quite understood this reaction. Bernadette suppressed the rebellious stirrings with the same gusto that caused Hazel to cringe on the last occasion. But doing so seemed to work, and in a very short space of time the old men were being coerced back into their individual place of work again. As they waited, watching her, Hazel had to admit privately to herself that Bernadette was a success in this field, and had more going for her as taskmaster than she would ever have. One old man in particular was known to Hazel and that was the one carried from the pool gatehouse. 'He is probably the one who has been stirring them up with tales from the village,' she observed to Annita.

By the time they returned, all four were feeling the strain and gladly left their horses in the stable area. They were obliged to enter the village over a temporary bridge, erected only that morning, and saw a huge gatehouse ball resting against the boundary wall ready to be drilled by the engineers. This was one day that would not be routine, they would not visit the pool, and nothing in the village would help them relax, food not being yet on tap in their normal haunts.

Freda was there at the very centre of things directing everybody in sight, and spared just time enough to hear their account before they too received jobs. Hazel she left until last. 'Come, this is a good moment to equip your hairdressing shop.' Freda led Hazel into Tanya's bubble house; this she had spared time to open up and fill time as she stood around this morning. Opening it served to maintain her presence outside supervising the engineers' effort, and keeping up a critical dialogue with Red whilst he was there in the village. There were items of Tanya's furniture, a small table and three chairs already separated from the disordered interior. Added to this was also a small pile of possible items she had displayed on the table. 'Look around and take anything that you want,' she urged before departing.

Freda retraced her steps, purposefully striding towards the little man who had been tailing her, and ducking out every time it seemed that their paths would actually cross. 'Leon, was there something you wanted?'

He looked at her with gratitude, the task was easier now, but he still had to tell a lie and he was not good at telling lies. Arthur has gone missing Ma'am, and I think he has fallen in the digester because the lid was off this morning. At the time I thought you ladies opened it up as you passed by, but now I think that's where he has gone all right.'

Freda took the short walk to the septic tank; such digesters she had always thought a hazard, quite apart from being an awful smell. Leon took the lid off, and the peculiarly revolting odour hit her forcefully. He looked down into its smelly, uneven, brown tarry content. 'I can't see him Ma'am, if he's down there he wouldn't have lasted long. I expect he will float later, all blown up like, but sure thing he's joined his missis.'

Freda turned away, appalled by both vision and smell. 'You had better close the lid,' she said faintly.

Leon swung the top section down until its metal edges met with a thump. He found a short rod nearby and held it up. 'It was due to be opened up yesterday and Arthur only had this to stir it with. The long one was in the village with the doors closed on it, so I guess he miscalculated and was just overcome by the fumes.'

Leon did a sort of sway towards the pot for good effect, but Freda had enough, she edged away before speaking. 'Maybe we do not need its gas now, I will find out. But be careful from now on, and have someone else standing by.' She turned, and made for the village, leaving Leon jubilant. He had carried it off; even the hiding of the long rod in the village just after the gates were open had not really been necessary.

Frances slipped inconspicuously through the engineers' gate-house and then met Freda face to face, which pulled her up short. 'We need the horses to push the gatehouse back into position,' cried Freda, very much as if she were expecting her. 'Can you bring them round now and enable the engineers to finish?' It was obvious that Frances didn't want to do it, and a whole lot of prevaricating in French was tried out to no avail as she searched among excuses. Doing it, they both knew, would stop her joining Jackie for at least an hour. 'That's just one of love's little disadvan-tages,' mused Freda, as she wended her way back to continue the supervision.

But the push took no more than half an hour; the big globe, still all lumps and bumps, did not need a lot of persuasion to resume its original resting place. Men removed much of the floor that was broken up inside, and began banging heavily at the worst dents bordering the outside door. After the expense of much energy and the bringing of further tools they had still made very little impression. Red stood with Freda, noticing her apprehension rise as they failed to find enough persuasion. He stiffened as through the clear material facing them he could see two of his men arrive with the heavy copper battering ram to hammer the curve back from those reluctant internal bulges. Whilst hearing the crash of heavy blows, and feeling his heart in his boots, Red felt rather than saw Freda slip away, her face taunt with consternation as she realized the implications of her discovery.

Hazel rummaged about in masses of stuff, still affected by the uncertain atmosphere that surrounded Terry in her mind. A conflict of interests and emotions began which was quite beyond her understanding. Through the mists of mind she saw piles of clothing, and scattered among it an occasional comb or other thing she might use, and such objects slowly kindled her into an overriding interest in the job. Such small finds as combs, cloths, scissors, even a candle for singeing were all worth having and slowly the tension eased. She had doubts about a bar of soap, but collected it for experimenting as dim memories told her that it did dubious things to hair and should be avoided. One thing she felt could turn out to be an asset was a personal stereo headset and tape player. What was on the tapes she couldn't be certain, but surely if the sound could be amplified then her shop could have music. There was more interest to be had in Tanya's domestic possessions, for bowl and water containers were likely to be of importance. Freda was there as she came out, and when shown the collection complimented her. 'I think that's enough to get you started, don't you? Can you use the Walkman?'

'I wondered if Terry or somebody could amplify it.' Hazel was feeling apologetic for an idea that had little to do with hair.

'Your Marc might be the right one to query that with.' Freda checked off what was on the pile. 'We could even get the engineers to make you curling tongs or curlers.' Freda knew she had spotted something vital that was missing. Almost talking to herself she carried on. 'I will speak with Jackie today.' Freda turned mid-sentence to face Red's back.

Red stood cursing as he viewed the main gatehouse with the crashing of the ram cum super hammer assaulting his ears with regularity – he should have foreseen it as the most likely tool to be picked out without any thought at all. His minions had not consulted him; if only they had he would have devised a scheme, but now was too late for recrimination.

Observing the engineer drove tongs from Freda's mind for the moment, and she said thoughtfully, 'There's something been going on that's very underhand out there. I have a feeling that we are a pace behind certain people, when in fact we ought to be one pace in front. We need something extra, something like the pit that nobody knew about, that pit may have saved us much more than we like to think. It is even possible, Hazel, that your men Terry and Marc, who are both into electrics and isolated here in the village, might be set the task of constructing an electric alarm. Assuming that we begin such a project now, in due course of time it will evolve into some kind of advance warning. This will need discussing at our weekly gathering because the others may have ideas. This evening I am due to see Eileen, Jackie and Annita, so if you have no objection about your men it will be discussed as a preliminary.'

The banging had ceased and Freda hurried towards the gate, leaving Hazel troubled, for the mere idea of trusting Terry with village security bothered her. Dinner would be late tonight; Freda had told her that Eileen had been dispatched to ensure all agricultural hamlets collected their midday meal a few hours late this afternoon. Apparently doing so would allow Maria to catch up with things, and placate the agricultural labourers whose work did not involve the restoring of village fortifications. And if the engineers were to have a deliberately delayed dinner, then the women could expect much the same in the name of security.

With the extra time available Hazel busied herself carrying her new table up through the staff walkway and into the room ascribed to hair treatment. Another series of trips, and bringing one chair along with several other smaller items, completed as much as the miserable girl wanted to do. Lacking enthusiasm she moped, sitting upon her single chair, in a room that was too empty to raise her spirits.

Relaxed now the long wait was over, Rose and Poppy waved Hazel to their table, bursting with excitement, for in Poppy's hands lay a heap of fine black mesh. Rose mouthed words that took time to sound, and when they did, they came with a rush. 'It's a petticoat for you, we couldn't do pink but we could do black.' Poppy let the fine woolly weave fall open, and whirled it around her with an unintelligible whoop. There was no getting away from them, it had to be tried on immediately, if not before.

Obligingly Hazel slipped away into her food house room and put it on, the heavy knit dress feeling a lot smoother than it did before. The slip between the layers made walking back comfortable and she glided in feeling like a mannequin, cheering as she saw everyone wanted to touch Poppy's creation. The stir she created heralded more loom work on the thin thread, as the idea was popular. Poppy had triumphed, her name now ascendant, with people remembering how they missed her odd plates, the ones so recently replaced with depressingly standard pottery.

Despite the successes of the day and the pleasures of being among friends, Hazel felt upset, desperately alone and quite unable to settle. Right at this moment she wanted arms to hold her tight; but Terry was a traitor and any idea of visiting him filled her with revulsion. Daytime merged into evening as she tried to sort out the empty room given to her for hairdressing, which was even more upsettingly not very far from his. Once again she sat upon her chair feeling all choked up and verging on tears. The afternoon's gains were there on the table, and she sat beside them without even trying to envisage how it all might fit together; the tears fell regardless.

Bernadette was with Marc as she returned to check on them, before finding her usual niche in the restaurant. She listened awhile at their door and the trivial teasing angered her. It would all end as a nothing that she could be sure, for the girl simply hadn't grown up or acquired a woman's appetite. The system here she felt had shortcomings where Bernadette was concerned, in her mind's eye she took Marc's part and felt angry for him.

Hazel sipped thankfully at the wine carafe brought to her by Maria, which helped to bury her own troubles and concentrate more on his. Her friends better knew the nature of Marc. Annita and Maria for instance had both contradicted her madman image, giving assurances that he was really nice. In a way this was irrelevant, because she was not sure that she had forgiven him, but she lacked Terry's strong arms about her and his were available.

The evening wore on, some hot rolls were sweetening the air, but today she didn't want them, such thoughts even made her feel sick; it was an odd feeling having your stomach replaced by an ache. There were doors moving. Bernadette emerged and seemed to float through the eating area. Hazel half realized it was her own drinking rather than reality that caused the girl to look inebriated. Marc arrived and quietly waited for her to rise; he seemed to be bulging into that costume of his, which she thought was predictable after Bernadette's teasing. Back home she clung, seeing Marc into his room and then tripping back a little later when she had decided to bring him the fleecy duvet as a present. That was shortly before

234

she accompanied him onto the bed to see if it were comfortable. Hazel alone now could free him from the pressures of his own hormones. There had to be some forgiving and now she thought was a good time to do it.

24

The Goldfish Piggy Bank

A succession of successful bank robberies monopolized the news; becoming instant headlines in all the newspapers of southern France. It was the sheer speed and brute force of the crime which immediately dictated the media coverage – three banks within three days. The papers were soon in full cry and by the fourth day they had turned to criticizing the police. That unwelcome jolt of public opinion came as a bolt from the sky for the many police chiefs comfortably situated in their citadel headquarters. So it happened rather late that Claude's superior began frantically collecting evidence from each crime scene and eventually arriving in the Lutz-St-Saveur Commissariat.

Each of the three robberies had made a serious dent in public confidence for the police. The shock was all the greater because these were otherwise quiet law-abiding districts that had been subjected to a gratuitous spate of multiple killings. The random-ness of these acts had everyone feeling insecure, and the acts of near lunacy alone commanded full media coverage. The crimes extended beyond the usual spectrum for armed robbery as the gang made other crude attacks at the same time; enabling press accounts to multiply into extra pages overnight and the editors of such papers started to make numerous assertions of widespread law and order breakdown. But it was a short-lived press bonanza, for this abnormal pattern was followed by silence, leaving precious little to fill the space besides much sniping at the police who had not arrested anyone. The police for their part had perceived all three raids as the work of one gang relishing unwarranted violence as their own distinctive thumbprint; for that there would be no quick fix. It had started in Bordeaux, involving vast sums, gradating down to paltry sums taken from the last bank raided at Lutz. But even there the violence continued at much the same level leaving just as many dead and dying. These were the factors that brought a top-level chief of police step-wise back through the more important police stations of his career – even to his origins.

Yes, Gabriel Masse had returned, bringing with him chaos to Claude's empire, not that the event would have much effect on Commissar Brie himself, for his staff were there taking the brunt of it. There was even pleasure in it, a freedom arising from his chief's return which constituted an immediate reprieve from onerous duties concerning the man's demanding wife. The burden of investigating a messy bank crime was yet another benefit quickly lifted from his shoulders by detectives fresh and keen to solve an affront to modern policing. It was true he'd had to attend a couple of meetings and introduce these hounds of justice to the locality police, but after that he was pretty much on his own. His boss had been appreciative of those past efforts in his domestic quarter because he mentioned it in an aside, one that somehow managed to penetrate the circle of advisers and minions flocking around him. They were, as Gabriel complained later to Claude, a full-time job of their own. His staff, the minions in the Commissariat were driven this way and that, becoming so confused they hardly knew their own business any more. Claude by contrast was able to rise above it all and go his own way, and by doing so soon became extra plump from eating undisturbed most evenings. For the day he procured a sign for his door reading 'Meetings in Progress'. Thus much of the commotion passed him by, and stopped well short of Claude himself.

On the far side of his office there stood a new filing cabinet, and it was to this the Commissar's attention was directed during the short duration of his self-imposed isolation. He had heard of Hazel Gray and Terry Hayes from the clergyman Charles Chapman, whose evidence had connected them admirably as innocent tourists; but now at last there was time to read all the confirmatory paperwork and fill in that extra detail. They were indeed the cyclists, as became more evident on examining the contents of letters; Terry's parents for instance had supplied photographs of him always showing a bike somewhere nearby. For Hazel, her passport had been left in her saddlebag among a jumble of feminine items.

These people were quite distinct from the big Belgian man Marc Casserta who had so angrily visited him about his wife and used mechanized transport to get around. There would seem to be no reason to connect them, apart from the fact they were all missing. However they did all go missing at roughly the same time, an event probably engineered by Georges locking his adversary in the caves. Marc, who had appeared to be robbing the till, was in fact acquiring the keys and had made off with them as evidenced by new keys bought by the management. The teenagers would need to use the spares once the primary set of keys had departed, and their responsible handling of those keys pointed to a quite benign, separate presence in the cave. For them to have escaped by following the engineer's route was entirely reasonable; it merely remained to see which bodies if any were under the rubble. If it were Marc then Jan Kee's charges would change to murder for the most basic of reasons. If it were the cyclists then everything would become very much more complicated. But from the evidence the cyclists must have moved on to reach the source stream for the spa 'bottled water' lake; if they were found dead – he'd need a new scenario.

There were small disadvantages to being second fiddle to an office on the busy side of Sylvia's desk he decided; coffee breaks were invariably late. But putting minor hardships aside, Claude indulged himself in writing letters and in particular corresponding sympathetically with the parents of his missing teenagers.

But everything good has to end; and just when Claude's life had settled once more into the comfortable rut of normality; his chief, complete with experts and 'yes men', moved on to solve other media prominent crimes. Their leaving had left everything, either wedded to, or unsolved, awaiting further progress by Claude Brie. The circus had moved on, and the chief's office was hardly clear of tobacco smoke before Claude's phone was ringing with Julia on the line.

'Mitzi is being buried tomorrow, and Gabriel said you might take me – as he can't be there.' She sounded fresh and intense still, as he so well remembered the warmth of her last kisses; they marked the issue of a Mitzi substitute; all unknowingly Julia was grateful.

Claude was short with her, sensing the danger to his newly discovered carefree existence. 'Sorry, I am inundated with the work your husband left unfinished.'

She made one last plea. 'It's close to town and it needn't take long.'

But Claude was not being tied beyond offering to pay for the taxi out of police funds. It was enough to quieten her; but did so in an unsettling sort of way. He disliked refusing a lady, as it was not in his character, but the treadmill would keep turning the moment he put a foot on it. Pacing the floor took him through all of the departments in the building; everyone smiled at him for they were all comfortably back to normal again – it was a very happy place this Commissariat. The repository for trial evidence was certain to claim his presence now, and soon he stood looking at Mitzi. The dog was a bit misty now, and still without a sticker to say she was not needed. Claude knew that one would be there soon, because the poodle parlour had pleaded guilty. If only the sticker had been on he could have raced Mitzi over to the cemetery, all ready for burial tomorrow. His mind toyed with how convenient and how much cheaper it would be if the two dogs could be buried together, perhaps one dog deeper in than the other. He begrudged police time and expense in having a later burial – all he wanted was a simple sticker. Claude reached up to the top of the glass cover of Mitzi's jar, and absentmindedly looked at the folded paper that rested there. It was not a sticker, but the Pet Cemetery blurb that the driver had left when the road casualty poodle was picked up. Yes, come to think of it he had put it up there personally, thinking that the dog's owner might insist on having it back.

Absently he looked at the writing; the cemetery enterprise was described as being the bright idea of two brothers, both stonemasons. The idea had caught on, and they now had four such cemeteries. As the place names met his eye, he caught his breath and moments later was running excitedly for his office. Regaining his breath for the telephone, he asked the operator to connect to another town police station some hundred kilometres further up country. It was a place of little importance rather like Lutz, but the other station had in its locality the first on his list of pet cemeteries, a town seemingly not robbed. It was as he had suspected, the town in question was subject to a less publicized, but similar, armed bank raid six months ago.

Not pausing even to gloat he rang Julia, saying that he would

239

very much like take her there after all. She was delighted and tried to flatter him with much sweet talk. Words failed Claude, he was far too excited over his discovery to start flirting on the telephone – but at least he had the visit arranged. Claude sat looking at the card, exuberant and unsettled despite the fact it was hard to award his own self much credit for spotting such a blatant coincidence; but as it had happened he must cherish it and be prepared to take full advantage. The advertising material had listed three towns in the very order the bank robbers had hit them: each town having a pet cemetery within ten kilometres. The money had not appeared in circulation yet, so what better hiding place to stash the loot for a while? Well of course he couldn't be sure, for it was still only a hunch, but the idea was strengthened a great deal by the fourth name. The fourth town he could see as forerunner of recent raids, giving him a reasonable degree of confirmation. With a dog's interment handy tomorrow, he would be able to visit the scene discreetly, for any visible interest by the police at this stage, might well tip off the robbers.

Julia was up early preparing a hamper for what she intended to be a whole day out. She bathed and applied delightfully cunning traces of expensive feminine perfume. The dress had to be appropriate: she chose a light summer dress decorated with highly coloured flowers, all of them accentuated with a black outline, giving her the excuse to wear black shoes and carry a black bag. Claude always appeared more malleable when he was standing on the doorstep below her – so she chose high-heeled shoes. The weeks of tolerating her husband had depressed her, and the thought of her dapper roly-poly gentleman, about to arrive, infused her with a gaiety that was rare for Julia.

When the black official car stripped of all police indications arrived, she was sure it was done especially for her. Claude even loaded the picnic basket as if he had no objection. She was cheerful, and carefree in her chatter throughout the short journey, opening wide the passenger window to breathe the fresh air and knowing full well that Claude was shivering without his sweater. Julia felt pleased he was suffering for her in silence; it was the mark of a true gentleman she concluded, for not a word was said. She sobered up when they passed the lodge gate, and began to think of her dog.

240

Claude noticed that the ornate lodge gate was set in a very ordinary fence surrounding the property – anything available within would be accessible at all times. His more immediate requirement for a car park area had him driving round its colourful perimeter of parkland. It was a cemetery that impressed the eye as well as being novel, a brilliant fantasyland of small coloured headstones. The mind was forever attracted and fascinated as if you were part of a three-dimensional scene from a Disney film. Soon a track leading towards the centre enabled a right-angle turn, and their car purred towards a tall structure in the middle.

A short man dressed in monkish trappings came out to meet them, peering as if short sighted towards them and clutching a Bible-like book to his breast; on closer inspection Claude noticed that it was a sales catalogue with a crucifix on the front. Julia identified herself as she emerged from the car, and the salesman led them into the suite; it was principally a showroom with an annex of toilets to the rear.

Inside the showroom the walls were lined with small coloured cement tablets that could well have featured in a cartoon. The salesman/priest said the ones that had brown backs were for dogs, and the black-backed ones were for cats – just for easy identification. They looked closer at the tablets, noticing that any message written thereon was decorated about its edges with paw marks of the deceased, the writing being set upon a blue or pink surface depending on whether it was a he or she. This part was just by way of introducing himself, as Julia had already bought the headstone. For the very same reason he dispensed with further explanations, leading them on past the clever click-lock, time-degrading plastic coffins, and then on to the coloured chippings adorned with a selection of vases that he hoped to sell. As a salesman he was persuasive and wanting the best for the dog; but even so Julia firmly rejected these latest offerings outright. Somewhat crestfallen and reproachful, the man decided she had forfeited any chance to see any of the other extras he had available and instead swung them sharply round to the book of remembrance for signing.

Claude professed to be merely the driver, a ruse to avoid entering anything in the book, and blithely turned a blind eye to Julia's hostile stare. Nevertheless her look was enough to have him reluctantly accompany her to the plot. The man led them through rows of neat, gaily coloured stones to a spot where there was freshly dug earth. Timed exactly to the second an electric truck pulled up beside them, it had brought the groundsman accompanied by a wood-imitation plastic box. The man first positioned an imitation grass strip alongside the hole, and then reverently placed the box upon it. Their look-alike cleric held his imitation Bible at arm's length and began to say prayers. Julia's eyes filled with tears, and by the time the two men began lowering the box, she was in full flood. Claude stood there gauging the depth, would another fit on top later? In fairness to Julia who would probably prefer her dog also to be there, he decided it just might. A few symbolic shovelfuls of earth were thrown, and a brown-backed headstone was brought over towards its destination. Claude, having finished estimating, decided that as a driver he had a freedom to wander and could well leave the sorrowing owner to her abject misery.

Moments after turning away Claude heard Julia's cry of rage; he paused in quiet contemplation of the blue-faced stone, bearing those sycophantic paw marks and the many poignant words referring to 'him'. He hovered there mere seconds before making himself scarce, cursing the sex of the road casualty as bad news; then wincing as Julia's penetrating voice reached him with ringing clarity. 'Mitzi never cocked her leg, not ever – you have altered my her to him!' The salesman, for that is basically what he was, tried to calm her, saying quickly, 'I saw him myself Madam, it was a male dog, and so we altered the words to fit.' Julia began to shout and weep at the same time, it sounded like it was going to be quite a scene – so Claude left it.

The car was not far off, it was at most two minutes later that Claude reached it still puffing heavily from the run; he reached inside and grabbed his camera before pelting up the steps into the showroom. The book of remembrance lay open. He photographed that day's page and the two that preceded it, then almost without pause entered the rear corridor to the toilets. There commenced a staircase able to test his stamina even more, and whence he passed immediately through a service door onto a flat roof. In a trice he was climbing the metal ladder found there, fastened to a water tower rising way above. Gasping from such unaccustomed effort, he hooked an arm through the ladder, leaning back to release the camera shutter several times, capturing the full panoply and instant geography of the cemetery as seen from his perch. Claude stopped only when his arm could not physically stand the strain any longer. Puffing his way down the ladder again, he could hear Julia's raucous voice still raging in the distance. Without knowing it, she was putting on a remarkable show and giving him all the time he needed. Hopefully with her tying both men down with sheer indignation he would even have time to look at the graves as he wandered back.

Julia had them in disarray all right, and some very unladylike curses coming from such a genteel person cowed the men; at one point the salesman held up his imitation Bible as if to ward off the evil in her words. Yes Julia was in fine form and she soon had them raising the coffin to prove her point. The men floundered about attempting an unaccustomed task for them; the heaving of a coffin out of its mud-lined hole was a job that soon had them gasping for breath.

'Well if it is my dog then, you'll open up that damn box right away, and prove what you say is true.' She raved on, and on, stamping an elegant foot, which promptly speared the imitation plastic grass web on the heel of her shoe. Julia angrily whirled around scanning the landscape for Claude. 'Where's that man gone!' With her shoe heel firmly trapped in the open mesh she tugged and shook it off angrily. Within that brief interval of her cemetery scan the salesman had taken fright and disappeared; Julia on returning to the fray found only the quaking groundsman to take the full thrust of her complaint.

The casket was manifestly not being opened. Aghast at this she vented anger upon the unfortunate groundsman, who gamely tried to help, pushing here and there at the smooth unyielding surface. Unknowingly he worked his way along the lid with fumbling hands, more to please her than knowing the secret of how the precisely machined lid latched into position. But then he took heart, on seeing his priestly colleague rise in the hole like some muddy apparition shouting good advice. Despite this the groundsman, all fingers and thumbs, still managed to get it wrong. With a scream of rage at the ineptitude before her Julia picked up the headstone, all twenty kilos of it, and demonstrated how to open a plastic imitation wooden box infallibly. Under the headstone's weight the otherwise frail box disintegrated, its collapse cushioning the stone's onwards progress to the groundsman's ankle, where it lodged and the man very promptly retrieved it. The salesman/priest also rapidly scrambled over the muddy sides, as he perceived the danger above that hole. First the lady's wrath had moved the very ground he stood on, followed in quick time by headstone tossing.

All the witnesses involved were present at the graveside when the shattered box revealed its secret, a rather smelly mound of white fur that was definitely not Mitzi. Julia began a fresh tirade about the unknown dog they had managed to put in Mitzi's coffin. It was a propitious time for the poor groundsman to limp off and tend his injury upon the truck, for there was a more experienced man to handle Julia's latest tirade single-handed. The groundsman sat dejectedly on the running board with a wet rag round his ankle, watching his well-muddied friend, wearing smeary trodden-on glasses, first calm then comfort the distraught but still unpredictable Mme Masse.

The unexpected length of the graveside hostilities gave Claude even more time; he struck off into the avenues of brown- and black-backed stones looking for empty holes, and on finding one photographed it. He now headed towards the more gaudy colours on the other side of the path, for they were relatively few. A bright yellow stone stood out, in fact bright yellow all over. Claude, strongly disbelieving the text of bereavement to a canary, reasoned colour both sides meant that they probably didn't even know what sex it was; but who in their right mind would bury a canary with a plush headstone? Nearby an ornamental bush caught his eye, with plastic covered hoops enclosing its space; he grasped one, pleased to see that it was based upon sturdy wire. Quickly he straightened it and thrust the resulting half metre into the canary's grave. The wire passed to its hilt, but no, there was nothing of any size buried near the surface. His probe searched about, bumping fingers into something just inches under the loose soil; he raked away the earth. There he uncovered not one but a number of small gold-painted boxes rather like one might buy a hundred grams of quality chocolates in – just the right size for a canary. Claude brushed the soil back, his query satisfied; this was merely a repository to dump your songster and stay friends with the kids – he nodded his approval.

Nearby were several orange coloured stones; reading them, he found without exception all were for goldfish, and once more the piece of wire probed, finding small boxes. That held until the last in the row where there was something hard at the limits of his reach. It was suspicious – unless the fish had been buried complete with pool. He jabbed the sharpest end down with force and twisted. The point stuck just enough to say it was not stone. Out came the camera again and moments later Claude walked off, smiling triumphantly.

Julia had by now comprehended what had happened, and met him along the path, her face contorted with rage. But as far as Claude was concerned she could complain as much as she liked, he was treading air and unrepentant.

He was blatantly honest about the dog. 'Well you wanted it, I didn't say it was Mitzi did I?' Julia gasped, lost for words and collapsing back into her seat glowered sullenly at him.

Claude said comfortingly, 'The casket can be paid for out of police funds, and then you can bury Mitzi. Gabriel will hold your hand, and everything will be just so.'

Julia was still fighting. 'He will never come back for that,' she snapped.

Claude smiled mysteriously. 'Oh, I think he will,' he said.

She sat in silence throughout the return journey, holding back her tears. It was not until Claude had carried the picnic basket back into the hall, and she had closed the door on him, that Julia let herself go.

Later the same day Claude sat in his office examining the enlargement prints from his photography. With some degree of overlapping they were good enough to provide a map of the cemetery and the areas being dug at present. His 'book of remembrance' photographs identified the fishy orange stone as connected with a signature on the day before the robbery; but on checking, the name did not correspond with the owner of the address quoted. There was good ground to believe that the robbery's haul in Lutz had been buried there, and it was only a matter of time before the criminals came to collect it. With a knowing smile, he rang his distant boss. Of course the man was embroiled in something more important; but even without embroidering the facts, Claude knew that he would cause something of a stir.

It was the very next morning that the circus was back. Claude strode with a beaming smile through a Commissariat now peopled with long faces, every vestige of happiness gone. Flushed with success and in an absent state of mind he was quite unable to detect the prevalent air of misery pervading this otherwise sunny outpost on Spain's doorstep. Reaching his retreat, he replaced the

'Meetings in Progress' notice upon the door and settled comfortably in his office chair. It would be a long wait, and now that the assembled throng could nibble away at something in three adjacent districts, his lifestyle would indeed return to being the bachelor's paradise it was.

25

Princess Elect

Hazel was summoned to see Freda. It was early afternoon, the time when Freda did most of her work – a time when everyone would be back in the village. Two months had passed since their private talk, and even after all this time Hazel was still unsure whether or not she was pregnant. The question, however important it might be, was unresolved; sure she felt a little sick in the mornings, but even that could be the new foods she was doing her level best to avoid. To be honest Hazel did not know what to say, beyond the fact that periods had passed her by.

Freda listened as Hazel struggled with her uncertainties, for there was more to her question than a mere passing interest. It was a matter that concerned them all and must be settled.

'You are not sure, but you have said more than enough to convince me. The next step is to call a meeting of everyone and make an announcement.'

Hazel thought this premature, because she was not relishing the fuss that everybody would make; she could imagine them all turning sideways on to look at her. She pleaded for privacy. 'Couldn't we leave it awhile, another month even?'

Freda became more emphatic, for as she saw it there was now little room for manoeuvre. 'I am sorry; I ought to have explained the consequences fully to you earlier, but when we spoke it was even more unlikely than the present time. Bear in mind that the last baby to arrive was St Lucinia's a good five hundred years ago. Back then it had to be a miracle, especially the way it happened; but the sheer rarity since then means that any baby born to you will be another miracle in the eyes of every woman here. It was upon the strength of this notion that the idea of having a queen was born, because the inhabitants had acquired someone who was native to this place and quite unlike anybody else. It was this quality

247

that put the baby in a category of its own; unmatched by anyone else it just had to be royal.'

Hazel cut in swiftly. 'I do not see how that should affect me.'

'But it does! Your baby will be considered just as much a miracle. And if we are to make anybody responsible for the future Queen, who could possibly be more suitable than the baby's mother? On that basis alone they will want you as Queen.'

Memories of Freda guiding the women through the last uprising beset Hazel. 'From what I have seen here already, nobody could manage anywhere near as well as you do. I am better suited awaiting my turn; so please let us agree to keep quiet about it, because it still might not happen.'

'That is a nice compliment you pay me Hazel, but the fact is I must shortly give way to either Frances or Jackie. I cannot hold on for another month or two, it is something that needs to happen and your name cannot be withheld as my successor.'

Hazel listened with a growing realization that it was out of her hands. She protested, seizing upon what was different. 'But it is a totally different situation, because I am far more able-bodied than Lucinia could have been. Cannot I plead for carrying on as I am? If there is a baby, then no doubt in due course it will get elected.'

Freda was pleased to see the girl was unselfish. 'I am glad that you see your position that way, but responsibility is paramount here. The fact that you are keen to ignore is that the baby when it arrives will be more of a responsibility to carry than your men could ever be. It will demand your full attention, much as the job of being Queen will, and the powers that go with it must be seen and fully understood by that child. We cannot keep the facts to ourselves, especially as your solution is unlikely to sway the vote.'

'Then surely, I don't need to be there!' Both the concept as set forth, and its increasing accent on responsibility horrified Hazel.

'You need not come, unless you want to; but the meeting will be called tomorrow afternoon come what may.'

With Freda's decision ringing in her ears, Hazel left feeling very depressed. There was going to be a lot of fuss and she knew it. What then of Terry? Would he discover from somebody's chance word somewhere that he had fathered a baby? However much he was out of favour, and he was certainly that, she still had a duty towards her subject male. And even more pertinent, what about her special friend Annita? Did she have to learn from the meeting?

From the sound of it, the baby – any old baby in fact – would blight Annita's chances of being Queen, so she ought to start by apologizing right now. The thought spurred her on towards the hunt cave, but then on failing to hear the sounds of conflict she halted. Despite a renewed friendship between Annita and Bernadette both met less often and probably were following their own devices today. Hazel found Annita eventually in the stable cave talking to Cauliflower and fondly patting the animal's neck whilst the contented mount chewed on a handful or two of hay. Annita found it hard to grasp that Hazel had got to this stage with not as much as a word, but seemed mightily pleased that it was so. 'Come back to my place,' she cried. 'Let's break open a bottle and celebrate.'

The rest of the afternoon was but time filled with their chatter, a bottle open and an optimistic Annita upon its delivery end. Annita, it seemed, was not bothered about sitting on the throne either.

'Anyone who takes on that job finds trouble comes home to roost from every conceivable direction, so I'm very glad they are not going to nominate me.' Annita's relaxed expression and eyebrow-twitching laugh helped to have the position accepted by Hazel as a genuine one, and she felt relieved to know that she could expect her friend's support in any elevation that they thrust upon her.

The evening brought the inevitable visit to Terry ever closer. There were customers in her shop now, even though it had taken some extra borrowing from the food house to bolster up the relatively few contents of Tanya's house sufficiently well to make things viable. Things like work surfaces were not commonplace as she previously supposed, they had to be made to order. Little as she thought of her abilities, they stretched to cutting and shaping of hair, and already a few walking bushes had become well-shaped advertisements for her salon. But as yet it was early days and her chance clientèle did not keep her occupied very long. Marc would be all right for hours now, so she descended through all the layers of bubbles to Terry's room. Hazel had quite deliberately avoided seeing him since the uprising, and this had led to her feeling doubtful about any encounter at all; but now she felt it had to be done. His door was facing her and tied as usual with a double bow on the outside. Shrugging off any inclination to knock she tugged

Maria's bow and walked in. Terry sat up naked on his bed. Hazel thought he looked pale and even smaller than he had previously.

'I thought you'd got lost,' he said at last, moving towards her.

'You stay over there!' Hazel exclaimed, recoiling through the door.

Terry halted mid-stride and grabbed at his clothing pile, not wanting to deter her. In many weeks of lonely evening hours he had thought of little else.

'Sit on the bed!' She said it sharply, re-entering the room.

Terry sat, mind in turmoil. 'Let me explain,' he pleaded.

'No, you listen to me, and comprehend that your clowning has brought about a baby.' Hazel stepped back, and shut the flimsy door just as hard as it allowed. There had been no mention of reasons for her absence, and as she tied the door she congratulated herself. His outline appeared on the door's other side, impotent and pleading. Hazel closed her ears to the muffled voice, finding to her surprise the facility of just shutting a door and walking away smoothed over everything awkward – and for this she was truly thankful.

No, she didn't owe Terry any more than the announcement she decided, and returned to her usual evening wait in the food house. Wearily she passed Frances and Jackie in the first division who seemed to be involved in some noisy horseplay. She prepared her chosen infusion to drink, still angry to have that traitor bearing down on her conscience, but confident that she had done the right thing, for any complicity with such a character would certainly prejudice her in the eyes of others. But, despite these thoughts of fact, how could her eyes stay so moist without reason? How miserable she felt sitting there in her usual place drinking alone. This was not the reaction she had expected, for surely they were unsuited; Terry was too immature for her and that was a fact she had known from the very first. Marc had easily driven Terry from her mind in recent weeks, even to the soft feather-filled sheepskin, originally intended to make Terry's lonely exclusion more bearable, but now it had become an essential in the frequently shared softness of Marc's bed. Marc fitted into all of the systems here, and if the village attack had not fortuitously alerted her to 'Terry the traitor' then she would have stayed out of step with everyone else permanently.

Annita had recommended this lifestyle to her in the very early days and it was a pity that Marc had already frightened her out of considering him seriously, otherwise it might have been very different. Hazel had taken to heart her remarks about Franz: 'When you first arrive here and feel really low, it is so wonderful that you are the one who is able to be comforted every night before moving off to your own bed.' Well that much was true, but in a way she was the Cinderella of the bunch because she had not chosen to have an evening with Marc. There were seven of them, a number difficult to disrupt, because between them they fitted neatly into the days of the week. Not that it mattered much for she was not looking for intercourse, but just happy to pick on any occasion that might allow a cosy cuddle. That worked well, excepting for Annita's night which was a special case and when she simply couldn't do it. Annita had so easily talked her into allowing that single evening date to be extended right through into his bubble.

Annita always brought a bottle of fruity drink as a thank you when the cord on Marc's door was finally tied. Hazel noticed after a while that there was often a black striped mushroom in his bubble when she left and that its upper flat surface had been cut off either side of the stem making a T shape of it. This was something she found hard to understand as she never saw it arrive. Eventually, through their happy late night giggles Annita explained the mystery. The mushroom shape she announced was a versatile sex aid useful for extending love right through into Hazel's abode.

This was a time when her friend was available for advice and would be able to discuss the odd problem arising such as Patricia. Sometime earlier she had seen scrapes and bruises on Marc's back, and she'd spent a good hour questioning him. Despite a characteristic reluctance to speak about it, slowly the truth emerged. Patricia openly despised men but emoted much on the fact that she was offering herself up to the god as a holy vessel – for that second coming of Itzla. First there was a blessing for the phallus, with much, 'laying on of hands' and praying. Then he must spear her womb and create a little godling, but only to be spanked over her knee afterwards in order to remove all the taint of earthly pleasure from the act. 'I must see that it's spiritual throughout,' she said. No wonder Marc had resisted, although with her, he stood no chance.

Pat's face and figure popped up in Hazel's mind and she could not restrain herself from laughing with her friend. She continued with her own recent experiences of cutting the prelate's hair whilst the woman described herself as the earthly tool of St Lucinia, and whose own prayers had halted the recent revolt. Patricia sat there wanting Hazel as some kind of disciple and confiding little things about the cave deity. She talked of changes to come, and cryptic remarks about moral salvation that would flow from a new saviour. There would be fewer men saved and a hardier lifestyle for an even more devout band of women. Annita laughed when Hazel mentioned it, saying Pat had never got over being Queen, never moved off the throne just wheeled it metaphorically into the church. She referred to her as the Red Queen. 'Orf wiv 'is bleed'n'ed,' they chanted, a chant Hazel had heard before. Despite laughing with Hazel over this Annita was quick to speak for all the women. 'But just keep this in perspective, for all of us are pressed to work hard and these are our toy-boys, who by their very being allow an individual to be her normal self and use this short relaxation time enjoyably. Concubines by their very nature are no more than seasonal goodies; as they stand no chance of holding their jobs down against any appealing newcomer that takes our eye. For that reason it does not warrant any over attention. Mind you this one needs his row of press-studs moving in now he's not so plump; and that's something that's right in your department. By contrast the other fellow, who I think you love, needs no attention and should last pretty well if you do not neglect him.'

Tonight Marc was with Rose; Hazel found difficulty in imagining the kind of relationship that must be ongoing. She knew Rose talked incessantly to him in her own lethargic way, and hearing that particular voice as a continuous stream came as something of a surprise. It may be that Marc was hers for the evening and no doubt a willing audience unlikely to hurry her. Rose's instructions and thoughts mumbled on and on inaudibly over the space as she eavesdropped. Perhaps it was more understandable than the utter silence surrounding Poppy, but the advantage of Poppy was she occasionally did not turn up for her night. The sound of doors opening interrupted Hazel's thoughts; Rose emerged looking self-consciously at her, a shy 'Goodnight' floated back as she exited.

Lately there was a further wait for Marc to appear, something new that happened recently, since Maria and herself had put heads together and arranged plumbing for Marc to have a shower in an adjacent bubble. The shower impinged upon no one's time but Hazel's, who found the wait somehow washed all other women from him. Tonight especially she needed comforting – for who knew what tomorrow would bring.

The conference took place so inconspicuously that on any other occasion Hazel would have been unaware of it. This time, however, she was acutely aware, and not left in the dark over long; because she was summoned by Freda immediately after it had finished.

'Everyone is delighted,' she enthused. 'They want you as Queen if all goes as planned, so I will stay on and show you the necessities of the job. You will need to attend the group of elders for meetings regularly, but you are free to go on working whilst you are fit to do so. Bernadette will take over work in the entrance chamber, and as she has enough tinies of her own you still have Rose and Poppy.' Hazel smiled, almost feeling the workload shift, only to be replaced by a wary look as Freda said she must now take an oath in the council chamber. Council chamber indeed, Hazel didn't even know they had one. But it was seriously said and shortly she walked into the church, with Freda talking all the time.

'Whenever you start as Queen, you will need to be well informed about what's going on, and to do this you will need to attend both the elders' meeting as well as our own. But you must keep such matters to yourself and not divulge the least thing to your friends.' The council room was right next-door to the communal meetings room; it was just the walls were hung more richly with skins, without the usual maps.

Maureen stood at the door welcoming her and then apologizing for Maria being unable to come because she was busy. With Freda, the two constituted enough elders for a swearing-in ceremony. The circular table seemed very small in the centre of such a large bubble and showed that in number they only filled five chairs. Upon the table lay a Bible, which Hazel was instructed to take in her hands and swear that she would keep anything she heard via the elders strictly to herself. She managed to do so in a clear steady voice, and seemingly pleased both of them. Having got that over she was all ready to go her own way; but no, the pair led her into the church where Patricia was waiting.

'You are perhaps more inclined towards the Bible, but here the established church is another aspect you have got to observe,' Freda quickly whispered as she stepped aside. Pat led the girl towards the statue of St Lucinia and there, kneeling, she repeated the vow. Speedily Freda rescued her, and in no time at all the

253

threesome exited the church. From the minimal conversation there had been with Pat, Hazel received the strong impression she was not on good terms with other elders. They mentioned her again, but only to agree on how much better she looked since Hazel had tidied her hair. As she left Hazel quizzed them about when the next meeting was due, but Freda was hazy about this because staff movements were normally debated and the recent unrest meant some necessary changes were still going on in the engineers' cavern. Freda would let her know when next to come, and on that note of dismissal Hazel wandered off, wondering what next to do in her rearranged itinerary.

26

The Devil's Colander

Behind the scenes in the food house, there was little room for manoeuvre when it came to putting escape ideas into effect. From very early in the morning Terry became caught up in Maria's yoke, and driven with little that could be called a break; by contrast Marc had it much easier as Hazel doted on him now, and left him undisturbed until breakfast. But however favourably they might compare to one another, the men felt the same driving force, one derived from having to feed people in an unremitting schedule of food preparation carrying them along relentlessly until their efforts became less essential in the mid-afternoon. Maria was a workaholic, driving herself with enjoyment in her efficient routines far more than she drove them, as is the way of people who get great satisfaction from such things. The afternoons were her prime time for indulging in the odd culinary triumph for which she freed herself from any other consideration. At this time she would forget her staff, for they were well versed in what to do next, turning her attention to experiments that kept the limited number of ingredients in Hades expanding over an ever-widening range of specialities.

As work finished in the food house for Terry, he was switched to collecting bats. The demise of Arthur had caused him to become ever more involved with the collection, climbing high on the purpose-built rickety frame to do it. Leon was intended to help him, but working the sewage job alone meant that the tiny man was always somewhere else. Soon Leon failed even to attend on the bats at all, and that was Terry's opportunity to drop the number killed. He could have managed with effort, but as Terry saw the situation it could be turned around so as to enable an escape. Maria, truly efficient as always, made an instant check on the reasons for a drop in the supply, but for this Terry was well prepared, using his new friends among the engineers to drive the bats higher at first light. Maria then witnessed the bats high on the walls and her lad collecting even fewer of them than he had the day before. It was a valuable food supply, one that could not be allowed to fail, and so she agreed with Terry that the bats had thinned, deciding that Marc must be spared to help with the bat hunt. His suggestions to remedy the matter she took seriously too; the frame would move better if it were fitted on large wheels, and needed additional ladders to extend its reach. The equipment Maria pursued at high level, and besides this enabled Marc to be brought in immediately.

Elsewhere the engineer's department was programmed to meet this emergency. The engineers, still feeling the results of Freda's purge after the village attack, were ill-placed to oppose extra work and any chance to increase their workload was being seized upon. Among many other changes, Red had been sent outside to take on Harold's team; and with him busy in a less sensitive place, tasks that reeked of punishment could be imposed upon the remaining engineers without particular thought. Even though they wrestled with a falling output neither Frances nor Jackie saw anything wrong in that, or even thought that it mattered.

Marc facilitated his transfer by obviously doing cleaning and polishing work until Freda realized he could be spared. But having arrived to help with bats he wanted his own way, promoting a scheme that was considerably nearer to realization than was Terry's. For him it had to be the best scheme because irrespective of whether it failed or was successful, it had to remove him from this place. In his capacity as waiter he was privy to talk in high places, and from what he gleaned his tenure was disturbing on the longevity front; many names of concubines were mentioned in conversations, but all had passed on within the span of those talking. Maureen, for instance, was apt to boast about how many her nursing skills had saved, but mentioned concubines as if they were on some other list. Why? he asked himself, and began plaguing Maria, the one who was kind enough to chat with him most, spending a considerable conversational effort trying to get the relevant facts out of her.

She part-answered his quiz one day in the kitchen by allowing him to watch the high-speed disintegration of some organ derived from a sheep before making it up to volume with creamy goat's milk. Here was his cold white soup, the special beverage flavoured with mushroom presented to him at regular intervals. 'Could these hormone extracts be part human at times?' he asked. But his inquisition had worn itself into a joke now, and Maria easily wriggled her way out without confirming or denying anything. He later found Maria was more communicative when he was with her in the evening and she told him many stories of her earlier life. He listened, but more concerned about himself and keen to find out why both testicles had been replaced by similar-sized spheres. The other men he knew had one testicle. Were his testes damaged somehow on entry? Or was his condition deliberately engineered? Maria was as frank about this as he was going to get. 'The women expect their concubine to have two balls,' she said. 'And that's exactly what you possess!'

From all of this Marc became convinced he was a eunuch and only likely to become more effeminate. His mind made the reasonable assumption that the extracts he was taking were intended to retain sufficient masculinity to suit his job. He felt with some desperation that there were signs he was even now beginning to fail expectations and needed to make an escape before his strength ebbed away or he was discarded. It was surely the winter season outside and there must be enough ice on the mountain to suit his scheme by simply reducing the river volume – this, as he had observed before, meant more headroom. But what stirred him into action was having the vital materials he needed virtually put into his hand.

Hazel had been circumspect about it when putting the request, as already Marc was committed to doing extra work with the bats. Could he do some electrical work for her? Can a duck swim? thought Marc, agreeing at once. And in a very short time she led him into a veritable Aladdin's Cave, except that Hazel called it 'Tanya's bubble'. Sure there were electrical bits in there, but ropes and torches as well, suggesting to him he would not be around for the actual electrics.

The engineers had witnessed many changes of late, and in the most significant Red had been replaced numerically by someone from the farming community. The replacement man had originally been a knife-grinder and was both elderly and small; he stood over his workbench with a hunched back as if stopped in mid-action. His new workmates called him 'the clothes horse', since he could crouch that way doing almost nothing but always looking as if he were on the job. 'Dobbin' had been the derisive name that was conjured from this, and when he objected it became 'Dobsie'. In the recalcitrant and generally obstructive atmosphere of the engineers, their new recruit had been set to work repairing generators which formed much of Red's old job because of their importance requiring such extreme care and precision as well. Already the generators building up from the bench had come to a complete stop. This task they all knew was capable of shutting down production everywhere, unless countered by the females running the show. To accentuate the men's contempt for the women running the place even more than this, their latest non-engineer replacement was simply passed over to the would-be escapees to carry a rope and tidy up after them.

One suitable afternoon, Maria's tiny workforce completed the cull in what Maria would consider an impossible time, then sneaked out through the engineers' double gates with the manure. Dobsie, who was a shepherd previously, well knew the way and shortly they were passing round the back of the waterfall out of sight. This was Terry's first view of the waterfall, causing him to gaze fascinated, and then even more so at all the engineering mechanism he saw on the other side of the falls. He was soon falling behind whilst at the same time admiring all the rows of protruding generators busily converting energy into electric power. From there on, the final short stretch of river was bounded by low walls on either side until it passed through a masonry arch, a place where Terry caught them up. On the front side of the arch the river gushed out and fell as a torrent into a large hole. The hole had recently been reinforced with sturdy materials, containing within a lighter construction from some earlier age. This buttressing with sturdier walls of greater height Terry presumed spelt a danger from flooding.

For his first descent Marc decided he would establish that it could be done, before going any further. He prepared to climb over the wall and descend using two ropes: a long rope with harness of about four hundred feet, and a much heavier rope reduced by their knotting to about thirty feet which ought to clear the drop. The upper end of the harness rope was tied to recent heavy metalwork, and then within thirty feet of Marc it was wound just once round a wide pipe; the pipe rose conveniently near, and

258

was used as a bollard before securing rope to waist. The heavier rope was dangled to wherever it reached by the falling rush of water, and finally made secure at its upper end. Marc gripped it and smoothly swung his legs over the low wall bordering falling water. Terry and Dobsie watched him submerge whilst paying out the harness rope: at thirty feet they felt Marc's signal as expected, and knew he had reached the bottom knot. They prepared to take the strain, and this lasted for perhaps another twenty feet. From this point the tension on the rope suddenly declined, and went loose round Terry's handy bollard with no urgent rope pulls to bring him up. The sound of a familiar voice behind him had Terry start nervously, because he felt he was doing something under-hand; but then realizing it was Red, he hastened to welcome him as someone who could share in the excitement.

'How long has he been gone?'

Terry slackened his hold, and turned to face Red idly inspecting the knots tied in the rope. 'He's only just got to the bottom,' he said.

Red looked critically at a screen of falling water, completely obscuring observation by virtue of its outward swing. 'It will be icy cold, your mate's a bloody nut case.'

Terry pointed to the big pipe he had been using, his curiosity aroused. 'What's that for?' An idea lurking in the back of the head told him it was for sewage. Red instantly dissociated him from the notion.

'When we burn off sulphur ores, the choking gases are drawn through it into the waterfall.' If Red had more to add it was lost, because there was an agitated sound from Dobsie; both Red and Terry swung round to find him fishing up slack rope. As they watched, the bent figure brought in the frayed end of harness rope from the water. It emerged, terminating at a knot drawn out as a thin remnant. Terry felt sick, as he recognised an already tied part of a rope that he had personally included in this section. Anything non-ideal he thought should have been placed at the other end and not the one nearest Marc; so from sheer incompetence he had lost Marc.

Dobsie just stood there. It was nothing to do with him, and he continued to stand in his bent way as the two began quarrelling over who should descend in a rescue bid.

Marc had imagined that the water might be cold, but not that it would have such a powerful numbing action; the torrent was immediately penetrating the sheepskin borrowed for the purpose and driving the heat from his skin in uncomfortable little eddies under the garment. As his head submerged it took such a battering that all other discomforts were eclipsed, even to the pummelling of his chest that threatened every breath he took. Immersed in icy cold water his legs had a leaden feel which grew worse as he slipped from knot to knot on the heavier rope, only to be taken by surprise when he reached a space beyond the bottom knot. The rope had ceased abruptly, and suddenly he was retracting his numb feet from nothingness whilst hanging on equally numb hands. Collecting his wits and curling his back, he paused there reclaiming the bottom knot. He jerked the harness rope to signal the others, before carefully winding the long rope of less substance round an arm, to take off like a parachutist and fall in an upright position that took him clear of falling water.

The buffeting at his head stopped and suddenly transferred to a strong push at the hips, his feet first striking, and then stumbling unsteadily forwards upon a bottom littered with loose ankle-bruising stones. Marc allowed himself to move with the current, until the rope abruptly snagged upon something able to stop him mid-stride; leaning backwards he pulled in an attempt to free the rope. But there was no standing upright in the racing water that swept his legs from under him, then spun him as he saw his legs surface in front of him – that was before whatever it was let go. Lying flat upon his back he shot forwards propelled by racing water and moving ahead at bewildering speed. Strange to see his feet just missing an occasional projecting rock. The torch he dimly recollected was responsible for this, as it was already turned on and strapped to his waist.

The torrent swirled him at breakneck speed round a shallow bend, causing a violent spinning in which water flooded his mouth. Flinging out limbs in a bid to stabilize he clouted one arm painfully against the roof and it was not until half a dozen knocks later that he was again on an even keel. He floated on his back feet first in the stream of water and the widening gap above his feet alerted him to brace for rapids. Feeling now more like an insect going down the drain he resigned himself to a death by battering, still mercifully numbed by the water. The sense of fall continued until he struck something hard that jarred his spine and continued on seemingly sliding along a rocky wall of rounded stones, the stones tore at his sheepskin. There was something reminiscent in this of being deposited on a stony beach by the surf. His painful slide continued forwards and culminated in numbed hands fumbling to free the torch which, thank God, was still functioning. The rest of the rope, complete with frayed end, lay behind him. He wrapped it around his waist and tucked it in, still not comprehending what saved him from the torrent.

The torch revealed he was standing up in knee-high water, with a beach ahead. Taking just two steps forward that were successful, in the next his leg entered a large hole requiring great effort to retract again. He made his way step by step into just inches of water bottomed by small pebbles, watching as the river water disappeared completely through the stones like some great big strainer. Marc splashed his way over to adjacent stones that were merely wet, both thankful and amazed. Upon either side of him the torch picked out sparkling white rocks; there was something familiar about them and memories of seaside rock confectionery stirred as he viewed the fractured ends with embedded delicate white tubules, except that these glistening threads formed the whole wall. Marc walked forwards, now seeing a continuous floor of similar nature to the sidewalls; there was much that was cave about this place. He was aware that it had warmed, and an intermittent rumble overlay the noise of trickling water. Underfoot the crisp shell-like material encouraged him slightly downhill, its surface sharp, scratching abrasively against his sheep's hide sandals. He touched a sidewall and promptly saw his finger run red with blood, leaving a mark on the pristine white tubular formation. Ahead the torch picked out a white wall stretching right across his horizon and completely blocking the way. His stomach turned as the beam of his torch stepped down markedly, despite the blur of light still being visible and penetrating as a yellow stab.

It had to be mist. Much relieved he wiped the lens, but hardly improved its light. Mist it was that had engulfed him, for then all was drawn away and the cave sparkled clear again. Marc moved further forwards, his torch picking out a dead sheep right up against the end wall. The sheep started to eddy away from it and moments later cold water licked over his ankles. All about him water sprang from the floor squirting and then gushing. The sheep

261

floated towards his light: there was little wool upon it, brown showed underneath as if the flesh had been cooked. The remaining wool would be better called fur, for its upper half was slicked down – grey and very dead.

There were rumbles; the waters unsteadily subsided and then they were gone. Marc hesitated, ignoring the strong impulse to move forwards and discover. Luckily for him, because there was a bubbling noise with the cold water rising just a little; that was before jets of high-pressure steam hissed through myriad pores in the rock. Marc stumbled backwards with a scalded leg, seeing the sheep suspended on jets of steam go tobogganing back towards the end wall. Superheated steam sprayed up, fogging everything; it was uncomfortably hot, and with a stinging leg he staggered backwards again as the squirting steam intensified. The walls and the ceiling progressively took up steam intensity, and a resulting wall of heat overtook him as he retreated from burning jets that intensified upon all sides of the cave. Feeling safe he watched mesmerized, until his flesh stung by the heat had him dance backwards just ahead of its leading edge. Marc was back now, right back to the loose, small, beach stones. That was when the jets ceased to fog, and from a safe distance he watched another cycle. Marc could see why the stones stayed back here, for they had not the sheep's buoyancy.

But hell, how could he muse on this? He was trapped along with the mutton. The thought hit him like a bolt from the black depths; here was a never-to-end cycle carrying on within a hollow perforated rock, and if he wasn't careful he would be part of it. One foot caused local movement as he stood uneasily on the stones; something had caused a shift underfoot. His weight when transferred to that place physically rocked the stones adjacent to his feet. Stooping he picked up a buried metal rod and held on to it as something useful, knowing full well that it must have been lost when that new wall was built. He had been denied the river's course by the stones in the strainer, and if there were any man-sized holes in it, going back could be suicidal in this strange place. Hemmed in by rock he grappled with the next move, his mind entertaining thoughts near to panic – he was trapped on a devil of a colander in a truly ferocious stream. Before long, if he let it happen, he would be rolling back and forth with the sheep. The torch took away such thoughts for it had dimmed, and without even a mist to blame this time. He switched it off, preparing his mind for going back against the flow; if he could he must chance standing near the freezing falls hoping to be rescued. How long should he stand here in the warm before he started back, any miscalculation would end in tragedy. Don't panic, he told himself and was immediately heartened by little more than a noise.

Terry felt he had to win the argument and put himself in danger as penance for the defect that was all of his making, so he pointed out there would be more strength in Red to pull them up. The memory that Red was not aquatically inclined made him the more insistent, realizing Red was methodical as well as strong. There would be a better chance of success if that man stayed up on top. As for his own wellbeing he had little care, having been on the verge of suicide ever since Hazel's abrupt and very traumatic visit. To go this way, ostensibly trying to do something heroic, was God-given. The heavy rope was hauled from the water, and another twenty feet cut from the harness rope to join it; to this was added a bundle of buoyant roots from the aerial plant before replacing it over the side.

'Dobbo, get that spare wire,' Red yelled. Shortly the bowed frame struggled over with a heavy spool of copper wire that had been left adjacent to the generators, something that Red just knew. It was wide-gauge stuff, perhaps even a bit too rigid, but certain to be more trustworthy than the rope. Red turned his attention to Terry, binding several yards of rope round his waist, and not content with that, laced the heavy wire through it. Terry began to entertain suspicions that Red was using him to rescue a friend by just treating him as an overgrown float – a float that could hold a torch. As a final touch Red took the whistle from around his neck, the one that he signalled his rock-handling team with, and tied it on firmly. 'Use that,' he said.

Doing it was more trying than Terry had imagined; the climbing out on the masonry wall and taking off like Tarzan clutching the chunky knots felt rather grand, but the accompanying deluge of ice-water did rather take the edge off things. Cold racked his body well before water drummed fiercely upon his head and each breath seemed hard to take as he battled down on the first part of the rope, with the water seeking to tear him from it. Maybe this ought to have been done by someone stronger. Alarmed defeatist thoughts strafed his mind, but it was too late now. Leaden sluggish limbs had him regret his decision to come and he wondered if he could hang on much longer; but inch by inch it improved, especially when his head cleared the falling water. Feeling half drowned as he coughed in the icy water he angrily asked himself how ever could this be the right time of year? But putting anger aside Terry had passed his worst physical experiences, and moreover had enough length in the rope to take him right to the bottom. Knot by knot his legs were progressing but making slow work of it. Higher up, the torch, wrapped in sheepskin nestled against his chest, had bumped on a protruding rock. Would it still work? Now as he turned his head upwards the opening was gone, only plunging light-grey water filled his view.

The down rope had pulled him out of the water, and he mentally thanked the bundle trying to float downstream for making the rope act so beneficially. Terry's feet, when they struck down, plunged deep enough into stones lining the bottom that they hurt his ankles, whilst the forward motion dragged him out of balance but slowing as he resisted by hauling on the rope. It was perhaps twenty yards before he was upright and walking. Terry took the torch from the sheepskin bag that immediately raced away from him, his fingers strained at the switch feeling clumsy. The light blinked uncertainly and came on, and ignoring the success in this, he groaned to see nothing at all ahead. He blew a blast from the whistle, a noise seeming puny against the rustling water behind him.

What now, do I go on? Will there be enough rope and wire? He pulled a couple of times above his harness for the next fifty feet of rope. After one hundred extra feet the water was high on his chest and still rising. He blew a further call on his whistle and then signalled for another fifty. At two hundred feet of line, he was fast losing hope, but at least the water level was reducing again: Terry shouted and blew his whistle.

'Terry!' There came a distant shout.

Were they calling him through the falls? Terry turned, to foolishly view a black space behind him.

'Terry, keep coming!' The agitated voice was coming from the other way.

He pulled the agreed signal on his line, and the restraining harness allowed him forwards, although soon he must be dicing it on wire alone. Terry waded forwards. It was almost another thirty feet before he saw Marc in the beam of his torch. Seemingly Marc was managing to make more steps forward than he was being pushed back, using a pole or something to do it. Terry pulled for more line and stepped out until the rope tightened behind him, standing quite still; he was bothered to know of its full extent. Their hands stretched out towards each other and painfully the gap diminished.

They touched and he pulled until Marc's arm was round his shoulders, standing right there in racing chill water. Marc grabbed the harness line on his other side and passing his prop to Terry set off back along the harness rope. Terry watched his retreating back for a while leaning his weight on the prop, and then used the prop to reduce his reliance on the line; Marc who moved faster was easily forging his way through the current now. Terry shone his torch occasionally, noticing that they were both being slowly reeled in.

Even so it was a good way before Marc reached the added bare wire; it was then that his movement had to progress at the speed dictated from above. Eventually he encountered the bundle of roots and climbed onto the knotted rope, taking the overload strain off Terry's line. Marc stepped up, very grateful to part contact with the bottom, and then feel the heavier part of their reliable rope in the struggle through the down-rushing water, only to find a proffered hand that surprised him to find it was connected to Red lifting him over the flood wall.

It was Terry's turn now: they brought the line in as slowly and as carefully as they could, being fairly sure that he would not be able to climb the rope on his own. To their profound relief, and a tangled heap of wire among much wet rope, the load on the line suddenly decreased. Terry had made it to the knotted rope, a sure indication that they could also drag him up, and this they did rapidly. He could be heard coughing even before they bounced him over the masonry lip. Terry had made it if a little bruised.

They had to hurry now, to be back before someone missed them. The friends parted company quite unable to discuss the matter. Marc asked Dobsie on the way back where the hot water supply originated and was shown a capped-off section in the engineers' cavern. 'It comes like bubbles full o'steam.' Dobsie pointed out the pipes. Marc could see the old pipe-work leading away in at least three different directions.

'That was where it was then,' said Marc, as much to himself as anything. But Terry was there, hanging on the words, and hungry for explanations. 'I think that there's one or more of those heat sources like in the destructor, only it is underwater instead.' Marc ceased conversation, the burns hurt and the sheepskin on his backside was tattered, exposing angry colours and an extensive graze. His injuries were going to be hard to explain away this evening, assuming an invented fall whilst collecting bats, knowing Freda as his date. He needed to think clearly, but could hardly take his mind off what had happened. 'There was a dead sheep down there,' Marc said, still with the carcass rolling about in his mind's eye. Dobsie looked at him with interest.

'The women did one o' them things they calls an audit, two days ago. We allus put a sheep t'other side wall, t' hide it. It stands there for a day easy, but the fools dropped it o'er the side.' Dobsie looked towards Mark, self-evidently proud of his intimate knowledge about the sheep community. He was difficult to detach, waiting whilst they collected their bats and headed for the village. Marc had the uncomfortable feeling that the old man was hanging on for them to tip him in some way, but then of course they were the poor in this community.

27

Empty Procreation

Gabriel Masse laughed, his heavily jowled features simulating a caricature sculpted in stone, a look carefully cultivated to stand out prominently among his other high-ranking colleagues but completely wasted on Claude. Only minutes after carrying his chair round the desk, Gabriel moved it in closer, deciding in quick succession to employ the latest fashion of speaking to one's junior at his own level, and then really close, to make it that much more personal. His hand clutched a bottle of cognac, and from it poured two tiny glasses

'Congratulations, you must be relieved to find your hunch had substance after all, and that I caught them. They were a nasty crew that lot, they could have done you any amount of harm; but give you your due, you had the good sense to know when it was in another league. That is why I decided you should be present when the arrests were made – your just reward so to speak. But all good things have to come to an end: they want me back in Toulouse now.' He struggled to achieve the right degree of grudging admiration for himself, experimenting for later embellishments of image in the accolade expected upon his return to the seat of power. 'With the robbers apprehended, and most of the bank haul recovered there is simply no excuse for me to remain here longer.'

His voice gained an inflection almost of regret, but he waxed even friendlier yet, his face lurching into another gear – a sort of hangdog expression.

'It is a hard life living away from home, and I really am thankful for any excuse to come back. What is it now – nearly three months? Julia will miss me dreadfully; the time has been long enough to even consider having a family so do not be surprised if she starts babbling on about such things. Just humour her, much as you did last time. If some kind of magic date is advocated, then I have no doubt that you will hear of it early on, so keep me informed – I might have to find her lodgings in town some night or other. But look on the bright side, everything may just return to normal.' His chief laughed, and clapped him on the back. 'I'm sure your best will do us handsomely.' He clasped Claude by the hand and held him fast by it, towering over the small man as he stood. 'The dog, I think, can be buried now; but preferably not in a pet cemetery. Advise Julia for me. I'm sure that she will see reason.' He released Claude's hand. The interview was at an end.

The Commissariat staff heaved a sigh of relief as the police big guns began to depart, and trivial chatter set in among themselves displacing matters of more import; so much so, that chance members of the public were undecided whether they had come to the right address or not. The euphoria peaked in Sylvia's office, set between that of Claude and the top man. Sylvia whirled around in some kind of jig upon her desk top, squirting puffs of aerosol conditioner through the chief's open door every time she came round. Her friends stood around the desk hooting with laughter and egging her on by making clinking noises with their cups. Into this light-hearted world came Julia; her knock was not heard, but as she came in Sylvia stepped to chair then to floor automatically – turning to the intruder almost as if she had just dusted a light fitting.

'Monsieur Masse has left for Toulouse.' Sylvia bit her tongue hard not to add, 'Hurrah.'

'It is Commissar Brie I want to speak with,' said Julia pleasantly. 'He has a notice on his other door which says "Meetings in Progress".'

Sylvia laughed, she still felt exuberant. 'He has had a notice on that door for the last three months continuously. There are people here who would disturb his thought pattern you see.' After being blunt in public about her remaining boss, Sylvia was sufficiently contrite to knock upon her connecting door, and show Julia into Claude's office.

'Ha, Madame Masse, I was just thinking of you.'

Julia peered about the office, yes, it was true – Claude was alone. 'I have told you before, you can call me Julia.' She said it kindly, pleased to note that the small man's features had brightened upon seeing her.

Claude came towards her, and smilingly sat her in a chair, amused for quite another reason; he was trying out his chief's technique on the man's own wife, whilst the seat was still warm. 'You have a problem perhaps?' he asked, bringing his own chair up close. He very soon regretted the additional confidentiality of a move that brought her so very close, and the euphoria within him faded away as troubles perplexed her brow then poured into his ear.

'Gabbie was to be available tomorrow, and he has deserted me.' Her eye creased, as if the thought might evolve into tears.

'There, there,' said Claude in a most admirable comforting manner, his holiday having worked wonders for him. 'I am sure I can find an hour or two if it will help.'

Her eyes brightened – all threat of tears vaporized. 'Would you really? Oh, that is so very sweet of you.' She was working herself up for that kiss on the forehead again.

Claude threw in his apologies to stay her lips. 'I am sorry about the cemetery. It came in the line of duty. If you want her, Mitzi can be collected, she is no longer needed.' That, he thought, would take the edge off her ardour. But though the kiss was staved off, the smile behind it broadened.

'Gabbie wants him buried in our garden, and if you could manage to come for lunch tomorrow you can both meet Dr Desprez, and also bury the dog for me.'

Claude was taken aback, burying the dog himself was not something he had contemplated, but the smile egged him on – yes he would do it.

Claude was there to see the jar containing Mitzi removed from the evidence room; she swirled reassuringly if not very appealingly as they moved her, with odd tufts of disturbed fur rising to cloud the contents.

'Can't we tip some of this out?' asked Mullet, feeling the weight.

'No,' said Claude, fearing some vital bit might possibly be lost, and besides, he wanted the others to suffer a little as he had suffered over that dog. 'Take it exactly where it is to be buried, and dig a suitable hole alongside.' He directed them very precisely, and even before the two men had started heaving at the vessel he was congratulating himself on forestalling the finding of it just sitting on Julia's doorstep.

There was a red car standing upon Julia's drive, as Claude backed in alongside. He had dressed in an old suit used for gardening, one that seemed just right for the task – a task he relished less the more he thought about it. Julia came out to his car. Her face wore that disturbed look again; she poked her head in.

'The doctor from the fertility clinic is here, she wanted to give Gabriel a medical and got ready to go when I said he was in Toulouse; but then I heard you arrive, and said you must be him.'

Claude felt decidedly uncertain about this new turn of events. 'Surely that is between Gabriel and you. I can't stand in for him, can I?'

Julia looked at him as if he was talking utter nonsense. 'Gabby has had children with his first wife, it's me that's the question mark she's come to verify – he is just a formality.' She banged the car with her hand, emphasizing each word in that upset way that characteristically Julia so often used to cause the world to cooperate.

'Leave it to me,' said Claude, feeling anything but happy about it.

Minutes later, Claude entered the house through a front door that Julia had deliberately left on the latch, and formally met the doctor in the hall. Dr René Desprez was neatly dressed in a trouser suit, and viewed Claude's dishevelled clothes with barely concealed disgust.

'Comfortable to travel in,' breezed Claude hospitably. 'Let us sit down.'

But his authority as man of the house immediately took a setback, because Julia wanted them somewhere else – there was a bite to eat. The conversation however covered his gaffe, and he stayed comfortably on police matters throughout the meal. Claude soon had the feeling that he had discharged the task better than if he had been Gabriel himself. Réné broached the subject of her visit, and that was when he started to feel uneasy for prying into something that should stay private. The couple had, from the conversation, been trying on and off for five years, a matter not helped by Gabriel's promotion, which took him away for long stretches.

'You are already following your cycle much as we suggested?' Dr Desprez was now talking specifically to Julia, who nodded her head in agreement. The doctor looked at her intently and with growing objectivity. 'And we have chosen today for a medical review.' Réné recapped the position, her voice betraying deliberations that heralded a further move. Again Julia nodded her head.

'Then I think another room is called for, a bedroom will do. If I may, I shall examine Monsieur Masse first.' Claude felt rooted to his seat. Réné smiled at him – she had seen it all before. 'Come along now, it's not painful you know.'

Julia led the way upstairs casting backward glances at Claude, would he hold out? That she couldn't say for certain, but at least he was doing it. Julia chose the bedroom that had been near gutted with the owl episode, on the premise that Claude would feel more acclimatized to that one rather than any other.

'Do you want to come in Mme Masse?' Dr Desprez asked, holding the door open; but received in reply an almost horror-stricken look from Julia as she retreated. What she did not see was an equivalent look upon Claude's face.

'Would you mind stripping off?' Réné turned and began setting up a small microscope on Julia's dressing table. Claude stripped, it was all second-best stuff, even his shirt had been retrieved from the ragbag – he screwed it up all together. As a medical it was brief: blood pressure, the chest was tapped, cough, she said, testing the reflexes – quite undeterred by anything masculine. But he was still not off the hook, for now it was the specimens: urine first, hardly was it off the production line before she began the testing. Réné had left him holding a vibrating apparatus designed to obtain seminal fluid. She finished her testing with time to spare, way ahead of him. Oh the embarrassment of her assistance! Réné was very objective and thinking nothing of it was very soon able to transfer his sample to the microscope – he could see it himself if he wanted. Taking just one tiny droplet from a flexible tube she set the slide up, and then stood to one side inviting him to see the hanging drop preparation which she thought might put him more at ease.

Looking down the objective, Claude was astounded to see such frantic activity, and the perfection of these microscopic forms, which swarmed into view and out again. To follow any one as it wriggled its way in and out of so many others was just not possible

271

at that speed. He felt there were enough of these little fellows to populate the world twice over, and was beginning to feel rather proud of his own potential. But looking through the microscope needed only one eye, and the other soon aware of a big rounded gut. With dreams of stud fame beginning to fade, Claude made for his trousers. Dr Desprez had said something to him and left whilst he was still enthralled looking down the tube at his assets. That she had gone to Julia he felt certain. Claude dressed and wandered into the upper hall where he could hear a murmur of voices coming from what was most probably another bedroom. She didn't ask me if I wanted to be present, he thought, amused at what might be Julia's reaction if he had said yes; but then of course he hadn't been asked.

Much as he expected, the back lawn was where he found Mitzi's glass flask; it was sitting beside the hole that his men had dug for her. Close by rested a click-together casket, and to one side of it lay a headstone with pink face showing. He noticed the absence of paw markings, the only thing missing, for although Julia had avoided a cemetery burial she was using all their standard gear. He read the text, it was a bit sentimental, but not as bad as some he'd seen. How the devil was he to get the dog out of the jar, getting the lid off alone strained his ingenuity to the hilt. Having exposed a chemical fluid with that strange almost earthy odour he knew as formaldehyde, Claude treated it with respect. Not far away there was a shed upon the vegetable patch. He entered and discovered a fork. However, Julia would certainly object if he spiked the dog to pull it out; reluctantly his hand retracted. Instead he chose a hoe, one that he could visualise dragging a dog from inside a jar, with ladies attending. A spade joined it as ideas flowed freely, and clutching both Claude retraced his steps, the plan clear as crystal. Reaching the lawn side of the jar, he began digging a shallow trench at the likely pouring distance. He was almost finished when both women joined him.

'You cannot just dig up the lawn,' protested Julia. 'That has been there for centuries.'

'It can all go back on top.' As he said it, Claude averted his eyes from the untidy line of irregular turfs that he had cut. Well, if she didn't want the fluid under the lawn, then it would have to go down the hole. Carefully he cleared the casket a measured distance to one side and poured a flood into the freshly dug grave; the vessel moved with considerable difficulty as he tilted, and the hole immediately became waterlogged.

Julia's neck craned to see the deed done. 'Hold it!' she shouted. 'You are just putting her back in all that horrid liquid again.'

'It will seep away if we wait,' yelped Claude, dicing with the unpredictable contents that had just reached a most critical stage; the dog resting so near the lip that it had cut off the liquid's egress. Now was the right moment to assist the dog out, and float the coffin upon waters that would shortly subside in the hole. He swivelled the flask whilst maintaining the same angle towards the coffin. Julia stood there, hands on hip behind the coffin – he would splash her. Claude abandoned his second plan.

Carefully standing the three-quarters-full flask upright, he then coaxed the women to either side of the flask, and tilted it slightly towards the casket now re-positioned at the centre of his part dug trench in the lawn.

'Hold on tight as I pull her out,' he snapped, facing his helpers as they tilted; but no, Mitzi had slipped back even further. Juice poured into the shallow casket filling it far too rapidly for fishing with the hoe – in a rush Mitzi splashed down into the coffin sending up a shower that wet them all. Claude, standing a good hoe-length off, having no more than touched the dog, got off very lightly. There was a squawk as the shower hit the women, and hands that held the flask forwards let go. It fell, tamping the casket down into the lawn furrow, leaving Claude directly in line with the formalin, which emerged as a tidal wave hitting him just in line with the knees.

Dr Desprez ran over to a hose reel at the side of the house, and turned the tap – nothing happened. Julia made frantic signals which took the doctor round the side of the house to where there was another hose reel, but in addition there was the mains tap. Her own face was feeling the bite of the chemical as she ran, so her first act upon turning the water on was to splash it on herself. Returning to the lawn side, she found both Julia and Claude at the rear hose with Claude gushing water in Julia's face. He had at last stopped her protests, and continued pleasurably drenching her until his own skin began to object. Leaving her to gasp, he stuffed the hose into his trouser waistband, and quickly drawing it out, bathed the area under his shirt. Bedraggled and sopping wet, they left Mitzi semi-floating in her casket, and headed for the house.

Dr Desprez realized that Claude was the one afflicted in considerable measure, and that his skin was decidedly at risk; quickly she had him sitting in a bath of tepid water. But there was more to be done, much more when she found the antidotes she was looking for.

Claude had hardly become comfortable in the bath when Julia knocked upon the bathroom door and entered carrying a pack of eggs. These she cracked one after another and carefully strained the whites into the water.

'Doctor's orders,' she said, but such words disturbed her concentration enough to let a yolk escape. It splashed into the bath and both gave chase. The yolk was more slippery than lost soap and Julia became immersed in hunting it, so much so that she seemed to have forgotten Claude's nudity – Claude uncomfortably wondered where she'd trawl next. Through the door came Réné Desprez, carrying a pot of something hot, which had Claude wondering how he'd managed to choose a thoroughfare with bath. Helplessly he watched as the steaming hot pot full of gluey liquid streamed into the water.

Réné took a hand in stirring the mixture. 'It is gelatin to protect your skin,' she said. 'It will react and harden with the formalin.'

Claude groaned. He could see himself set firmly in a bath-sized jelly tablet.

Réné asked, 'Do you itch?' Claude was sure he did, so she set off to discover what other remedies there might be in the house. Julia remained, fully determined to be his nurse, and crouched low helpfully circulating the water with her hand as paddle.

Claude saw the clarity of the water as excessive, and dignity not being preserved considering Julia's close proximity. Mousy memories of their night together in this very bath could have given rise to some very unpredictable female emotions, and if today she was tending an imaginary nest then he would rather not be in it. A bar of soap was soon in his hand, improving the water's turbidity, whilst he thoughtfully reminded her of her own splashes which surely must need attention soon. This was something she was evidently hesitant to do, for once having entered fully into the spirit of nursing she was now set upon putting him to rights. There slithering near his foot was the yolk, he dug his toes into it and much appreciated the rapidity of water clouding over his assets.

Through it all, thoughts of that beastly formalin concoction were uppermost in his mind – he could see the skull and cross-bones upon the drum in the evidence room. Surely the formaldehyde in it must have been diluted for use? If he assumed it was one fifth of full strength, and that it had been in contact with him for perhaps under five minutes, it didn't sound nearly so dramatic – he would very likely survive without all this tribulation.

'I am all right now,' Claude remarked to Julia. 'If you just dry off my clothes, I'll go home.'

Julia wasn't so keen on that; the doctor had remarked the condition might be serious, and besides she knew that this delay in Réné's schedule would help persuade her to stay overnight. The delay would be even more convincing if she had a patient and so with all things considered there was the strengthening prospect of company tonight. 'There's nobody else to be with you Claude, I think you ought to stay where you are until the doctor is satisfied.' Julia put her ideas into action by seizing his clothes. 'You are right, these things do need drying; but first they have to be washed. I will go and put the machine on right now.' Julia left immediately taking his clothes with her. This was more comfortable; Claude reached out to flip the latch, and relaxed once more into his gluey bath, undisturbed and peaceful.

The bath water had cooled; they were neglecting him. Claude drew himself from the bath and wrapped a towel round a body that was feeling decidedly sticky. The quick look to see if towel fluff was sticking to him was, he knew, no more than an excuse to see the damage. No fluff; but his thighs did look abnormally white. Poisons did that, but perhaps also excessive sitting in a bath? The best way to check would be to recline on a bed for a while. Claude made his way across the hall to the master bedroom that he had used earlier. It was so very pleasant here just drifting away; he could wait for his clothes in comfort. Julia's ornaments were above him, as if resurrected upon their original shelves. The Dresden china figurine caught his eye, the head looked really well stuck on from where he was – all of the other pieces must be new.

A muffled knock roused him. Réné Desprez entered with a cup of hot chocolate. 'It's time for a little refreshment.' Putting the mug down, she resumed her role as medic. 'I had better take another look, we cannot be too careful can we?'

The 'another look' was critical, and the patchwork of white blotches on the pink looked threatening to Claude. 'I have been

275

sitting in water,' he said defensively, knowing that a whole swathe of skin itched abominably.

'Drink the drink,' she said firmly, and left the room.

The faint light of day showed through the thin curtains. Claude turned in bed and struck something soft; his eyes came into focus, the shape was human – the shape was Julia.

In a rush he was wide awake. A small panic seized him, where are my clothes? He lay, not moving, his mind awash with the events of yesterday; settling decisively on that chocolate drink, it must have been laced with something to make him sleep. Oh yes, it was for the skin irritation. Moving just one leg out of bed, he was relieved to see only pink, the blotchy white patches had gone. Relief for this merged with apprehension as the mound with back towards him stirred.

'Claude. Are you awake?' The mound was turning with bed-clothes clutched so as to turn with her. A swathe of bedding twisted towards him, and the bleary-eyed face of Julia emerged looking directly at him, but was in fact even more tangled up in her own guilty thoughts.

'Claude, I have to tell you,' her voice quavered unsteadily.

Claude wondered what was coming such was its import. Well, what could matter? He had survived a chemical deluge, and was ready to go hunting criminals again.

'Dr Desprez put your specimen into me – she thought it the right moment.'

'Where is she?' His words thundered anger across the room.

'She was too late for going anywhere, so I put her up in the other main bedroom, otherwise I would have used it.' The voice was gentle, showing how much care and consideration she had shown for him. Julia stared at the man's back as he rose; his head looked quite bald from here. The baby would look like that to start with, all pink. Jogged by Claude's back view, maternal thoughts blossomed and threatened to sweep her away.

Claude moved from the bedroom. He had been in this accursed house too long: walking naked and uncaring through the house he ran his clothes to ground in the kitchen. There was a dead bird on the lawn, and no wonder for what he had left out there was a hazard to everything ecological. Hesitating only to retrieve the bird as company for Mitzi, he found the hose water still running from

276

yesterday, and ran it into the coffin. The flask, now empty slid easily across the wide surrounding colour contrasts of the lawn; it was ready for collection. Tipping out the coffin's excess water, Claude clicked on the lid and heaved the whole thing forwards, until finally it dropped into the hole prepared for it. He stood surveying the casket, which had fallen upside down. Only his foot encased in a damp old shoe moved, leisurely nudging muddy earth from the pile to fall in – sufficient to disguise the coffin's untidy configuration, simple to do but decidedly satisfying. It was a tranquil time; he stood uncaring, but pondering irrelevant early morning thoughts.

The worst troubles in this world could be put at woman's door. His scheme to just tip out the flask onto the lawn with adequate drainage would have left the corpse handy and dry enough for slipping into the box – but no, he had let himself be browbeaten into a situation that fast deteriorated, until ultimately there was no practical sense in it whatsoever.

Seeing his back and him still on the premises brightened Julia's morning. She smiled happily. 'He really must care for me.'

28

Twins for Charon

Hazel was getting a little too round to sit on her horse, and morning patrol became increasingly Maureen's province. Released into Freda's company, Hazel found the queenly life demanding in just about every direction for which her earlier life experiences had failed to prepare her. After her routine village morning Freda enjoyed walking, and so together they strode through the more habitable caverns; besides Hazel missing her horse, on these occasions she quite often missed her intellect as well. Walking was not naturally one of Hazel's strengths, and quite early on her condition slowed them appreciably, causing Freda to look around for some other activity on which to unload her companion. Meanwhile they walked a shortened route in the afternoons, and for the mornings spent a while discussing current affairs as they waited for the morning patrol to return. One morning however, Hazel arrived as usual and was turned away by Freda, who asked her to come back later.

Whiling away the time, Hazel chose to visit her workforce whom she expected to be working at the loom, but the space in front of the machinery was vacant. Even after much prying about among the materials being worked, she was still none the wiser; that same beaten feeling supervened, the one she found so easily these days. Hazel moved off, quite convinced that slack behaviour was creeping in and that she ought to be stricter with her workforce. But on passing the entry cells to return, a noise caught her ear, a metallic clanking that could only be Charon in action. The corridor between the cells leading to the Styx chamber was her instant destination, but remembering Freda's words she resolved not to actually enter the chamber itself. Framed in her view from the walled corridor was Bernadette doing a crab like walk towards the sentry, and ahead of her upon the floor was a heap – a human-shaped heap.

Despite all prior reservations Hazel was moved forwards by sheer curiosity to stand level with the cave entry point. The few extra paces widened her angle of vision sufficiently to see Rose and Poppy in their quaint pointed hats. The hats were of bright copper, and a woven mesh hung down over the shoulders, particularly so at the back. These she knew had been passed down from a long line of tinies for protecting the head, but Hazel's mind still could not divorce them from the fairies she had imagined on entry. Not that she, in her present state of knowledge, saw the hats as any sort of protection, but maybe the tinies felt psychologically better for wearing them. Both seemed well adjusted to the chamber, with Rose actively involved in stripping clothes from the nearest man and Poppy putting together his bundle of possessions. Climbing gear, thought Hazel objectively, impressed that at last Bernadette was collecting herself a workforce. But beyond being a spectator she was of limited use here. A much better use of time was to convey the news to Freda.

Freda was quite obviously displeased to see her; she clearly meant her wish not to be disturbed to be obeyed; but disturbed she was, being run to earth in the concubine bubble whilst putting books on shiny metal shelves. The shelves had been delivered today, and the impact she wished to make on Hazel by enthusing her into maintaining a library failed – for Hazel walked straight in. Hazel's estimate of the news being important still told her that it was right to intrude even if Freda's reactions were off-hand. 'Bernadette has found two new arrivals in the entrance cave,' Hazel said excitedly, expecting Freda to be pleased.

Instead Freda's face bore the troubled expression of hearing bad news. 'I was hoping that we would have more time before that happened,' she said flatly.

Hazel puzzled much as to what was the matter, but said nothing. Freda had an intellectual approach to many things, which occasionally took the dairy off the best of news. Freda was disappointed in her and chided the messenger bringing bad news, but mostly for not knowing that it was. 'You must now make up your mind whether you are still Charon and the men rightly yours. They should be, as you were appointed to do the job and Bernadette co-opted to be your substitute.'

Hazel could hardly believe what she was hearing. 'Of course they belong to Bernadette, she's brought them in and will naturally

279

expect to be their boss.' Hazel envisaged fighting with Bernadette over them, and shied away from the very notion – that was not something she was capable of doing.

Freda looked at her coldly, and said with hardening voice. 'Then you must call a meeting. It is very good practice for a new Queen to influence everyone when there is some change in circumstance that needs a ruling.'

The voice still sounded hard, if not actually harsh, and Hazel slowly began to comprehend that the bitchiness hadn't anything at all to do with the library. 'Why do I call a meeting?' Hazel was still completely baffled.

'Bernadette missed her place as Charon, she was too young. If you have reinstated her rights in the matter, then either of those men can be her concubine and your man must go. It is a bit soon seeing Marc has hardly got into his stride yet – what I would call a plain case of wasting manpower needlessly. The matter concerns everybody, so it will have to be thrashed out in an open meeting.

'To me, Bernadette has not earned her place yet as Charon for she is still too immature; but that is a question you must put to the vote.'

As the implications began to dawn upon Hazel, she drew in a sharp breath, and her drawn face betrayed a whole train of consequences hitting home. What then of Marc? He would have to go. The memory of Franz with arrows embedded in him assailed her; and worse still as Marc's owner she would have to do it.

'The duties here sometimes pull us apart,' said Freda sympathetically knowing well what was in her mind. 'As Queen you have to set an example, obey the law and think responsibly for a whole community.' It was clear from her tone that Freda was unhappy to consign Marc to the destructor; but at the same time she must have been looking ahead, because she added, 'If he is doing the electrical alarm system, then you had better hurry him along, he is best used in finally taking our secrets to heaven with him.'

The pathetic collection of thin books in various languages that sat upon the shelves were a reminder of how deprived this world really was. Paperback novels they seemed for the most part; and these shared the shelves with pocket diaries part gutted to expose their information sections. In one block the inevitable Bibles, small and portable, occupied a whole shelf. Freda's own huge Bible, the one that related to the cave history, lay by itself on a lower shelf, too large and too different to be included with the others. Hazel looked inside and saw it was written in English upon leaves of hammered goatskin, and the collected pages bound together in a neat leather cover. At the back was a list of women's names in order of arrival date with Hazel as the last entry. On the two shelves beneath this definitive volume were the original writings; at best indented on baked clay tablets, descending through a whole range of materials and languages to mere scratching on slate or stone. Through the turmoil of upsetting news that had ravaged her mind, Hazel had the grace to compliment Freda upon her library idea – it was an impressive achievement. They were her first words today that had seemingly gone down well.

Freda had engineered the opening she needed for Hazel's task, and now explained how all the cheap novels in Tanya's bubble were reason enough to house the collection in one place. 'There is much light work to do in Tanya's bubble,' she observed. 'I think you may find recovering books, or anything else in there, is very good occupational therapy.'

Hazel's earlier experiences of Tanya's bubble as a supplier of materials had already aroused her curiosity, and knowing now of the diversity therein it seemed to open up prospects of what she could do with this permission. She was soon entering into what was an already familiar bubble to see more exactly what the job entailed. The heaps yielded little to her superficial poking about – apart from clothes. Her drift round the interior suddenly took on new purpose as her eye alighted upon the chance piece of silk cloth; thoughts of Poppy were instantly aroused, spawning ideas. What if her workforce were to use this material collected in yesteryears, and adapt it to the requirements of everyone as their turn came round for another smock? The stuff could be simply dropped into one of several hot streams, and be collected later freshly laundered for dressmaking. No one was so religious that their clothes had to be uniform, it was simply dictated by the wool ready to hand; Jackie already wore non-uniform clothes. But an idea that would have fired her any other time was not ripe for today, whilst every so often huge feelings of unease bit deeply into her vitals. The idea was destined to be postponed and as she became ever more preoccupied with impending disaster, Hazel soon gave up on the heap altogether.

Her round of duties with Freda had already accustomed Hazel to the women's collective meetings. Freda could work them so cleverly that she usually got her own way, and such thoughts consoled her. Hazel understood it even more thoroughly, because she was being made to take an active part, rather than just sitting there as she had invariably done in the past. Even that was not the end of it, for they would go on discussing the meeting, and discussing the meeting again until her brain was sick of the detail. The afternoon walks always saw off this tail end to whatever meeting had taken place, taxing her brain as much as the exercise taxed her feet. Her meetings with the elders was even more of a failure as Freda frequently did not attend, leaving her as the least voice among the more powerful women but still having to account for it afterwards.

Freda's afternoon wandering, apart from meetings preparation, she said had a definite purpose. To be wandering about in the outer caves long after the four had departed was a valuable way of spotting dangers before they materialized. It would be very soon known for surveillance rather than wandering, if it were used obviously, or petty crackdowns took place afterwards. No; she said such information had to be used intelligently, by countering any-thing undesirable without sign of a direct connection. Freda saw no point in pursuing things her managers had missed, like hiding livestock or brewing beer illicitly from grain stolen right under their noses. The afternoon walk enabled Freda to assess how well her little empire worked and provided facts enabling her to sum up the performance of the woman responsible. Additionally doing things this way enabled her to understand fully what was going on in the caves. 'If you do so and are not very clever about it, just remember, Hazel, that they will very soon keep a special eye upon you, and after that you will not see anything at all.'

Among the earlier elders' meetings that Freda did attend, there were many references to size manipulation even of the women and this Hazel found did raise uncomfortable recent memories. Freda pointed out her friends almost certainly half knew what was routinely done, but it was wrong of her to confirm any outrage they might be feeling especially if that could blame the manage-ment. 'Early in our history we realized that certain fungi were responsible for the small stature of the miners, in fact all who lived in these caves. But there is an advantage in having an appetite scaled down by smaller body mass and our forerunners found this an essential for supporting extra people. It is a practice inherited from the past, which we have refined by using another ancient discovery, that of the somnambulistic mushroom able to prolong sleep or if you prefer it unconsciousness. Combining both of these influences an earlier society balanced all newcomers to the available food supply upon entry. It is a process that we still cannot afford to dispense with,' said Freda. But then noting Hazel was still looking indignant she was pleased to point out that her size in particular had been so small that there was little need to adjust it overmuch and she was released early from treatment. Even so Freda succeeded in only slightly mollifying her; and quickly moved on to detailing how the men were adjusted to suit their allotted place in society by manipulations upon entry before recovering consciousness. 'They must be considered objectively, and much as a farmer fits livestock to his requirements, so do we.'

By the time Freda reached the one selected as concubine, the subject matter had so electrified and astonished Hazel by its sheer invasiveness, she had quite forgotten any slight to her own self.

On another occasion, they sat looking over the fishpond to be, from one of the many diggings entrances in the cave wall behind it. Freda continued her dissertation on the food supply, wanting her involvement long term. 'The fish pond took us ten years to build. It was our brightest idea, and one promising to use very little power. When next there is a volunteer suitable for obtaining the fish needed, we will be able to improve on our present diet. When you arrived so easily, I saw you as the first choice to leave and do so. But now it is you who will need to watch out for another candidate; there's no hurry even if it is years, the facility had to be there first just waiting for fish.'

'Is it easy going the other way?' Hazel asked. 'I remember tripping over a lot of creepers inside the Styx.' The hazy memory of a tiny skeleton, too, was still there provoking shivers.

Freda's glance was not sympathetic. 'Most of those selected are successful, and my map will help whoever decides to go. The creepers are only plants and could not stop a fast-exiting creature, presumably bent low to dodge the strong fields set up in the rocks. Those huge fungi owe their development to historic graveyards about that spot. Inside the gully stunned creatures cannot rise without other knockdowns, and assisted by gourd roots tend to remain there permanently, eventually becoming very good fertil-izer. The gourds must have evolved such a degree of movement by competition with each other, in fact rather more than any other known carnivorous plant species. If you look at them they are enormous, and that raises suspicions in me that they are the source of the bubbles we live in but perhaps fossilized a very long time after they die. Personally I would say that if one is aware of them, they are not a factor you would worry about.'

Quite separately from these diversions Hazel found herself gradually drawn towards the role of Queen. Freda launched her into everything and wherever she went Hazel went also. Eating was good: Marc waited on the table, and the augmented royalty ate delicacies that flowed from Maria's afternoon specials in the food house. Hazel was well into dreaming of royal life and all without making a start inside Tanya's bubble, when Freda burst in on her.

'Let us go and see those new arrivals, they ought to be progress-ing well by now.'

Heading out of the village they soon passed the women's reception cells and turned into the path that divided them. Freda halted Hazel there, and strode into the Styx cave towards the body of a large male. His general physique was of good condition, and this she discussed with Maureen who reported him as closely matched with that of his companion. Her next stop was to examine their belongings, watched intently by Poppy, who had picked up the spirit of her scavenging admirably. Freda looked very thought-ful as she returned to Hazel who was finding it amazing that she had watched here for months and seen nothing happening; so why should flesh and bones suddenly pop up now on the floor like some conjurer's magic trick? Two very blond and good-looking fellows who could well be Scandinavian, she decided.

Freda spoke with more urgency now. 'You may have trouble in convincing the girls these are to be workers. I suggest you hold the meeting, and that it be commenced before they are influenced by a sighting.'

Upon her return, Hazel feverishly began organising the event, notifying everyone still about the village, knowing full well that the crunch would come in getting the four present also. As it happened everything fell into line, and all were available that afternoon; that is, all but Freda who was elusive. 'You can have my vote, but it's

time you handled something so very important all on your own.'
Hazel pleaded, but Freda was adamant.

They held the meeting in style, for the conference room in the church was always available. Hazel was there first but still lost for what she would say; they arrived little by little as a ring of curious faces across a marble table. Remembering how Freda managed things, she stood to command their attention, and welcomed them to the debate before coming to her subject matter. 'As you may already know, this morning we were fortunate to receive two male climbers, who are hopefully going to be part of our operating strength. The reason that this meeting has become necessary is because they have arrived during a period of handover. Bernadette is acting for me as Charon.'

There came a squeal of rage from across the table as Bernadette began to get excited; it was the prelude to finding words that suited this outrage. Hazel banged upon the table with the petrified combination near to her, the one so often thumped by Freda, and spoke firmly to her friend. 'Bernadette, you must listen to what's being said before jumping to conclusions! All of you here decided that I should understudy the Queen, even though I had no wish for it and found no advantages in doing so. According to the same rules Bernadette understudied me, and should not receive lasting advantage from doing so, or at least until the whole handover is complete.'

Bernadette decided it was her turn now and interrupted, her voice rising emotionally deep in brogue. 'I s'pose you t'ink t'aye are yours!' Her excited voice quivering with emotion turned heads towards her, before they all transferred back again to Hazel as if it were some game of tennis.

'No, I do not claim them! But surely they must wait for the handover, only then can they be yours, Bernadette.' There was a note of desperation in Hazel's voice.

Bernadette nodded to Hazel, as if she accepted the position and the problem looked to have been largely resolved.

Maria raised her hand, and Hazel indicated for her to speak. 'If so, what will they be doing? Bernadette seems to have lost her concubine prerogative.'

'We have lost several workers lately, so that is open to suggestion.' Hazel smiled reassuringly, pleased she had side-stepped the next question.

But Maria came again. 'You called the meeting, is not that a royal prerogative? And you eat like a Queen.'

Hazel's smile faded. Before she could reply, Pat had joined the battle. 'Yer doan wanna-nuvver conkeybine, that's wot!' Yer wan' wot yer got, doan'cha?'

The room erupted in noise and Hazel saw the meeting slipping from her grasp. If she let go then Marc would feel the brunt. She knocked the gavel and said firmly, 'This meeting was instructed by Freda to give you all a voice in the matter. I should add that I am quite capable of doing a manning when I have to, but what I do not believe in is wasting the men that you put so much effort into saving; unless of course there is a very good reason.'

Annita's voice joined hers. 'Hazel does not have to prove herself. She will be OK when the time comes.' Noises of support also came from elsewhere, what could only be Bernadette.

Jackie showed a hand and commented mockingly with perhaps a touch of self-interest. 'I like the manning idea, for he will leave a gap and you without a male to plug it!'

Hazel smarted, countering this with an apology. 'I'm sorry to disappoint your expectations of me; but I have never been a very sexy person and lately find even less enthusiasm for it. To me the concubine is a responsibility, which I am confident of managing. Not until I am a full-time mother will I allow there to be any chance of a conflicting interest.' She looked apprehensively about her and particularly at Jackie, whose sparkling eyes and impish face showed she enjoyed the dilemma she had arranged for Hazel. But no responses came and Hazel had a strong feeling that she was winning. Maria still had a look of distaste on her face; she of course was one person Hazel knew had seen the newcomers, one who was able to dispense with Marc in their favour. Very well then, she would trump her with royalty. 'It's not just me,' she said triumphantly looking round the table. 'Freda says that is what the agreement in question actually was. I have her vote to use if necessary, she supports making an arrangement with Bernadette.'

Pat jumped up from her seat. 'She stays 'ome, an sends 'er girl ter do 'er dirty work. Cause she carn' face us!'

Maria's voice came again in that same ominous tone. 'Freda is behind this isn't she? I doubt if she also told you that the new arrivals are German, and she wants a lengthy trouble-free life for her countrymen as workers.'

The room filled with uproar, and everyone trying to be heard at once, but angry voices now evidently all set against the motion. Another voice came clearly over the top of the hubbub, even as Hazel raised the gavel again; it was Maureen. Hazel paused holding the gavel's stem aloft not knowing quite whether to react, as Maureen's firm voice was heard.

'I propose that Bernadette gets her concubine, whether she wants it or not. The situation will give you a chance to do the manning, show your baby full attention and be properly one of us. Then you can be sure of undisputed acceptance as Queen.'

Hazel knocked repeatedly. 'Is there someone who will second the motion?' Hazel's voice did not penetrate quite as it should. Poppy put her hand up and said something indistinguishable, but whatever it was could only be taken as support.

Hazel banged her gavel. 'Who is in favour of it?'

Hands climbed aloft all round the table, except for Annita and Bernadette. With a hoarse throat, and feeling weak at the knees, Hazel declared the motion passed. Her two friends stayed close to her as the room emptied. Annita said as she commiserated, 'I'm afraid you put your foot in it there Hazel.' She wrapped an arm round her friend's shoulders, for Hazel was well and truly ready for a cry.

Freda too was upset, when Hazel disconsolately admitted her dismal failure in bringing the meeting to a satisfactory outcome. Hazel said nothing about the German men, somehow it seemed unfair to mention what clinched it; the consolation was that the meeting had not taken issue with her personally. There was not much more said about it, because Freda recognized the hazards of deciding things at meetings better than most, knowing that they do sometimes go awry. Her advice was to concentrate on seeing that the execution took place cleanly. The last words rang in Hazel's ears as she came away. 'Practice shooting in the hunt cave whilst there is still time; Annita will show you how.'

In the next few days Hazel took much practice with the crossbow. Annita raked over the old targets in the hunt cave and underneath discovered the straw shape that she had used. It was tall and the shape was human, this they stood in the opening where the fugitive would emerge, whilst Hazel practised shooting bolts rapidly into it. Her condition did not matter overmuch, as the bowstring was drawn taunt by a removable winding mechanism, one that had been modified and passed down through the ages. A second bow sat close by on a stand, ready wound for the follow-up shot. The technique for practice was to turn about suddenly, and put two bolts accurately into the straw form; this was her exercise and soon Hazel became quite adept at it. After two days Annita left her to it, and bolt after bolt thudded into the mid chest area of the dummy.

Up to then she had deliberately disassociated the fugitive from Marc, but as her technique became more certain there existed more imaginative thoughts of Marc in her mind. For the ump-teenth time Hazel swivelled round, and at the very point of releasing the bolt she started, as the dummy suddenly seemed to animate in a terrifying vision of Marc, like some grisly time echo of things to come.

29

Where Eagles Fly

Two bright copper fifteen-foot ladders were carried into the bat cave, and that was the trigger for Terry's escape attempt. There was time only to admire the ladders as sturdy entities that could be used in combination, before realizing that everything had to happen without delay. The moment Maria knew of the ladders' existence, there was a strong possibility that Marc might be withdrawn from bat collecting and so weaken the chance of success. Anticipating the immediacy involved, every stage had been planned to match the ladders' construction and their personal progress on clearing ground. At one point they had even stopped the engineers for a while whilst the women held a series of unexpected equine events near the stables. Already the collection frame had been mounted on large wheels and was able to move easily to the spot they wanted; but having wheels the whole construction possessed a disadvantage in being less stable once ladders were placed on top. The frame, which stood some twenty-five feet high, needed to be wedged level with stones underneath before use, and the lower platform weighted with rocks to make it firm. That much they could prepare for earlier; so it only remained for the ladders to be carried over the uneven stone floor and into position underneath the bat run.

This was Terry's project, and although both rope and wire had been saved from their previous adventure the need to use rope he thought unnecessary, for anything tied to the waist would end up all bunched behind the feet in a real tangle if he reversed. Marc reasoned that he needed the rope; why not loop it over the shoulder and only carry it forwards? But that matter was only furthered when they combined their efforts to haul up the ladders and assemble both sections upon the frame's top deck. Marc was soon wrestling with the task of getting near to the hole, as the ladder barely made it. At least he was ready to extend the ladder as far as possible, with the help of a stepladder placed on the top deck.

His adjustments continued until it rested some three feet under the hole. However this made the angle with the cavern wall acute; in fact much too narrow for Marc's liking, so he tied the already existing spare length of knotted rope so as to connect both upper ladder and staging before being satisfied. Marc had become more interested in the bats' entrance hole since setting his friend Red to watch how they used it. Red reported back that the bats flew in and out as if there were no restriction, so the hole which looked quite tiny from the ground, might be a reasonable bet.

All that remained now was for Terry to climb the ladder, despite his fright the moment he saw it from the ground; somehow it reminded him of an acrobat's workplace without the trapeze. By the time he reached the top of the stage he was already pretty high in the air and reluctant to set his feet upon such a long ladder. But he could not back out now, and hesitantly started to climb the first ladder, which swayed alarmingly under the scared novice. The old harness line was visible at the other side of the ladder, for Marc had tied it loosely three rungs down from the top, first insisting that he agree to carry it looped high on one arm. Marc insisted because Terry needed it for safety higher up, and signalling his intentions was also important if they were to act together. Any success and he knew Marc would be following shortly. Terry's forearm carried a torch with batteries refreshed electrically. At his waist hung a weighty pointed tool that would dig chalk at one end or alternatively hammer it with the other. He had the equipment as suggested by Marc, who in truth was the most competent person to use it, but this was Terry's initiative and he meant to hold on to it.

Marc found himself watching critically from the platform's high level, steadying the frame and ropes, but occasionally having to shake his head at Terry's ineptitude.

Terry's arrival on the upper rungs of the top ladder caused the portion that rested against the sheer wall to bounce a little, which because of the fear that this brought, even helped him into his signal/lifeline which he now threaded through the second rung and over his shoulder. His movements became more purposeful as he reached the point of transfer, knowing the lifeline was primed to preserve him, even so he dared not look down. Terry slid his body upwards beyond the ladder, slipping hands vertically over the surface rock and stepping up to the penultimate rung he balanced there erect. Reaching out above him his arms entered the hole, and once in it became committed to a search forwards for some kind of grip among the felts. Terry paused hanging in there before reluctantly bending his head into the dark hole festooned with grey fluff, but he was still well short of entering fully and his feet scraped their way up to the top rung where toes butted against the rock surface and where fear aroused a perceptible whole body tremor. He stood on tiptoes still sliding his weight forwards and upwards over smooth vertical rock; then daring one foot on the topmost ends of the ladder he finally drove his ribcage over the ledge.

Everything felt knife-edge as he hung there in a black hole caked with loose dirt, hoping his fingers that were scrabbling along mercifully irregular walls would find a better hold somewhere. He wriggled his shoulders along the top surface and by degrees passed more of his body into the hole. His feet left their support and scuffed the bare rock, at which point his shoulders met the roof. Relieved about this he was soon concentrating on fingers which had located crevices behind loose felt and having scraped clear of the soft cover found points of leverage to wriggle further in. Terry was soon lifting his pelvis through into the space with feet kicking rock as he trod the air; but now with shoulders reliably wedged much further inside, his centre of gravity ensured he had arrived. Now he could bring his head and neck into play, there was more leverage, although there was no rest for him until his knees had encountered and raked their way over the sharp edge.

Unable to fall out now he switched the torch on, heartened to see the way ahead had widened if anything. His body, now all on the same level, progressed easily, but he suffered much in his mind from thoughts of what might be flying towards him; such ideas, he told himself were ridiculous at this time of day. These patently trivial thoughts were soon dispelled by something more positive, as dirt and stones dislodged from overhead. Nothing as large as him had ever crawled through here before so it all could collapse, and that idea did bother him enough to extract the tool from his belt and carry it in front of him. Such thoughts had replaced the bats, but he was relieved to see it was all white stuff falling. The fault itself was deep in chalk, and even though there were difficulties it was heartening to see the stuff around him crumble easily away from the hand tool. He had anticipated that the bats had room to fly all the way, for if there were places where they just crawled, the tool would not be equal to the job. These worries diminished as loose stuff stopped falling and the felts he encountered remained soft all around him. But the dust remaining from the fall had powdered an already dry throat and so he was grateful for the breaths of fresh air wafting through; not to mention the coldness he felt on his face for surely that must come from outside. He turned the torch off to conserve batteries and wormed his way forward to a blurred perception of light, perhaps another fifteen feet of movement. If anything the tunnel was relaxing from his shoulders as he moved, light twinkled ahead and getting stronger, it looked like genuine daylight. It was well over to the right; he checked the dark side wall with his torch and found another division to the left!

This was a point to signal: two tugs to signify OK, then a further four to say he was turning left, a move intended to seek out the cave he vaguely remembered hearing bats before that final glassy tunnel; a memory still strong enough to motivate. It was hard to move away from the light, its grey blue could only be sky. Purposefully he turned inwards moving through the decidedly larger orifice that had opened up into the rock. He had moved another twenty feet or so when abruptly his arms descended into a soft dark deposit that subsided beneath his chest, causing an avalanche of dust and dirt to cascade into the hole beneath; he dug in the chipping tool but lost the torch in an effort to stop sliding with it. The total distance since his turn was small compared to that last glassy approach tunnel; no way was this his cavern destination.

The cleft appeared deep according to the delay before hearing the bottom thumped; but however near the bottom he was, without the torch he could not go forward. It could not be done. Reluctantly he signalled their agreed code: two pulls he was OK and six pulls he was coming back. Easier signalled than done, for he was facing downhill and powder fell away from his arms as he levered in a soft friable substance that wanted to go forward. Terry soon felt hot from exertion and besides being very frightened, he was stuck. Releasing the loop from his shoulder he passed it in front of him until Marc got the idea and the rope firmed up; now he could lever on it with his arms, squirming and worming back until he was seemingly on the level with much rope lying in front of him. It was an unusual motion that he warmed to, and become more adept until a cold breeze struck at his feet. Terry humped himself through the last inches feeling the narrower aperture's resistance repelling him as he reversed into it.

The light of sky was again ahead of him when he felt the nearby rope jerk, it was clear that Marc had sensed a stop. Two quick pulls to say OK, then five to say he was turning right. It was an easier task now with vision; he retrieved the loop and wore it over his shoulder before going forward towards the light. His arms propelled him forward on a slope going downhill, he used the tool to brake as it steepened but still the hill promoted a fast pace. The hole and the cold came faster towards his face, and as he dug deeper to slow himself his tool was increasingly losing contact and passing over anything solid. Stopping to signal again was not an option as the other arm sank in a depth of felt, loose and pillow soft it surrounded him. Other undulations appeared in front of him cracking open as finally its whole substance began to slide, and he with it still on the rope; but now there were yards of slack from his reversing. Like a rollercoaster, the guano/flock slipped over the edge disintegrating as it went, leaving the human component to fall head-first into thin air.

Suddenly he was jerked to a stop, with the rope almost taking Marc off the high platform at the other end before snapping taut to where the slack was wound. The rope bit into Terry's shoulder and inverted him in mid-air, whilst its loop skimmed along an arm skinning it until it reached his hand where it stopped hard, snagging at the wrist. The other hand dropped the tool and urgently caught hold of knots upon the loop. Terry was yanked to a stop with an inefficient grasp on the rope. Suddenly all his weight hung on hands, with one shoulder stabbing pain and a wrist in sheer agony, probably dislocated. The sound hand struggled to take more weight as he found himself hanging in space. An icy wind turned him and cut like a knife at all exposed flesh, he could only hang grimly on to the rope. His rope swung and turned in gale-force blasts of wind, and from here he took stock.

Terry looked up to where the rope lay across a huge fan shape, now almost clear of its centuries of build up; the rope would not fray, but climbing back was impossible with his shoulder, or perhaps impossible anyway. He wished that there were knots to make the climb worth attempting, but lacking them, he must do something else before he froze in the icy buffeting wind. Terry looked down below, and made out the twiggy outline of a bush, perhaps only ten feet down – beyond that it was hundreds. Gritting his teeth he raised himself slightly on his good arm, and checked the injured hand could release the rope. Hanging on would not get him there; he would have to work up enough swing for the mere foot it would take to do so. Numb from the cold, and with the rope barely moving, he worked his bottom half until by degrees the line swung inwards almost colliding with the rock face. Then came a chance extra shove from the wind, and he knew that it was enough, letting go without even looking down. The plunge stopped at ten feet as planned, and glancing off the rock face he struck an eagle's nest which moved under his impetus towards and over the edge; the forward motion taking his favourite raptor's offspring with him to plummet down together with the sickening knowledge that the next contact would be fatal.

Marc instantly realized something was wrong: he mounted the ladder, and negotiated the transfer with the natural ease of a trained engineer, his problem mainly one of extra bulk. Could he squeeze through too? It was hard going at first, but shoulders and pelvis were soon easing away from the walls, and in a surprisingly short time he was at the junction. A wide hole yawned in the direction that the rope went, and beyond that was yards of slide. Judiciously he collected the long rope; it was lightweight and the loop for Terry's shoulder when it came was bloodstained. Whatever happened was unsuccessful; there was nothing more he could do beyond the hope that somehow his mate had survived.

Marc well knew that Terry had wanted to turn to the left, and certainly it seemed wider in that direction; to go back would be very difficult for him personally as progress with his extra bulk had already told him so. He wormed backwards and was rewarded by a fall of loose grey-brown dust that had him coughing. Let's press on, he said doubtfully to himself, and to his relief moved almost immediately into a wider hole. In his hand he clutched Terry's rope dragging it to the left with him, and in the wider section looped it about his shoulder, knowing full well that the end of it was tied securely to a weighty climbing frame.

It was not so very far before he encountered signs of Terry's first collapse, and moving with care upon its funnel shape his torch picked out what the inevitable dust cloud would have hidden from Terry. There across the divide the bat run continued; but before and below that there was a chimney of converging rock leading into untold depths.

To Marc this was a heaven-sent opportunity, if only to turn about; he pulled yards and yards of rope past him knowing that it would have to stop sometime. Eventually a solid resistance abruptly countered his pull, and then with all excess rope hanging in the chimney below him, he tilted forwards slipping head first; but only to turn over clinging on to the rope. He had cleared the bat run. Marc hung there collecting himself, before abseiling down into the depths. The chimney seemed a long way down, fears about bottom-less holes loomed large in his thoughts – it would be just his luck to find one. But no, the other wall was approaching, and quite suddenly his feet dipped into a sea of dust and fluff. Halting his descent to view the scene he slowly became aware of Terry's small avalanche. There seemed to be light to one side of him and that initiated a difficult traverse towards it; alongside there a narrow cleft terminated in a space that was lit, and before long he was into it. Once Marc was outside the fault in the rock, its content of black, evil-looking, fibrous dust was behind him; at an estimate it could be anything over a ton. He tugged the submerged residual rope into the space at the bottom and weathered the resulting cloud of dust. His feet next hit the rocky floor close to where the rest of his rope had landed. It was a real relief to leave the felt heap trapped like soot in a hopper. The rift above was just visible, over a mere crevice extending right through to the floor.

He looked round the cave to his extreme right where a row of holes provided low-level illumination. His torch would not be needed so he switched it off, observing that he was at the far end of quite a large cave, one that had a mass of stalagmites at its centre rendering it completely inaccessible; as a result he headed for the luminous holes. Ahead, in a deep recess, something fibrous that resembled dried leaves obstructed his path, and through it a brighter if still subdued light percolated. He pushed its light frame aside and found himself standing right in the line of Hazel's fire.

Hazel was astounded; the bolt bounced from the rocks above and she looked at him in a mixture of shock and incredulity. It took some minutes for Hazel to recover her composure, in which time Marc hurried over to help her. She leaned heavily on him, white faced. 'Where did you spring from?' Her eyes searched a face lit by the glow of destructor minor.

There would be no point in lying, Marc pointed to the place where he had emerged. 'I am looking for a way out of here, and found myself in that cave.'

'But there's no through path in there.' Hazel's voice quavering and questioning, she did not believe him. Guilt at being caught in the act was overwhelming; but he couldn't know?

Marc led her back to his chimney crack allowing her to see and believe, for to come in at that height was not how she would describe an entrance. There still protruding from a mere crevice at shoulder height his coil of rope lay on the floor in a sooty heap, Marc lifted it and chucked it up out of sight a sure sign he had entered just there. 'I must go back to the village,' he said. Marc was worried now; he had a feeling that he could square it with Hazel, but there would be others far less understanding.

'The loom is working out there.' Hazel was suddenly alive to all sorts of possibilities and even helping him to escape might atone for the murderous rehearsal. 'I'll take my workers out of your way for a minute or two, but promise me that we talk about this tonight.'

Hazel looked at him, and not for the first time he detected a loving expression; for that there was only one answer. 'Of course, I will! See you then.' She pursed her lips, and he was there for the kiss, dirt and all; they clung for what seemed far too short a while before Hazel set off.

Marc followed her easily enough, for her walk was ponderous and slow. He waited near the cave mouth following her every move as she spoke to her workers. With an abrupt move the women headed for the end bubble of the men's cells. Marc's foot struck objects lying on the floor, and possessing enough time to investigate, found himself two pairs of rock climbing boots and a couple of loose pitons. It was too good an opportunity to miss, and in a trice he had the best pair laced together over his shoulders. Stealthily passing the cells, he could hear the chuckles of little women demonstrating their copper hats to Hazel.

He was not out of the woods yet. It was afternoon and women-folk would be present at every stage of his return. It was with much caution that Marc crouched inside the pool gatehouse only minutes later, waiting for the chattering figures he could see mistily through its fabric on the village side.

There was increasing noise from the other direction, and with a start he realized that there were more of them coming out of the pool approaches, singing as they came. Marc was driven to move sharply from his hiding place into the village. Stepping quietly through the door, he noticed with relief a nearby figure talking with her back towards him, and even better pointing with an arm in another direction.

Marc slipped very speedily behind the two nearest bubble house combinations. Very carefully he lingered between the shells that were Cora and Tanya's apartments, with no fear they might be occupied, but hoping all the time that Maria was not watching him from the upper storeys of the multi-bubble food house. The swimming party arrived and moved through, but still he had to wait for the gossip to finish before legging it to the engineers' gate.

As Marc exited the gatehouse he could see Leon working at the digester, a heaven sent opportunity because he was now faced with more than he could handle. 'Leon, for God's sake come and give me a hand! We have lost Terry!' Leon was stirred into coming with him but had to rush along behind. After passing him Marc paused only when he reached the foot of his borrowed ladder. Cutting all the ropes free he was able to rattle the ladders down, leaving the dragged line dangling from the hole. Passing the stepladder over the side to Leon who laid it flat, the new combination ladder could be laid on the frame and trundled over to a suitable wall, where Marc grabbed two dozen bats, dispatching them to a suitably dark bat heaven. With a tolerable pile of carcasses to hand over, the new ladders were spirited away to the engineer/miner cavern where they were laid inconspicuously against a wall. Marc untied both give-away ropes from the mobile frame, and when he came to detaching one half the heavy knotted rope left from the waterfall an idea presented itself. Straight away he handed the part rope to a surprised Leon. 'When you take your load of manure out tonight, hang that over the falls for me.'

'There's not a full load yet – I'll take it tomorrow,' whined Leon, thinking how inconvenient it all was.

Marc had enough obstacles for one day, he grabbed Leon's sheepskin top threateningly, and drew him towards his face.

'Bloody well get on with it now – do it now!' His bulky shadow loomed over the tiny man menacingly. 'Take the rope to Red, and get him to tie it over the falls like it was the other day – tell him it is urgent.'

Leon hung the rope on his cart knowing that his work pattern was changed.

Maria looked critically at the bats that Marc had deposited. 'Where are the rest of them? Are they with Terry?'

'I don't know where Terry is.' Marc was being deliberately non-committal, but knowing full well that Maria would not leave it there he ventured an opinion. 'I saw him earlier today with the food trolleys, but I don't know where he has gone since. We should be able to make up the deficit tomorrow, because the new ladders have arrived.'

Maria's face took on a smile, and he left her diverted into a happier frame of mind. Too soon Marc was arriving in his room, haunted with the memory of losing a friend and annoyingly finding the floor strewn with electrical parts, just as he had carelessly left it. A legacy of weeks struggling with the village alarm system, for which Terry had been an indispensable part of solution finding besides the overcoming of many obstacles, and now he would be there to the bitter end, completing everything alone. Together they had fused wire connections into glass or wax in making permanent fixtures instead of solder, and that had been difficult. But they had succeeded in this despite having relays and detection switches that had so many problems. From the junk available, tiny speakers had been extracted and used to resonate far beyond their usual limits as alarms. They had even discovered a tiny transformer in a portable radio able to supply the low voltages necessary for working an entire circuit. For all these things Terry's involvement had given him the back-up he needed.

But seeing the pieces of his favourite electrical puzzle, however much they bugged him, helped to take him out of depression, and he sat for hours juggling with the pieces.

30

Blud

Freda invariably avoided contact with Patricia if it was at all possible as the woman was too crude, and beside that too illiterate for her liking. To cap it all, deciphering the meaning of her usually twisted sayings surpassed even the effort necessary to understand Poppy. Queenly prerogative counted for little when it came to manipulating the one who moved on the second highest level and considered it supreme. But here was a meeting Freda couldn't avoid; important issues were at stake and several voices drove her to contest them. An invitation to lunch seemed the most amicable thing she could do to learn of Pat's intentions first hand, and that she did.

Many had said before that the woman was unhinged; but even under this label she was also respected for carrying out the religious leader role wholeheartedly. No matter what religion each woman entering the caves started with, Pat had a knack of converting them all to the religion of the caves. For as she would contend, all routes to God are through some martyr or other and the caves had one that was their own. Her attributes were feminine enough to please a female flock, and what's more suggested a realistic route that prayers might be seen to reach God via their holy lady.

It was Maureen who first alerted Freda to their churchwoman priest's more extreme reaction, after having had a stormy encounter with her. The prelate had chosen to discuss the fact with her that Hazel was about to have a baby. According to Pat it was the colony's very own baby, such a happening could be none other than a second coming of St Itzla herself. Pat had foreseen it in a dream, and had been saying prayers for the event ever since she came into office – except that she had expected the baby to be her own. The cave spirits whispered to her of a brave new epoch, one that would begin shortly with the birth of a sacred mistress, a mistress Pat intended to serve faithfully. The coming would herald a dream existence for women, and this dream world would revert to using genuine castrates for menial tasks. Maureen would play an important role in all of this because the men would be likely to oppose any such a move; she would become a soldier woman leading the fight for church and domain.

That was all the support she required of them; devout people setting the stage ready for the reign of 'Itzla the Second'.

But it was more than a bigoted drift of conversation that had upset Maureen. 'She talks about childbirth in such a way that makes me doubt her claim to be an experienced midwife. We have no way of verifying any claim that she makes, and I for one believe she shouldn't be anywhere near a birth.' Maureen went on to hint that there were even wilder things that Pat had said which revolted her from any thought of allowing Pat to be trusted in anything crucial. 'But you will have to hear her yourself before you will believe it,' she added thoughtfully.

Hot on Maureen's heels had come Hazel, bothered and upset with Pat's latest visit to the hair salon. Hazel it seemed had sought advice on how she ought to prepare for the event. Pat announced grandly that she was carrying the baby god Itzla; the deity would manage everything nicely and all that she needed to do was pray at the altar. Pat's talk had been frightening, particularly when she added that the child would be taken into the church for rearing. These thoughts stayed very much in Freda's mind as she pushed and pulled at the latest batch of novels, found by Hazel in Tanya's bubble; she managed the task with scarcely a single thought for it.

There was someone outside. Freda opened the door to Maria, whose face showed the strain of coping without help in the food house, for this had been her first chance to emerge and consult with top authority. 'Terry has gone missing! At first I thought he was doing electrics with Marc and didn't miss him; it was only much later that we searched the place without finding any trace of him. It will be hard to cope without him, and I am particularly bothered because his talk has been so suicidal of late.'

Freda spotted the figure of Patricia coming towards her, and quickly closed down their conversation. 'I will get everyone out this afternoon. Leave it to me, and between us all we shall find the explanation, this should not be your worry at all.' Freda stood aside for Pat to enter, but patting Maria's shoulder consolingly.

Pat sat at the table, impressed by the food upon it, and in part for being waited on by Freda's lackey – who she knew intimately from her evening experience. The dinner progressed to the accompaniment of smalltalk, until Marc had served the beverage most resembling coffee. Freda saw he could now be dispensed with. 'Marc, will you go now? See if you can assist Maria. The usual bat collection may have to be postponed today.'

'Yes Madam. I'll leave the pot ready to pour.' Marc was already aware that this would be a confidential talk – nothing unusual about that in the royal apartments.

Once they were alone, Freda was quick to raise the subject, knowing that she was treading on delicate ground now. 'Hazel will be ready soon for her baby. Her women are already weaving the gown.'

'Itza the sekend, yer mean?' Pat's answer intimated there was to be a battle.

Freda drew a sharp breath. 'It's a baby, not a god. It could even be a boy.'

Pat shuddered as if the very idea gave offence. 'Boys'ud not git pass yer sen'ry – us gels git up agin. Nah, it's Itza 'erself awlrite.'

Freda shook her head and spoke very sharply. 'The child will be brought up here in the palace, with Hazel as Queen. You will move on to do Maureen's job!'

Pat shook a spiky head vigorously as a decisive negative, driven by the fervour that sprang so naturally from her. 'Nah, 'er muvver is only 'er wrappers. Wen I cuts the liddle gawdling aht, she is brung up wiv me – you kin stay Queen!'

The throw-away position angered Freda. 'Hazel will have her baby elsewhere if she is not safe in that church!'

'Er 'ips ter narrah fer a gawd – so we gotta cut er aht, ain't we?'

'Where did you do your midwifery?' Freda's voice cut through the patter.

Pat paused as if in thought, before she replied. 'Lunn'on, a big 'orspidal, in Ormon' Street.'

Freda did not believe her. 'Maureen and I will stop you attending the birth. Together we will prevent any bloodletting.'

'Yer mus see – she's 'er liddle gawdlings sacrifice – ain't she?'

Freda thought it time to take some measures to combat any impending tragedy. 'We need to do this with the church facilities, however much I disagree with you. So you will set the dormitory

301

suite aside for Hazel and friends, including myself – that is an order!' Freda noticed that Pat was looking at her in amazement.

'Oo sez we carn' ave a mart'a? Itza's awlreddy in 'er natral barf – awlreddy ter rinse erself orf in 'er muvver's blud!'

Freda tried another tack. 'Hazel, the one who has made your hair so attractive, do you really want to kill her?'

'It's fer Itza – carn' 'ave er – wiv nuffing offer'd up.'

'But Hazel will have milk for the baby.'

'So 'ave the goats.'

Freda was quick to take this gift. 'Why not sacrifice a goat?'

A disdainful expression spread over Pat's face. 'Nah, awl uver faifs can 'ave goats; but ahr's is real, ahr's is.'

'How about a man then,' said Freda. Pat made a spitting gesture, enough for Freda to abandon that tack. 'Well then, there's the father,' she said.

Pat's expression softened visibly from its existing confrontational mode.

'Oo's the farver? Arl 'av im – if it bovers ya.'

Freda paused, Terry was a doubtful contender at the moment; but Marc had not long to go in this place so she was deliberately imprecise in her final choice of words. 'All I will say is that the father serves you personally in the food house. Nearer the time you can arrange your own dirty deeds, but not before. We shall concern ourselves with protecting Hazel and seeing that she does not come to harm.'

Freda talked on for a while, time was needed for the conclusion to sink in and be affirmed. Opposition had aroused Pat's indignation, and Freda did not think she could trust the woman to keep her side of the bargain. She took time to soothe her, cautiously working the conversation into calmer waters. Inwardly she was furious, but doing her level best to be polite as she cautiously brought the visit to an end.

Freda's first move was to reassemble the four, and begin a search they kept from Pat's ears. Marc was questioned, he being the last person to have seen Terry. According to Marc, Terry had decided to clean the food transport bikes before doing a bat cull: his answers then set off a hunt on the agricultural side of the village. The bikes had indeed been left clean, enabling the hunt to move forwards from that point. Consequently it was within the next hour that a rope was discovered hanging in the waterfall. Freda made her way there on foot, because she had some serious thinking to do. How do you manage a religious maniac when in truth your side of a bargain has mysteriously disappeared? A confinement somewhere else would be the correct answer, but given the beliefs of the entire community through untold ages this was a special event. Every woman in the caves would be against her, particularly if she tried to hustle it through over the conference table. The birth would have to take place in church, and be protected by sheer vigilance. It was a detail really that the birth would have to take place upon the altar; but whether or not you stripped it of any religious significance it was still the best place, only needing a few sheepskins to make a decent couch of it. What she had to guard against was any distraction; Maureen who had nursing experience must be allowed to take all the decisions, and maybe between them they could sideline this overzealous priest. Marc was now her favourite choice as honorary father, and more especially so as he would be the only male food house attendant known to Pat.

The rope was still there facing the rush of water, it had not been touched. With no more ado Freda pulled it up, watching bulky knots emerging from the waterfall at intervals. At the extreme end it had been cut off recently with a sharp knife as evidenced by its white centre. Such huge knots in the rope suggested to Freda that they were tied to enable a descent, but surely that made it too elaborate to be a suicide's rope. Also the cut did not taper away as she imagined it should, if cut whilst bearing such a weight. If Terry had stolen away to escape the caves by this very risky route, the cut end was only feasible if after descending the cut off part could be used later; this supposition suggested that the other portion was by now downstream somewhere. Terry she had already ascertained was desperate and suicidal; but a suicide would only need to jump in. This had to be an escape attempt if it was anything at all. The alternative was that he was still about, and the easily portable rope that she could see was cut and dangled in the water to mislead.

So it was that Freda remained suspicious, although at the moment she could not think of anyone fool enough to immerse in near-freezing water simply for verification. There was little she could do to further her suspicions, but these were enough to continue a low-level search. In these circumstances she must first try to exclude the possibility of the rope being a diversion and the man himself lying low. Freda decreed for her troops, and everyone else for that matter, to keep their eyes peeled for either the man, or the other end of this most distinctive rope.

Hazel was upset upon hearing the news about Terry, knowing that she was responsible for his suicidal feelings. The news arrived promptly enough, because Freda requested her to release Rose, who must now resume work in the food house. Hazel wept and fretted awhile over her love and then entered Marc's quarters for consolation; but these were empty, he had donned his goatskins for collecting bats – and left.

Marc had overheard Freda's conclusions, and with his senses reeling into all sorts of alarm he set off immediately. People were looking for Terry or the other end of the rope; for sure they wouldn't find Terry, but the other half of the rope was still very prominently tied to their new ladder. Worse still Maria was already keen to see the newly acquired equipment and would certainly decide to visit it in the very near future.

Hastily he climbed into his dirty gear, outwardly to complete the usual afternoon job. It was after normal working hours, but he knew the women could hardly do anything except approve of his intention to collect bats, in pursuing a belated attempt to make up the deficit. Soon a limp pile of furry bodies were being carried into the village, but in addition secreted under his hairy jacket Marc's body bulged with many turns of heavy knotted rope. At the entrance to Cora's dwelling, which even to this day lacked a front door, he ducked inside. The place had sensibly been abandoned because of its heaps of items spoiled with mottled brown stains. The stains, bearing witness to a former tenant's violent death, were in addition responsible for the heavy sickly odour, which had long deterred all comers. Divesting himself of the rope he pushed it under one of the piles, but it was resilient enough to push right back at him. He kicked it back with vigour, not knowing that the heap had moved appreciably upon its other side.

31

Batman

The snow was beginning to retreat from the St-Saveur ski slopes, and now it was only a matter of time before the local skiers, having brushed up their skills, would begin an annual migration northwards. Today there was a fair sprinkling of enthusiasts, all able to see an extensive grey cast on the valley snow, most simply felt dejected to read signs that the thaw was chasing them along overmuch this year. Individuals who had bothered to stop, however, were able to make out a well-defined central point where the discolouration intensified, visualizing a dead sheep at the centre of it all. But it was not until an elderly ex-officer with binoculars discerned human arms and a leg that matters moved along. The little group of bystanders on skis grew with the news, and somewhere else a climbing party was diverted to recover what was thought to be a hermit's remains.

A local off-duty policeman happened to be one of the climbing party charged with the mission. He was still on the accident site when he passed the news to Claude Brie by portable telephone, and for once the Commissar was informed well in advance of the newspapers getting the story. He was soon on site attending the corpse, which was immediately recognisable to him after having seen extra large photographs sent by Terry's parents, who thought the sheer size would keep their son in mind. Terry now varied from his portrait, in that he possessed a well-trimmed beard and a short hairstyle, neither of which suggested that he had been living rough.

His death was destined to hold other puzzles for all those involved in the subsequent forensic investigations. Stomach contents gave many clues to his diet. The fats extracted led on to DNA investigations and the results of intensive testing revealed that bat tissues were prominent, as was mutton in the meaty residues. The

305

vegetable component yielded cells of mushroom-type character, coupled with potato starch and microscopically many quite unique spores of unknown fungi species. Other investigations might be debated at length, but these results at least were straightforward. The physical injuries, apart from those of the fall, were recent abrasions suggesting exertions upon exit rather than any sort of foul deed. He was well nourished for his size and wore goatskins, rather than the rags they would have expected to find upon him. Whether he was wearing such skins under the cycle cape he was last seen in was much debated in the newspapers, for he might have intended to become a hermit all along. But then, of course, the existence of goats upon a mountain is not something improbable enough to need a cycle cape theory. Shortly however, all of these things paled into insignificance when it was realized that Terry was now nearly half his original height, and that was an inexplicable finding for all concerned. His bones were examined closely, but apart from exiting injuries the only other abnormality found was that of a well-healed partial castration.

It was not long before the national newspapers were giving space to a sensational story, and doing so despite the reluctance of local police to release any fact whatsoever; still the news gave rise to much fancy. 'Bat man plunges to death' was a common thread that ran through the headlines of local papers, which did report his widening of the normal exit for the bat population high in the mountain. But the news was soon in national papers, which have more ways of extracting extra detail. Consequently the news soon moved from headline sensation to the inside pages, in which his proximity to an eyrie was found more astonishing, and facts about Terry were embellished with suggestions that he lived in a climber's hut on the mountain slopes and collected eagle eggs for food. The facts well embroidered with speculation appeared in most papers as a mystery that needed to be solved, and producing at least one article of interest whilst offering theories. For the newspapers Terry's story worked miracles for filling much empty space in the present time of little news.

Soon Gabriel Masse was on the telephone, alarmed that the story could build up in the press inevitably causing the police force to be blamed for inaction at the very start of things, and so he threatened a return, blaming Claude for making so little progress. 'This is the consequence of ignoring the cave disappearances,' he claimed, ranting on and using all the benefits given by hindsight and newsprint.

Claude for his part held his temper, just listening and well knowing his boss would himself never go anywhere near a cave, especially for a one-off backwoods event that didn't involve promotion. It was supremely non-significant, non-political news, able to hurt nobody not even his own self; that was something Claude felt very sure about. It could not help being the kind of story that whips up a public interest one day and is dead as a dodo the next. There were no benefits Claude could think of in having his boss around, as recently time had been all his own since the insistent spate of calls from Julia ceased. Of course, he had checked to see she was all right, but when he did so, he found the doctor's red car parked on her drive. In fact prime among the benefits of not having his boss here was to avoid being the one stampeded towards doubtful joys of living among uncut rock.

There were some choice moments of biting invective present in Gabriel's long-distance call, which roused Claude sufficiently to bite back. 'The man fell off a mountain – surely that is a failure of the police helicopter rescue service? Let us think even beyond that, sir, and more about probable future victims. If there are others about to drop off into my lap beyond the one that has, then that is something preventable if you authorize me to make use of these helicopters. I know that the service tends to keep clear of police work, but we do know now where to look, and rescue does appear to be the name of the game.'

Gabriel bumbled along trying to dismiss this extra dimension, but realizing that other possible further unpleasant incidents were able to arise, along with the whole lot of unwelcome publicity that could be expected with it. These were thoughts he hadn't previously had and which brought the pressure full circle back on him. Being a zealous guardian of the police purse he had the answer – and here he had the preferred scapegoat, the one responsible for past police inaction. His subordinate he saw as volunteering in so many words to shoulder the future responsibility for any failure. He said in the driest of voices, 'How many hours do you want?'

The cautious voice pulled Claude up short; he had wanted an open cheque. 'Four hours a day maximum, after two weeks we can review it.'

307

'I will give you ten days, and at the end of that I shall expect results.'

The permission had been given, albeit a reluctant one. Feelings of enthusiasm and excitement welled up inside the little man, as here at last was an opportunity to get somewhere. He replaced the receiver, talking exuberantly to a filing cabinet picture standing opposite his desk. 'Hold on we are coming to get you.' It was but one of the cave victim pictures, put in place and changed with much dusting daily by Sylvia in her latest attempt to influence him. Hardly was he off the telephone than he was back on it again ringing mountain rescue – a subsidiary service he now part owned.

Next day the mission started in earnest, with the landing of a helicopter upon a strip of park land not so very far from the Commissariat. The arrival happened with a high-decibel racket of rotors bombarding the surrounding streets; both Claude and a local expert climber found themselves running towards the helicopter. Within minutes they were scrambling into a noisy cabin. Lift-off was so immediate that Claude's personal plumbing had a post-breakfast alert, he grabbed for a seat and levered himself into it. From his inoffensive look neither the pilot, nor Jon the climber could imagine him as anything more than a passenger, and to press home the point, they engaged in an over-technical conversation to his complete exclusion.

Not that it bothered him; for countering the shattering roar of the engine and the retention of his breakfast had left Claude completely preoccupied, he rode the sky holding grimly on to his seat. The craft wheeled and bucked its way southwards, approaching within minutes the place where Terry had been found. There was little need for opening a door to view closely, because right above the marked spot a whitish flared shape punctured the central regions of the mountain and from this protruded a loose blanket of flock waving in the breeze. Above it towered the mountain; the helicopter soared for thousands more feet, with the Commissar at last taking interest in what was visibly present.

The climber shouted and waved his hands towards the rocky mass. 'Over there is a cave famous for its ice-laden waterfall, it completely freezes over in the winter.' Claude winced, feelings decidedly aflame after that very inappropriate and distracting travelogue got under way. Somehow both pilot and climber had to be detached from their own particular delights as this was beginning to resemble a specialist pleasure trip. Claude yelled, overcoming the noisy space between them, urging the pilot down to hunt about in the vicinity of the opening. He was being unrealistic if he thought he could approach the place so easily, both the pilot and expert climber told him so. Claude was adamant and stuck to his guns, knowing that they would almost certainly be returning to base having just gone through the motions, if he permitted it.

The craft descended as close to the mountain as its wintry updraughts allowed, and from there they viewed the space level with the hole. The helicopter flew this way and that; then moved over an indent, floored with a gentle slope. The pilot nosed his way over it to the accompaniment of excited shouts from his climber companion, who was pointing towards a fissure in the rock wall. To Claude the fissure appeared to be not much more than a mark, so he was surprised when the wheels touched down and the rotors ceased to howl above him. There was no need to move, the door was open and Jon the climber outside, leaving the little man struggling to breathe in exceptionally cold rarefied air. The climber seemed to be gone quite a while, and in that time Claude settled down to be almost comfortable in his bucket-like seat. The pilot shouted at him, pointing through a side window. Behind this the figure of Jon stood beckoning. With a rush that had him colliding with seats and tripping over discarded belts, Claude made for a sliding door over on the other side of the aircraft and almost fell through it in his haste. Stumbling and slipping upon patches of ice after his big step down, he wheezed over the loose stones towards Jon who remained standing in front of the fissure. Jon watched him approach and as he neared the climber stepped inside the opening.

Claude stepped onto the flatness of a boulder, and was immediately marooned by a goodly drop on its other side; he looked for the climber to help him down, but Jon was gone. Claude sat with his legs over the edge, then turning to face the stone he hung there a moment before slipping slowly down over its smooth rounded face. Then dropping half a metre he crashed down onto stones that were set in solid ice below. Claude rubbed his leg before rising and looking back as if to query, how do I return? There came a shout from behind him and Jon was beckoning almost angrily as if he were holding things up; Claude felt affronted, if the man wanted him to hurry then he should help.

The opening loomed large as he entered; nevertheless he was still suffering the doubt about such instant luck and success. Claude found he had moved from the biting cold air but into the sudden darkness of a chill-free interior. The light in Jon's hand was switched on, but impinged as a weak illumination on the dark walls, far too weak for Claude who was already feeling he had had enough for one day. Unfortunately the reverse was true for his companion, for he was growing steadily more interested by the minute. The tunnel divided, causing Claude to hurry and catch up with the light, fearing he might get lost. For Jon the paths showed clear signs of use as he followed the most frequented of them, in this way their path soon chanced upon a beehive-shaped cave, a cave that was strikingly uniform but had four un-symmetrical exits. 'This looks promising,' Jon shouted over his shoulder, his voice ringing all round the cave. 'There are foot marks through this widest opening; see how it goes down.'

'Stop,' Claude shouted, fearing that the man would continue on ahead. 'There is enough here to justify a search,' he said officiously. 'We will come back with equipment and examine these tunnels more objectively.' He nodded appreciatively, taking his surroundings in from the frequent light flashes; the beehive cave could well be his office, policemen or cavers could go in all directions before reporting back to him.

Jon looked at him as if he were some kind of spoilsport, but then, realizing the calibre of the man he was dealing with, kindly helped Claude to find the right exit. His shoulder too shortly bore the imprint of Claude's shoe as he helped him over the difficult boulder. The pilot too was helpful; tomorrow he could arrange a generator for lighting and other gear to help search the caves.

Within minutes he was putting Claude and the climber down again near the Commissariat. The Commissar immediately consulted his watch, wondering if he could carry over the unused time from one day to another; he could so easily be cheated out of time if he didn't count it. Claude felt triumphant, for he had succeeded in entering the cave system, and not so very far from the disturbed fluff.

32

Cradle Craft

Freda fully accepted the fact that she had no alternative but to be firm with Hazel, and insist upon having the confinement in the church. Driving this decision was the social importance of the event and the many religious implications stacked around it. The practical considerations of finding room for the interested parties to gather in one secure place, as well as having everything necessary within reach, seemed to make church the only real choice. She made a point of visiting the multi bubble with Hazel, to make sure that the girl's objections were fully overcome. Regrettably Pat was at home, and drifted by smiling to herself like some shark in waiting; such smiles took away the beneficial serenity of Lucinia's countenance and threatened to depress their mood before they even started. The one beneficial thing to come from this glaring defect in arrangements, was for Hazel to realize she had to come to terms with it, and accept that Pat's experience had to be included wherever they put her. There were now only days to term, and this time Hazel saw the altar slab ready prepared in a carpet of sheepskins. The very sight of it made her nervous, but it was an ordeal that she couldn't be too choosy about.

Freda carried on gamely, countering every objection she thought might arise, explaining the altar's essential role in the arrangements, and trying to ease her mind. 'It is just the right height so anything surgical always gets done here, simply because it is the most convenient ledge we have. The only problem with the altar, as I see it, is that it is an altar, and a good sprinkling of religious nonsense surrounds it.'

They inspected Hazel's room, finding that it butted on to the end of the dormitory bubbles that stood in one long line along a corridor made from demolished cells. These were last used during the brief siege, and she remembered her room as being the one in

311

the middle. Her new room offered advantage beyond mere near-
ness to the altar, in that it had an offshoot bubble growing
externally from the wall. The tiny offshoot had been opened up
for her especially; it was a sort of translucent crib enabling her to
see the baby's outline from her bed. Looking into it she was aware
of an odd disturbance in the light from outside. Hazel was at once
suspicious, resolving to check her baby's cradle from without. Her
own bedding looked comfortable, and indeed she couldn't fault it.
So generally speaking Hazel was very pleased with the arrangements, and then suspecting rightly that Freda had much to do with
it, thanked her most sincerely.

Hazel dallied near the church steps as she left Freda. The fact
that she felt much like a cargo liner shouldn't stop her checking
on important things, so she headed on round to the secluded side
of the church – the side out of view of occupied bubble homes.
Two engineers were drilling a door in one of the spheres near her
crèche. She could see then from checking the bubble divisions
that the work had no relevance at all; just that her job had been
extended by Pat for something of her own, as so many of these
women did.

Marc headed for his evening appointment with Patricia. Hazel, he
knew was staying a couple of nights with Annita, and so tonight he
would be home alone. Pat never missed, he could always be sure
she would be there and as domineering as ever; in fact she was far
worse tonight. Measuring little above her chin he was dwarfed by
her well-fed bulk, and was powerless to fend off the grab that
stripped his tunic from him in two quick moves. The very fierceness
of the encounter was unusual and that had him sexually aroused,
for she came at him like some predatory beast. Retreating from
her, he was gathered up into an embrace, which sent both crashing
backwards, as she overbalanced onto the padded patch furthest
from the door. Crushed by the fall Marc watched her rise above
him.

'Yer gives 'er the litt'el gawd – an' me nuffink,' she snarled
down at him. Seesawing herself into some kind frenzied ecstasy
state Patricia cried out as she moved in sex, ripping with fingernails
that grasped his back. With energy soon expended, the ponderous
heavyweight lay upon him disinclined to move until fully recovered.

'Ow me gawd – yer back's awl bleedin'. Old on – ah kin git

somefink ter make it be'er.' Pat rushed across the room, and returned in moments with an old mug, twisting a waxy-looking spiral of ointment from it with a blunt-looking knife. 'Git over on yer belly, ever so quick, it is.' She applied a liberal helping to the cuts.

Marc lay flat; this priest woman was full of mercurial moods and her balm certainly worked, for it had a peculiar deadening effect on the scratches. Pat left the room, and he was conscious of the fact she had gone for a 'wee' as she called it.

Pat re-entered the compartment; her man seemed fast asleep and now she was a little scared. Had she overdone the fungi in the unguent? Were the fungi more potent than usual? She seized his shoulder and shook him vigorously – he mumbled sounds.

'Yer gotta larst – yer carn' snuff it nah.' Quickly Pat wiped the abrasions dry with a cloth, then avoiding this area, began coating every inch of unbroken skin thickly, using all the rest of the pot. She smiled. Absorption would be slow now. Marc's press-studs were clipped together, almost unnecessarily so as his tunic stuck firmly upon the thick grease. But for Pat he was handier now and she heaved him to his feet, where he stood propped against her ample figure. They moved slowly down the ramp and out into the village, where Marc lunged drunkenly towards Hazel's bubble.

'Yer carn' go nah,' Pat admonished, straightening his trajectory. ''Azel's avin' er liddle gawdling. Cum 'ome wiv Patricha insted – ay luv?' There was no perceptible resistance beyond that point for the man could barely drag his feet along. They passed the entrance to the church, only to stop further on round its exterior. Pat opened the newly prepared door and gave him a good shove forwards.

'Nah yer kin be a blud doanin' daddy – yis – I s'pose – awl of it.' Shutting the door Pat wired it in position with heavy wire: the blood baptism was safely stored awaiting her to pop out and get it.

Hazel stayed the night at Annita's place, and so Marc was not missed. Annita, she found, had an empty concubine bubble that was fitted with a comfortable bed. Annita said the bed was there for visitors, but in reality it had been the result of wishful thinking back in the days of an unfulfilled desire to sleep with Marc in her own dwelling.

The pains came periodically from midnight on: Hazel had been calm up until then because yesterday both Pat and Maureen had visited her separately with independent assurances that the baby was in much the right position. But now in the late hours when everyone else had left was when the contractions had started – exactly as she might have predicted. Hazel was scared; how could they all expect the baby to wait on them whilst they had their sleep? Very soon there would be a battle for existence and their inexperience in such matters might well let her down. There would be no rush to hospital for her, although to be fair about it, wherever she was it was still up to her. Even so, this must be the worst location for childbirth against any country in the world – at home it would be classified as primitive where high risks of mortality in childbirth were unacceptable. And then what kind of future was there here? There were no other mothers with experience to guide her through all those early snags, or other children for the child to play with. Older and more experienced women, the ones who had previously had children, were the ones she missed most. It was a pity that such women of mature years did not have the adventuring streak or the fitness necessary to reach such a remote system of caves.

Hazel did little more than groan, bewailing her pains from the bed, but unknowingly she became increasingly noisy until other movements in the home bubble heralded Annita's arrival. Her coming soothed away all of the worries, for Hazel knew then that her friends were on tap for her and could she want more than that. Their talk rambled on until the lighting change heralded morning, a signal for a whole series of mugs containing hot drinks.

Maureen was there early with more reassurance for Hazel, and was soon hurrying off to make arrangements because there were only hours now. The pending event stopped all aspects of normality in the village except for breakfast; this was a day the four would not go on their rounds. Soon those at a loose end were rounded up to tend the food house trolleys, as the workforce still needed feeding. Marc had gone missing and in short, Maria demanded help.

The village came to a standstill as Hazel's contractions came closer together, with everybody deciding it was time for church. Like some flabby spider awaiting her prey Pat hovered in the anteroom, welcoming the little knot of friends one by one as they entered. Hazel was helped to sit up on the altar slab with her legs swinging over its edge; her friends chatting to her about anything and everything except babies, all talking excitedly in the wide foreground space under St Lucinia's benevolent eye. Pat penetrated the group to ask if Hazel would like a beverage, and on getting her acceptance bustled off to prepare it. Maureen followed her closely into the kitchen; there would be no powders used to promote an inexplicable collapse in childbirth, a collapse requiring Pat's preference for a Caesarean section.

The beverage, once delivered to a seemingly cheerful Hazel, was the signal for a watchful Maureen to fetch Freda. On arrival Freda's first move was to carefully secure the church doors and Maureen assisted in this, ignoring the surprised looks of those who saw. Having assured complete isolation both women had to rush because the waters had broken. Hazel was coaxed into a couch-like mound of sheepskins, and Maureen settled near her head, suggesting she breathe deeply and push down on the pains.

A small throng had taken seats on the benches just short of the altar; these were privy to the integral noises of labour, noises that they were never destined to make and very likely never to hear again. But for a one-off event it was not destined to be an easy one, and after considerable interval the birth progressed as far as the baby's forehead appearing, then all forward movement ceased. Maureen urged and there was much manipulation, until at length Pat reached for one of the sharp knives that lay on a tray nearby, her hand being instantly stilled in Freda's grip as she stood there with her eyes now switched towards Maureen. But the small blade with a rounded back commended itself to Maureen who nodded her head in approval, whilst at the same time she moved to be closer. Both hovered upon either side of the priest watching as she handled the knife, either ready to pounce if there were the slightest sign of untoward movement. Moments later the audience heard Hazels squeal of pain as the perineum was cut. Maureen was already back comforting and holding Hazel by the shoulders very tightly.

'Push,' she said urgently. 'Breathe, and bear down on it.'

Hazel gave the one big push that counted, and the head was through, turning all by itself to permit the body easy passage through into Pat's supporting hands. She raised the baby abruptly for all to see, wet and shining in the light, and then with a scream of frustration made as if to dash it upon the stone. Freda grabbed the child from her – it was a boy. The unintelligible shouting intermixed with sobbing drowned out the baby's first cries, as Pat releasing her hold turned to face the stone figure of St Lucinia, lamenting loudly.

'It is a boy,' shouted Freda to all those assembled, her face jubilant radiating the great pleasure and relief that she felt in having a successful outcome.

Maureen moved in to take over, cutting the cord and binding the cut end with cotton rag; materials she had been careful to obtain earlier from Tanya's place, all of which were washed, dried ready for use. A further wipe with more cotton cloth had Hazel relaxed and clutching her precious baby, wide eyed, bright and happy. Somewhere to the side of those attending Hazel, a prostrate figure offered prayers at some interminable length to St Lucinia, asking forgiveness for bringing a male child into the world along with the profanity it had brought into her one and only sacred temple.

There had been a few groans of disappointment from the benches at Freda's announcement, but even so only two decided that they had better things to do elsewhere, and began somewhat dejectedly unbarring the door.

Not that Hazel was aware of detracting movement in the church, relief that it was over hid all that, and holding her unique bundle of joy tenderly saw only Annita and Bernadette bursting with pleasure at her good fortune. Her friends were not in the way either as a wait was now necessary for the placenta. Others crowded towards Hazel, for a great sense of relief had seized all waiting in the church and brought them close in to fill the space about Hazels delivery slab. There was little time to concentrate on being hurt and Hazel was still mostly unaware of losing blood.

Not yet finished praying and crying in anguish the half-demented Pat managed to stay out of the way, until eventually she regained her composure enough to beg Freda's pardon for her show of emotion. Freda's reception of the plea was frosty to say the least and left the religious leader in no doubt that she must bend herself to the task of returning to favour. Pat now appeared to be making amends for her behaviour and departed to make them all a hot drink, this time unknown and unsupervised. In her own way she had done a vital part for the complications would have thrown anybody else into total confusion.

316

Realizing the contribution Pat had made and aware of her total commitment to religious belief, both Freda and Maureen were anxious to dismiss her as any kind of threat. Especially after hearing such an abject apology neither felt able to hold it against her, as overall they still rated her as a harmless ignoramus. Released from these very particular pressures they wallowed in their other worries, underlined by the carrying of heavier armament that nestled in a fold of material about the waist. The priest was once again a nonentity.

Mother and child waited for transfer to the nearby dormitory, whilst Maureen had the nail-biting job of suturing the wound, again there was pain for Hazel despite some minor relief brought about by fungal-derived sedation. Bernadette took the baby, her face lighting up as if she were transported to heaven, waltzing across the floor and whispering nothings in the baby's ear. More cotton cloth was produced, and Annita attended by the round-eyed Bernadette folded cloth into a nappy shape to fit their precious blue-eyed boy.

The transfer to a comfortable bed for Hazel, with the baby resting at her breast, meant a relaxation of tension inside the church. Freda detached the friends from Hazel and led them into the corridor. It was now time to give Annita and Bernadette their instructions on keeping watch. Tonight they should sleep in the bubble room adjacent to Hazel, and not be so sure that all danger had passed. Her young troops had other ideas and looked through her as if she were transparent, their minds were blank to any wider implications, for they were in festive mood and any amount of her irrelevances wouldn't keep them out of their old bedroom.

Freda's instructions droned on awhile, until completing her spiel she left. As the church door closed behind her the two friends lost no time filtering back to be with Hazel. Pat moved in, and out, still with that same fixed smile which even now managed to give Hazel the shudders, raising her tense state. The baby was wrapped in a woollen shawl, Poppy's thoughtful gift, and stowed safely in its comfortable recess. Reaching into the tiny bubble crib, two petri-fied mushroom halves were visible, comfortably bridging the bot-tom curve and ready to receive their tiny load. Here Hazel rested the baby, tired and sleepy enough now to close those wide, bright eyes; eyes that had previously looked with curiosity surveying those who presented themselves. The pink, slightly wrinkled face relaxed now, and looked all serene in a niche that was just the right size. Hazel, who wanted to be sure, drew herself over to the opening again gently arranging the ample shawl to pad the baby's support layer. Even this effort was painfully exhausting, causing her to move back and recline on her own bed; she was beyond chatter for the moment and her bedchamber emptied.

Annita and Bernadette made themselves scarce, each gripping a bottle of wine that Pat had supplied; they knew well their own favourite bedroom and headed for it. The church was quiet now for not only had the crowd moved off, but Maureen as well, heading for urgent discussions with Maria over the disappearance of Marc. The whole place soon became still as a mausoleum, with Annita and Bernadette lolling upon their padded heaps of bedding imbibing wine, telling each other jokes and sniggering at the smutty ones, which gradually became plain dirty. A couple of hours had passed before there was a cry of sorts from the baby. Hazel was there instantly, taking the child to her own bed and proffering an optimistic nipple. The cry had roused her friends who swept into the room, and before very long Bernadette was swinging the baby round in a circle held fast in her arms, watched anxiously by Hazel who was aware she had been drinking.

Pat, the root cause of her friend's latest unprovoked merriment, appeared out of nowhere bringing more bottles of wine. Hazel refused her own bottle, but by the time Annita had got through all of the toasts fancifully supposed to celebrate the birth; she found herself sipping her friend's glass to join in. The baby was put back into its bubble, and the revelry tended to quieten after a while, only to be resurrected when Freda looked in to see how Hazel was getting on. Freda had brought with her an armful of pea plants that were in flower which added scent and colour to the room. A signal for the slightly tipsy Annita to begin proposing the same toasts all over again. Freda tried hard to understand their position and was very tolerant, merely taking them aside and stressing the inadvisability of drinking before she left.

Freda had good reason to be worried, but at the same time successfully concealed the news of the missing concubine for Hazel's benefit. The loss of another man from the village had put her mind to red alert, and that was precisely where it stayed throughout Hazel's delivery. If she counted Arthur as well, that meant three-quarters of the village men had vanished, for there was only Leon left. Space here was too limited to allow people to disappear so completely, even if they succeeded for a while they still would have to eat. Was this some kind of new plot that would shortly burst in on them and take them all by surprise? She could only continue to rack her brains and check on the principal happenings at the moment, such as Hazel who somehow seemed to be at the centre of things. Having checked Hazel and friends were securely in one place, she was free to gather her forces together and begin an armed, far-ranging search. Even so Freda left the church hesitantly and not absolutely convinced of doing the right thing. Pat obstinately remained in her mind's eye; suspicious behaviour coupled with a degree of lavishness in hospitality that was somehow out of character, this combination made her reluctant to leave.

It was mid-evening when Hazel's friends completed their visit and finally retired to their own bubble bedroom. Bernadette took the baby off to see her bedroom in such a lightheaded flight of rather stupid fancy that Hazel and Annita were both left laughing. Hazel was tired; but relief came abruptly when her friends finally turned their backs clutching yet more bottles of wine, she herself was feeling awful. Pat's response was to bring her a heaped plate of her favourite yogurt, and that had her eating.

Pat sat in the church meditating. Hazel had been asleep for two hours now, and her friends were flopped out murmuring sluggishly one to another. Hazel would sleep well, for she had been careful with the sleep inducement in the yogurt; the girl must wake when wanted but in the meantime must be as insensitive as possible. Pat was still smarting from Freda's disbelief in her Great Ormond Street experience; but she had shown them, hadn't she? Her mind buried itself deep in the unappetizing past; if only she had been born elsewhere and spoken without the local dialect, she would surely have made university and not ended up here, for everyone agreed that she was clever, even calling her an intellectual. However, those in authority were convinced that her old school's reputation also reflected her potential, and so possessing non-ideal paperwork the best position she could get was a probationer's job in a children's ward of Great Ormond Street Hospital. Here was her chance to make a contribution, even a small one, but her work colleagues shied away from any idea she proposed, and it was only a few stormy months later that she was out, having expressed her thoughts too forcefully. Of course there were other hospitals that were impressed with her professional experience, much enhanced for the curriculum vitae – hospitals she knew by now didn't check. Soon she was back on a ward, but this time dealing with babies in incubators. So many defective lives were being saved – ones that Mother Nature would surely have rejected. As a member of her team she tended them all; nursing the contents of clear plastic boxes, the little bodies important to someone or other plumbed in with masses of tubing. It was a case of humans playing God, urged on by crazy life-pressure groups that demanded nothing be switched off. Incubators they tended were all kept busy collecting imprecise events from malfunctioning parents, events all spiralling downwards and taking with it the whole human population of Britain. Soon, when these defective specimens interbred, hospital culture would spread and monsters be destined for every family tree. She saw the dangers arising from selfish parents and used her ingenuity to counter the worst of it. It was sick to be spending so much from the public purse detracting from the quality of life – and then, so little on nurses.

Her actions had nudged the team towards lower success rates, which in turn first caused investigation, and then much politically correct repercussion which soon settled on her personally. She had been hounded even as far as France. Here in this remote part she evaded persecution, seeking solitude in out of the way places – so different to Cora or Poppy, who had been attracted by a religious film and come all this way from idle curiosity. By contrast St Lucinia had guided her there, to a shrine that put natural birth at the centre of things, and just seeing it had fired her with enthusiasm. The story she heard recounted had her plunge into the caves full of fervour and belief, with food very much the second consideration. And when close to irretrievable starvation she chanced upon a unique cave society, Pat knew that this was nothing short of a divine miracle. She had entered a world where there was no need for birth whatsoever, and she could leave all those damaging theories of hers behind. Fit individuals presented themselves every so often for integration, and from then on it was merely a process of assimilation. She had followed the founder's ideas on maintaining a well-balanced society and had done so brilliantly until now.

Her ideals were not going to change and the day was coming when she would again lead her flock.

Pat put aside immediate plans to rectify all these matters and looked forward to regaining approval from her god. Hazel was sleeping deeply, thanks to a priest's knowledge of fungal extracts and her friends also slept soundly, part drunk on the amount of wine they had supped. She stopped at Annita and Bernadette's room; they were out to the wide. Next stop was Hazel's room, where the new mother sprawled part out of bed but looking comfortable.

Pat picked up a saucer spread with a mutton fat into which several stumps of candles had been pushed. She lit them and walked off as quietly as she had on night duty in a hospital ward. The baby was breathing easily and slept without other movement in its recess: Pat lifted one half circle of the base, and placed the saucer with candles lit underneath. The candles burned evenly when she replaced the half section without overmuch disturbance to the baby. Moments later Pat had moved out and cut the creepers, which formed the hinges on an identical next-door bubble. Then, free from any need to hurry, she smeared the doors thin flexible convex side heavily in her mutton fat extract – applying the door to stick over a very similar wall surface just outside the baby niche; this provided an airtight seal so far as she could see. Pat sat near at hand, waiting. Nobody stirred and nothing much appeared to happen, just the candles extinguishing one after another. She was too experienced to hurry, knowing that carbon dioxide causes breathing to strengthen for a while.

Pat removed the door only when she was certain it would be too late for resuscitation; true the baby had made a cry or two, but the cries were muffled and Hazel had not moved a muscle. Silently Pat took the door away to stand loosely adhering to a corridor bubble further on. Returning immediately she removed the candles, wiping the heavily fatted tell-tale smears from the wall with a few of the cotton nappies. She returned to St Lucinia in order to pray – for now she was sure her God would forgive her part in the earlier insult. As for the colony here she had saved them a future battle, for the men would only see the lad as a king in waiting. Right now it was a birth unworthy of making a false queen of Hazel.

Freda had retired for the night but was sleeping fitfully; the day's events were on balance disquieting, and added to that for some odd reason Patricia's face kept bobbing up wearing that unnatural sly smile of hers. But surely Hazel had been kept safe and ought to stay so, as Pat would not have reason to claim the boy was a second coming of Itzla any longer; besides this Hazel had her bosom friends standing guard. The day's search had been fruitless, and everyone slept with weapons to hand. Despite this the village was so well secured that there was no reason at all for unease; why then was her mind disturbed? There had to be another reason. There was something not quite right in the church and that seemed the most probable reason for her disturbed night's sleep; but if there were reasons then they were far too deep for Freda's brain to resolve. All that she needed to do to satisfy her doubts was to cross the perimeter path; there was even a bed she had reserved there.

Freda pulled on her dress, and barefooted through the night's low light levels headed straight for her destination. There were faint noises of Pat, how devout of her praying into the night at the altar. The priestly woman rose as Freda approached, almost as if she was expecting her.

'They're all 'avin a kip – why carn' yer jus' nod orf?'

Freda was not there to bandy words. She hurried to Hazel's room where all was quiet, just the laboured breathing of Hazel who was now even more out of the covers.

'Let's see 'is nibs then,' cried Pat, lifting a floppy child out of its recess.

'Aw my gawd, 'e's ded!' Pat put the child to Freda and shook Hazel roughly. 'Yer baby's 'ad a cot deff,' she cried out loud.

Hazel sluggishly responded, her eyes opening only to fill with horror as she espied the still form in Freda's arms.

Freda rightly felt that Pat had used her, but not quite sure what to do about it she laid the tiny baby upon the bed at Hazel's side. Staring eyes convinced Hazel, her babe was no more, and she began to sob uncontrollably whilst bent over the small still form, then hugging it wet with tears.

Pat had seen it all before. She turned to Freda. 'Yer uvvers is drunk tergevver in bed.'

Freda turned on her heel and angrily hurried off to see her troops.

Pat looked back at Hazel as she left also. Hazel was still weeping over the body, in a less than presentable condition – with a body droopy enough to imagine her collapsing over the child. There was the sound of an outburst further up the row of dormitories, and Pat sidled away to the stone mother figure where she commenced praying, but voices in the background increasingly intruded as they raised with emotion. She had been very careful, and doubted that there would be evidence left pointing at her. But Bernadette's scream of rage unnerved her; girls could let immature maternal feelings get out of control at such times – Pat decided to make herself scarce.

Finding your way about in the multi-bubble church was difficult if you didn't know where you were going. Unlike the food house, the bubbles were less regular and tended to be more translucent, making the doorway path not so easily seen. Her knowledge had Pat feeling safe, she could let things cool down before she need put in another appearance. The place she headed for would not be found easily, for in that location individual cells cramped together forming a spiral that tended to take on a silvery tint. Once there she would safely close a particular door and not be seen through its silvery haze; the thought was something almost as comforting as the metal thing she kept next to her – a gun from the armoury.

The girls were in a cosy huddle, fast asleep on the bed, and Freda's coming woke them; their senses still reeled from celebrations and neither one seemed to know where she was. News of the tragedy hit them hard, Bernadette especially so, for the baby was the nicest thing that had happened to her since arriving in this godforsaken place. Their noisy arrival and concern triggered Hazel into crying again, for in that space of several minutes the drugged state had supervened. But now given the presence and concern of her friends Hazel wept uncontrollably.

'Where's Pat?' Annita was now feeling objective.

'She left,' said Freda, not wishing to pass on her suspicions. But she did not need to; the fact that Pat was not there was itself suspicious.

Annita began to examine the tiny form in Hazel's grip as closely as she could. There were no signs that suggested foul play to her. Next she turned to the tiny bubble offshoot where the tot had been laid and put her head inside. 'It smells of candles.'

Freda put her head in and agreed. She was moved to pick out one half of the bottom, underneath it there was nothing, but her hand came up greasy enough to need wiping. The finding didn't get them anywhere at all, for it may have been greasy all along; but certainly this was suspicious – even more so, upon turning back to Hazel they found her asleep.

'Pat's at the foot of this,' cried Bernadette. 'I'll kill her!'

33

Creepy Cathedral

An hour had passed: the tiny twisted cell had a bridging cross-section in metal as a seat, and although Patricia was duly grateful for her discovery of this priestly cell of solitude and contemplation, it was decidedly uncomfortable. She fingered her necklace of gold with its flat representation of St Lucinia holding the hand of daughter Itzla. The daughter was sharp and angular compared with the beautifully rounded shape of Lucinia herself. In their own time they had stood up for what had become the normal way of life, and now, perhaps with a touch more guile, Pat felt she had faithfully followed their example. St Lucinia it was that had guided her actions throughout, for she was that god's earthly representative!

Pat felt sure that the first baby was no more than a test by her god; the truth had turned out to be just as she always thought. Itzla's second coming would be her own baby and that was the miracle still to come. It was a certainty now that she had passed the test with honours. After all, enough girls were destroyed when they did not suit other cultures, so there could be nothing wrong with a boy not fitting in with the ethos here and being erased painlessly. She had been right of course, and people about her must already be realizing that the boy would grow normally and be unaffected by normal entry factors such as restricting growth and masculinity. Whether or not her flocks attempted to correct things beforehand the men would still have a Messiah and be inevitably sliding towards war. So why sit here in this stuffy place like some criminal? There was work to do now, she must prepare for Itzla the Second, and for a start she must restore Marc in case the virgin birth needed helping along.

There had been movements, for vibrations travelled easily in this thin-walled entity where only the filled-in floors dampened it

325

down. Little of Pat's arachnid instincts were needed to know that all such movement had ceased, so why sit here in isolation? Fully attuned to her surroundings, Patricia's next moves were quiet and methodical. She must step cautiously, and not go unarmed; for who knows, the quiet might be a trap. Bernadette, although such a little girl in matters of the mind, relished hunting above all else; a bad trait in an unstable character that was awash with strong emotions. Adding to that, recent events had left the girl unhinged and dangerous. Twisting the loaded pistol into her waistband, Pat reflected on the state of the armoury when she last looked; it had been devoid of the best guns, which in turn led her on to wonder where the others were and who had them.

Pat trod the way back cautiously. Her route was complex, she moved only where upper solid floors cast deep shadows upon the corridors below. Had they all moved off and left her in peace? She peeped in at the end room: Hazel was fast asleep on the bed, and on the floor Freda slept, barring the door with her body. Pat crept away from that room to enter the girls' room where again a scene of slumber met her eyes, and there again she silently stole away. But as she left the room, turning towards her own quarters in the rear end of the church, Pat's next step was impeded by a barely visible wafer-thin rim. The rim she walked into moved with her as she stumbled forwards, causing another part of its wafer circumference to catch her next footstep. Pat lost her balance and crashed headlong into a door shell positioned mid-passageway. Scared that everyone would come running, she froze prone inside its curved inner surface, not daring to move a muscle. Patricia faced the floor through the inside of a door shell and she lay there motionless listening for noises beyond her own rocking. The only sound that broke the silence after that was her own breathing so she struggled to rise, with every move tilting her unstable boat shape.

She twisted about only to find a lump sticking awkwardly into her back, Pat then wriggled round to sit elsewhere and avoid it, whilst the slippery eggshell shape rocked like a boat and kept her slipping about, quite unable to balance everything with her weight alone. She picked up the bundle intending to throw it out, but cringed back in horror as she dimly saw the baby. Realization dawned; it was the door she left which had slipped off the corridor wall and then been discovered as a place to put the baby in, out of sight of the mother – who would no doubt be upset by it. Pat judiciously climbed out, now juggling her moves to retain the baby bundle. She propped the door against a wall curve and stuck it hard at the wall, it would not slip off easily again. There was now a thick ridge of greasy wax round the pressed in door shell, too visible and too incriminating to leave; alarm bells rang in her mind. As the bundle of the baby came naturally to her hand, she wiped the junction of wall and door, using the baby's shawl. The shawl was plastered thickly with grease in places, but on turning provided fresh surfaces to wipe everything clean again. With the door invisibly stable for the time being she made tracks for the altar. Upon its handy surface the loose wrap on the baby was removed, only to find the grease was heavily smeared over the baby – the whole thing must go.

A few prayers first: Pat always prayed to Itzla, reasoning that if she put her prayers through the goddess's daughter it must be a good way of keeping both her deities informed – it was her short cut. Patricia replaced the baby's shawl and laying the tiny corpse upon the altar knelt to pray. There came a scream of rage behind her: Bernadette was running towards the altar, clutching a dagger that gleamed wickedly in the light. Pat levelled the pistol at her and the girl froze mid-stride. Pat grabbed the bundle and backed away towards the anteroom. She kept moving until the cooler outside air of the village swept over her. Bernadette was not following, her shadow was retreating, but it could only be to arouse the others.

Patricia hurried towards the engineers' gate and entered as far as the small neck where the rock joined with the rock of the bat cave, and the septic tank digesters sat in a row. She pushed the one ready for loading open, flinging the shawl-wrapped baby into its murk. She whirled about to face noises originating in the gatehouse. Annita and Bernadette would be the ones making that particular hurried entrance through the gatehouse. She swore softly to herself as she heard their raised voices close, knowing then for sure that they had guessed her direction correctly. Both trained all of the time as killers, but Pat in her career had done precisely the same. She watched them coming knowing that her chances against such fit youngsters were slim. Even as she looked they separated, so Pat waved her gun first at one and then the other; the pistol was old, but it still could be deadly and to reinforce her visible protection she shouted, 'I ain't dun nuffink – jus' a cort deff. 'Azel knows awl abaht it!'

Bernadette barely paused, edging round the extensive cave wall bulge, giving the woman a respectfully wide berth, but looking dangerously incensed. By contrast Annita still held back, despite moving towards the digesters on her far side. Pat wavered, not able to cover both, but recognizing Bernadette as the greater danger pointed the gun directly at her. Annita's flail struck the digester immediately to her rear causing Pat to take a fleeting look, enough for Bernadette to capitalize on this and run sidestepping towards her. She had dropped her arm to appear less offensive earlier, but now her knife struck home. Pat felt a numbing pain as the knife drove upwards under her ribs; she had withheld her fire unsure of Bernie's intention. It was now that her finger jerked upon the trigger despite the girl not being in the right place. There was a loud explosion; Pat saw distorted lights, and the stitch-like pain blossomed into warm hurts all about. For a moment she writhed in agony against the metal-clad edge of the still open tank, weak and dropping; but then rose miraculously towards her god, taking a suffocating last breath that was about to launch her into paradise.

The gun had blown up in Pat's hand, and pieces of shrapnel mostly embedded themselves in Pat, but some also in Bernie's hand and arm. For one moment Bernadette thought she'd been shot, but seeing her opponent bleeding and collapsing, grabbed at Pat's middle attempting to push her up and over the lip of the vessel. Suddenly Pat moved up with great ease for Annita was there also, and their combined lift merged as joint effort, dumping Pat's dying body complete with Bernie's knife into the sticky, sickly mire of the pot. Not wishing to see Pat's terminal movements Annita quickly closed the lid and threw the locking lever. That Bernie bled copiously was a self-evident emergency, and so the remainder of Annita's time was spent in getting a hold on the pressure point to stop the blood flow, at the same time maintaining arm elevation until they were back in Hazel's bedchamber.

The irony of Bernadette dodging the bullet, but being instead a casualty of shrapnel from the priest's defective gun took away any possible sense of triumph. It was only later that they could celebrate their successful two-pronged attack. Initially Annita was too glad to see her friend still alive to be bothered by mere wounds. Her first aid had been interrupted by a sudden bang upon the lid of the digester, which was ignored, as were the diminishing noises lapsing into silence. Together they set out, retracing their steps with Annita trying not to let too much blood leak out along the way.

Freda was in the act of assuring Hazel that apart from Patricia, nobody else would have wanted the baby harmed and that the whole episode was one that couldn't have been predicted. Her assurance was abruptly ended by the dramatic appearance of a bloody Bernadette, with one arm held above her head and Annita moving in step clamped to the pressure point. Instantly minds turned to first aid, and the one thing Hazel could help with was plenty of cotton waste. Before long pressure pads and bandage strips were applied leaving Bernie looking as a casualty should, but facing up to a Freda inquisition.

Annita whiled away time, waiting for Bernadette's twin woes to conclude, by talking to Hazel whilst looking casually into the fatal recess. But Hazel was aware and wanted the mystery solved; for in her mind something else had stirred. 'The engineers were drilling holes from outside near the cradle.' She would have gone on to explain that it hardly could have any connection, but already the more mobile of her friends was out of the door. So it was then that the insensible form of Marc was found in an exceptionally greasy state. Again Hazel's store of rags was raided and soon completely exhausted in the sizable job of cleaning him up also. For Hazel there were just too many interruptions here. She retired to her own bubble, leaving the bed supporting just Marc. For at the moment he was barely in the world of the living.

No one worked out how Pat had done her foul deed, but they all knew she had. Annita had to admit to Freda that she became caught up in Bernadette's passion, a passion that could have killed them both. 'But Pat running away like that swayed me, although afterwards I could see no reason why she did, for killing a male was never a reason to run. If she'd only toughed it out, we would not have had reason for chasing her, or be threatened by a gun.'

Freda agreed they had every reason to tackle her, but was not sure either about the motive for running away. 'It has to be some trait connected with her past, but I for one will not miss her. What

Bernadette did too was very wrong, for now we have another martyr to contend with. And if that were not enough, the pontiff's priceless necklace has gone with the woman.'

Freda was rather more scathing about the youngster's action when the upper council met to decide; for it was Bernadette's second misdemeanour with a knife. Her own knife had been confiscated so it was an even less forgivable offence. From now on Bernadette would be banned from carrying a knife of any sort; a crossbow maybe, but not a knife. Such a weapon was too immediate for one whose temper could at times get the better of her.

The same meeting also put the birth of a boy into perspective, and the secular law that Pat had never considered overmuch was found to hold all of the answers. This being a matriarchal state, succession was matrilineal, and a boy would never even be considered for the post. As Hazel did not produce a girl, the same verdict ensured she would keep her original place. Such an outcome would make Frances the rightful new Queen. So it was that Freda was elected as both temporary Queen and prelate for the period of transition; she must guide Frances, whilst taking up her new post in the church at one and the same time.

Even the weekly meeting agreed unanimously with the verdict that Pat should have been arrested, so she could argue it out. But then most of these members had not experienced her at first hand in a dark church, and for those who had this was a much more satisfying result. Hazel alone was beyond relishing Pat's fate. Even as this second meeting got under way, Hazel was still not recovered enough to be there, and so sparing her the lengthy concentration on what had happened.

Freda now had the task of breaking the unpleasant news to Leon: he had bodies in the digester, and they were likely to be unconsumed as yet. He looked very shifty when she reminded him that he was the expert at this kind of thing, having already had the experience of Arthur's remains. His answers were less spontaneous this time, and Freda eyed him ever more suspiciously as she finalized her instructions. 'Anything recoverable must be collected and yielded for a proper ceremony at the great destructor. The gold necklace you must retrieve as soon as you can.'

None of this appealed to Leon, so he fastened on her remark, 'any remains recoverable' and worked the digestion four times normal, making quite sure that there would not be any. Having done so, he now carried out the other half of his instruction, and was relieved to find that the gold had survived. A well-riddled wide-mesh sieve yielded up a marginally thinner gold badge of office – shining brightly there, despite representing the doer of dark deeds in the church.

34

Father To Be

The Commissar sat at his office desk with coffee, having yet another planning session; he was fully engrossed in what anyone else might call a daydream. The departed mind had leapt that inconvenient boulder near his cave entrance and was grappling with the many intangibles beyond, able to do so because he had long since saddled the rock with a not so imaginary ladder. His mind comfortably probed the cave system, believing he would brighten the chances of a successful outcome by constructive quiet contemplation. It was an easy place to visit by airborne senior officers, so he must prepare thoroughly, by turning his beehive cave into a model police station. Any such visitor must see everything fully under control, and his authority stamped indelibly on everything and everyone. He would be seen detailing men into a confusing hub of radiating tunnels, after which such policemen would reappear at the centre having run like black ants through an incomprehensible maze of tunnels to do his business. These were the endless daydreams that filled the day, always well-lit ones; because early on he realized there must be floodlighting to remove the dark tunnels witnessed first-hand. The lights to come were already stacked ready at the airport, as was the odd bulb on a lead that might be needed among unexplored tunnels. In fact they were all very helpful with these minor matters as his recent daily contact with the heliport showed. The advantage of so much delay elsewhere meant that he was well rehearsed enough to know his ultimate office inventory down to the last paperclip.

This had been his answer to an annoying series of reverses, and helped to keep things in focus as he marked time in the Commissariat, marooned there for a whole week waiting to hear news of the next airlift. Nature's last gasp of winter had been a light dusting of snow, and this was seized upon as adverse weather by the predominantly unfriendly air rescue control staff. 'Too windy to land on the spot you have in mind,' they said. But behind their bland promises of future help, the position was rather more complicated. The Commissar's project had every available pilot on unofficial strike knowing that his original pilot was the airport's resident daredevil, and at the moment on holiday. What other pilot in his right state of mind would try to go one better and attempt that initial trip with a heavy load? Not that anyone bothered to inform Claude of this fact, he was just kept waiting until the right man's name could appear on the duty roster – the original one. Lately the telephone talks with the airport were beginning to sound more promising, but without the fact emerging that his special pilot had become available.

Claude's mind continued grappling with every conceivable situation, invigorated every so often by seeing his short collapsible metal ladder leaning against the far wall of the office. Immediately facing him stood another sign of progress, and that was Sylvia's new filing cabinet, which had recently undergone a revision of content. Now its lower regions were heavy with essentials to make the task more easily performed, the job was not worth doing if he couldn't relax. Claude was quite prepared to take his whole office with him if it made his slim chance of success any more likely. His dreams dissolved into thin air as his door opened, revealing Sylvia.

'Doctor Desprez to see you sir. Monsieur please meet Commissar Brie.' Sylvia ushered Réné in and departed.

Claude sat her in a chair, before going back to his secretary in some small dudgeon. 'What do you mean, Monsieur – can't you see that she is a woman?'

Sylvia recoiled from the onslaught. 'Sorry, I got confused.'

But that was not the end to it. 'Why not call her doctor then?' Claude rounded on her savagely. 'There's no appointment either! You don't just put strangers straight in front of me!' He stormed away unwilling to hear her excuses, and paused a moment's breadth, his face undergoing some small metamorphosis in the space of the single doorway. He entered the room with a friendly smile. Ahead was the dreaded Réné. And yes, her trouser suit did make her look mannish. To his surprise she began apologizing before he did.

'Julia rang through earlier, so I rather barged in. Sorry if I inconvenienced you, but there is some urgency. Julia's just confessed to me that you are not her husband, but rather the dogsbody he leaves behind in charge of things. I realize that it was not only her that deceived me into thinking that you were him, and find myself surprised at how a man in your position can be so easily led astray.' Claude weathered the barely concealed insult and waited with bated breath to see where she was going with this sudden change of direction.

Réné gave him a withering look and continued. 'Did you know that Madame Masse is suing her husband for divorce?' The Commissar's face moved, visibly losing some of its assurance. 'From the test we did today, it is very likely that Julia is pregnant, and so the deception that so obviously pleases her, has profound implications for both you and me. It is important therefore that all three of us find out for sure, and so I have arranged an urgent specialist clinic appointment for tomorrow morning.'

'You will let me know the result?' Claude's concern showed.

'It is Julia who will wish to keep you, her preferred father, informed! As for myself I am outraged that you, a senior policeman, could get me involved in a sleazy divorce case. However I shall pursue this urgently hoping for a negative result; but if we do have to stand in the witness box then you can be quite certain I shall make specific and serious complaints to your superiors.' Réné went on to slate him at length and Claude had to sit it out and take all she threw. Then having trampled verbally upon him the outraged female left, slamming the door shut on a stunned chief of police, who stayed put for a considerable time abjectly miserable.

The following morning dawned fine and clear: Claude put his troubles behind him, and better dressed for caves this time took Mullet along the road with a vanload of office furniture behind them, not to mention his home comforts. They sat waiting on the road adjacent to nearby parkland, and that proved a good setting for explaining the strict orders circulating in the Commissariat to Mullet, whose mind moved a little slower than the rest. Mullet learned there was an exercise in mountain rescue going on, and there must be no details given, especially to reporters.

As soon as Jon and his two helpers arrived, Claude moved off to join them carrying his small lightweight ladder out into the open. Immediately he was surrounded by his extra troops – their questions only abating when they heard that he did intend to pay them.

334

Relaxed, they collected as a small group watching a noisy fleck on the horizon getting nearer; within minutes it was time to stand well clear as a helicopter landed along with its own attendant gale. The small interior was crammed with passengers and equipment; too crammed by far for Claude's special vanload. The van would have to remain standing on a side road in Mullet's care, whilst the Commissar went ahead.

The pilot tut-tutted a bit as the ladder came in sight, but they found room for it somehow, and all crammed tight together for the short flight. Of course the last-in ladder had to be first out, which was how Claude managed to pass the rock, and be strolling leisurely with Jon towards the cave mouth in weather totally devoid of ice and snow. The pair soon outstripped the others, all concerned with disgorging the necessary equipment. Better prepared this time, Claude was more ready than he had ever been, carrying a brand new heavy-duty torch and wearing a shiny safety helmet on his head, the helmet gleaming unnaturally bright in polished metal. Soon they were in the beehive cave again, and Jon was drawn to exactly the same exit as before.

Claude reluctantly followed him along the arguably used trail, finding that it led steeply downhill into a cavern, and at this point their lights barely touched its centre rocks. Even without much probing, it was immediately evident to Jon that this was the strategic centre of the area. The place came alive with possibilities, except to Claude who saw it as totally out of character with a dense thing like a mountain. He expected his mountains to be solid and not something made out of big bubbles. The huge spaces inside were something akin to fraud in his estimation, and he was quite sure that this fraud perpetrated by nature was a big deterrent from carrying out his exacting plans. But viewing the vastness of the space before him and having walked the several discernable openings off it, he very soon realized that he was ill equipped for this foray.

Jon found history repeating itself, as the mission rapidly vaporised with the small officious man wanting to go back to the start for a rearrangement. They returned to a beehive cave that was dotted now with lighting equipment. In this gloomy place several technicians hung about hoping to follow whoever knew where they were bound. It was starting to be busy; hardly had one load funnelled its way into the cave before the short flight involved saw to it that there was another on the way. Claude's own bits and pieces had arrived and standing among them was Mullet, a man chosen for his muscles rather than intelligence. He was the first of Claude's black-ant brigade, for which he had so many exciting tasks in mind. The brief was precise because the Commissar had it all worked out and knew exactly how he wanted his office to look. Mullet had problems with this and it took much explanation before he bent his back in any kind of obliging fashion, leaving the diminutive police chief searching through the piles of tackle for a roll of official yellow police ribbon.

Jon viewed the chaos as more equipment arrived bottled up in the inadequate small cave, whilst the Commissar appeared to be involving himself behind a desk. He decided to put his time to good use with the lighting technicians by leading forwards down the slope, and out into the big cave, which was obviously where it all had to go. Claude when he was ready found himself following behind the heavy-duty lighting, and for him the procession trundling down the hill was painfully slow. In the cavern, the first of three floodlights was already switched on, and he could see clearly now that the cave must be nearly a kilometre long and very high indeed. Jon, who had taken the initiative besides completing the direction necessary for positioning lights, turned as the Commissar approached, pointing high on the walls.

'Look, you can see bats up there. We may even have to climb for your survivors, if we assume that they were living off bats.' Claude looked at him bewildered, for he had already inspected the openings on to the cavern and stretched the police tape for numbering them. It was the number of openings off the ground floor that had already divided his anticipated time down to days; it was too convenient a flash of inspired mental arithmetic to throw away on somebody's chance objection – was this man pinching some of his strategic time plan? To him it was even more fundamental than that; to do the search on level ground was his own terms for being here. Survivors deserving rescue should walk, not swing down from the rafters. 'Why should they climb,' he muttered sourly: here was an expert trying to confuse him.

'They may have arrived on any level up there,' said Jon, rubbing salt in the wound. His lamp swept over the many upper holes in the cavern. Claude groaned; the side wall might have passed for gruyère cheese, had it been the right colour. Too confusing by far to see it as the upper storeys of a police station, it was more your average coliseum with damage. He drove the upper levels from his mind; Jon could find climbers for the upper levels, he would concentrate upon the area he had under his feet. In fact this area had certain similarities to the ground floor of the Commissariat, except in scale, and soon he was moving along the walls amending the police 'No Entry' stickers with a jumbo marker, and putting in names on gaps corresponding to doors on the original. What he had here would be instantly familiar to him and his staff. Tomorrow when they began operations, he would find his way about better than the experts.

Claude wandered leisurely back to the beehive cave to find out how Mullet was getting on with the office. Mullet didn't look very clear across the poorly lit space, even though an individual lamp shone upon his face. Perspiration still hung damply on his brow as he slammed home the last desk drawer, moving over so that his boss could inspect the managerial seat. Mechanical noise was simply overwhelming as three diesel generators for the floodlights thundered in the middle of the cave; they produced exhaust gases that turned Claude's initial words of complaint into a prolonged wheeze. He dropped into the padded seat intending to recover enough breath to tell Mullet off properly, and promptly knocked his knees on a twisted hill of wire connections which rose on a distribution assembly right under his desk, before fanning out. Bruised knees promptly suggested to Claude that his man had purposely followed orders exactly – just to see them fail. He was getting back at his superior, Claude decided.

So far Mullet had shown real genius by finding the one position in which to site the desk that combined every possible evil. Well he would suffer for that behaviour; for this incident had helped to strengthen his feeling that there were better places to put the centre of managerial direction.

Professing remarkable forbearance, Claude led his constable down into the cavern, explaining that he would show him a better site for the office in the main area. 'Do not plan on leaving, until all is transferred,' he said warningly. But then of course he was moved to arrange other help for his man, for there was no way that Mullet could have moved the office contents all on his own. At the far end of the cavern Claude had earlier spotted a small blind cave. He returned to remove the no entry tape, and instructed Mullet accordingly. And as the constable's back receded he commandeered one of the floodlights to point into the cave. Then with painstaking effort he built a small cairn of loose stones in its long, low entrance – strategically placed to avoid clumsy feet, and bearing his own specially made plaque – Commissar C. Brie.

35

Sentence of Death

The very idea of Hazel relinquishing her bed to Marc was quite unacceptable to the others. Resuscitating him in the church was perfectly reasonable, but that was where tolerance ended, and once the first aid had been administered he was immediately ejected. Groggy and barely conscious, Marc was transferred to the food house into Maria's tender care. There he spent two days on Terry's uncomfortable board of a bed, after which he was properly awake. No move was made to press him into his usual job, and gone was the tunic contaminated with grease; he was supplied with simple sheepskin garments. Freda it seemed had pulled her rank, insisting that the electrical work was vital and done before any manning took place. As a result, cross words were already being exchanged with Maureen, for it was she who had the difficult job of holding back a new intake, even though their consciousness was well advanced in readiness for training.

Soon Marc was busy transferring the materials he had amassed to an unused bubble high in the food house, a place allocated to him as the security control room. There he drilled a single hole through its tough skin and pushed heavy wire through the transparent wall until it touched the ground. Alarm speakers once connected to this were drawn back up again, to butt against the bubble: secure and out of reach. There were more holes to drill, this time in the top of the bubble, enabling the sensing wires to run hidden in the illuminated suspended ceiling. For existing security reasons, access into that zone required a ladder to be put up from the centre of the village, a step requiring Jackie to be there and personally supervise him. Individual spools of fine wire he deposited there, ready for moving on to security points, as yet undefined. In the control room to be there was a confusion of wires, all intended to go somewhere and be dealt with later. The parts to drive and prolong the alarm were his first concern, for that was the crucial part. His work was a challenge that drove him just as much as the frequent urgings of Freda. Apart from the satisfaction of succeeding, the job gave him excuses to be outside the food house; an essential if he was to prepare for his next escape bid.

Marc already thought he knew the best times to enter the hunt cave, but these had changed for Maureen was now often in the vicinity. He noticed that this woman in particular always took special heed of him, and besides concocting cover stories derived from his work he avoided passing every time she was visible. Besides her, the whole area had become more uncertain, for now there was a rash of other women frequenting. Waiting to emerge from the cover of the hunt cave, he could see that there was a distinct pattern of behaviour for such visitors, each stayed only a short time and peered into the men's cells from a side chamber. The two new men were the source of attraction – these Marc noticed had become pink.

He stole wire or anything else that might help and his collection inside the hunt cave grew, well hidden among the central area stalagmites. These extras were also useful for sweeping away the give-away dust from his frequent climbing activity into the elevated rocky split. He made a secure rope connection high up in the bat cave, then climbed it in the hunt cave end to hammer in the pitons that would facilitate his exit: eventually he had a rope coil secured to the top and bottom of the chimney all ready for leaving at a moment's notice. The climbing boots needed to be fitted with padding for his small feet and those he brought back to the control room. The ropes Marc checked swiftly to assure himself that they were dependable, knowing now that the bat ways were not necessarily continuous or level. With a frequent check for women in the outer caves, he hammered in any extra piton spikes he was able to find. Marc had now achieved favourable conditions for ascending the creviced chimney rock, and when the time came he could move off in an instant.

It was not long after regaining his feet that Marc heard of Hazel's bereavement, and decided to say his goodbyes to her now rather than look for a way nearer the event. Being awake early was a natural consequence of being anywhere near Maria, so his best time to visit was very early indeed – the deficit side of doing this was completely missing breakfast. Carrying a huge, almost empty spool of wire as a diversion, he headed for Hazel's bubble. The simple door tie was soon cut through and rearranged once he was inside; there was a continuous silence, and no movement to suggest she had become aware. A sound of sobbing became audible just when he was beginning to think of her as asleep. He moved through the space beyond the point where he was permitted to be, and then passing the remaining bubble approached her bedchamber quietly. The humid atmosphere clung unpleasantly as he stealthily crept into her damp surroundings, attention centred on the figure ahead, but she had lapsed into silence, stirring uneasily. Marc wormed his way along the bed material and reached his arm out over her head not knowing how she would react; after all, he had not been into her bedchamber before. Hazel clamped onto him like a limpet, her wet face buried somewhere between sheepskins and chest, convulsive shudders coursed through her. Marc put an arm round the shaking heap, every minute expecting her to cry again but she didn't. They cuddled a long time, long enough for Marc who was suffering cramp before he moved again. The fact dawned that it must be time for him to be at work, and as she was fast asleep he gently disengaged: departing he cut and remade the clip of wire securing the door.

Whilst in her room his eye had been attracted to a bright red shape at the other end of the room that he recognized as his cave lamp, and close by were a number of batteries. Marc left feeling elated, at last he had run to earth another important item that would have him better equipped when he left, and it was marked in his mind as something he would repossess when actually he did manage to say cheerio.

Hazel was deeply depressed: her baby had been murdered, whether by connivance of them all or just the one mad woman, it was immaterial – her baby was dead. But the father was dead as well and all because of the words she so deeply regretted saying – words that had to be the explanation of Terry's suicide. She was to blame, there was no excuse for her, nor was there any way that she could atone for the deed. There was not even a baby remaining that she could make amends to – her family gone forever. Despair beyond even that, because the baby was quite irreplaceable; another would not be possible here or anywhere else for that matter – she was barren. Guilt, remorse and every other miserable thought hit her mind, deepening the depression further and taking her ever lower.

Annita and Bernadette visited, but each time their presence hardly touched the surface. Each time the crusted accumulation about her eyes felt worse, and the fringe hair about her face registered vaguely as a worsening wet tangle; all signs she knew of but was powerless to control. These outpourings of grief took every ounce of energy out of her, listlessness enough to allow all friends' visits and pleasantries to fail totally. Hazel dimly found herself not wanting visitors, and failed to put any effort towards making them feel welcome, even for that she despised herself. That was yesterday, but today Marc had cuddled her, and the cloud had lifted – despite everything someone still loved her. The tears had dried and she was receptive to Annita, calling to cheer her for the fourth day running. But then something Annita said gave her a dreadful shock, one that totally altered her perception of things, for there was yet another tragedy impending.

'The girls chose their new concubine yesterday.'

'Oh, I'm not really ready yet.' Hazel's face showed how startled she was.

Annita had a consoling smile for her. 'There's no need, Freda has said she will stand in for you. She simply feels the need to brush up on her archery skills, and has told us all that it gives her an excuse to take some pre-retirement recreation.'

'I want to do my own manning, thank you. But it's very good of Freda to want to take my part – I must see her right away.' Annita's words had hit her in the pit of the stomach, prompting an instant reply. A response immediately followed by an oddity; a laugh. In the moment that it takes for mind to connect events, there was her regret for failing Marc as he so rapidly approached execution. But then there was also the vision of Freda training a crossbow with typical Teutonic efficiency upon an exit hole, out of which the concubine was expected to dash. But as Marc would simply move up into his bat run she was due for a shock. There would be such a consternation among the savages, with their flails and stones all a-flutter, everyone convinced the man must have committed suicide on the way in, but really not too sure about that either.

'Are you sure you are all right?' Annita was staring at her incredulously, as if she had just seen the first signs of senility.

'No! Really I am fine.' Hazel smiled reassuringly. 'I must see

Freda at once.' But Annita had already become concerned enough to accompany her for a couple of bubble houses down the line, leaving her at Freda's door. Freda was at home, and Hazel lucky to find her, because she had just returned from an early afternoon walk.

'Why, Hazel you are looking so much brighter! Do you feel it?' Freda smiled happily because she really was pleased to see Hazel emerge from her self-imposed hell.

Hazel set the question aside. 'Annita has been bringing me up to date, and I came to discuss both the manning and the rearrangement of my job.'

'It is early days as yet. You had best concentrate on resting until you are fit and well.' Freda was being both defensive and wary, for Hazel still looked supremely out of condition.

'I have been thinking, and I would like you to discuss it with me right now.'

'You had better come in then.' Freda ushered her into the dining area, where they sat down at one corner of the elaborately decorated wide table.

'I don't want to put Bernie out of the Charon job again by returning to it.'

Freda listened saying nothing and waiting for it all to spill out; Hazel's thoughts could be tortuous. 'What has happened has left me unable to come to terms with living here. You said a volunteer was needed to go out into the world, and willing to risk living a very short life. I think that's how I can best contribute otherwise I am sure you all will find me insufferable.' Hazel pulled a pathetic face, a face that matched up with the debilitated state of her physique admirably.

'There are better contenders for being insufferable than you, you know.' Freda sensed the emotions driving Hazel on, and tried to jolly her along.

'Not better ones for going past the sentry though,' said Hazel quickly.

'We must fatten you up first, at least put you in good shape.' Freda's mind was already more than a little bothered about the diminishing number of women, and so dissuading this unbalanced but able-bodied soul from instant action was clearly a necessity.

'I have a job to do before then,' said Hazel. 'There's the manning to do.'

343

'There is a queue for haircuts first,' Freda quipped. 'But, if you are really set on going, we can sort out the concubine problem. Wait here, I have a suggestion for you to think over.' Freda moved into the back section and brought out the pair of dancing figurines in gold. As Hazel took them, the original feelings of wonder returned and the ornaments' sheer perfection stirred her profoundly; she stood there entranced as overriding the gleam of beauty came Freda's voice. 'Give it a month, and if you still feel the same you will be fit enough to make the trip. The dancers can go with you, even one of them should buy the many things we badly need; the other would be yours to keep.' Freda noticed how Hazel handled them so lovingly before handing them back, and that was enough to reassure her that Hazel was not so depressed she could be written off.

Marc was astonished to hear that Hazel had eaten a dinner already and these were words that disturbed his concentration, giving him strong signals she was up and very likely to interfere. Her visit coincided with a time when it was most disruptive, with the man standing knee-deep in wire, totally preoccupied in where it was all going. Marc struggled with the necessary receptive words to make it sound as if she were welcome.

Hazel had things to say however, and was not being put off by him being busy. 'I have arranged with Maria for you to return to our bubble,' she said.

'Good, my bed over here is that hard, you would never believe it.'

Hazel knew exactly how hard that particular bed was, but was not going to waste words on things other than his escape attempt. 'You must go tomorrow afternoon.' She sounded bothered, in fact 'panic stations' would better describe her state of mind, knowing that she was no longer part of the execution schedule and that it could happen any time without her knowledge. Common sense really, after losing her boy friend and then the baby – they would hardly expect her to shoot a concubine as well.

Marc had no wish to be hurried; here he was at the very climax of his ingenuity with complex electric works, and she expected him to drop everything and leave it all unfinished. The feelings Marc had were certainly not of loyalty to the village, or anything like that, they were aroused very simply from curiosity into whether all the clever things he'd done would work. 'Give me another day,' he pleaded.

But Hazel had made her mind up: they were already in the danger zone. 'No, it has to be tomorrow. Can we go and see the chimney? I may even come with you.'

Marc looked at her, absolutely thunderstruck, why this sudden whim? If so, it wasn't very clever. 'It's not something I think that you could do,' he said at last. 'Terry died in that bat run.'

She looked at him wide-eyed, as if she were hearing things. 'But he went into the waterfall, didn't he?'

Marc groaned for he didn't want to dwell upon Terry's death. 'He crawled into the bat run a good while after we had failed in our escape through the waterfall. After his death I had the choice of two equally possible fates for him, and of the two, I couldn't have them paying attention to my latest escape route.' Marc sounded unhappy, he didn't want to deny her anything at all; but the chances were high that she would louse it up. Even he could not be certain of getting out successfully – so why make extra complications! But complications remained a threat for the moment, because Hazel insisted on hearing every detail of their two abortive attempts before letting up on the inquisition.

'Don't worry, Marc,' she said when she had heard it fully. 'It just so happens that I have my own way out.' Hazel was then driven to explain her own meaning as she had immediately aroused such an intense interest in Marc.

His interest soon turned to horror when he heard of what Hazel intended to do. Strong memories of creepers tearing a man apart assailed his mind. He could see that she was surprised at the necessity of justifying her intention. So it was only gradually that he calmed down, whilst she went into details to explain her odd immunity that had already selected her to go. It was the shortening of life from here on that gave her more to wonder about, and whether it would be barren as expected. But with all this he was leading her into discussion and away from stark reality: Hazel wanted decisions right now.

'Can I look at what you intend to do? This evening I know you were due to be with Bernadette, but she's in pain from an inflamed arm, so we could spend some time together in the hunt cave.'

345

This was all a bit too sudden for Marc, as he saw his own scheme for making an exit speedily becoming less sure. 'I suppose so,' he said reluctantly. 'But there's all this electrical work to finish.'

Hazel was exasperated. 'Let's discuss that some other time,' she said abruptly.

Marc watched her go. He too felt exasperated; the female master species were a pain.

Hazel was feeling brighter, in fact a whole lot brighter since the revelation that Terry didn't commit suicide after all. Those last horrid words of hers couldn't have affected him and his aims too much. The fact that he had been genuinely trying to escape was a relief, and even heartened her now that she believed it. Feelings of tiredness gradually became uppermost; she lay down for a while feeling absolutely drained of energy. Her mind was buzzing, whilst her limbs gratefully relaxed and rested, leaving her almost aware of the dull aches receding. Hazel calmed down, aware she had reached a pleasant state of inertia, one that was able to suspend active thought for a while. She snapped awake after what must have been little more than twenty minutes, departure thoughts already ringing in her mind. She must see Poppy. A much-refreshed Hazel headed for the loom: Poppy was not there. Unbeknown to her, her entire staff had been diverted to other more productive pursuits. Almost by chance Hazel then peeped into the Styx chamber and saw Bernadette about halfway along doing archery practice. The girl's figure stood rather near the target for the Bernie she knew, but the bulls-eye was as well pierced with arrows as ever. Eventually Bernadette turned, and seeing Hazel there waved a free hand, wincing at the quick unpremeditated movement.

'I'll not be jumping out on you as yet,' she said cheerfully, her arm hanging limply by her side. 'It's for sure I'll be here, even to me bed.' She pointed to a soft mound on the floor.

'You are sleeping in here? cried Hazel, aghast!

'If it stops it flaming, I'll sleep anywhere.'

Bernadette chatted on about things other than her injuries. She was putting on a brave face to cover the hurts, and quite evidently using the known but dangerous recuperative power of the chamber. The hurt arm had been well disguised from Hazel when Bernie visited her, but doing so must have been very difficult.

346

As she left Hazel swore all to herself. The last thing that she wanted was someone camped out in her direct path to the sentry. The finding left her feeling tired again and she returned to her bed. Hazel rested, until the next thought in line hit home, motivating her in the direction of the stables. Parsnip's nose nuzzled in her hand for the inevitable titbit and she was soon promising him all sorts of delicacies, once she was on the outside.

Annita was grooming just a horse breadth away listening to it all; Cauliflower's bulk shifted towards Hazel whose imagination was in full flood. 'If its parsnips for him, I want a cauliflower.' The voice was intentionally deep, and enough to startle her; but too recognizably her friend for the hoarse voice to be anything but a joke. Even so, when Annita did bob out from behind her own horse's body, Hazel was very nervy and jumped. 'Are you really going out?' Annita's mouth gaped, her face a picture of rapt attention.

'Give Parsnip some hay and I'll tell you,' laughed Hazel. 'But don't tell anybody else, it's a secret.'

'Secrets have got to be worth more than that. If it's going to be a real honest to goodness secret, and one that I really have to keep, then it should be worth at least a hair-do before you go.' Annita was evidently in a sort of wry humour that drove her to exploit this discovery just as far as jest would take her.

'I'll do it this afternoon,' promised Hazel, without giving more away.

When they met somewhat later there was much talking with an air of normality that was not present earlier in the day. Besides putting Annita's hair to rights, Hazel used the gossip to make her move sound not quite so immediate. The conversation sharpened her wits, and with it came even more release from the cloud she was under. There was pleasure in the task, she must be back to her old self again, still tired but that was all. A further rest and she would be ready for a whole evening with Marc

They met in Tanya's bubble where the heaps were now tidy piles ready to disperse. Hazel was insistent that she must check the way ahead first; knowing Bernadette might need to be countered in some fashion. She loitered on the Styx cave approach, blocking any view that her friend might have had, until Marc had passed her by; remaining there long enough to look in on the two new

347

men who were no longer lobster-coloured. One of them was awake. The sight panicked her: Marc's execution must be imminent. She remembered the last one they dressed up for, there had been very little notice – it just happened.

Marc was waiting in the open mouth of the cave. He was carrying the combined torch from her room; the torch that had given her peace of mind, expecting increasingly to use it – the only preparation she could boast. Hazel held back any expression of annoyance that arose; it died on her lips, for after all he had the most hazardous journey to do.

'Marc, promise me that you will wait at the other end of the tunnel. Otherwise I am lost in the dark, for I know I couldn't find my way out like Terry might.' It was said so charmingly, and in such a damsel in distress kind of manner – Marc's heart went out to her

'Don't worry, if it's the last thing I do, I shall be there.'

The only thing wrong in that, decided Hazel quite unable to suppress the thought – his last deed might well happen before he emerged. She remembered the little skeleton on the way in and shuddered – it could be either of them. With an effort she tore her mind away and put it to practical use. For a start there was his huge mound of rope. 'Is there any rope left behind for me, or have you got it all?'

Marc grinned, 'You certainly won't find any in the village – how much?'

She seized his hand and took him to the cave mouth. 'It is about twice as long as this corridor.'

'Will half as much do?'

Hazel looked dubious, and hesitatingly nodded her head. They returned to his crevice and pulling the rope forwards Marc reached behind it.

'Will this do?' Marc dragged a spool of heavy copper wire forwards.

'No, I want my rope.'

She sounded like a little girl about to throw a tantrum, so Marc did not haggle further, but paid out more than enough to measure Hazel's minimum need for the Styx cave and then on to the next knot – a fair distance. 'I suppose you will let me keep this.' He said it more as a tease, whilst coiling up the cut bottom portion of his rope; but as he did so, a thoughtful look supervened. 'There is one way that you could be useful, if you were here. You could free the rope when I have reached the end of it, because it is unlikely to take me all of the way now. It's a fact that I don't know how high the bats emerge at the other end.'

Hazel began to think that they were getting too rigid in predicting what they would or wouldn't do, when it was most likely that an emergency was going to trigger his first move. She found her stroppy voice to direct him – squashing many of Marc's preconceived plans. 'Marc, after lunch tomorrow, you must move off without saying anything to anyone. If you see any ceremonial bits of stone or flails, you will depart immediately, even be ready to climb in from the bat cavern if your way is barred.' She met his astonished look, stony-faced, and meaning every word. 'Promise me that much now. It is important!'

Grudgingly Marc made noises she could take as yes, but he had already burned his boats. In any event, a repeat crawl in the narrow bit was the last thing he would contemplate. If he added the scrapes and the perils of that to another unknown section many times as long, he would have a choice recipe for failure.

Hazel moved off with her rope to hide it away, and as she disappeared from sight Marc tucked the bright red torch under his own heap. Even so, the inevitable afterthought had him high up knocking further climbing irons into the other side of the chimney just in case he had to do the unthinkable.

The return to their own abode was not so direct as there were people about; but they made it uneventfully and this time Hazel made no attempt to segregate Marc. He was made welcome in her quarters. The night too was the most carefree one that Hazel had spent since returning, for her head had cleared, and regrets about Terry, or even the baby, were no longer persistent in her mind.

36

Pick up Styx

The morning lights had switched on well before they were awake, and sluggishly they cuddled together for last moments in bed before retreating. Marc left it late rising, and he had to hurry away when they did move, for soon Freda would be progress checking. Today Hazel moved off very soon after, for her constitution had to be properly back to normal before she could consider herself fit enough to leave; an appetite for breakfast did give her the necessary boost to start being optimistic.

The pool wet her, probably for the last time. It was a familiar delight that she had neglected in these latter days. The preliminary underwater tour swept her round its illuminated depths, passing their new addition on each circuit; it was a stout metal grid covering over the dark gap. She was heartened to think of it as her contribution. The swim was a bonus, which she could enjoy in solitude because all the others were at work, in fact just like those pleasant, early days when she first arrived. Now that she did not intend to stay, Hazel felt more appreciative of the pool than she had. The pool was as good as any she had ever used; it was clean compared with the swimming pools at home, and you did not smell of chlorine afterwards. It was one of the better aspects in this cave world, not that there weren't many other good points that she would miss elsewhere. She had made the right start, and her last day had begun as well as any day could; Hazel relaxed, comfortably drying in the warm air yet composing herself for what was about to happen.

The swim was almost forgotten by the time she had dressed and set off for Tanya's bubble. In the part-ordered interior Hazel hunted fruitlessly among the well-sorted residual heaps for a torch, discarding many gutted parts of torches, none of which were worth having. In desperation she entered Cora's wreck of a bubble, and walked round the heaps of mouldering brown fabrics. The place repelled her as a place of violent death, and one that retained its own particular odour. She was unsettled, but aware that failure to find what she was looking for would fatally flaw her exit. The search took her into the third bubble depth before finding a complete working torch, but having done so, she emerged thinking perplexing thoughts quite unconnected with her departure. Something had inadvertently tripped her up, and rigidly protruded from one of the more substantial heaps. At first it was shock with alarm bells ringing in the mind, but slowly the pieces reassembled and she fully understood. Returning to Tanya's abode, Hazel gathered armfuls of sorted fabrics and headed for the loom. These good intentions took a setback on finding only Poppy working; she had forgotten that interpretation depended much upon Rose, and that Rose was now working in the food house. Although she knew from prior experience that Poppy would understand what was being said, this was not so good; and to help things along she proffered individual fabrics to augment what she was saying. Hazel just nodded her head as Poppy replied, for without Rose the interpreter it was all nonsense at the pace it was delivered, and however disconcerting now was a little late to start learning the lingo.

Hazel turned to go and saw figures a short way off. Maureen was standing outside an occupied cell talking to Freda. Close to the women stood a wheelbarrow heaped with sand. The observation stabbed Hazel's consciousness as unusual, firstly because it was morning and Freda had left the village unattended. Then there was the sand, and that was what was on the floor when the last concubine was executed. Beyond these pointers, there did seem to be a quarrel going on between the women, and as she passed them by Maureen's voice rose in an aggrieved fragment. 'What am I supposed to do with them then?'

That Maureen was keen for progress was very evident, but why should Freda want to oppose her? Hazel's mind worked on it, and then it was obvious as she remembered Freda's words after her own disastrous conference. It's that perishing alarm – she wants it done before he goes to heaven. Whatever either of them might agree as a result, she had no idea, but supposing she ate as soon as practicable, then she would be ahead of them and better prepared for whatever was afoot. If it was a manning then they would do nothing at all towards it before the four's midday return. This decision still left her with over an hour before lunch. And so having decided on the best course of action, the next hour could be entirely inactive; she rested in her bubble house until an early lunch was feasible. Before retiring Hazel examined the small torch. It looked almost new and still bright – she tucked it in the fold of knitted dress material that she had round her waist.

Hazel headed for the food house. Eating was her next priority and there she encountered Rose. Meal times for the caterers were different, and this was Rose's lunch break. Having joined her Hazel decided upon chicken as the food most likely to stay down during her ordeal. In any case the roast lamb no longer attracted her; ever since her taste buds had homed in on a trace flavour from the chale toadstool she had disliked its ever-present taint in the meat. Despite this those same taste buds had thankfully failed to detect its flavour in her favourite yogurt. Rose did not react as Hazel joined her, but sat quiet for several minutes as was her habit. Hazel, with thoughts racing through her head, was quite glad of this break until eventually the thin figure spoke. 'Poppy and I were ever so sorry about your baby, we both cried.'

Hazel hated any reference made to this, for it undermined and weakened her resolve to concentrate on the matter in hand, but then she had to expect it. Thanking Rose, she asked after Poppy, but in doing so managed to cram in all of the details she wanted to impart.

Rose laughingly called it 'Tanya's rag bag'. The message had been received. She meditated in that slow world of hers before speaking, as if the thought had just materialized. 'Have you heard about the meeting after lunch?

'No.' Hazel's mind snapped into instant attention.

'Maria's just told me, and says we all must go – it's important.'

This was the final confirmation of Hazel's fear, for such a meeting would be required when repeating what happened last time; she might not even be invited to attend. Last time they had emerged from the meeting to fetch their flints and flails. Marc must be warned, because from what she knew of it the chase alone could cause serious injury. She sat there watching out for him, as despite his electric work he still took Freda her food. Hazel not only watched the palace area for him, but on watching relished the tinted clarity of the food house view, with its warm beautiful village scene arrayed neatly beneath her. It was a beauty that put a lump in her throat, and tugged at her heart to think she would never see it again. They talked disjointedly whilst Rose so very slowly ate her food. It was a good quarter of an hour later that Marc's white woolly garb showed up exiting the six bubbles; quickly Hazel made her excuses, and near running met him in the entrance vault.

'Marc, when you have served this course, meet me in Tanya's.' They passed, hardly slowing as the instruction passed from one to another. Hazel then went directly to Tanya's place and waited, for she knew he would not be long.

Marc slipped into Tanya's bubble, his face bearing an expression of incredulity and also stubbornness; plainly he thought that Hazel was taking this a bit too far. 'What do you want,' he said brusquely.

'Marc, your life is in real danger now, for they have got their new concubine ready. We have got to go at once, so cut that meal as short as you can and start out from the bat cave.'

'That route needs preparing; I can't move the stage or get the ladders elevated in under two hours. Why not use the hunt cave? It is the best place to start.'

'If you must, you must, but go carefully and wait for me in the chimney then. I'll be there in an hour's time. If you have to go before I arrive, don't forget to meet me at the other end. I'll send Poppy straight off for an early lunch, right now.'

Marc spontaneously kissed her, and dashed away to move on the dinner.

Left to her own devices again, Hazel headed for Poppy. On the way there she looked in on the Styx chamber, and as she did so her heart missed a beat, Bernadette was back from the patrol and already practising. Moments later she passed the men's cells, spotting the figure of Maureen moving about inside talking, but as she passed by the door was suddenly thrust open.

'Hazel, can you fetch me the special soup from Maria? I am stuck here for the moment.'

Hazel complied in haste; there were now two further hazards she recognized contributing to making Marc unsafe, and she fumed that he had chosen to come this way. Short of breath, she returned for the task of instructing Poppy who had probably already been told, but extra shepherding by Hazel would not be seen as out of the ordinary. A veritable minefield of tangled talk ensued before the nimble fingers ceased; Poppy started back happily walking with Hazel. On the return trip with Poppy, Hazel noticed that she was once again under observation; Maureen's awareness appalled her, the woman was easily the most obvious danger that Marc faced. He was dicing with danger if he came through here, for as the village military chief, Maureen would be doing the briefing on tactics and liable to intercept Marc the moment she saw him in the wrong place. In no time at all he would be penned up in one of the men's cells. The more she thought about it, the more certain Hazel became that the woman didn't want to move away from here because she was watching.

Hazel's brain raced as she shortened her pace to walk with Poppy into the village. What would move Maureen? The eagle-eyed one who would be alerted by anything out of the ordinary: the one who had to be distracted in some way. She had too good a view of the hunt cave approaches in there, and even if she was not actually watching there was a likelihood that she would emerge at just the wrong moment. Whatever the diversion was, it had to be important enough to justify the disturbance, and that meant really important! Hazel racked her brain, wandering round the village like a zombie, but then she caught sight of Cora's bubble and moved inside rapidly, her mind in overdrive. Entering the gatehouse soon after, Hazel waited for Marc to arrive, and when he did she intercepted him with quick whispered words that caused him to let her move off first. Moments later he saw her hurrying round the bend into the line of cells – holding her excuse.

The outline of Maureen was visible near the cell wall, bent slightly forwards as if in conversation with someone unseen, but her head still moved watchfully. It was evident that she had to go through with her diversion as planned, and even though the plan seemed increasingly tenuous she launched herself into it. Hazel moved close to rap upon the door, and knowing that she was bigger than this powerful woman and standing so that she obscured the greatest possible coverage of the exterior. She felt, rather than knew of Marc's passing – and as the door opened, hers was the initiative.

'Yes?' Maureen's voice was harsh. No one should disturb her at this delicate stage.

Hazel allowed a tremor to enter her voice. 'I found this in Cora's bubble.' She raised the cut rope that Marc had hidden, an object which she had found quite inadvertently. Maureen viewed the cut end with instant interest, and then with something approaching alarm as she saw a differently spliced end where it had joined another rope. Her voice was astonished enough to lapse into her native brogue.

'It is not the one we found, is it?' But then she went on to provide the answer herself. 'By the sins o' Patrick – 'tis another half it is!' Maureen, normally a most exacting linguist was quite evidently shaken by the find. She moved out rapidly to join Hazel, closing the door upon her pudgy-looking charge.

Hazel's lack of fitness showed as Maureen moved apace towards the pool gatehouse. She was yards behind her as the rope arrived so very speedily at Freda's place. They caught Freda still having her after-lunch beverage, and so in that instant she was able to bear down her full intellectual powers upon the rope, and then upon Hazel.

There followed such a barrage of questions that Hazel's head whirled; but she backed up her tale to Maureen admirably. The rope had been just lying there for anyone to find, and that was quite unshakable, because it was true. The fictional reason for why she was there at all felt shaky, but her feigned interest in finding needles for a material-based idea got her through.

Freda, who had been nursing so many doubts all along about those mysterious and suspicious disappearances, was consequently very keen to accept Hazel's account. She had prior ideas of how she might test the waterfall incident further, but so far there had been insufficient reason, and in order to do so now they must ride there right away. Her inspiration was based upon a reel of fishing line she had recently unearthed in Tanya's abode. Very soon they were arriving at the exit waterfall, and found their cut rope exactly matched the one still resting there. Freda tied a heavy stone to her fishing line and heaved it in. Such was the length paid out that even both halves of the knotted rope looked insufficient when Freda lined them up on the ground. She pointed to the cut ends. 'For another thing is obvious to me, a suicide's weight would give this heavy rope a jagged edge, and not the straight cut it has. These observations suggest that the rope has a more complicated history than either a suicide or an escape attempt. This rope is a deliberate plant, so we need to call a meeting of everyone.'

Hazel found herself returning to spread the news of a meeting that must now take place an hour earlier, leaving everybody just about enough time to feed if they hadn't already done so. Her recipients for the message were found rapidly, leaving her thinking with some little amusement on how Freda would not miss Marc now – she would be too busy. In this assumption she proved to be quite correct, and indeed she could apply such reasoning to the whole village, because the residents were now all going to be too busy to worry about concubines at all. Whilst they were occupied finding something to eat, she could pass the time with Marc. Hazel felt optimistic, but perhaps it was early as yet to think that she was winning, because on the deficit side of sorting things out for Marc, she was rapidly being enmeshed in the very scare she had started.

Marc was sitting in the chimney assembling his gear, and shod now in out of proportion climbing boots. Boyishly he showed her a cold chisel, previously stolen from the engineers, it was a tool that could be grasped as he moved and ready to dig through any narrowing or chalky projection. He was dressed in skins, with the fleece turned outside, and there was over twenty feet of wire coiled around his waist, just in case Hazel could not be there to cut him free. Hazel was glad about that; for with all the fuss she'd started, she couldn't be sure of being in place later but she would try. 'Give me another half hour before you start, I will be back if I can.' They arranged signals just in case he was crawling in the bat ways when she returned. A quick kiss, and she was off again. Marc consulted his watch – another Hazel contribution. There was little to do now but wait.

The conference was set to take place in the church, a place that stirred bitter memories for Hazel. It was to be a serious affair and Hazel was taken aback at what she had started in order to move Marc just those few feet. Freda was being dramatic in exhibiting both halves of the rope and pointing out the inferences of finding the cut end hidden in the village, the one that supposedly had accompanied a suicide's body down the watercourse. Clearly Terry was in circulation and possibly even Arthur, for his death too was uncorroborated. She pointed to signs of unrest lately among the men, who seemed ripe for any kind of plot whatsoever. These were the enemy then, their village men who had both the inside knowledge and current invisibility, enough to threaten the whole community. Their search had to be swift in the closing part of today; a snap head count in all open areas, coupled with a physical search in the segregated ones. A statement that Freda followed up, detailing exactly where each individual should search.

Everyone was given familiar territory to scour. Hazel, to her immense relief, was allocated to her own area – which from its geography must suit her run-down condition and easily be the safest of them. To do so she could have Poppy as company. Her orders were to survey the area beyond the pool gate, after which they were to patrol the village.

Among areas given to the others, Hazel was relieved to hear Bernadette allotted to checking out her staff of tiny fungi growers; to have her out of the Styx chamber was an unexpected bonus. Freda concluded the external operation would be completed when all three sections outside had been searched and the village gatehouses closed.

Freda took pains to impress upon them all that this was serious. 'The man must have been lurking for some time in Cora's bubble because that is where he planted the giveaway rope. So our first task is to search the village thoroughly, remembering that both men know the village extremely well. Hazel you may start your search whilst this is going on, because you must be back guarding the village while we are away. There is not much of today left, so you will all have to move yourselves.'

Listening to the enthusiasm of her friends, especially Bernadette accepting to be part of it with her arm painfully resting in a sling, Hazel felt her own part was that of Judas, knowing that the men would not be found. She was glad that the meeting was so short, and that Freda had chased them all off very promptly. Quickly Hazel collected her weapons with everyone else, and joined the trickle dispersing from the church. The four called across their greeting to Hazel as they headed away; Hazel waved her crossbow back knowing that she had betrayed her friends, and met the thought by promising herself she would make up for it all.

Things had fallen right into her hands; speedily she disposed of Poppy, sending her to search the pool area. Poppy tried to convince her to go as a twosome in case of danger, but artfully Hazel failed to comprehend and sent the exotic flower off on her own. Hastily she returned to Marc who was getting ready to depart regardless of her, and there was another bout of hugging and kissing before the off.

Hazel sat close to the chimney listening to the shifting of soft skins beyond the screen of dust falling over the accumulation, noticing that there was still a lot of rope to go. She opted to leave and hurried back to meet Poppy. Instead Freda stood waiting in the gatehouse, giving her a nasty shock. Freda it seemed had decided to check on their safety whilst knowing she had an ample reserve of women on hand searching the village. Trying to look open about it, and not in the least surprised, Hazel moved into the gatehouse fully aware of Poppy on the return path. 'We have done a preliminary search, and it is all clear,' Hazel summed up, breathing heavily and deliberately looking unfit, lest Freda pull her away for something more pressing. In her mind's eye she could see coils of rope departing, and then to add to her intense frustration Freda began to linger.

Freda walked along the line of cells and entered the observation bubble, the one bordering both men. 'They are looking great!' Freda cried. 'This time round you must take part in our little party and be properly one of us. While the men are still newcomers their soft parts match us for quite a while, so don't miss out, and to hell with embarrassment. We are all grown women.' Freda knew well what she was advocating; largely it was worries over Hazel wavering, and the wish to predispose her towards staying that motivated her. Hazel's smile accompanied with a quick nod was her only response, so Freda returned to the present. 'When you are finished out here, bolt the pool gatehouse door and occupy the agricultural gate-house. The engineers' gate is already bolted, for if I have a definite mistrust in particular, it is in that direction.'

Having delivered her final instructions, Freda looked again into the cells and strode off towards the gatehouse and Poppy. She had not gone many paces when she beckoned Hazel to her. 'Have you seen the Styx chamber tonight? It's a mass of excited lights. You can see two of the gourds quite clearly and their lateral arms busy wiping organisms from the walls.' She pointed and was gone.

Hazel breathed a big sigh of relief. She rushed back into the hunt caves and found she was out of breath, even over that short distance. When it came to feeling unfit, she didn't need to act. Feeling exhausted, she pushed forward on legs that had become shaky, and moved over to the chimney. There was still a turn of rope to go and so she collapsed into the place where Marc had sat before. Thankful that the rope had lasted out, Hazel watched it moving upwards for a while and then pulled it twice. The steady advancement of rope ceased and what was spare began to depart upwards into those dark regions of flittering bats. The remaining turn of rope sped forward of her hands, and as this came to an end she felt three pulls. The knife was ready – Hazel severed the rope, and the cut end snaked away; this was her point of release also – she was free to do likewise.

'Steady now, mustn't let it go to my head, let's get out of here sensibly. Thoughts raced through her mind making the next stage hard, for she had not considered it well enough. Relief at getting over the main hurdle had worn her down, and there was not much that she wanted to do for the present. Poppy was pleased to see her back at the gatehouse; a bit like the pet dog who stops you from doing what you would have done, and just like a real pet the conversation was all one way. Hazel talked on about nothing in particular, intent on calming both Poppy and herself. Soon the talking became a cover for her intentions as she walked Poppy to a vantage point in the village; here was a place that Poppy could watch both the pool and the agricultural gatehouse, almost, but not quite, in accordance with Freda's direction.

With Poppy established, Hazel was able to head for the palace apartments and in particular the gold room. Freda was not at home, but this was just as Hazel expected, for she would be well away now supervising her troops – who would have moved to the extreme ends of their domain and become bogged down on head counts. What she had started was going to be a right turmoil for everybody – the day would be a long one.

Hazel entered the gold room and immediately the dancers caught her eye but she knew they must be left, rating to her as priceless works of art. Instead she would take the hippopotamus. It might be antique but for her eye the work was not detailed enough to call it priceless. Its weight must be a nearly two kilos and in gold that must be worth a great deal of money.

The library was her source of writing paper, there were blank leaves in some of the cheap novels, and soon she was writing to Freda on them; she scrawled a message in unaccustomed handwriting.

Dear Freda.

I am leaving – I hope to pass the sentry in a few minutes' time, taking your gold hippo for purchasing supplies. I shall return in seven days with the fish supplies if successful.
There's a rope halfway down the entrance chamber, and if all goes as I hope it does, there should be something for you to haul in after 4 pm on that day – so wish me luck!

Terry is dead, of that I am certain. Marc tells me that he died in the bat exit fault; hope Marc used it successfully elsewhere as he will be my map.

Note: I found the cut rope and used it as a diversion!
Sorry, Hazel.

Hazel rearranged her dress fold with the hippo butting onto the torch. Her ruse with the rope had not only assisted Marc, but had removed Bernadette from her own direct path – warmly congratulating herself on that she arrived at the mouth of the Styx chamber. But a setback was waiting for her there. Sprawled on the cave floor were two bodies: one had fallen a few paces from the sentry approach and was still clawing at the floor; a second protruded from the bend where retrieval was just about feasible. Frustrated she stood fuming; there would be no race past the sentry for her now, not with those obstructions littering the way – it was one of those times that she found herself swearing over and over. The rotten cave had denied her all along. She had to make the trip right now to keep her word to Marc, but simply stepping over the bodies would not do. Her brain weighed up the facts; how long had she before Freda came back and stopped her? There was no way of knowing, and she certainly had no wish to be around when her note was read – its contents would lead to so much aggravation. Hazel cried out aloud in exasperation but there was nothing at all she could do about it. She must set to and rescue them.

The thought struck her that whatever she did must be planned, and then integrated into a scheme which would not peter out simply because she had forgotten something or other. Slowly she retraced her steps through the hunt caves, back to find Marc's chimney recess. Yes, there was the large spool, still with the remainder of the heavy-gauge copper wire that she refused earlier; wire that would back up the rope just in case it was too short, for

360

after all bringing supplies back was an essential principle of going. Hazel rolled the spool through into the forepart of the Styx cave. Soon she was drawing her rope through the spool's centre, where simply tying a bulky knot arrested it. Tipping the spool over trapped the rope underneath and to her mind that made it permanent.

Next it was Poppy's turn, the gatehouse watch could be abandoned – and just pray that Freda didn't arrive. Hazel moved into the first of the men's cells where the retrieval suit was kept, and with Poppy's aid dragged its parts out into the Styx cave; soon Poppy was helping her into it. Clattering along she trudged many weary steps into mid-chamber and there stood stock still collecting energy for her next move. She paused watching the heightened display on the walls and also the creepers which were jerkily withdrawing from sight. Taking a few deep breaths she set off again with determined stride to approach the fallen woman, turning to shield her with the wings. Then grabbing into the shoulder of her coat Hazel dragged the considerable weight over the uneven ground to Poppy. Taking another rest in mid-stride, she set off again to bring back the male figure from close in to the sentry rock. Here she could feel the vibration very strongly, and turned about to drag her load rather than pull it, using the entire wing shield to face the gap. She was surprised to find how much the influence diminished. She took a grip upon the person's hair and dragged, grabbing an arm as it emerged to get more purchase. The body moved easily enough although a train of adherent creeper root followed it. Hazel bent to her task of pulling the weight along, opposed and restricted by the heavy plates of her suit. It was more of an arc that she trod, and not exact like the first rescue; but she cared much less now. Her eyes divided their attention between the brilliant flickering on the wall and the fact she was also dragging several of those disgusting creepers; one by one they detached and fell away from the person as she moved forward. Hazel looked high up to a huge ghostly gourd that must be ultimately joined up to some of those creepers from its recessed ledge, but did seem completely divorced from it all.

Once clear of noticeable influence, she made a further stop for the fuzziness to depart her mind, and then even more rest until something in mind told her that time was precious. Hazel finally discarded her survivor well short of Poppy, who was stripping the first. Next she dragged the heavy spool further in towards the centre with the rope still trapped under its central hole, depositing it just on the edge of the safe zone. She took more deep breaths, staggering a little as she returned, only to realize that taking off the suit was simply time going to waste. It had proved beneficial in cutting the field around the sentry entrance and time would be saved if she kept the suit on; particularly Freda, the complication she feared most, must come soon. If protection were what the suit conferred, then she would borrow it. Wresting Poppy away from her work, she told her carefully what she wanted her to do, but first and foremost to pay out wire from the reel as she moved.

Poppy complied but nevertheless stood there looking bewildered, as she watched Hazel swaying away from her along the chamber dragging both a rope and the wire. Hazel headed for the sentry, having twisted her ends of wire and rope about a wrist; her gait she imagined spacewalkers might find familiar, apart from her suit being the heavy one. Hazel ploughed her way on flapping the forward arm to balance, and keeping her back towards the sentry rock; the hook bend arrived with sensations of increasing heat and oscillation in the metal plates, a sort of wave. Her ears were making strange internal noises but ignoring them she decided to move faster, and that's just what her limbs heavy with shield failed to do as the suit slowed every effort. The sentry's strong field which she had felt was being blocked from the rear was now tangible at the front; both sets of rock must be part of it. But it was the metal behind her that was getting hotter, was she cooking between the two plates she wondered, perspiring uncomfortably. Hazel wondered if the suit might do her damage, by charging her plates into some sort of microwave, but it was far too late to worry about that now. She was becoming over hot and moved urgently, aware her mind was growing fuzzy again. There were odd singeing vapours of hair and clothes, whilst her ears heard frying noises.

Tripping on through the tangle of creepers underfoot she staggered forwards to bounce off the curved wall that had been her goal. She hit the floor with an enormous clang, one that cut through all the noises going on in her ear. The reflections from cellular light at either end lit the floor badly and there in virtual dark Hazel lay with trembling building up until she was shaking and aware of weight much too heavy to lift off. She was dizzy, barely knowing where her limbs were, and spewed sick somewhere,

362

her mind barely conscious beyond the retching. Splayed out there on the rock bottom, cool low-level draughts impinged on warm metal surfaces, until the heat retreated and chill tremors coursed her body. Eyes open now and conscious of blurred, shiny, wet ground, Hazel saw her hands clawing vomit as did the woman seen earlier. The sight incensed her to move and Hazel turned over, her back plate slithering on hard brambles; the brambles that had caused her to trip and of which there seemed to be a whole network clinging to her back. She moved and found two that had penetrated her from below clutching like claws. Hazel tore at the smooth, hard tendrils curled up inside her, realizing they had entered a chance orifice and tightened into it whilst she was virtually unconscious. Hazel grabbed at the stems but they were curled over, and hardened into hooks; she eased herself into a sitting position and tugged at the stems between her knees which dug in hurtfully as the blood trickled down so as to wet the floor.

She began to scream and grabbed at the woollen strip that dangled heavily at her middle spilling out the weighty hippopotamus; this she grabbed and used as a hammer regardless of ornamentation. Screaming and inching away, her blows rained down on the brambles flattening their stems into mushy wafers on the floor as she wriggled backwards on wobbly arms that barely supported. Hazel dragged herself clear, sliding on her back and guided by the curved wall of rock she rounded the acute bend of mere yards, before reaching the space that opened onto the approach tunnel. She subsided there amidst all of the junk that lined the walls and collapsed.

A while later, Hazel opened her eyes to the odd part-light that diffused through those slime-laden tunnel walls, realizing slowly that she had made it, and what's more all in one piece. There was the torch, spilled out near the hippopotamus. She reached forward into the dimness at the foot of the sentry rock and collected them; the creepers were gone. There seemed to be more light produced by these walls than in that distant arriving memory, nevertheless what a relief it was to switch the torch on successfully and with the light came a lessening of anxiety.

Hazel eased herself out of the gold armour taking a rest every now and again, until at length it was all off. The rope still had some slack in it, and this she separated from the wire binding it to the handle of an old-fashioned flagon and piled the heavier rubbish about it. Now she took the wire and threaded it through every individual part of her suit, then saying a silent prayer she pulled urgently at the wire; jerked and pushed alternately upon its stiffness so as not to move it overmuch. She was pleasantly surprised when an answering tug came. Her heap of treasure started to move and soon she was judiciously guiding it into the curve, watching as it went clattering on its way. Hazel retreated to hold the ropes end tightly and prevent it being drawn along with the movement of her armour, and which surprisingly kept her informed about progress of those heavy objects; the danger of a tangle was soon past and she was able to relax. Turning firmly away from the sentry Hazel set off along the algae-misted, glassy tunnel; going this way it twinkled with light into the distance, but for this she was weary and past caring. Much lighter now, her legs bore her on towards the tunnel mouth where Marc she hoped was still waiting, for surely she had been a long time coming.

37

Mythical Prescience

They had all departed and the helicopter was returning for him at 6 o'clock: Claude Brie stood looking into his depressing office of stone. The arc lights warmed his back making a pleasant introduction to its uncompromising depth. He peered uncertainly from the periphery wondering where he might put a foot. Between him and the back wall, the floor was packed with desk drawers and cardboard boxes; somewhere out in the middle of all this, and quite unapproachable, was his desk looking much like an island. Such a configuration Claude recognized as further evidence of Mullet's inappropriate humour; he mastered rising feelings of indignation and bent his back towards transferring the excesses out of his path.

A whole heterogeneous collection lay in nearby drawers, displaying little that could be called order. He directed his first moves towards approaching the desk by simply stacking up the drawers on either side with those in his path, laying them flat and ready for insertion. It was pleasant working there with the lighting playing hot upon his back, but hardly a dozen drawers had been transferred before there was a whiff of cooked coat tails, and his bottom was decidedly warm. He began to move more hurriedly having made little progress into the drawers at his feet, but then as he bent again there happened a splitting sound; his over-hot trousers rendered tight by good eating were coming apart on a rear seam. He straightened his back, bending the knee to make the next transfer; priorities were changing now, something must be sought for the repair.

The desk, he must reach the desk, Claude seized the drawer in front of him and put it in the space behind, speedily increasing the gap behind him until he reached the desk, fortuitously gathering himself bottle of cognac somewhere along the way. The split had worsened, but now he could sit on his chair comfortably, weighting the two halves of material together, whilst at the same time contemplating the next moves in the reassembling of his desk. The twin lights shone on him unable to heat now, but of course the light was blinding instead; it was another Mullet triumph of positioning – but why was the chair so near the desk? Cautiously Claude checked for obstacles between the two, and before long a smile creased his face; Mullet had missed a trick. Already thirsting after six hours in the caves, not to mention the exhaustion he felt now, Claude looked for the home comforts so painstakingly pro-vided – he craved coffee but nothing familiar protruded from the visible drawers or boxes. Rising above it all, Claude attacked the bottle of cognac, relaxing in his chair and countering the blinding light by merely turning the chair. Even in this relaxed posture, the chair legs scraped abrasively on hard rock and he missed the comfortable slip turn as provided by a real office; the whole comfort idea was beginning to lose lustre.

He cradled his head in hands to think, awkwardly aligned to the desk in a decidedly uncomfortable posture, but it did make him more objective in a befuddled sort of way. He counted off the eight days left to complete his investigation, knowing the next step as the most difficult, perhaps even impossible. After musing on this and its sheer unpredictability for some minutes, he turned to a more tractable subject – Julia. He did admire Julia's knack of getting her own way, and he suspected she would deal with the baby issue her own inimitable way and suppress any baby news in a court of law, if it ever got that far. That left both him and Réné depending upon her doing either that or simply declaring Gabriel the father. For sure he was the sort who would get quite nasty without much provocation, and to be cuckolded might easily upset him in a big way. Divorce would be a certainty then; and what about that delightful property, the promenade house? It would feature in any settlement perhaps, although he understood it was Julia's family bequest and therefore safe, but if not, then the bloodsucking would commence – probably his, if a baby was in existence.

Such thoughts made him feel trapped, particularly here with a sea of obstacles around him, and especially now when he couldn't be sure of being sober for the way out – the grope back began. He bent his mind to the necessary game of draughts with the boxes on the floor. Gone were the thoughts of putting the desk back together, the drawers could stay there and rot. He wandered out into the cavern; this was a far more stimulating place, what a pity that he had not yet located his video camera. Claude strolled past doors of his imaginary police station; he knew them every one, and would as long the sticky tape held firm. But what about all those other holes high up where Jon would be looking? That lot was a maze, in fact it all was one massive maze, and then underneath faced by this massive array of different caves was the central rock formation. It had looked somehow bovine before, but now with two bright lights mounted on what could only be horns, it held almost mythical qualities. In such appendages he saw a Minoan bull standing out from a sea of darkness, the most appropriate centrepiece for such a vast maze – and this for him completed the picture, a picture representing his extended territory. His mind blankly roved through the minotaur myth seeking any further similarity that might bring enlightenment of a divine kind to his enterprise and point the way. All these openings were his maze of police tunnels and he the high chief of the black ants, if slightly worse for wear, and just approaching his own icon a bull at the centre of it all. The pagan hero he could discount, for he was already in the morgue – the shepherd type who fell off a mountain. As Claude saw it the fellow had already dodged one fate in the bullring, by meeting the chief black ant posthumously without his fabled ball of string. Yes, he had forgotten that ball of string, for wasn't the hero supposed to be an assassin following it? Surely there couldn't be another hero assassin out there waiting in the dark and this his supernatural warning? The very thought made his flesh creep, for he was alone and vulnerable in this vast, creepy hall. In the myth a cunning priestess had plotted, laying a trail and guiding the man on to his target. Would his particular priestess be a pregnant one he wondered? No of course not, that was another avenue entirely. His trouser seam destruction lurched into yet another avenue, and the garment loosened about him – Réné came to mind: she was far more likely to curse him.

Claude could feel the pair of them closing in on him, his brain befuddled and preoccupied with torment, eyes barely focusing ahead; but they reacted now to something changed. It was something whitish and sheep-like; he shivered involuntarily, sure now that it was more than a dream – the bloody caves were haunted. Just across the space separating them, a miniature youth wearing sheepskin sat un-moving in a doorway, just one up from 'lost property', a coil of thin strands resting over his shoulders uncomfortably completing the illusion.

He must be awake and sober for his shuttle. Claude hesitated to pinch himself; surely he would not be feeling so draughty and uncomfortable in his trousers if he were dreaming? Cautious from a combination of all previous thought, Claude approached to a safe distance before addressing the youth, who sat cross-legged upon a dirty brown mat. 'Where did you come from?'

The youth almost carelessly pointed up the tunnel. With a surge of rage, Claude noticed one of his no-entry tapes stuck to the mat. Before he could say a word, the small figure looked him right in the eye, and Claude beheld a countenance that seemed familiar. Marc smiled across at him.

'I remember you – it is Monsieur Brie isn't it?'

The penny dropped, it was Marc Casserta deep in beard and filthy of face. He took one more step backwards, remembering the hulk that had left him threateningly on bad terms. Marc stood and stretched out his hand, the surprise was that it rose upwards from beneath chest height. Claude looked down, wondering where the brute Marc Casserta had gone – it was a mere pause, then politeness took over and he moved in to shake hands. 'Better come into my office,' Claude said, wondering whether the fellow was lousy. He certainly looked very dirty.

'I had better stay here,' answered Marc evenly. 'I am waiting for Hazel; she will need my light to see her way.'

Claude's heart leapt within him, was this the other lost soul – the Hazel of matching knickers fame? 'Why didn't you come together?' Claude struggled to understand.

'I came a different way; this way would be quite lethal to me.'

The Commissar's eyes strayed back and forth along the holes in the cavern wall, before he queried, 'Which one?', fully expecting that it would be one of those on view.

'I will show you, but first we must direct more light into her path.' With a surprising show of vigour Marc hurried to the pair of low-slung floodlights outside Claude's office, and with it all swaying dangerously over his head, he slithered the tripod legs until the parallel lights faced into the mouth of his tunnel.

'Come,' Marc said, all ready to go; but then stayed behind to help Claude retrieve his topcoat from the stand near his darkened office, using a smart combination light to do so.

Claude chose to face him as he dressed. The creature might not be an assassin, but its woolly whiteness was still not ready to be taken as something other than a subterranean ghoul.

Marc followed a trail of wires leading to the two generators in the beehive cave. Not all were still working, and so most of the way up was covered by a number of oil lamps. One generator stood silent as only two of the main lighting circuits were being left on overnight. It was not long before they stood in the beehive cave's noisy fume-laden atmosphere; but then only to step smartly from it again into one of the other holes flush to the cave floor. Something clanged as Marc walked into the dark. 'I hit that coming out,' he complained rubbing his shoulder, the light going all over the place. 'That's my route up there.' His torch picked out a tiny hole with fluffy dirt hanging over its bottom edge.

Claude looked in amazement. Did the fellow shrink further to get through it? Besides it was way off the ground. His powers of belief were strained to the utmost limit. 'You came through there!' he said, disbelieving.

Mark turned on the fluorescent element, and pointed upwards. 'Like them,' he laughed, indicating bats clinging further up the wall. Then switching back to the beam again he illuminated a parallel hole that continued onwards just across the narrow cave. 'That's OK for them – but I preferred to get out here and walk.' His light outlined the sizeable coil of rope he had left on the floor

Claude was suitably impressed, the rope had its own pile of dirt and certainly enough to accept what he'd been told; but then his attention suddenly turned to the familiar metal shape of his own filing cabinet. There were also several chairs that had been pushed in here out of the way, presumably until tomorrow. He might have known Mullet, the man who gets tired easily, would find an easy option if there was one; especially with the office superficially full. Tomorrow the man responsible would have excuses galore, so he wasted no more thoughts on Mullet.

Opening locked drawers Claude inspected their contents, and was pleased to see his files on the missing people were handy. A video camera and his home comforts lay in the drawer underneath. 'Would you like coffee?' Claude asked.

369

Marc accepted, looking as pleased as if Claude had offered him much more, and even after finding himself loaded with all that Claude thought important, his enthusiasm continued unabated; mainly on account of a severely dust-laden throat.

Soon they were back, and plugging a heater for coffee into the spur sockets of the floodlights. They allowed the lights to remain where they were, for this was now the most convenient area to await Hazel's arrival. Rearranging, they made their surroundings more comfortable using a table and chairs salvaged from Claude's office.

Despite having the longed for comfort, Claude looked about him strangely, his unease quite apparent.

'Is there something wrong Monsieur?' Marc's voice sounded concerned.

'No it is a very small matter; I am wondering whether I ought to photograph the location for police records.' But this reply was far from the truth; for he was still countering the effects of an earlier thought pattern. Julia was in his mind and uppermost right now – her smoke-laden, 'man-lure' perfume he sensed as being right under his nose. Claude broke free of such minor distractions to pan the camera round him, and fix it securely pointing at the table from that very convenient lighting pillar. He looked at his watch. 'I really must hurry coffee and then dash. The helicopter should have arrived by now, but it can wait for our refreshment.' The aroma of coffee arising from cups dispelled any lingering ghosts, and both men heartened to a brew that soon put Claude's hallucinations to rest. He was keen to know of the danger in the tunnel; for his men's sake he ought to be aware. Marc told him of the swift but agonizing knockdown that had reduced him to being a servant in a village populated by women. Marc speedily changed the subject as he saw the Commissar was looking upset at these words, and instead admired the camera. 'That's an ultra low light camcorder you have got there. It was still in its experimental stages when I set out to find my wife.'

Claude was much too preoccupied to answer; he looked at his watch again and rose hastily. 'The helicopter will be giving me up for lost; I must go and speak to the pilot. You stay here. We can chat further when I get back.'

Hurrying along the poorly lit cavern walls, Claude was thinking furiously as he went. If he took Marc's initial words seriously, then

370

there were dangers further up the tunnel for any search team, and the fact that the man was waiting at a safe distance tended to confirm what he was saying. Claude made a decision that he would curb his own adventurous spirit, and not be too much of a leader when it came to venturing into tunnels. Soon the fume-ridden beehive cave was endured and passed by; Claude emerged into the cold night air wishing the strips of cloth that waved round his bare legs were whole. Mounting the short ladder over his stone he ambled over to where the helicopter stood with its blades quite at rest. The pilot he recognized as one of the team, who earlier moved equipment into the cave. It was an aviator who looked very annoyed, having been kept waiting a good twenty minutes only to hear that his passenger was staying a while longer. 'What about the two ladies sir? Are they staying overnight also?'

Claude whirled upon the man. 'What do you mean, two ladies?'

The pilot winced as if he had been hit. 'The two I brought up with me. They said you wanted to see them.'

Claude was silent, his mind chaotic. He banged his head against the aircraft deliberately as if relieving some other pain that needed knocking.

The pilot tried to add detail, just in case this was set to rebound on him. 'They were waving a piece of paper about as if it were important.' He added, 'I told them to follow the cables, one of which specifically directs its illumination into your cave office.'

Claude groaned; a big audible groan.

'Why? Did I do wrong sir?'

Claude collected himself together again. 'No. Just supposing I want you back here tonight, is there a number I can reach on my portable telephone?'

The pilot scribbled a number on a piece of paper, but warned the Commissar that he would have to act soon, because he was shortly off duty, and another pilot might easily refuse to undertake the non-emergency but still tricky flight. 'It could be that the ladies will be stranded with you until morning sir,' he said respectfully. With that he handed over his note. Wasting very little more valuable time on the Commissar he waved Claude Brie to one side and then took off.

The progress back was slow, Claude reached the beehive cave cold and deeply depressed; his exploits in the caves had arguably saved one, but in doing so he would seem to have lost another two.

It was only then that the full import hit him, and the laugh that began in a small way gathered momentum and was destined to reach its peak in the beehive cave where he collapsed helplessly within its fume-ridden depths. He emerged coughing but only to collapse again over the next handy rock surface – a place where he could grip and laugh uncontrollably, allowing the tears to water its surface. For the women had entered a village where they would never come back; never stand him in court; never ask for child support. Moreover it was a place that perfectly suited Julia, with men there to tend her every need – a place without even a telephone to ring for himself. He could not even feel sorry on her behalf, because she had tricked him; this was a measure of divine justice. At length his chuckling subsided, enough to realize that Julia had passed by whilst Marc and himself were inside the splinter cave. After all, hadn't he caught a whiff of her perfume? The faint possibility that they may be still be stumbling about in the cavern gave him a nasty turn; he hurried into the depths and strode about the complete circuit, realizing as he did that he was not dressed for meeting anyone unless it was Robinson Crusoe – but that did not matter, they were gone.

Marc was practically asleep, sitting propped against the wall upon his mat. For Claude it was vital to learn more about his world, and to be reassured that Julia would not come tripping out of that tunnel instead of Hazel. The draughts impinged uncomfortably on his legs, pity the safety pins were not among his office comforts. Discomfort drove him to seek them in his official cave and grope among his office possessions equipped with a mere torch. He sought the distinctive shallow drawer from his desk; and upon finding it, emerged carrying a bundle of safety pins easily surpassing all expectation. More comfortable now and with a long line of safety pins running up his trouser legs, Claude dragged the coat-stand into a more useful position, and hung up his outer coat before making more coffee in readiness for the Marc Casserta interview. To find someone smaller than his own self was a prime source of amusement to Claude who was enjoying a good humour tonight, and the sight of a sleepy Marc sitting on a normal-sized chair with his feet off the ground, raised his curiosity. Also knowing what a big man the fellow had been – how could this possibly be? He roused his midget with more coffee before probing to elicit the exact nature of the world he had left behind. The Commissar

372

found it incomprehensible to talk of a place where men fell insensible for weeks, and then on waking found that they were chest-high to women.

Claude's mind conjured up a line of pretty Snow Whites, each followed by her own set of dwarves, and was moved to ask, 'How can this possibly be? Surely it must affect both sexes equally, are you sure the women weren't deceiving you?'

Marc shook his head uncertainly. 'When I entered that passage I thought I was coming out into sunlight; to someone immediately behind me the sensible thing to do would be dash forward through the danger spot on seeing me fall. Had there been a third person in line then retreat could also have been an option. As I see it women invariably let the man go first wherever they meet an unknown, and because of that fact, I think their exposure would always be considerably less.

'Weeks my friend, you said weeks, is that also consistent with your theory?' Claude looked blandly across the table at him.

'That's how I saw it; there are other interpretations because the truth is, we don't know. The women tell us that it is due to a fatty layer under a woman's skin – the one that makes them so shapely. Beyond that they are unwilling to discuss the matter, except that it is a protection they naturally possess, and the one that makes them the nurses rather than us.' Marc looked at the man facing him as if to say try that one instead. Claude made no comment at all, so he continued. 'Hazel believes herself to be partly immune, for after passing that stone she even had a baby afterwards, something nobody else has ever managed to do.'

Marc's talk confirmed the Commissar's view that he must do nothing in haste for although there were people to rescue inside, the hazards were so undefined as to put any would-be rescuer in danger. Was he really so set upon rescuing people who were miniature in build and fully adapted to a cut off world? Why mix them with normal sized people at all; and might they not possibly prefer their specialized world enough to resist if he did go in? His best course of action was to await Hazel and hope that she could throw better light on the facts.

What Marc went on to say took Claude by surprise; his inform-ant was a man who had privileged access to the top women, in what amounted to a woman's world. Claude was soon opening the cognac and steadily oiling the man's throat with it; but stuck to coffee himself, lest it worsen his own condition. And when they had progressed far enough to be talking about electrical phenomena he was delighted that his stab in the dark had also produced an electrical expert who worked in that field. But for all his up-to-date knowledge, Marc was soon admitting that he had met something that strained the technology of his own age. If he were to hazard a guess, he would say that it was based on some unusual chemistry going on there, and so extremely borderline that even a new wave form or natural laser emanation could not be ruled out. But putting fancy aside, here was an unusual energy source, which however derived must be responsible for the hot streams and other oddities he had witnessed inside Hades, perhaps even to the unusual indigenous vegetation.

The Commissar was impressed, for he already believed the solution must be something fundamental given the changes he had seen wrought on Marc; a right bull of a man, cut down to this little half pint fellow who could barely sit a chair. What had happened along the way? Where did all the rage go?

'You were looking for your wife in the caves, were you, Monsieur?' The question was quiet, but on a quite different tack.

Startled, Marc looked at the Commissar. 'What do you know of her, has she been found?'

Claude was irritated by the counter-interrogation, he wanted his own questions answered first, but seeing the fellow was in poor shape and instantly anxious he buttered him up. 'She is at home now, an infatuation had carried her away – it was much as I suggested to you at the time. But tell me, you went looking for her in the caves, and dynamiting our deep holes, is that so?'

'Yes.' Marc sounded much deflated – hindsight made his actions regrettable.

'Are you familiar with high explosives, do you use the stuff?'

'No, it seemed a good idea, but it didn't work out well in practice.'

Claude warmed to his natural role, with questions disguised with information. 'A man called Jan Kee has been charged with the theft and the explosion. You are either party to defrauding an insurance company, or simply the target.'

'I know little or nothing about his business – but target? No, I cannot even believe that.' Marc looked confused, and more than a little uncomfortable.

374

'Jan Kee was living with your wife when he gave you the explosives. Explosives he did not intend personally to see used inside a cave.'

Marc looked like a sad if shocked minstrel sitting with mouth open, his blackened face bearing a distinct ring of white where he had been drinking. Claude judged that he would not get much more that was sense from the man, and felt moved enough to boil water for a wash. Acting upon a whole succession of ideas, rather than kindness, Claude rummaged for his electric razor and a pair of scissors, which he proffered as Marc's ablutions moved towards conclusion. The cave man still wore skins and had long hair, but looked acceptably clean-shaven.

There were voices: Claude urged his sleepy eyes to open, and raised an arm to trigger the video camera suspended above his head; his protesting stiff neck creaked reluctantly to cover the two figures embracing upon Marc's mat. Hazel was looking tired and drawn, but shortly she smiled towards the stranger, standing up with Marc who introduced her. She was bigger than Claude had expected, but pleasurably shorter than he was himself. The grey woollen dress was somewhat too large for her, and protruded abnormally about the middle. Though standing proud of Marc she was child-sized, with the facial features of an adult. Her resemblance to the passport photograph of Hazel Gray, the one found hidden in the bushes near a bicycle, was so striking as to leave him in no doubt about the identification. He was quick to offer coffee, which she drank as if it were some kind of relief.

Claude immediately put his vital query, had she passed two other women on the way out?

Hazel answered confidently. 'No, it was a man and a woman. I pulled them in to safety myself.'

Claude smiled. Hazel was not the first to be fooled by Réné's masculine appearance. Thanking her, he left them both enjoying the coffee; hurriedly he grabbed his coat and moved away smartly, knowing the helicopter might still be on call. Soon he was braving the cold outside, but this time some thirty safety pins stopped the draught whistling through his underpants. He still couldn't believe his luck in completing the mission, even before it was due to commence, even the helicopters were still on tap and fallen in line with his winning streak. A jubilant Claude remembered other necessities on his return path, revisiting the filing cabinet and acquiring saddlebags. One of these would be Terry's, but with Marc looking like a refugee from the stone ages, anything in there might help, or so he thought.

Terry had little in there, and soon it was evident that Marc was already wearing more substantial skins. But dipping into the bag, Claude took up a capacious shirt and encouraged him to wear it over the top. 'The result might look hilarious in the daylight; but I suggest wearing it, anything that counters the cold out there is worth it.'

Hazel headed away into the dark only to make a similar discovery, finding that nothing fitted; two woollies she dragged over her head, and ended up wearing both since the extra padding helped to fit better the bump under her dress. There was a comb in Terry's bag, from which she sprinkled the teeth, but still managed to put her hair into a semblance of order. She was all ready to go, Hazel the woman, rather than creature of the rocks.

They waited for the helicopter just inside the cave entrance, facing the cold night air. For Claude there was the need to use his telephone once more, so he moved out into the cold to track down his boss. To do it he needed to pull rank, and reached Gabriel via a police switchboard; the operator put him through, though she would not part with the number. The female who answered had a voice that sounded sleepy, intriguing and sexy. She listened to him with minimum of comment, and then passed the phone over to Gabriel. Initially the wakened man was cross, but warmed admirably to the idea that Julia had wandered into a place of no return. When asked whose territory contained the offending caves, Claude was free of hesitation, for he had already ascertained in his conversations with Marc that they belonged to Spain once. He recited what he had learned about the approaches having collapsed, pointing out there existed only one highly dangerous approach hole on the French side. Gabriel's laughter punctuated his report. 'She bloody well deserved it, let the Spaniards dig her out, if they must.'

Claude received a verbal pat on the back when he mentioned rescuing the missing two. But this was only a prelude to a request to call in and keep a watchful eye on the high promenade property for him. Gabriel sounded keen enough for Claude to have more suspicion that the property might rightfully belong to Julia. But whomever it belonged to, Claude saw the task as a hazard, rooting him firmly to the spot where Gabriel's wife had gone missing. If the press ever got hold of the story, the rescue would be as nothing to the dirt that would wash out in the newspapers. Then this might move internationally if he was meticulous and not blocked officially when reporting the loss of two French citizens over the border; a matter for negotiation now in the modern European community.

The helicopter's arrival prompted his thought that two women had flown in, and so two women must be seen to fly out again. Accordingly he climbed his ladder over the boulder first, hopefully blocking the pilot's view before leading his flock to the aircraft. The pilot was yet another airman, and one whom Claude gladly and lengthily thanked for coming, whilst at the same time contriving to direct both Hazel and Marc into the rear seating. Having occupied the man's attention throughout the flight, the Commissar was soon insisting that the pilot land on a lawn near two isolated houses; night noise being best avoided in respect to the town centre. The others remained unaware the journey was not as prearranged, and talked in low voices throughout the short trip. As they disembarked Claude was grateful to see that Marc's shirt over his sheepskin apparel conformed exactly to his original intention of confusing gender. Before the helicopter lifted off from its patch of strangely coloured turf, Claude was rescuing the spare door key from its hiding place in a nearby shed.

Julia always kept a good larder, so it was very soon that they were sitting down for an evening meal. The cooking Claude felt inclined to do, as the others appeared much too weary. He was dead right, for they were off to bed very soon, mumbling excuses. He found himself alone with his thoughts, and not long after followed their example, raiding the house linen to make up the spare room bed.

Yawning, Claude turned comfortably in bed for his mission had been accomplished successfully. But then of course he was still on a tightrope, for having confused the people around him about Julia and friend, trouble had been averted until later. Tomorrow he had to find the solution, or it would all rebound on him and this made the future look even more unsettled than what had preceded it. What was it Hazel had called the place? Yes, the place was called Hades – and he could think of no better place to put Julia.

38

Dilemma

The rain drummed against the windowpane, mixed with an occasional rattle suggesting intermittent hail. Claude woke to unaccustomed noise in a strange bedroom, and on finding it was still two hours to dawn tried to sleep. His cloudy mind filled and was swamped with recollections of yesterday; that in turn was met with a period of sustained suppression before a shallow sleep engulfed him. It was sleep but so thinly spread as to leave him aware throughout its length that the sleep was insubstantial. Events swept past him, all those exuberant and euphoric achievements, they arose and for a mere moment in time formed a triumphant dream. This upbeat moment soon blended with the nightmare of so many deficiencies collected. He skimmed through dreams, about the house without an owner but marking time on the impossible position Gabriel had put him in. Drowsily, he was soon wearying of semiconscious ideas that might progress what he'd started, and how he might extract the latest two who slipped by him. Still struggling with the impossible he surfaced in a sweat and at last managed to escape a veritable sleep treadmill. His waking mind dismissed the problems outright for he would know later today whether the cave operation still had to be done. The cave equipment would still be there if he wanted to return to it another day, for only he could wind the operation down. But he should beware, for whatever he did now might well come under official scrutiny at some later date, or worse still in the public spotlight; his personal future had to be locked up in this somewhere. Luck was so far on his side, having withdrawn the two refugees from the caves into this secluded spot where informed decisions could be taken. Most crucial in all of this, was the reaction of the two he saved and that he would elicit today. If they wanted to bask in the public spotlight or not at all was the crunch question; everything could be so undemanding if they did not.

His mind had shrugged off the sleep urge completely now and knowing it was still early remained where he was thinking out his most pressing problems. Becoming more objective now, he concentrated upon his newly found missing persons and what were their likely motives regarding publicity – could he rely upon himself to swing it favourably? The trousers full of pins caught his eye, draped across a chair, reminding him that he must aim to be an official-looking figure for the coming interviews. There might be an old pair of Gabriel's trousers he could borrow; particularly he wanted his debriefing interview with Hazel to go well.

He ventured out into the upper hall, one bedroom door stood ajar and its double bed had not been slept in; they were dishonest those two in accepting both rooms, then stealthily coming together in one of them. Their dishonesty had done him out of a decent bed. They were lovers then, this pair that he had rescued – or was rescued too strong a term, perhaps he had only part rescued them? Claude slipped inside the empty room and opened wide the wardrobe; inside a single dark suit hung from the hangers. Grabbing the trousers he put them on. They fitted him well at the waist, but there seemed to be an extra quarter metre in the leg. He tucked the extra to be inside, but this was uncomfortable so he searched out a pair of scissors and did the job properly. Today needed to be a clear one – first free himself from the Commissariat. Claude hesitated with hand poised over the phone before deciding against it, helped on by a lull in the weather. He reached for his coat instead, and moved out on to the lawn with the mobile phone. From there he rang Sgt Vierne, and arranged for the whole days operation to be postponed, with but an airborne visit from the inspector to check on police property and supervise turning the lights out. That he managed to arrange without declaring his own whereabouts.

Having put the operation on hold he found he was still the early bird, there being no sign of life upstairs. The Commissar then made himself coffee and consumed a light breakfast in an otherwise silent house. Finishing a meagre bowl of cereal he looked for and found a room more to his liking, one heavily into books. Claude Brie reclined in a leather armchair having found a better and more intellectual atmosphere for doing battle with the factors involved today. Whatever the outcome was, he wanted the pair of them away as quickly as possible. Of the relatives, Mrs Gray was his most persistent caller, always enquiring for news of her daughter, and so he felt fairly sure Hazel would be off home to mum very shortly, or the insistent mum would come and get her. Marc, by contrast, was more in command of where he went; but it was the man's reaction to the first mention of his wife yesterday that suggested he would be back home to sort her out very shortly. The door rattled with newspapers arriving, causing Claude to abandon the project and hurry through to intercept them. Anxiously he scanned the front pages and was relieved to see no mention of a recent police activity. He mentally patted himself on the back for diverting the helicopter to land on Julia's ancient lawn; that had been a brilliant move, for almost certainly there would have been arrangements for spotting a return flight. The headlines could be predicted: 'Commissar Brie rescues two in caves' – local hero and all that. But even if their cameras had missed all the safety pins, the debunking that happens when another newspaper scoops the first, could mean – 'Commissar Brie expends boss's wife to find lost dwarves'. He shuddered, the sooner these matters were settled the better.

They arrived with enough noise to bring him in from the side room: there was an air of excitement about them, and their pleased expressions made the exchange of morning greetings pleasurable. He decided to make coffee for them, whilst Hazel raided the refrigeration units and gleaned enough ingredients to cook a large omelette – very good it looked too. Marc inhibited the flow of exuberant talk between the three by sitting very close to Hazel, after which the couple seemed more steeped in themselves and not so communicative. Claude got the feeling of distance and almost of matrimony in the air. How easily he forgets the wife, he told himself. There were beginning to be factors he had not considered earlier.

A squall hit the building outside, and rain gushed over the windowpanes. Rain was a novelty to them, and like children they hurried to the window. He had to squash their intentions of going out into it; a desire that needed firm handling – they were enjoying their freedom and wanted to feel the elements. Claude was insistent that they keep a low profile, but at the same time realized he must find something more than talk to keep them occupied. Close proximity already had him aware that they were as badly dressed as on arrival. Hazel did not appear to be bulging in the middle now as she had, so her knitted dress sufficed; not that this altered the fact he need arrange medical help for her. But there was room to do more for their clothes.

Claude left them eating, and headed for the bedrooms. The other double bedroom yielded two more wardrobes, containing the quite different fashions of Julia and Réné respectively. In between them a dresser was sandwiched, with drawers full of women's underclothing. The dresser he identified as Réné's by the letters resting there, already knowing Julia's was in the other room. Without hesitation Claude read a letter, finding it was from Julia, providing the terms of agreement for lodging at her place. Reading the whole correspondence, Claude gathered that Réné lived over a surgery which was about to be refurbished. With this pearl of enlightenment exciting his grey matter, the Commissar carried an armful of assorted clothing downstairs, which he then piled in front of Marc as Hazel cleared the space in front of him. 'Turn that lot over, and see what could be altered to fit you. There is a sewing machine upstairs, and I am sure that the pair of you can improve on what you are wearing.

'Hazel, I think that it is time we had a chat.' Claude led her wet hands and all into the study. Her interview was necessarily long and tedious; a process not helped by their separate tongues. The Commissar had only half accepted that this miraculous something, having knocked you down, could miniaturize you in the process, and so he was better pleased to be presented with an alternative version. Hazel initially proclaimed the same scientific wonder, but this time a wonder divided into two parts.

'There is first some kind of shock wave that knocks you down unconscious, and leaves you for dead among cannibalistic plants, unless there is a rescue. But once you have been rescued you have to eat what's available, and that is why we became so small.' Hazel shrugged her shoulders it seemed straightforward and logical to her.

'But he is smaller than you, not just thin, but scaled down on what he was before.' The Commissar had seen Marc before and after, which ensured his expressed disbelief would be definite enough to cut through the wide-eyed innocent female look.

'The women had a better diet which included more of the usual fungi than the men ate. Some varieties shrink your bones; the men just ate more of them than we did.'

'What are these plants? Are there any we can name?'

'Most of them I had never seen before,' Hazel replied truthfully. 'Some looked like everyday mushrooms but grew in damp areas very near to the rocks that knock you down. Others were brightly coloured and strange. That place is supposed to contain boron drugs able to both affect the mushrooms and alter the chemistry of our bodies. It is something a scientist trapped there reportedly said in the past.'

Claude still puzzled over size differences that were disproportionate. 'But your other friend was not so muscular, the one called Terry, but he shrank to very much the same size as Marc on the same diet. They appear to have been tailored for you; how can that happen?'

'The men ate differently, and lived somewhere else; they were not the same.'

Hazel was reluctant to be drawn into the fine detail, having already fathomed that it would be viewed none too kindly by officialdom.

'The man accompanying you now; he is not your holiday companion?'

'No, that was Terry. He got the idea of crawling through the bat ways, and we lost him.'

'The men, did they fight for the love of you?'

Hazel's eyes sparkled, someone was willing to believe she could be fought over – the femme fatale of the caves. She suppressed an inclination to giggle. 'No, they were very good friends; but I didn't see much of Terry.'

Claude smiled to himself, for even if there was no evidence to support it, he had to pursue the possibility that Terry's death could be foul play, rather than accidental. Having ruled it out to his own satisfaction, he turned to a subject just as likely to be sensitive. He swooped across the room, to return with a little bundle housed since the caves in his greatcoat pocket. These unrolled on an occasional table to form several pairs of ladies' panties. 'These are yours, would you say?'

'Yes,' Hazel blushed as she admitted the fact.

Claude held up two pairs clipped together. 'These blocked the spa water plant filters. Was it fun that took you swimming in the spa's underground lake?'

Hazels face exhibited surprise. 'We didn't see a lake, only a small pool early on, it rose up over the rocks during the night washing away some of my things.' She turned anxious eyes on him, evidently dreading the next question.

Claude tactfully passed over the bed of newspapers, the defective contraceptive, and the floor strewn with gutted candles; instead he asked in an understanding voice, 'You had a baby in that place, is that so?'

Emotions rushed to the surface. Hazel looked ready to cry, but nodded her head bravely, barely able to hold back the tears.

Claude, expecting distress, had a box of tissues ready, which he passed to her before continuing. 'Was that why you left?' He got a nod for his question; but there was evidently more to come. He waited, whilst Hazel struggled with her emotions before adding more.

'They want me to find supplies. I was given gold to pay for it all,' she said bending the truth very slightly. Hazel excused herself and left the room, shortly afterwards returning with the gold hippopotamus which glinted richly wherever the daylight caught it. Claude took it, examining the heavy object closely. Here was an extra complication, be it a very handsome one. The work was ancient and valuable, that he was sure, even if it did have recent damage towards the tail end. 'If you want me to, I will introduce you to a jeweller friend of mine, and authenticate the find for you as I believe I can witness that it derived from the caves.'

'Would you really?' Hazel's voice rose excitedly. This policeman, he was really nice she decided; for quite how she might sell gold in somebody else's country had bothered her every time she thought about it.

Claude dismissed her thanks easily because he would be simply giving a friend the chance to make a swift profit. 'But I would be grateful if before I speak to both of you a small point could be cleared up,' he said. 'Did you or Terry know a clergyman by the name of Charles Chapman?

Hazel looked bewildered at first and then less so. 'That sounds like the fellow my friend Eileen met in Lourdes; he was very religious so I suppose he may well have been a preacher.'

The Commissar nodded his head thoughtfully, and asked her

to send Marc in as she exited. His balding head remained bent over pages of writing as the door opened again, but nodded to acknowledge Marc's presence.

Settling in Hazel's still warm seat, Marc waited for eye contact.

Dwelling upon the relative size aspect which still bothered him the Commissar questioned Marc upon the subject which Hazel had apparently shied away from and found it richly rewarding. Marc was quite sure that there was a definite trend towards uniformity in size for the men although both sexes declined with age. He went even further, pointing out they formed an underclass that was manipulated from the moment of arrival in the caves. It was more than inferior food they suffered. The men he knew all had only one testicle and one of them who rebelled was castrated. He made no mention of his own defects, they were personal, but went on to describe the fate of Harold, the man who was expelled. When the sickening consequences of passing the sentry stone were made clear to Claude, the policeman became less sure that he wanted to give the go-ahead tomorrow for otherwise sound men.

'You will be wondering about rescuing others in the caves no doubt?' said Marc, and then interpreting the resulting grunt as encouragement continued. 'Since we spoke earlier, Commissar, about my own observations of electro magnetic emission from those rocks, I have been hearing how Hazel came past the sentry stone in a metal recovery suit they use. It is provided with a distinct tail which scrapes the ground and that may be a necessary feature to properly earth the discharge for any shield your men use. It would avoid knockdown; assuming that there is an electrical exchange between rocks triggered by anything moving between them.'

Claude's look was a sour one, which gave Marc little optimism about rescuing the men. 'My brief was to find you both, and not one that included prospecting for new worlds. What happens now is unlikely to depend upon police authorities reaching a decision. The caves are situated in border territory and you are entering into the realms of international cooperation and politics.' Claude stood and ushered the small man out, aware unashamedly that by widening the parameters he had crushed the other fellow's hopes of extricating his many downtrodden friends.

Hazel had by then reheated the coffee and placed biscuits

together with the necessary crockery upon a tray; her question was quite simply, where do you want it?

Claude's demeanour was instantly affable, arising from a feeling that he had survived the first hurdle. 'Why not serve it now, and we can all three continue discussing our future plans in the lounge.' Upon making his suggestion, Claude entered the rather less formal room and sank into a huge, oversoft armchair.

They were assembled and after wincing a little on Marc's coffee, which had stewed overlong, Claude began to feel his way. 'You both need time to recover from your ordeal so I suggest that you remain here for today without drawing attention to yourselves. I shall answer the door until this evening, and as we are on private property neither of you must show yourselves; just turn a deaf ear to the door-knocker or to the telephone. This afternoon I will arrange a doctor to see you both, and a jeweller friend of mine will call to view Hazel's gold.

Claude launched himself into the hoped-for dispersal discussion by producing Marc's passport. 'Monsieur Casserta, your wife awaits news in Belgium, do you want me to telephone the good news, or are you going?'

Marc looked uncertainly towards Hazel. 'Not yet, I think I have to see this through first.'

Claude looked visibly peeved with him, although he suspected even this morning that Marc would not be detached from his new love quite so easily. All depended now upon Hazel, a definitive answer must be obtained, his full attention shifted towards Hazel. 'Mademoiselle Gray here is your passport. I have no doubt at all that your mother is anxious to have you home. Can I tell her that you are safe?'

Hazel's face clouded. Yes, Mother would be here on the very next flight, there would be no refusing to go; unfulfilled promises suddenly became dubious. She shrank from making any answer. 'Can I recover a little before you do? She is due for shock enough on account of my size. I really do think that I should be more myself first. And then there is that promise I made to provide live fish for stocking the cave ponds.'

Claude nodded his head, with the crunch question on his lips. 'Then there is one final matter on which you have to decide. From the outset I have not informed the press about a police initiative to discover your whereabouts, and as you more or less rescued yourselves, the position is very much the same as providing transport from the caves. The question is; do you want such publicity? It will create a great stir and everybody will be very happy for you; but then you have to accept that your relatives would know immediately and will want you home. It is not a good thing for the caves, publicity will lure sightseers into them and that can only be harmful so I for one am against it. As you said yourselves, it is a dangerous location.'

The answers were immediate and definite – No. Neither of them wanted the spotlight of publicity to fall upon them for a variety of reasons. A further realization had only started this morning, when they exposed a full-length wardrobe mirror and were horrified to see themselves puny and diminutive. Public exposure would best wait until they could identify with the image they had before them. For Marc this factor had bothered his mind a lot recently; what future did he have with the beautiful wife that had already left him once? He was better off pursuing his present lover who already accepted him. Hazel was less preoccupied with being somewhat below her usual height, for already she felt committed to the mission of improving her friends' lot in the caves. Neither one was a factor that Claude had banked upon to get a no vote; but both had a decisive effect upon the negative response from both of them.

Claude warmed to them, feeling that he could now be helpful. 'If that is your decision then we must watch out for reporters, or even gossips able to attract their attention. Because of them, you will need to move from this locality as soon as you are able, but until then I assume you will stay here, keeping well out of sight. As soon as it is feasible I will take you to a large specialist fish retailer just outside Toulouse where you can order your fish. And when I close down our cave activity the rescue service will still owe me many hours of flying time. It is just possible that I might cancel some of it if they lift the fish for you.' Claude saw two faces break into smiles, and knew he had saved them much trouble in keeping to Hazel's deadline. The interview was at an end, much to the relief of Claude.

Claude had been busy on the lawn with his telephone, and the tangible results of this were soon apparent. First to arrive was a posh-looking car, and a gent who chatted long and hard with the Commissar, before meeting up with Hazel and Marc. He viewed their gold hippo with interest. The man was a jeweller called Monsieur Zoub who on close examination became quite excited about the hippopotamus, attributing its craftsmanship to some earlier civilization, possibly even Egyptian. For the time being he would value it as metallic gold, but soon perhaps it may be seen as an art treasure and be worth much more. A cheque for such an amount would be forwarded to M. Brie, if that were acceptable to them. Hazel, who was very relieved that it was all done, simply accepted the receipt instantly.

Throughout the day Claude answered the door to numerous merchants who normally delivered Julia's supplies to the house; it was apparently her day for paying them. He cancelled all accounts, arranging to pay every one, saying that the lady of the house had gone away, and in due course the house would be up for sale.

For Hazel the doctor's arrival was the biggest surprise of the day, for he was well over six feet in height; the four-foot-three woman looked at him with some amazement. Seeing the Commissar as being a normally sized person had sugared the pill regarding a proper relationship with other people, and so it took but one tall man to make her in particular realize the position was quite as bad as the wardrobe mirror suggested. Apart from this there was little other interest arising from the doctor's visit, for he was not reporting to them. Only the removal of Hazel's stitches was his lasting contribution. His final words to her recommended convalescing for a week, a timescale that in the event meant nothing, as events took a helping hand.

Claude made his way home upon a bike he had noticed in a shed outside the kitchen, congratulating himself on a successful outcome today, yet at the same time aware he would have to be vigilant to keep everything on course. Before going to bed he stood admiring the new trousers, they must be lucky for him must they not, and despite gathering a little cycle oil they would suit his wardrobe admirably. It was time now to resume living, but endeavour to avoid all those little misfortunes that tended to dog his footsteps. Julia would presumably remain out of the way, for he knew that any honest report produced by him would be suppressed – the chances now were good that he might at last be free.

His hand caught upon the rear pocket with the sort of noisy scrape that suggests something extra. He pulled a ticket from it and gaped at the 120 euro price tag. Even worse, the date of delivery from the smartest tailor in town was only a week ago. He preserved the stub. Gabriel would have expected two pairs of trousers with the new suit surely; Claude's face brightened, he would point out the tailor's misconception to the man concerned, on his way to work tomorrow.

39

Hen Party

Anger left Freda near choking with indignation as she read Hazel's note, but swamping all else was the realization that she had been fooled. The girl she trusted had connived with the men to outwit her. Today the women's efforts had been disastrously short on time, and upset the male populace so much that she had been embroiled in a near mutiny from her unhappy troops. This new blow coming on the heels of that could only serve to undermine and rebound on her personally – in effect this would put her firmly on the way out.

She had been deceived, along with much plotting in the background, deceit stretching right back to Terry's death. Hazel had been careful not to shoulder the blame for the deception, and so reading between the lines Freda realized that the instigator had to be Marc; the one who had served her at every meal with disarming demeanour and charm – characteristics which in retrospect had given cover for the underhand way he was living. The bat-ways had come into it early on. She remembered Maria consulting her about a drop in the supply of bats, and that happened soon after Terry had taken over collecting them. Marc's part involvement, and release from some duties, to her were all very suspicious manoeuvres now. Leon was the first move in the job sequence relating to bat culls; and here at last was one she could interrogate.

But it was several days before she encountered Leon; strange, for him to keep such a low profile, he being an everyday part of village life. Freda intercepted him and pressured him to talk about Terry. He must have seen Terry in an unusual spot, preparing for the long crawl out. Leon was full of his denials, but gradually she wore him down with patient questioning. Before long he was admitting that he had seen Terry up there, and Marc also for that matter. Having come clean about it, Leon assumed that all would be forgiven, and demonstrated to her how the new ladders fitted into the escape plan. Freda found some difficulty in believing anyone in their right mind would tackle a height like that, and especially on something so unstable; it had to be a measure of their desperation. She turned her thoughts from the sheer folly of it, and listened again to Leon's whingeing voice. The authors of this trouble had gone, leaving him with all the blame – they were bigger than him and their threats had kept him quiet – what else could he have done? It was no business of his, he just wanted to be left in peace and do his work.

Marc had not left from this place, because the ladders were stowed away, and Leon denied taking them down in a voice that held the certainty of truth. Could Marc have left by the bat ways after all? Freda was uncertain and looked elsewhere. It was only a matter of time before Maureen's observations connected Marc to visiting an area near the loom, and after that his dirt piles in the hunt cave soon came to light. A piton spike to reach the crevice chimney was sufficient proof of his departure that way. She was astounded by her discovery. All that remained to be decided was Leon's punishment and his future. By virtue of his daily job in the village he was trusted, but could he still be? Under the control of his wife Leon had been an asset, but now she was gone and he was a loose cannon. It was time his job was restructured around the various composts that he compounded, for these he was their last remaining expert.

The newcomers now in the reception area affected her position as head in the same way that Hazel had, and as she would probably be displaced as Queen there was little point in resigning. Not that the throne would be missed; she could comfortably move on to the church, leaving Frances their rightful Queen. It was the task of coaching her that Freda shrank from, for without possessing a common tongue it was not similar to being Hazel's tutor. Frances scorned English, despite it being the standard tongue that everybody used. The woman would find herself isolated by this idiotic foible from those she had to rule. Frances must largely find her own feet; luckily she was close enough to Jackie to have her advice and a better chance of survival. It would mean a weak Queen perhaps, but why should that matter with such a strong military leader as Maureen, backed up by her own self in the church? Yes, the church would be her base now, for certainly much of their military might was dependent upon it and that was a strong card to hold.

Freda was aware that her new thinking must apply to Bernadette as well, because she was confronting the same language barrier with both the new arrivals. Surely it was time to exchange Jackie and Bernadette, enabling the newcomers to be reliably instructed by Jackie. Bernadette could then revert to her former role as one of the four, losing nothing, as she had received her full complement of men already. Two men she had, and only one of them for the long term – still that was better than nothing.

The balance in Hades, she could see was changing: in the new couple Freda saw a step towards older folk. They spoke French and that should trigger a change but not advisable now, because holidaymakers and sporting types of various nationalities were the arrivals these days. This may need to be raised with the elders, but the questionably lesbian influx changed nothing. However for them to have penetrated here suggested the outside world must be indulging in some kind of mechanically assisted climbing. Through all the thoughts of changes to make there was pleasantly in the background the prospect that she was exchanging the throne for a pulpit, and that could be thoroughly enjoyable. In lighter mood and that frame of mind she was soon setting off with a few possessions towards the church. Already she had established where her living quarters were going to go, and all she had left to decide was the best place to put her new library. These transfers could take their time, but completion had to await the impending return of Hazel because despite all she still had belief in the girl. The return of their gold recovery suit was indicative of the girl's intrinsic honesty, making it more likely that the fishponds stood some chance of completion. This was the one initiative above all the others that she had progressed and one that Freda hoped to see completed.

Tonight was the initiation of Bernadette's concubine, the much-admired climber they had named Adam, his own name being difficult to pronounce. Maureen had struggled mightily with this one, and only reached an agreement with the man by relying upon Freda's writings in his own language. With him, everything had been delayed, and nothing gone to schedule. They had missed the timetable, foremost because Marc had stayed too long to be

391

harvested along with the old crop. And the time wasted over his incomplete electrical work had severed the ceremonial connection with seed planting, traditionally linked to initiation. One of which was a bad omen from the religious aspect, and the other more an annoyance.

Julia was another who had been quickly pulled clear in the Styx cave, and for whom Freda had special plans. What was interesting about her was a certificate found among her possessions, which said she was an expectant mother – mad to think they might have a baby girl queen in waiting yet again. Julia must not be allowed to fraternize as Hazel did, and so it was important to bring her fully into their accepted customs if she could be hurried along. Julia's companion had not yet recovered consciousness, a drawback of dressing up in masculine attire. Hazel had dragged her well short of the safe zone, and there she had remained for hours, awaiting a gold suit recovery. Her papers suggested that she was called Réné; Bernadette in her ministrations had further deduced that she was a doctor; wishful thinking perhaps, remembering the shrapnel embedded in her arm.

From its very nature, the evening party might have been expected to appeal only to those who were heterosexual – apart from Poppy who nobody properly understood. Freda on entering noticed Frances, the one who disastrously caused problems once before, had already arrived, and was seated with Julia their newcomer. Julia looked ill fitted to her surroundings, but this was to be expected on a first outing, where she might be expected to meet everyone and gain confidence. As Freda watched, Maureen slipped in and headed also for the vicinity of Julia. It was evident that the resident homosexuals were set to discover Julia's true orientation; the woman would be lucky to avoid getting conflicting messages here tonight. Her mind battled with present reality; lesbians ought really to be excluded from this event, but it was rather late for her to legislate against it now. If this became a direction the new society was taking then none of them would be keen on laws that diminished their rights. Her train of thought was broken again, as Poppy entered and approached Maureen closely. There was a sharp exchange of words; Freda anticipated some kind of brawl; but then Poppy headed over to sit near to herself, and sat watching the group across the food house floor.

392

More were entering and gathering around tables in the food house restaurant, most flicking a soft kind of decorative flail and wearing a flint chip brooch – the appropriate dress for such occasions. Annita in this respect was different in that she carried her usual double-ended flail, soft at one end and hard enough at the other to grip as handle. Some were chatting, some drinking, and some even singing a little song. The song swelled as more took it up, until at length Maria opened the far door and the assembled savages poured through it. The 'concubine elected' stood at the furthermost point wearing the usual sheepskin garment. At the end of their celebration ostensibly for the new planting of seed, Bernadette would have the duty of fitting their man to his new tunic, a man that would be bulky and awkward to fit in carrying out her privilege as Charon. But now Bernadette smilingly quaffed wine with the others, joining the swelling song as the last of the savages was trickling in.

Freda watched, not entirely disinterested, but all the same, avoiding taking part in the activities; the man was a German and she had no intention of making things any worse for him. He stood there: in her eyes noble and proud, but in his eyes a confused look, one that told of sedation with fungal herbs.

The flights of individual women kissing and cuddling caused him to flinch sluggishly, as in turn they dashed towards him. All singing the same time worn but teasing French song – stopping only to take some speedy liberty with their communal man and then dashing off on its snap verse. Across the room Julia had got the hang of the melody, one she knew of old and doubtless appreciated the words more than Freda; being suddenly carried away by them – sweeping over to join in, although she probably thought that it was the kind of hen night amusement as seen on TV. Julia then won an elevation to the top of Freda's list, much to Freda's surprise. For not being aware of Julia's predilection for small plump men she was for once slow to promote a name on the slate, whilst her attention was diverted pleasurably as she watched the whole party of lesbian persuasion troop out. This was surely a good time to invite Julia for lunch tomorrow.

Finally Freda would record her own name along with the rest, for she had no wish for preference on a list that was set out in order of foolishness: her aim was simply to ensure she could spend a regular evening with her compatriot. Like so many others before

393

him, she knew that the bulging flesh would eventually take up proper proportion with the rest of him, and the desires of her friends would change from lust for one, into lust for the next concubine chosen.

40

Deadline

Hazel had only a brief glimpse of the retail fish park, snatched whilst Commissar Brie dropped Marc off to arrange their purchases, then relentlessly the police car bore her over the last kilometres towards Toulouse. Hazel was in disgrace, and the long-held silence between the Commissar and her was maintained. Minutes later they pulled up outside an ornate house in a fashionable area, where Claude's widowed sister-in-law lived; the one he prevailed upon to give Hazel and Marc lodging. Even before they had time to knock, a tall angular woman opened the door, and greeted Claude in a voluble stream of French. The Commissar spent a few moments introducing Hazel to his relative Mme Brie before continuing his chat in a way that effectively sidelined her. Hazel took the hint, her luggage was not his prime concern, and soon she was unloading their almost empty suitcase from the car. Standing conspicuously to one side with it, Hazel awaited the austere woman she understood was a wealthy private detective's widow, who so quickly detected her presence and whisked her upstairs to their room.

The room was unimpressive and bristling with knick-knacks, but at least it was clean and smelled strongly of polish. Did she have any choice of room? Hazel doubted it, and was so out of favour she dared not ask. Her police chief was passing money to the woman as she came down, and upon seeing Hazel kissed the rather gloomy face goodbye. Claude hurried Hazel back to his car and in the short drive back to the retail fish park he broke the ice at last, making a curt excuse that he must leave rapidly now for his days work still awaited him back at the Commissariat.

She was pleased to be leaving him: the Commissar's displeasure was still fresh between them – for she had disobeyed one vital tenet of his command by answering the door to a window cleaner.

Defending her action afterwards, Hazel said the man had seen them inside, so to answer the door and pay him the money she found secreted in the kitchen was natural; he would have thought it mighty peculiar if she had not opened the door. Claude's response, even with such a good explanation, had been to whisk them off after only a day in the high promenade house. And now, with a quick goodbye, he was moving away; she watched as his black car slid off into the distance.

Now to find Marc among these acres of gardens; surely he would stand out because of his radically different stature? But no, nothing small moved on her horizons. She was near exhausted before spotting his back view through a large window of the main building with all the luxury of a plush office gathered about him drinking coffee and being entertained by top salesmen. Hazel lost no time in finding her way in for her rightful share of the hospitality, although knowing that she could not contribute very much at all. Their needs were not that of the usual domestic customer who wanted interesting fish; they wanted food fish of which there would be a comparatively small selection in the park. With a cool drink in her hand and a comfortable seat under her bottom, Hazel was again excluded by her imperfect French, not that it mattered a jot with Marc speaking the language so fluently and besides knowing precisely what was wanted. Her turn came when they had to choose from the many rows of plastic tanks, for she had recent experience of space in the sentry corridor and both of them knew the tank needed to move with an easy clearance round the bends. Without hesitation Hazel chose three strong polycarbonate tanks, a metre long by half a metre wide. Marc supplemented her choice with directions on how they were to be packed for transport. With firm assurances of the due date being easily met, they departed.

Now they had to sit back and wait for completion – Hazel visualized convalescence. But it was not to be. Claude's sister-in-law was a house-proud woman whose bony frame seemed incapable of stopping, and this bustling preoccupation with cleaning was difficult to live with. Hazel in particular had a peculiar knack of being just where the woman next wanted to clean. Uprooted by Mme Brie's regime, they left early each morning, determined to return as late as possible for an evening meal. This time scale proved fortuitous, as their priorities began to expand.

Most essential was to open a bank account and deposit their cheque. For this they needed the letter of introduction provided by M. Zoub, which secured for them a warm reception in the bank – much as it already had done at the fish park. With money, so much money to spend, they fully expected to enjoy town. This again was illusory, blemished by the number of people determined to take over their pavement space by threatening to walk right through them; midgets were evidently not regarded as equivalent citizens. Even to ask directions would have the informant stoop and use simple language as if they were intellectually challenged as well. Hazel thought their clothes might be part of the reason, because her quick alterations in Julia's house would lack the impact of real tailoring. Clothes were the answer to her perceived problem and that started a major shopping spree for her, although very soon it was obvious that the clothes had to be handmade for them specifically. Very soon she had found a dressmaker, and that dressmaker proved to have all sorts of other contacts available; helped on by finding she was about to be paid in advance. After Hazel had sorted her immediate needs, they were able to relax in a gay round of fashionable shops. To be a customer in a quality shop meant getting the same treatment as everyone else, and so soon they were only using such places and having to be wary of rejoining the street. Hazel soon spotted she needed the extra protection from having the unquestionable bearing of a well-dressed but dignified small woman, preferably holding high a parasol.

Their ways soon divided, for although Hazel got herself annoyed with Marc for even broaching the subject, she had to admit that there were less glamorous items to be bought, letting him go. The body of a midget bugged Marc much more than it did Hazel, for his affliction well outdid hers. His hair could be bettered to be more acceptable so he found a barber quickly, and following a shave and haircut he was pleased with the result. Whilst he was waiting Marc's eye caught sight of a newspaper column headed 'Lutz Caves'. Closer inspection revealed a critical report on the police withdrawal, claiming nothing had been achieved. The police spokesman pointed out that that they had gone as far as they were able owing to a rock fall at the Spanish end of the caves.

Interesting it may be, but today there were things to do, pursuing things more essential to their mission. He visited work-

397

shops of fabricators in metal, particularly those firms specializing in motorized remote control. Having found a number of addresses on a list of aeronautical industries based in Toulouse, one he visited impressed him as having the technology required. He soon became a favoured customer, one who paid cash, and as such placed an urgent but exacting order for delivery to the fish park – it was a high-sided, gold-plated trolley of his own design.

In this part of town there were electrical shops where he indulged in things the caves lacked, even such as modern components for burglar alarms. Merely escaping the job he began had not been at all satisfying to him; it would be a nice result to reward Freda's trust in his expertise by finishing the job, even if it was by proxy. As a person she was high in his estimation, and as there was no way that the women could hide his electrics from the men who did all of the maintenance, in his thoughts he was not preferentially helping the women in any meaningful way.

He found himself now in the part of town for practical hardware and as that part really appealed to him; soon he was foraging among ex-army equipment stores. There he chanced upon a pair of field telephones. They would make Hazel's contact with Freda so much more efficient than any exchanges in writing. The thought was immediately acted upon and he made a purchase. Then there was a lot of essential but uninspiring purchases, with things like rope, tarpaulins and backpacks to consider.

First expenditure had not made any real dent in their bank balance. Marc found himself drifting along with money to burn, and so he followed up his first excursion with a far more expensive shopping spree. Driven by no more than a whim, he caught up with the Commissar by purchasing an identical video camera. There was a real expense to follow, because his next move was to buy a mini saloon car. The drawback being that they would not use it in town, because there were radical modifications to do before a person of his dimensions could drive it.

More concerned now as to how their bank balance had dwindled, he turned his mind to things that need not cost anything. Red was uppermost in his mind. Was there nothing he could do to promote his friend who remained in the caves and so decidedly out of favour? That the Hades world succeeded so well today was due almost entirely to the generation of electricity, but the generators they possessed were obsolete and failing. He could supply new machinery, and specify that only Red was technically able to fit it. This would result in such a boost to power output that the cave dwellers would immediately see benefit. Simple for him with the contacts he had; and who knows the sale might even have future benefits for him personally as his old employer would appreciate something like that. No sooner than the idea occurred to him, than Marc put thought into action and phoned his old secretary Stella – she was astounded to hear from him.

'Marc, where are you? We all thought you had not survived.' She was very evidently concerned about him, and this was something Marc had not anticipated. In many ways it was like yesterday to him.

'I am in Toulouse, and very much alive, but it will be a week at least before I am back.'

'But, Marc, they couldn't wait for you, I'm afraid your job's gone.'

'Not to worry about that now, I have an order for you and I want it delivered to a fish specialist here within two days.' Marc quoted the address and product specifications, which might have sounded gibberish to any bystander; but it was run of the mill stuff to his secretary who was well used to the jargon. Eventually their technical dialogue came to an end.

'Marc, I am puzzled. The friend who took over your job lives at your old address, is there some kind of exchange going on?'

'Whose friend are we talking about?'

'Your friend, Jan Kee.' Stella's bombshell took him unawares.

There was silence, apart from spluttering noises at Marc's end, as unpalatable fact after unpalatable fact hit him in quick succession. 'Say nothing to him Stella.' Keep this matter between us, I promise to tell you later what's going on. But for the moment, quietly give the sales office my order.'

Marc wandered away from the phone, mind reeling, eyes glazed – he found himself walking into the very people who would normally walk into him. The talks with Commissar Brie had made him aware he was lucky to get away without being charged for the dynamite affair. Jan, by contrast, was still awaiting trial; he had imagined him to be still in Lutz-St-Saveur, but instead he had taken over his life: job, wife and home – the lot. Temper flared, his face reddened, grunting savagely he strode wildly along the street, where for once, most people tended to avoid him.

In the middle of town there was a coffee bar. For days now they had met in it at midday. As he approached, Hazel arrived from the opposite direction, looking very trim and doll-like in her new outfit, tripping along in a chic Naples yellow suit, she was stunningly visible. Then as if to accentuate this even more she held aloft a colourful parasol, which had an immediate effect in reserving pavement space – stunned pedestrians giving way to such a vision of loveliness.

Once inside, they were soon comfortably settled in their favourite corner, and Marc was able to vent his frustration. Ever since the doctor had towered above him, he had known his future had a direct relationship with size, diminishing expectation of Greta's acceptance. But size had no hand in her rejection, he had been rejected without that – certainly it was at odds with the Commissar's rosy picture of her waiting at home.

Hazel commiserated with him and said together they would deal with it, but for today the last afternoon they needed clear minds for a grand shopping spree. The afternoon, as might be expected, proved inadequate when it came to all of the shopping she wanted to do; suddenly it was her friends that were important. Marc found he had been taken over in a host of small purchases. The car was ready for collection, and soon the boot was full of vegetables leaving just enough space to pack in the other purchases. Tomorrow they would also need to use the back seats for Hazel's three suitcases of wardrobe, Marc's contribution to this being hardly worth the mention.

Tired and hungry they returned to Claude's relative, the worn-out, bony-looking woman who had slaved the whole day through on her small home. In their eyes she had one saving grace, she was a good cook, and could be relied upon to provide an excellent meal in the evening. But this evening was different, it was their last in Toulouse, and had to be special in some way; so they took themselves off after dinner, to enjoy coffee in their midday haunt. The café was a place that provided enough seclusion to discuss recent happenings, and agree upon a plan of action.

Neither had discussed their homecoming in any depth, but it had not been quite as they had imagined. First there was a lack of police to guard the police equipment as they emerged from the caves. Then the house they were brought to happened to be a remote one and even then belonged to a victim in the Hades caves.

This Hazel had discovered accidentally, when she opened a drawer and saw the photograph of a mannish woman described as doctor, and recognised instantly the one she had rescued in the Styx cave. Curiosity impelled her on to examine the other personal belongings giving evidence of Julia Masse, a top-brass policeman's wife, currently suing for divorce. The police presence seemed to be a one-man affair, which coincided exactly with their emergence nine months after being lost. It was evident the police couldn't possibly have known that they were coming, that must be chance. Was this local police operation fortuitous for them because a top official's wife was being taken out of circulation? Commissar Brie's less than public treatment of them suggested that he had something to hide; but given the kindness and consideration that suited them so admirably, was it right to question facts which seemed suspicious?

This would have been the topic if it were not for Marc's news, which swamped everything else. It was late that night the two returned to their lodging, having constructively considered the outrage from every angle. Marc thought that there was little that he could do, but nevertheless didn't want to take it lying down.

Hazel was not so sure he couldn't get his own back. 'If it will help, I shall stay on. How about that?' The answer was affirmative and sealed for either party by clasping hands under the table. Encouraged by this, Hazel moved the argument further on. 'If high-ranking policemen can dump their wives, I don't see why you cannot just as easily dump yours, and with one added in just for luck.' The resolution was carried, and later with an excess of emotion it was sealed on the doorstep with a profusion of kisses. The purposeful bout of kissing served to strengthen the bond between them even more, entwining and combining their wish to see revenge done to the full. Having gained momentum, the kissing began to find reasons of its own to become infectious, and as the infection developed even the curtains above them were motivated by this curious phenomenon to move occasionally.

Next day they were off after breakfast. Mme Brie would not hear of being paid, so the pair hoped that the Commissar had adequately covered their expenses, and just in case he hadn't, they presented her with a bouquet of flowers extensive enough to cover the presentation box of chocolates held beneath. It was a gesture that took Mme Brie very near to tears, which she covered by kissing them both.

Then there was no more stopping before the fish superstore where they were able to view their purchases swimming about in a number of separate tanks. Nearby was the rest of their order awaiting airlift, which included Hazel's three plastic tanks, each one equipped with a complimentary book on fish and a net for transfers. Marc's gold-plated trolley, large enough to hold a single tank, also stood there, but this he had already seen since purchase. Beyond them, and set to one side was a robust generator and near it a heavy-duty pump of similar construction, these were the items he was most relieved to see present, having arrived earlier. Their goods were all correct and in good time for the flight. The bulk of goods required were rapidly transferred from the car to form a heap, but in it the vegetables created such a mound that Marc could foresee it straining their relationship with the Commissar. The little car seemed much lighter for having left so much behind; gladly Marc swapped the vegetation space for suitcases, leaving room to set their backpacks on the rear seats. Journey's end was the promenade entrance to the caves, where Commissar Brie was waiting.

Claude had already checked on Julia's house, and was very pleased with their punctual arrival at the agreed time. He busied himself to be helpful, opening up the caves with a large key and saying something humorous to Marc about not blowing up the repaired section. Their language was just a bit too quick for Hazel's French to get the full import before the heavy door slammed behind them putting them in the dark.

Amid Claude's keys rattling Hazel remarked to Marc, 'As a policeman I'm sure he must be used to doing that.'

But stone-faced Marc didn't laugh as he had at Claude's comment; instead he laughed when she next spoke. 'I suppose you do know where you are going?'

They set off at a cracking pace for the first few hundred yards just to show that he did and arriving at the junction that had previously been under a pile of rocks. Marc held the light high showing the elevated bridge now intact and gleaming – there was not a trace of the rock fall, or of the flood she remembered. Minutes later they had climbed to the central plateau, a place convenient for picnicking; the trip had taken under two hours. A spirit stove boiled water, whilst they set out their packed lunch upon a sleeping bag.

'Did you travel in this kind of luxury last time?' Hazel scolded, remembering the smell of bacon frying and her own painful journey there on sugar water.

'Not quite everything,' he replied with a mouth full of food, there was a pause before grabbing her. 'I didn't have you.' Hazel protested ineffectually, as he began to make up for this omission.

The journey was so direct Hazel realized that Marc's claim to have surveyed the caves and all the routes leading to them was no idle boast. However direct it might be, the journey there still took up the rest of the day. Early tomorrow was the airlift, and that would fit well with their 4 pm deadline, so indeed they were ready in time. Entering the familiar cavern with its distinctive outcrop in the middle, Marc headed for an opening that Claude would recognize as 'lost property' and set down the sleeping bag; then from somewhere to their rear he collected more items, sliding a much larger sleeping bag beneath Hazel's.

'Extra padding,' he laughed.

'Where did you get that from?' Hazel sat on top appreciating the extra depth.

'This is where I used to leave my gear when I went exploring.' Marc shut off his lamp and said with a chuckle, 'It's dark in here – what do you do when its dark?'

'Sleep,' said Hazel feeling her way along the bedding.

'No you don't, you know.' Mark moved in so quickly, he was there before she could slide in.

41

Santa Hazel

It was a week since Hazel had departed, demanding that Freda attend the rope end left by Hazel halfway down the Styx chamber; and she made it early enough to compensate for any time differences with the outside world. The fact she waited made her doubt, although now she had little room left for doubt as to Hazel's intentions; it was more a fear that things may have gone wrong for her. She arrived well before 4 pm according to Hades time, and straightway had to retrieve Hazel's rope which was too far forwards for Freda's liking being way beyond the halfway point. She advanced several steps beyond what was her usual boundary and drew in all of the slack available before retreating.

This would be her last act as Queen, a thought Freda found very pleasant, for she would now be released to throw off everyday problems, and concentrate on new projects. She had much more to do in making the caves a better place for all to live, and alongside military supremacy there would inevitably be opportunities for her religious changes as well. Her thoughts had been evolving in response to a few days of near isolation, and actually living in the church. The time spent had been profitable in that it had given her extra horizons, with strange new thoughts such as extending their church to the men. Uniformity of religion created allegiance, a route well proven in history of many empires, and if she put her mind to it there was surely room to accommodate small gatherings of men in places other than in the village.

Her reverie was interrupted by a tug on the line, which she promptly answered: more quick pulls and the line went slack. Carefully Freda drew in the rope, noticing there was none of the snagging she half expected; the drag also was less than she anticipated. Framed in the sentry's opening, bows like that of a ship slowly emerged – a 'v' shape in canvas. The tarpaulin, which she continued to draw forward, was secured through eyelets set high along its top edge. Something glistened inside that was large, transparent and box-shaped. Freda dragged the sheet well into the safe end of the chamber before peering inside – the rigid see-through outline of a large, dry tank contained several objects, but nothing reminiscent of fish. There was a telephone handset, a long-handled net, a cardboard box and a bucket, which itself held a shiny black instrument. Her expectation had been a small vessel with water containing tiny fish; sheer distance would preclude the transfer of very much else. There was something odd about this – her busy mind avoided the term 'fishy'. What might there be in the cardboard box? She flipped open the ends to find three volumes of the same book about keeping fish, each printed in a different language. With annoyed frustration at the waste, an uneasy Freda raised the handset.

Hazel's voice crackled excitedly in the receiver, ascertaining that she really had Freda on the line. 'We have got so much here, and it's so complicated, you will need half the village to help you.' Hazel's voice carried her message firm, but with such a confident and forceful tone that Freda knew she meant serious business.

'Where are the fish?' Freda asked anxiously.

Hazel ignored the question; the tank must be right in front of her. 'Freda, will you take the fish tank off for me? In the bucket there's a video camera, to show jewellers in Lutz your gold, so put it carefully aside for the moment. Photographing what you have to barter will be necessary for any future purchases. The fish are ready to be sent through, but you will need at least two more people to handle the weight. Particularly I want Bernadette, if she is at hand, because she can use the camera. I know that, because she said her dad had one.'

'I am moving the tank now,' said Freda. Her erratic breathing was soon bearing witness to an effort being expended as the tank slid off the canvas on wooden protective skids. From there she pulled it without difficulty across an uneven floor. Freda called disjointedly towards the telephone, which lay presumably not touching her ear, 'It is off – I am on my way to get help!'

The empty canvas slipped back along the floor; there was now much work to do at Hazel's end, which was just as well, because Freda took some time in coming back.

It had not been quite as Freda had expected and she was suspicious, a legacy perhaps from Hazel's previous twisty dealings. She asked herself, where could such a bulk come from? She walked, mind in a whirl, and working overtime to see any undue implications in all of this; each time coming up with just one word – Gold. She struggled absent-mindedly with her task of collecting people, and after an interval she was back with helpers who stood about admiring the large plastic tank. Freda was immediately back using the telephone. 'Tell me, Hazel, how many are there with you?'

'There's only Marc, who's helping me with the fish; besides that he has built you a better burglar alarm, and wants to tell you how it fits in with what you have.'

Freda was still uncertain; the mere mention of Marc was enough to floor her confidence, but so far there was nothing tangible to feed her suspicion. However there was much sharper edge to her voice in the next question, when she asked about the camera. 'Why do you want the pictures? We could just barter any piece we chose.'

'Some of your ornaments could be very valuable. At least let us tell you what they are estimated as, before you part with any of them.' Hazel sounded very matter of fact.

Freda's voice came still decidedly hesitant, but with more confidence now that she had expended her main query. 'All right, we agree to that! Who do you want to speak to first?'

'Thanks Freda, I would like to talk to Bernadette. But meanwhile can your people part-fill the plastic tank with water – the one you pulled in?' There was a crackle as Freda handed over the handset, a pause, and then a mumble of voices before Bernadette's hard Irish voice sounded in Hazel's ear.

'So much blarney, surely it's all a con you'll be trying on us?'

'That's unfair, there isn't one. I promised I would come back, and I have.'

'Traitress you are! Should I be believing you now – tricked us, didn't you?' Bernadette's voice betrayed a temper on the rise.

'Come on, Bernie, you know me better than that. I did what I had to, and even now I am not well. See what's offered first. You will not accept anything you don't agree with, will you?' Hazel's words obviously produced a calming effect, for when she next spoke Bernadette sounded a little more restrained.

'What do you want me to be doing?' A truculent note persisted in her voice.

'Rescue that video camera before they manage to wet it.'

There was a blip of noise, as Bernadette laid the phone down suddenly – a pause preceded her exclamation. 'B'jazus – me dad kept cigs in a box like this.' Her voice came back on line, more recognizably Bernadette now, as she forgot her grievance in doubts over handling such a compact modern marvel.

'Yes, Marc says they have improved them out of all recognition over the last few years. There are instructions there, as well as two batteries – use one battery trying it out on the fish transfer, and then check over the replay to see you are doing it right. When you are sure, go and make a video of the gold room with the other battery. It is so we can check up on the value of each piece with experts. While you are doing it, show a bit of the village for me, because I want something out here to remember.'

'I'll have a go.' Bernadette sounded less sure. For having said she would had simply put her in at the deep end; how did one use the tiny thing without breaking it?

'Have they got some water in the tank yet?' Hazel was pushing for some progress.

'It's near to half filled; Leon's got his hose running up by the cells.'

'That's plenty full enough; can you put Freda back on the line for me?'

The phone crackled as it was handed from one to another, and the sound of Freda's comparatively laboured breathing had Hazel talking immediately.

'Freda, can you take up the slack on the rope, then when you can see gently guide the steering from your end? It is a motorized tank half full of water, carrying fish.'

Freda laid the phone down and called to Frances and Annita. Together they pulled on an altogether slack rope, finding only a slender white nylon cord tied to the other end. Freda collected this in personally, finding that there was still nothing that she would call resistance. As they watched a gold-plated box on wheels entered the Styx chamber moving apparently without effort, follow-ing in the general direction of the cord, whose angle appeared to control it. With a start Freda reinstated her grip.

To Bernadette, wielding her tiny video camera, the gold-plated trolley that enclosed the tank looked very uninteresting through the black and white viewfinder, but then her eye moved off to the genuine article and saw something befitting a pantomime – a gold thing gliding in on soft white rubber wheels, rather like a royal coach. No white horses though, unless they were there as wheels, whilst the plain grey dresses guiding it in made lacklustre coachmen pulling on the reins.

'There's a thermometer floating in it,' shouted Annita beckoning her forwards. Together they read the stem, and Annita transferred it into the water that was waiting.

The rest stood there looking in wonder. Most were good-sized fish: trout, perch, carp, chub and bream. With an effort Freda tore herself away from the spectacle and took the initiative, dipping the bucket to start the operation, only to be called away moments later for the telephone. An anxious Hazel wanted to know that the fish had both survived and arrived, for there were yet more to come.

They began work on a damp job with vigorous livestock that splattered them with water; until eventually when everything was transferred there was the instruction to lift the plastic tank out of its trolley, an effort for the whole team. To the surprise of everybody there the trolley was able to reverse out entirely under its own motive power – evidently having been set to reverse through exactly the same path via a computer chip.

There was another transfer now about to take place, and as water began to splash outside the Styx chamber, Bernadette was coming to her own individual decision that she had mastered the simple technique of camcording, and before long she slipped away towards the village.

A second lot of fish arrived, and this time the gold-plated trolley sailed uneventfully over the entry route memorized entirely from the last trip; traction came from batteries that sat upon its rear end. Once again contents had to be transferred into the first tank, which already contained water and fish. The fish operation being virtually complete enabled Freda with her helpers to take the last plastic tank out of the trolley, along with residual water slopping from one end to the other agitating a few remaining eels as they did so. It was ready except for Bernadette so the others stood watching the fish swim. It was as if this was an aquarium to look at rather than inhabitants to be in their pools – fish on this scale exceeded anybody's furthest thoughts. Freda gazed part-hypnotized by the fish before returning to the telephone.

There was a small 'hurrah' at Hazel's end when they heard that all of the fish had arrived – the operation it seemed had warmed Freda's whole being. But unknown to her all was not over yet, for Hazel still had much to send in; and beyond even this she wanted a chance to discuss what happened next.

Freda deduced she was offering Marc's services. 'No, I do not want to speak with him,' she said flatly, all of her suspicions reawakening. Suspicion then translated into another channel. 'However did you manage to bring so much to us?'

'We escaped from here only to walk into the arms of a police-man, who helped with a helicopter, but they left after losing two women. What we have purchased was bought with the gold hippo.' Hazel ineffectually launched into more detail but Freda became wary she was starting up on another far-fetched tale and sought to excuse herself. 'This is my last act as Queen, so what Marc has to offer needs from now onward be decided by Frances – hold on and I'll call her.'

Frances was unintelligible, and had to be put on hold until Marc, who had wandered, could be brought back to the phone – he must explain it all by himself.

Frances was pleased with what he could offer and receptive to his every word, after all she was Queen now and not as prejudiced as Freda was. 'Yes,' she said. 'I quite agree, we must afford up-to-date machinery, those repairs have always been a headache and are fast falling behind.'

Marc knew that, he awaited an answer.

'How much will it cost, and how long will it take?' Frances was being objective.

A whispered conversation between Hazel and Marc culminated in Marc's reply. 'Three weeks from now I will return to deliver,' he said and rapidly moved on to the crunch question. 'Who have you got there who's competent enough to install them?' The line remained silent at the other end, it was clear Frances didn't know. 'How about Red?' he asked knowing full well that Red had been a firm favourite of hers.

'Yes, it can be Red, but you still haven't said how much it will cost.'

Marc's reply flabbergasted Frances, but she was soon won over by his assurance that it was very little in terms of golden artifacts.

Bernadette had returned, and once she put the video camera into the trolley, Frances was dispossessed of the telephone. Soon the neat trolley moved off on battery power, throbbing into action and exiting almost noiselessly. But when it arrived into Hazel's care there was something unexpected inside, a package tied up in straw. Full of curiosity Hazel unwrapped the bundle, and looked uncomprehending for a brief moment as a fine gold chain found its way into her hands. The chain was threaded through a hole drilled in an irregular nugget of gold – the pendant promised by Annita had at last been delivered. Hazel hung it round her neck and reached for the telephone.

Annita was only too willing to come to the phone. She had been left out in the cold overlong, considering that it was her one and only special friend who was there at the other end. A good ten minutes lapsed and the pair chatted on. Marc had by then decided that the pictures were acceptable, and began preparing a tarpaulin stacked with plastic bags of vegetables. Apart from tea bags and instant coffee, most of the weight was potatoes intended for Maria whose own supply was minuscule, all the rest was either based upon Hazel and Annita's whim for the horses, or fish food. Marc coupled up the rope, signalling for it to be dragged through, all without disturbing the chatting duo. However, the tarpaulin's arrival at the other end caused the tongues to cease wagging abruptly – Maria had her eyes on the lot.

Annita's hasty departure brought Hazel back for she had not yet finished, she still had her specials to do, and the trolley had its last run. Freda was shattered to receive several weighty books of reference for her library and some writing materials too, the top page of which was already written.

It was Hazel's apology for her devious retreat, coupled with a thank you that appreciated all the kind things that Freda had done to smooth her path. Quite distinct and separate nestled a plastic box addressed to Bernadette, who found little containers inside, besides surgical instruments. Again there was a little note inside from Hazel.

Dear Bernie.

I discovered that you had the good fortune to receive a doctor into your care. If she is as capable as I have seen papers that say she is, then you ought to get those bits of scrap metal taken out of your arm. The little aerosols are ethyl chloride to freeze out some of the pain. I do hope it doesn't hurt too much. Get well soon.

Love Hazel.

Even then there was one parcel left for Freda, two metal boxes with a number of wires emerging at one end. It was a complete burglar alarm system wired by Marc to fit what they had and simple directions for connecting, enough to ensure that Freda could complete her project with ease.

Bernadette was first on the telephone full of thanks, to be followed immediately by Freda who had been completely bowled over by it all. But Hazel was not by any means finished yet, the tarpaulin arrived bearing all of the things Hazel saw as necessary for the hairdressers, and plentifully supplied with home permanent wave kits. Again Freda was thanking her; but this time imparting news which had Hazel realize that she was truly redundant. Poppy had taken over the hairdressing, and the designs were absolutely fabulous.

Hazel hardly comprehended the news, which any other time would have floored her ego, but the feeling of elation in providing all these things that she had so longed for only weeks ago completely overrode it. It was for her a heady pleasure condensing all that was nice about giving at Christmas or birthdays. The tarpaulin moved through sprinkled with all sorts of toiletries including much soap, toothbrushes for all, and razors for those men who might just happen to want them.

The impact of Hazel's bonanza would be remembered for long, as a sort of Christmas out of season, one that marked the point in time when things began to brighten for everyone.

42

'The Uninvited'

As Hazel made her way to the back of Julia's grand house, feelings of trespass were very much to the fore; and these soon gave way to feelings of guilt arising from her upbringing, bothered that she had entered the realm of a common burglar. Stealthily she took up the key from its hiding place, and on entering the house was only part reassured by its familiar surroundings. She hunted around for the mains electricity switch, and having found it, a second hunt began for the mains water tap – it must be rendered serviceable for Marc's arrival back from town. The cupboard below the sink was a likely spot, and so Hazel sank to her knees and crawled to look inside; annoyingly the back door creaked and banged behind her – the latch couldn't have quite closed. She reached further into the cupboard, and translated her ire into action upon the just-discovered but over-stiff valve. Instantly water gushed into the sink. A shadow disturbed the light percolating over her head. She froze, there was someone close behind her – it couldn't be Marc yet. In one convulsive move, she threw herself backwards, catching a soft body strongly with her head. There was a sharp cry, and her startled eyes beheld the Commissar, who had fallen backwards.

Clutching his midriff Claude was sat upon the floor with legs pressed against his belly. He composed himself. 'Whatever brings you back here, young lady,' he said sourly.

Hazel was aghast and hastened to help him up. 'Marc was hoping to edit his tape of the village here, and show the gold ornaments to Monsieur Zoub. He has gone to the shops, and I was supposed to be making the coffee. We didn't intend to stay long,' she wound up lamely, still feeling she had not found excuse enough.

Claude eased himself into a chair. She was a hard-headed one

412

that girl; but at the same time it was a relief to know that his burglar was a benign one. 'Well don't hang around with it, fill the damned kettle then, you are wasting water,' he grumbled.

He sounded so cross that Hazel complied immediately, harnessing the gushing water with a purpose. Soon she had made coffee, and saw her visitor relax to look more at home seated upon a kitchen chair. The Commissar appeared in a more friendly frame of mind now, asking how they had got on yesterday with the fish transfers.

'Marc was coming to report to you,' she said. But having said so, Hazel filled in the awkward pause by giving her version of the many contacts in the caves.

Claude complimented her on the coffee, and even noticed her new necklace.

Marc's arrival seemed just as fraught, because when he appeared, staggering in with food, and boxes of electrical equipment for editing the tape, the two men started to quarrel.

The Commissar had not said they could not stay, so Hazel left them to it, and departed to make up a bed, an activity that led naturally on to the discovery of a vacuum cleaner in one of the cupboards. This in turn caused her to begin smartening up the dusty-looking rooms. She was working in the hall when they called her back in; both were smiling now and all animosity had departed as if it had never existed.

Claude Brie stayed to an evening meal, both men finding time to tease her. 'She knocked me to the floor,' said Claude affably. 'I thought that she was praying there on her knees, not that it was just a springboard for knocking the wind out of me.'

'Yes, she is quite aggressive,' laughed Marc. 'I think that it's the company she has been keeping, every one's an Amazon there.'

'The bright outfit should have warned me,' said Claude. 'Whatever strikes you without any provocation is often bedecked in warning colours.'

Hazel relaxed and took it in good heart, it was better than hearing them quarrel.

'It is her gaudy umbrella you have to watch out for,' said Marc incautiously. 'That is where the forked tongue lurks. I discovered a cap covering a sharp spike upon it, and as a consequence my finger bled for ages. Just think yourself lucky she didn't skewer you to the wall with it.' Hazel glowered at him; that was a disloyal thing to say.

413

Claude mockingly thanked Hazel for sparing him; but just as Hazel anticipated, added words of warning for her to be less precipitate. 'Normal folk lack sympathy with us short ones – so beware, you need to adapt to your new circumstances.'

The Commissar departed, and Hazel found within minutes Marc had spread his video equipment all over the floor. As he squatted down enthusiastically she was soon convinced that this was a prime example of the way adult men play; it was no more than a replacement train set that so nearly revisited all their boyhood pleasures: still the same flashing signal lights, and the same individual entertainment, intended to please just one. So given the nature of the diversion, it was not until they reached bed that Hazel was able to discover what the men's quarrel had been about.

At first she probed. 'Was it that he didn't want us here?'

'No,' said Marc. 'But he did want to know of our comings and goings, because he's looking after the place for the owner. I made a mistake in saying, surely the owner was now imprisoned in the caves, thanks to a police plot. But I was wrong about that. The Commissar pointed out that Terry's body precipitated the hunt for us. He said it was my act in rearranging the lights to shine down another tunnel and light your progress that caused them to take the wrong cave. Finding you in the house was really the secondary annoyance; he was already annoyed about his airlift having to make two trips.'

'That means you were wrong, three times in a row,' chortled Hazel, thinking now was her time to tease.

'What do you mean by three times?' He demanded.

'Your heavy machinery, you looked really guilty about that.'

'Not a bit of it, they complained of bulk, and that means your vegetables.' His energetic nudge to emphasize the fact tumbled Hazel out of bed.

The following day, Marc spent most of the time squatting upon the floor with his back to her, working continuously with the house video coupled up to one of his own. There was much cussing, swearing and reference to manuals of editing machines as the day wore on. Hazel could tolerate this well, because although the cuss words were recognised as such, they were less objectionable expressed in some language other than her own. More annoying was his arrival for meals, which he took for granted, remaining blank as if in some other world not yet vacated. Bed, she imagined, would bring him round, but no, he was still glassy-eyed when he hit the pillow.

Marc's aberration ceased early on into the second day; he was quite himself when he arrived for the coffee she made and was quite complimentary about it. He told her as he drained the cup, that his task was over. After that there was but time for Marc to scribble a short note to Greta before they moved off. Besides calling in at a courier office on the way, they delivered a tape showing the gold treasure to their jeweller, Monsieur Zoub.

The next stop may have been a comfortable one for Marc, but it was certainly a cliffhanger to Hazel, who found herself parked in his car outside the Commissariat, weathering the occasional outburst of successive policeman who tried in vain to move her on. Marc had strolled from the building as if he owned the place, engaging her latest oppressor in a little lighthearted chat before driving off; what a pleasure not to be English!

With the house key returned to Claude, they moved on, for there were other needs that were overdue – called relatives. The next stop was a motel in the middle of nowhere, and after that the Channel Tunnel which sped them towards the Grays' house.

Hazel preferred to go home rather than have Mother come and fetch her; besides which she was bringing the man in her life home with her. How would Mummy view a daughter caught up with a married man? The thought left her feeling uncertain of approval. Hazel became even less sure as the journey progressed. Perhaps she should have sent her mother a postcard, but telling Claude to stall for a while meant it had become an indulgence which could be delayed infinitely. There was a certainty that her parents would be home, because Dad had become redundant before she left; only her mother worked part time. Then there was her sister Heather, who had left home shortly before her own fateful holiday; but where she was living Hazel had no idea. Her mind contemplated the compact house they were heading for. Marc's accommodation would be the bedroom she used to share with Heather; it would be fun to share it now with Marc.

The train pulled into the station to unload the cars; afterwards they ate with Hazel getting progressively more nervous. Not that she could put her fears to Marc, because she didn't quite know what they were – but she was very apprehensive indeed.

43

Golden Lure

Blanche stood upon the doorstep knocking patiently. That Greta always put obstacles such as front doors in her friend's way had to be one more symptom of the envy Greta felt for one who did not go out and work for a living. It showed, too, in the cross and harassed look of Greta when she finally opened the door to her friend. All of these foibles were becoming more pronounced lately, and she surmised Jan reinforced them, by disapproving of close friends who were only too well accustomed to invading their private abode.

Blanche excitedly held out a small package. 'This came in today's post, it's from Marc!'

With a feigned indifference, Greta took the parcel and put it upon a side table.

'Aren't you going to open it,' cried Blanche. 'You haven't heard from him for nearly a year. Go on, open it,' she made encouraging noises.

Greta reached out as if undecided to its brown paper exterior. 'It is only one of those tapes he takes into work after doing outside jobs,' she said, dismissing it.

Blanche knew all about that, her address was its usual destination – a price she paid for by always being at home. 'There will be a message inside there, intended for you,' she said.

Greta appreciated that there was sense in Blanche's comment; she was curious to find out herself, but allowed Blanche to sweat a bit first. The letter opener made a neat incision along one edge, and neatly painted nails teased out a folded page, presumably ripped from a notebook. It had been sited betwixt the wrapper and flat black video plastic.

Darling Greta
I have wandered these last months in caves searching; but am relieved to hear you are safely returned home. My trek

416

has been a hard one, but with its good fortune too. You can see just how much from the accompanying tape. But please wait until the 27th of May before you view, for by then I expect to have achieved everything and be ready to come home.

Love you, Marc.

Hardly had Blanche heard the contents of the letter than she was urging Greta to play the video; but that was a step too far for Greta.

'There are still ten days to go Blanche. Besides which, it is a half-hour tape and I have a meal to cook.'

'Hadn't you better see what's on it? If Marc comes home and finds that man here, there will be no end of trouble. He was like a raging bull in Lutz-St-Saveur.'

Greta calmly let the discussion die with a dissuasive comment. 'He won't do anything before the 27th otherwise he would have brought the tape home himself.'

Blanche left. She could see that further encouragement would get her nowhere at all.

Jan arrived only too soon after Blanche had departed, for unlike Marc the office didn't hold him. That was something Greta put down to her own influence; he couldn't keep himself away. Today however, she felt uneasy with his presence and tried to hasten the meal, but even so, her preparations in the kitchen had not seemed to progress before he was back with the part-opened video.

'Just put it down, I shall tell you later.' She repulsed his second foray with a single preoccupied kiss, clutching the notebook page in her apron pocket. He failed to progress the matter during the meal either, and then again as they prepared for an evening's television. He was taken by surprise when she brought him the note, and leaned close as he read it aloud.

'Well, put it on then.' Jan expected her to view it automatically, but in that respect he was wrong.

'No, I shall do just as he asks, and on the 27th you may see it, my darling.'

Jan looked at her startled, was this part of a return to her husband?

There was something about the note that promised rewards; but from the unconcerned face he could see her mind was made up.

For both of them, the evening seemed very flat after her refusal. Greta was restless, emotional stability was not her strong point, and now new influences between them threatened what little she had. The unease persisted into bed, where Greta tossed and turned; he seemed restless too. At some stage of the night she was drowsily aware that he had left the room, for the bathroom perhaps. It seemed an age later that Greta woke, but this time with a start. Her hand swept his part of the bed; it was an empty space and a cold one at that.

Greta padded quietly out of the room, instantly spotting a slit of light coming under the living room door, and besides this her ear detected the noises associated with television. Was he watching a late night programme because he couldn't sleep? She doubted it; more likely he was looking at her personal thing – the video from Marc. Greta became angry, and burst into the room intent upon turning the set off. There on the screen was a circle of gold and silver artwork, reflecting bright metallic light into the yellow surrounds. It was just a programme after all; she had misjudged him. Greta cuddled for some seconds, bringing her softness near to bear on him, bent on attracting him back to bed – they would be better suited soothing his restlessness there. Then Marc's voice spoke and she was galvanized away to the set, switching it off at the wall.

'You silly bitch,' said Jan. 'Don't you know what you have got there?'

She pouted her lips defiantly, and looked down upon him as contemptuously as she could. 'No! And neither should you.'

He urgently worked the remote control, and the rewind on the video started.

'It's our future, we can be together always, and rich besides – see the tape from the beginning,' his voice was pleading and agog with excitement. Jan stretched his arms towards her.

She relented, tamely switching the wall switch on again – the television fizzed into instant life and moments later the tape began all over again from the beginning. Marc's head and shoulders were visible and he was talking to her – her alone. His quest had been to find his lovely wife, seeking her long and hard in the bowels of earth; starting from the place she was last seen, and ending not so many miles away. For months he had been lost, he had chanced to stumble upon a remote and quite independent subterranean

418

world, one caught up in the no-mans land between France and Spain.

'It was a world that had evolved from miners, a world gaining its power inefficiently from a waterfall. But having stumbled upon them, I found the engineers in that place keen to do business with me. Soon they progressed to trusting me for bringing things from the locality into their remote location. To start with it was live fish, but now it has moved on to modern high-flux density generators. They paid for it with an ornament, a heavy one worked in solid gold, as payment for the fish.' The image of a golden hippopotamus appeared upon the screen, with Marc's voiceover continuing without interruption. 'The hippo seemed a rich reward for bringing food fish into their world, for there is a lot of change as profit so I guess the next stage must be even more advantageous.'

There were shots of live fish in a tank, mounted upon a sort of sledge, and being dragged through a wide cavernous space before entering a tunnel – the woman doing it looked pretty. Despite being draped across Jan's lap, and him fully aware, Greta screwed her face up in some sort of inner rage.

Accompanying the picture, Marc's voice sailed on quite unaffected by emotion. 'This is Hazel, my assistant.'

Jan grasped her arm. 'Look at this next bit.' The scene shifted to a shiny enclosure, revealing a space packed with golden pieces and interspersed with silver – the camera moved in among them. Marc's voice broke into a short laugh before continuing. 'Now it is agreed, they are willing to part with lots of this stuff in return for generating capacity. It is a fact that their world can be made a very comfortable place indeed, if they have the plant to make it so. Gold is of little use to them; it is iron that is scarce here, and they see little practical difference between the monetary worth of one they have in plenty compared with the other. Gold they believe is not worth extracting for they are well supplied with copper, what exists is old stuff – I believe it's been referred to as the "Green Nun's treasure".' Panning up and down the many gleaming yellow artifacts, the camera dwelled upon each piece in turn, the point where Greta had entered. The camera at length emerged into a most peculiar place; a collection of dwellings that were all translucent yellow spheres, and these identified by Marc as the village.

The scene switched to two items of heavy machinery. Jan had been interrupted by Greta before this scene and not seen it, he craned his head this way and that to see, reversing and re-examining the tape – despite fresh objections from Greta. Then there was a closer shot and Jan whistled; an inadvertent escape of breath. 'They're ours; they're bloody well ours!' He shook his head in disbelief. 'Where did he get them from – that sort of thing is arranged by me when it happens.'

Greta laughed at him. 'Marc had more contacts in your firm than you had girlfriends. He was dull, but I'll say this much for him – he was a success.'

Jan whirled to face her; she had struck home with that one, the end of the tape came and departed without notice. 'You have to decide who you are going with, and you have only the week to make up your bloody mind,' he said angrily

Greta's eyes filled with tears. 'I left him because I loved you; but you have so many women that they make a very good reason for staying with Marc.'

'Staying with Marc – you have already left him, and when he finds out where you were whilst he was blowing himself up for you, then you will be in real trouble.'

There were tears that came, and came, as the vast lake available to her eased out of the waterworks, some falling, but most wetting Jan's shoulder, whilst he, oblivious to salt water, manipulated the remote control to see the end bit again.

'That cave, I think I know where it is.' Jan's voice penetrated the wetness that hemmed her in. The picture now framed an obviously new, gleaming, specialized pump and generator; but revealing also the peculiar ridges of the nearby walls that were characteristic of the beehive cave. He returned to the shot of a woman dragging fish, and saw a cavern that was as individual as any he had seen. 'I know that place too,' he cried. 'I have seen it way back in the past.' Greta's crying had subsided, the wet season was turning humid; she too began peering mistily at the screen, then Marc's voice came again.

'I have put off the delivery date for a week, because I am due to see Commissar Brie tomorrow; he has some serious questions to be answered about a cave explosion, which I regret did me no good at all. If I make due allowance for my condition, another fortnight should see the business complete. Even if you cannot restrain your curiosity until the 27th, you will be pleased to know there is already money in the bank, and beyond that, prospects of being seriously rich. You can start planning for my retirement now, as I have injuries that have left me a little stunted, and quite impotent. You will need time to adjust your ideas to a new life for us; that's why I am sending you this tape because what's left of me badly needs to partake of your own particular brand of tender loving care.' Marc stood by the chair he'd been sitting on as the camera zoomed away.

Greta shrieked, as she saw what was left of her large and powerful engineer.

No way did she want him if he were that size, and only part functioning. She shrank from meeting him and having to refuse his proposition. He could have all the riches that wealth might confer, but her mind was made up, he was not having her. Greta clung to Jan as he passed monotonously up and down the tape by remote control; her tears dried and she was beginning to feel an emotional upsurge towards the man beside her, the one that was so very much in control.

Jan could hardly wait to get to work next morning; the motors had to have an explanation, and one that he in particular was best placed to find out. When he rang on an internal phone the sales office immediately said his own department had made the order. Swiftly he transferred his ire to Stella whose arrival he now awaited impatiently and with developing indignation. So much so that his secretary had hardly removed her coat before being escorted into his office. Jan suppressed his rage just long enough to query the order for electrical plant.

Stella's response was immediate. 'It was Marc Casserta who made the order.'

'Why didn't you ask me?' the heavy man's voice thundered.

'Mr Casserta is an authorized person, the order didn't need confirmation. In this respect his word is just as good as yours, sir.' She looked him straight in the eye, as if to say, 'sack me if you like, but that's the position'.

There was little he could do but talk of preventing a future recurrence. His rage had to modify now, because of all the further things he wanted her to do. For the time being she was off the hook. Rage turned into haste, for soon he was dashing about the building and seeing all manner of departmental heads to fix a rush holiday.

It was on the following day that Jan and Greta took the train journey across France to arrive back in Lutz-St-Saveur. There was no time wasted with hotels, in fact Jan had no wish to be seen there at all.

Greta rang Blanche in a hurry from the station, and they had a few last-minute words before the taxi arrived. The taxi deposited them at the upper promenade cave entrance; keys were not a problem – Jan had one. Greta still had misgivings about this latest move. 'What if we meet up with Marc in there?' She nervously put her query before entering the dark.

'He's in no position to argue with us,' Jan laughed. 'If those motors are to be sold, then I have the authority to sell them. Marc has ceased to represent the company; I checked that out this morning.'

The journey was not as direct as Marc's, for Jan had never bothered with maps, he did so entirely from memory and that was near enough. At length the two of them stood in a cavern with an unusual rock formation at its centre. The beehive cave needed to be sought, and having found the place, there dwelt both pump and generator, much to Jan's pleasure and satisfaction. He dragged them one by one down the path, churning up stones under the little platforms they were on, pleased that they were no longer in their original bulky crates. Jan was more than physically equal to the work of dragging the heavy plant as far as the tunnel that he remembered so very precisely from the video. As they entered the final approach tunnel the considerable exertion necessary diminished, for now the generator tended to slip more easily on what seemed to be a part glassy surface.

Directly in his path lay a tarpaulin like the one seen moving fish tanks on the video. Jan stopped; it would be even better to slide the skid's weight if he ran them onto it. Slowly he positioned the generator on the tough material, pleased to see there were ropes at every corner. He yelled for Greta, helping her to a rope; then together trudging forwards shoulder to shoulder, they headed along the remaining slightly curved tunnel until seeing eventually a patch of light ahead that was soon to join their own. Across the cavern a small camcorder switched off as they disappeared round the tunnel's natural curve – Marc had put to good use his latest hobby.

44

Travelling Dwarves

Hendon seemed comparatively quiet after the heavy traffic of inner London, but still busy enough at the junction of major roads in the central area to confuse them. It was at this set of traffic lights Hazel insisted on giving local directions as any knowledgeable resident might; but fell down in a practical sense from being the pedestrian that she had always been. Marc was soon gritting his teeth, as she tied him up in traffic, and before long managed to return them to the same junction but on a different set of lights. Her angry outcry after he ignored all further instruction ceased only as he parked in the family's quiet backstreet. Hazel alighted, but to see her home location through somewhat different eyes; it was a grey image not now softened by familiarity and identification, a street she could no longer feel proud of being associated with.

Holding a bright bunch of flowers she knocked. The door opened flooding her with food odours. Mrs Gray did not immediately recognize her own daughter, and when she did, she just stood there dumbfounded.

'Hello, Mummy,' called Hazel cheerfully – wondering at the lack of response. But when Mummy did respond it was with tears and hugs, those hugs mutually missing their accustomed resting places. Mrs Gray in particular was aware of losses from Hazel's natural upholstery, and betrayed confusion by her many uncertain interrogative looks – was this some other being she held or her chicken? But even if the proportions were differently set out, emotions were plentiful enough to bring mother and daughter joyfully near to tears.

Marc received the bunch of flowers that Hazel rapidly passed to him to be out the way; he pointed the blossom downwards and looked dispassionately at Hazel's mother. She was a round and chubby woman, poised on high heels, the high heels being in

423

harness via a strap underneath to black slacks. Her bright sweater was slashed through with horizontal circular rings, giving the overall effect of a ball surmounted by black glasses, rather than a woman. Whilst waiting his turn to meet Hazel's mother, he better observed the house squeezed in between the other houses of a terrace – eyes peered at him through a triangular space in the net curtains next door – it was all a bit alien.

'This is Marc, Mummy.'

The woman still towered above him, despite the fact she had stepped down from the doorstep. Marc handed her the flowers, which also seemed small by relation to bulk.

'I am pleased to meet you.' Marc said it with a slight bow and a handshake.

Hazel whispered to her mother. 'He is my partner.'

'Fred,' the yell penetrated the depths of the building, as Mrs Gray bounced up the doorstep into their vestigial hall. It was a cramped place to meet the father, and here again Marc needed to wait for all of the hugging to cease. Mr Gray was a wiry, gone to seed fellow, with silvery hair and glasses to match. The man of the house turned eventually to Marc, and smiling broadly shook his hand.

Fred's other hand arrived upon Marc's shoulder, and pointed him through into what must be the best room of the house. Hazel continued along the hallway towards what they referred to as the kitchen, and from there their voices penetrated the hall, rising excitedly every other moment through an open door. Mr Gray closed their door as the fluctuating sound level was conflicting with his trawl for facts, which he did under cover of much inconsequential chat. In these circumstances it took longer, but nevertheless culminated in the deduction that Marc was a married man. The fact was evidently communicated in the fussy disruption created by antics of the good woman in warning they were about to receive tea in best china. Hazel ceremoniously carried through the tea some minutes later. Mrs Gray chose to sit one side of an occasional table, squashing up to her husband upon their three-seater settee and clearly making room for Hazel, who completely ignored the gesture and faced the teapot alongside Marc by pulling a matching armchair from the corner. Mrs Gray talked incessantly on numerous trivial topics in the news until the suggestion arose that they ought to begin finding a hotel for the night.

'Of course you must stay here, I wouldn't dream of you going anywhere else,' declared Mrs Gray vehemently. 'You can have your old bedroom, Hazel – and your gentleman friend can have the spare bedroom.' She threw a disdainful look towards Marc.

Hazel's face questioned the fact. 'Is Heather at home then?'

'Your sister is a one parent family now; she has a flat all to herself.'

'That's fortunate, because Marc and I are living together – you do not need another room.'

'You are not living here in sin! Not under this roof you won't. Marc is very welcome to stay, but there is still a guest room that can be put at his disposal.' A puritanical note entered the voice of Mrs Gray, and Hazel knew she faced overwhelming opposition.

Hazel thought it unfair. Her elder sister, living it up with an arty crowd in the city, now had a baby illegitimately, and the consequences of that frowned on by the local council to the extent of giving her a flat. With Heather's dubious moral behaviour, how could Mum take that particular attitude towards her; was she clutching at the remaining straws of respectability? Hazel considered whether the hotel could be raised again as a valid point, but hesitated to introduce a sour note to an otherwise sweet reunion. But such thoughts had to be shelved because the questions had started in earnest.

'How did you get like that, were you ill?' Hazel's father turned an inquisitive stare at his small daughter, who was struggling to keep her feet on the floor by sitting close to the armchair seat edge.

'We were lost in the caves near Lourdes. There were fungi to eat, and the rocks all about made us feel unwell; but we had no idea of becoming smaller. Marc's wife had left him. I suppose it was simply the hardships there that caused us to join forces and find ways to escape. After all those experiences we are now very close.' Hazel said it with emphasis on the 'very close', thinking she had made it all sound so simple – surely Mother ought to relent when she understood?

'You won't get a well-paid job you know; better register as disabled, that's your best way to get the money you will need to live.' Mrs Gray warmed to her subject with a quick look sideways at her husband, who nodded in a docile manner as he had to all of her pronouncements. 'I'll go down with you to the Social, first

425

thing tomorrow.' Mrs Gray looked benevolently at her daughter, but lofted her gaze from the sawn-off, older man she had in tow.

'I don't want a job, Mummy. Neither do I want to apply for anything. I just came to visit you and be off again.'

'But you must do something about it, darling – we do not mind having you back to live at home. There's probably some way you can be compensated, sometimes there's somebody responsible – let's take it to law.'

'I don't want to sue anybody either. Oh hell, can't you just let it alone!' Hazel with agony in her voice turned a red face to Marc. 'Why not bring our bags in, I cannot just leave right now, besides, it might be convenient staying overnight?' Marc pulled a face, which fully conveyed his opinion of what he thought about that before setting off with Mr Gray to the car. The man helpfully took hold of Hazel's sizable case; whilst behind them there was the sound of confrontation – it was inevitable Hazel and her mother would fall out.

For Marc the place was airless; he sat in their best room with Hazel's dad who had taken off into the realms of newspaper and magazine following a preliminary gesture towards Marc encouraging him to take one. This he did but couldn't help noticing the prominent television set displaying a silent soap programme; a quite different one he noticed upon first setting foot in the room. There was a change of room for dinner, supposed to be healthy eating despite Hazel's mum cooking it. The wait was punctuated by cooking odours and the frequent optimistic rattle of plates from the dining room, a period otherwise marked upon his mind as several hours of tedious boredom. In the evening he sat with the family watching soaps, but this time with the sound on – everyone was ultra polite. Where was the famous British television? It would seem that the select band of quality screenings he formerly might have expected had disintegrated into several slots for trash. He was relieved eventually to escape the utter politeness and move into his room.

His bedroom was tiny, with a bed that fitted the entire far wall as exactly as if it were made for it; the door facing the bed groaned and creaked a protest on part-seized rusty hinges as he shut it. Windows too resisted every attempt to open, but here the draught was enough to move a curtain. When at last he did climb into the bed, the tinkling of springs under his slight weight astounded him.

Any turn or movement upon it was amplified into a whole orchestra of metallic noises. An hour passed, before the thuds and uneasy noises from the adjacent parents' bedroom subsided; he waited a further quarter hour before looking at his watch, it was 12.30. Just before the general retirement, Hazel had whispered. 'See you downstairs in an hour.' But how the hell did you do such a thing? He clutched at the rigid metal frame and eased himself from the bed. The clinking noises continued at low level as slowly he put more weight on the rigid frame, prising himself out of the mattress. With a sudden unnerving ping the springs closed behind him, and he was on creaking boards groping for the door. The door groaned and its handle squealed, as with bated breath he cushioned its return squeal. Noises at this point could be excused for he could merely be going to the toilet, which forwards faced him. Crawling through the bat ways was more predictable an obstacle course than this one. Hearing not a sound his heart thumped as he set about the stairs, their creaking noises were even worse than the landing; but additionally interposed were severe deep cracking noises that had him divert each foot towards the support ends of each step – with him moving like a snail. What would these people think if they caught him now? They could only think he was robbing them.

The slight chill on the house was only just apparent through his thin dressing gown, when some ten minutes later he arrived at the foot of the stairs. The handle to the front room door moved silently – thank God it was the only solitary thing that had. Subdued light attracted his eyes, and there looking lovely in her night attire was Hazel, reclining upon the sofa.

'I didn't hear you come down.' Marc was astonished, he was sure he was first; however did she run the gauntlet so quietly?

'I was here already, I came down straight away.' She laughed, a little tinkling laugh, and held out her arms to him. They cuddled up on the cushions, his hands soon finding her body, and hardly needing to go beneath her nightdress at all because it was so remarkably thin. Hazel was that much more provocative for being at home in her own surroundings, and able to tease him exactly as she had been accustomed to teasing her more worthwhile boyfriends, she untied his dressing gown and fluttered it above them. Soon the nightie joined it onto what had become their tent. Her fingers hardly paused before tugging at his pajama cord, then balancing the whole lightweight top layer upon her back slid down

427

over his chest so that her hard nipples slid rake-like over it. Hazel was proud of her breasts, they had been full since the baby; and when Marc's hands rose to intercept them she shimmied herself about so as to tantalize him to a maximum. A gold nugget dangled from her neck, the chain piling up on his mouth until it dropped in to twist upon his tongue. She was using her own mouth to lovingly play drag and drop with mouths using the chain, as hands joined forces in a prolonged exciting game underneath the covers. This was not the place for completeness. Hazel knew that sex was for somewhere else; she was merely catching up with all of that courting she would surely have done from home had they met earlier. Marc was going to be left hungry for more; what finer test could she have for him than an under the covers courtship in her parents' home!

There was a sudden bump upstairs: Marc part sat, his tense nervous state returning with interest. There was a series of little thuds then silence.

Hazel's head poked up provocatively under his dressing gown and laughed at his expression. 'That's only Mum getting out for a pee.'

'I left my door ajar, the whole thing made such a noise.'

'Don't worry, she's got a pot under the bed, she has a weak bladder.'

Hazel's hands pulled him down. 'It's a thin ceiling. If you listen you will hear her piddle.' She laughed, favouring him, whilst betraying a noise that would otherwise be missed.

Even so Marc froze, until moments later the overhead patter back to bed reassured him. There was another hour of petting before they decided to retire; she first, moving like a shadow up the stairs. Marc heard her tackle the toilet door before setting off himself, and on the stairs he waited at the bend, standing still like a statue until she cleared the tiny room. That was the moment when he pounded the intervening space with heavy foot, and went noisily into the toilet, flushing the overhead cistern as he came out. Going back to bed he swamped the place with sound. The young woman snuggling down on her pillow smiled to herself, Marc had chosen a safer strategy to return.

Everybody was on best behaviour the following morning. From next door the radio blared fortissimo, driving the two out for an after breakfast walk in the fresh air. It was a chance for Hazel to wear one of her more colourful suits, and they paraded about the local shops before taking the tube to Hampstead for coffee. The area was more to Marc's liking, almost cosmopolitan. But it was in essence only an attempt by Hazel to find her sister, one that failed abjectly as there was no response to all to her knocking. As the knock became heavier, an old lady in the flat opposite opened her front door and informed them her neighbour was out at work. Dropping a message for her sister through the letterbox, they found a coffee house close by and within the hour were on their way back.

The noise of rap music had still not abated when they returned; Hazel's parents seemed totally unaware of it. This was the point when Hazel muttered something about helping her mother and left, whilst unknowingly he talked loudly with her dad. Feeling neglected he heard her busy with the telephone in the hall, giggling and chatting. Lunch was a frugal affair, and as they ate Hazel explained she had contacted one of her friends, the girl was coming to see her after lunch. It was to do with her friends locally, and the fact that she was apologizing for the neglect of them, due to her mobile phone with its entire number list being a casualty of the caves. The day was a hot one as May sometimes is causing Marc to expect an afternoon walk, one that might enable them to find a hotel or even perhaps consider leaving altogether. As a consequence he was pleased to shortly hear this old friend of Hazel chatting at the front door. That much was pleasant, but when the two walked off for a couple of hours he was furious.

The foreign radio music ceased and Marc found himself listening to Fred Gray's fishing experiences, which began when Mark showed his interest in an angling magazine. Marc had searched it from end to end for any idea of the light levels necessary to maintain fish in good health. His sole interest, besides whiling time away, had been to see the natural habitat of fish supplied to Hades recently and perhaps get some idea of their relative adaptability. There was information galore on fishing, but nothing that threw light on aquariums. Fred it soon transpired knew nothing about rearing fish, and gave up talking when an entirely different source of music from the other side interrupted their chat. Eventually Marc gave up and just sat there.

Hazel rescued him by returning in time to bring in the afternoon tea. Through her friends she had been trying to trace Eileen and that was not a subject Marc knew anything about. Eileen it seemed had married the fellow she met in Lourdes and as Mr and Mrs Chapman had moved home because of the unaffordable house prices in London. The name Chapman stirred in her mind one aspect of the conversation with Claude Brie that had surprised her. Using her friend's mobile she contacted Eileen and learned the full story of an impersonation intended to gain more attention for the missing friends. Apart from swanning about the teashops a short bus ride away, and besides consuming many expensive cream cakes with her friend, Hazel had sent off a thank-you card for the Chapmans. Still exhilarated from her brief return to former haunts, Hazel now saw the boredom that had engulfed her man whilst she had been living it up.

Marc needed resuscitation as well as the tea she brought in, before there was any more of the same. 'Let's go and get the afternoon papers,' she suggested.

'Yes, let's.' Marc put his cup down, and said adieu to the parents.

Hazel left any discussion until they were out of earshot as she felt a definite lack of loyalty to her family – for what had seemed like home before, was distinctly dull.

'We need to move on, Marc. But if we are to see my sister, it will have to be put off until tomorrow morning. Could you stay another . . .' Hazel's plea was never completed, for ahead of them a crowd of senior school boys had dismounted from a bus, and were fully strung out across the pavement, most carrying their jackets over a shoulder. The bus was drawing away, as a boy pointed towards them.

'Oi, look at that bint over there. I reckon it's the fricking Queen o'Sheba.'

Another voice joined the first 'Where's your circus luv?'

A raucous voice answered. 'More like it's a tart for Picadilly Circus!'

Marc swung Hazel round, easily crossing the road in front of a single oncoming car. On seeing their move the boys began crossing also, but moved as a body strung out carelessly across the road, completely disregarding the approaching motorist, who hooted at the youths. He then needed to brake extra hard and stop short of those who chose to defy him.

The nearest banged the car's bonnet with his hand. 'Piss off, you four-eyed fucker,' he shouted, strolling belligerently ahead.

The others fanned across the pavement cutting off any way forward for the pedestrians, with a stream of offensive jocular abuse.

Marc continued towards the line that was forming ahead of them, 'Let us through,' he demanded.

No one moved. ''E's foreign,' went up a shout. 'Bet 'e's a circus clown. Do us a somersault, mister half pint – give us a larf.'

The tone changed abruptly. ''Ere, yer not pushing me about you foreign git!' The yobs strode into them, pushing with their combined weight and driving the couple back. Hazel continued to be pushed back along the pavement by two towering youths who broke free from the others; a remainder paused encircling Marc, that is, apart from those still parallel and leaning on the motorist's bonnet.

'Ger'us yer money, an' we'll stop 'em bashing yer bloke up.' One acne-studded face wheedled, before pushing Hazel full in the chest with both hands.

Hazel inadvertently stepped back, but lowering her parasol canopy brought its upper end downwards, striking the boy's head in one continuous scratch. Still descending, a rubber shape popped off at its tip, exposing a sharpness that dug a tramline in the boy's face from forehead to chin. Hazel's mind was already elsewhere, distracted by a flash of steel ahead – one of the lads had produced a knife. She sidestepped the one now squealing with face in hands, prodded the other with her point and raced towards the main group. Marc was bent low in there; her heart missed a beat, he was her everything. A row of backs fenced him off, and in front of her a foot retracted preparing to kick. All of her battle training came to the fore, as she drove her lance, for that was what the umbrella had to be, plunging it into calf muscle and retracting it even before the cry of agony hit the air. Hazel whirled to meet heavy footsteps sounding behind her; the lad now holding his face with one hand, swung a brick at her with the other. Instantly she stepped away with the point raised to meet the descending arm. Speared flesh involuntarily dashed the parasol out of her hand, which under its own weight dropped to the pavement with the brick, releasing a fountain of arterial blood. The blood pumped forcefully, squirting in time with his heart, the line of shirts in front of him broke away and began to scatter, wetted with a liberal coating of very red arterial blood.

Marc had not been doing too badly himself; at first sight his height should count against him, but arm muscles can only hit efficiently at anything above elbow height and Marc was below that point on all of them: he was additionally too close to make any blow effective. By contrast Marc's muscles although small by comparison were extremely strong as his tough livelihood dictated, and as the lads crushed in, their bellies were just ripe for a powerful solar plexus punch. Several in front of him backed away doubled up, clutching their middles, but from behind he was vulnerable: a knee crashed into his back and he fell forwards, whilst a boot struck home, assisting his plunge to the pavement. Suddenly they fell back, and many began to run; a boy was standing there holding his face, whilst squirting an intermittent jet of blood through a hole in his shirt. Marc grabbed the arm and dug his fingers into the armpit – turning it off like a tap. Hazel was there immediately, picking up her parasol and heading for the car.

The man in the car yelled at him. 'Jump in, you bloody idiot, or do you want to spend a night in the cells.'

Rapidly Marc picked up the brick and squeezed it down under the chap's arm: he scrambled towards the car, a door opened and they were moving away. In the middle of an empty pavement they left the stricken figure, holding his arm firmly down whilst his face streamed with blood; seconds later their car passed a ragged string of uniformly dressed schoolboys moving away. Faces turned to see them pass but none raised a voice towards the victors.

'They may have attacked you, but that will be as nothing in court, I fear you are easier targets for our police than they are as juveniles. The law demands you restrain these overgrown school- boys whatever size you are. That's the best our justice system will offer – so best avoid being caught in the middle of it and jailed. That you stayed to help might be a mitigating circumstance, but only in respect to your sentence – which still leaves you the guilty one, and ripe for suing by the boy's parent's using tax payer's money. That is as I see it – so the best thing I can do is drop you here near the tube station,' said their driver. 'I must go back as a witness,' their new friend continued. 'And the less I know about you the better. But thank you anyway – those obnoxious children needed a good lesson and they got one.'

432

Purchasing an evening paper from the station they returned to Hazel's house, with their minds set on instant departure. Hazel began a protracted goodbye with her mother, who entertained preconceived maternal ideas of her little girl not being the guilty party, suspecting Marc as being the reason. 'Let him go back home, Hazel. They won't look as close as this, will they; and if they do you are small enough to make them look ridiculous in court.'

Mr Gray evidently disagreed, but though visibly wilting from his wife's eye, was also concerned for his daughter Hazel, producing words of warning. 'That may be so dear, but can you rely on the judge. They are so much into politics and the jails are so full that you can never be sure who it is that's being tried. And then of course these are children, so politically correct emotions come in to see that nobody else gets a fair hearing.'

Taking advantage of her parents not seeing eye to eye on the matter; Hazel hastened to finalize her goodbyes and dress in less exotic attire, with the result that their car was soon off to an accompaniment of much waving. London was not the route for them as Marc did not trust his companion to use the map so he set off for Ashford on the M25, and before long their car was traversing Kent.

'We will not to stop anywhere, or if anyone gets out of the car, it had better be me,' said Hazel. 'The police will be looking for midgets, and that means you, so if there's any fuss, don't get out unless you have to.' But their departure posed no problem of any sort – just a report on the car radio to say that school children in North London had been attacked by dwarves from a circus who had left them bleeding in the street. Marc had earlier been a little slighted when Hazel did not introduce her friend to him and now from what she had just said he wondered if she was ashamed of him, a feeling perhaps induced by her mother.

There were several days to spare before Brussels, so they stayed in France, enjoying quiet hotels along the way. Delightful at first and devoid of the many pressures that had been pushing them along hitherto, it was all holiday.

Marc had time now to prepare for the career end of his life, and besides this dispassionately continued his earlier thoughts in mid-Kent, reappraising the relationship between Hazel and his own self. There was no sense in going back into the dreary

433

workaday rut that had blighted his life with Greta, he must live a more adventurous outgoing life. To enter into it, he must first decide whether Hazel was an asset or an encumbrance. She was ever quick to direct him in almost any given circumstance and always displayed her authoritative opinion, almost as if their previous relation still held. Fair enough for him to assist when she was completing promises to those in the caves, or be polite whilst she handled the interface with her parents, but there was no way that she could be allowed to continue taking every decision to herself; not that he didn't appreciate her support in the odd battle. There were other danger signs he was now aware of, namely the characteristics she held in common with her mother. Marc began to realize that he must change Hazel's self-sufficient mind or he'd be just another Mr Gray. She had learned this self-reliance stuff a little too thoroughly to be the person you could always feel at home with – he must see it unlearned. The honeymoon trail gradually disintegrated as Marc attempted to assert himself, each stop along the way taking them further into his own territory.

45

Home From Home

The meeting with his principal squatter returning the key enabled Claude to resume a whole train of events suspended in the background, ruefully considered by him to be his own life. Marc he saw as his close friend and the time taken having coffee in his office was not rushed at all, despite knowing the man's car was an obstruction on the main street and the way several other events were competing on time. So it was early afternoon before he was able to head for the Masse residence, concerned that his friends had left the place much as they found it. But pressing his mission might be it still came to a full stop just before journey's end as he decided to visit the high promenade's new exit turnstile. It had taken a good month of argument with the local council to bring about the heavy doors' replacement, assisted in no small measure by first banning M. Kee from his end of the caves and all of the associated maintenance work. Court action was not yet finalized, but there were enough offences already to enable Claude, aided and abetted by his friend manager of the Source Minérale Plante, to demand a very simple remedy for preventing entrapment in the caves. The turnstile type of exit would see an end to documenting people lost in the caves, at least while this elopement custom was still part of local lore and attracting others. In his dealings with the many officious people in council offices, Claude was made ever more aware of the fact he was the acting Commissar, whilst his boss carried the official title and always had to be referred to, resulting in a most inefficient three-way negotiation.

He was familiar with the property and on driving into the grounds felt much like arriving at his real home. That was the nice part, which disguised the fact that he was responsible for it and now was the time he had to put to rest all doubts and uncertainties about how his friends had treated the place. Any small doubt he had however was soon dispelled as groundless. Hazel had very evidently spent the whole period doing housework, keeping the impact of Marc down to a minimum; so much so that the entire house looked spick and span, there had not even been time for a fresh coating of dust to settle. He wandered through the rooms remembering Julia Masse in a more affectionate light now, for despite all his keeping of her at arms length, their various encounters had been a defining characteristic of the place, perhaps even she had succeeded in softening him emotionally. Only now that she was not remotely a threat would he let his mind dwell on the baby, and hope that its chances of survival had improved since Hazel's unfortunate experience. He felt the peace of this place much as ever and wandered contentedly considering the issues to the point of satisfaction before contacting his boss. Upon the site of Mitzi's grave he used his mobile telephone, reinforced somewhat by feelings of support from the deceased who he felt owed him a favour.

They met two days later in the courtyard of the house, M. Masse carrying a big bundle of plans for the estate. Awkwardly they entered the front door, Claude feeling he had to lead his chief on to the set position of a tray set with beverages, but his chief was working to quite another schedule and decidedly treating him as a mere helper, led the way through his own house. In fact they wandered a good deal before Claude managed to get his own way. At one point they stood looking at a huge patch of yellowing grass, and in response to the unasked question, Claude simply said 'helicopter landing site' and bending over a wheel indentation sniffed at it, perhaps kerosene he said. The many references to the papers Gabriel carried, prompted Claude to ask was he intending to sell the property? His chief merely nodded, looking critically at the house before entering.

'I rather thought that this was your wife's property,' opined Claude, showing him to a comfortable leather armchair, knowing definitively that it was her property.

'From what you have told me there would appear to be little prospect of her return. Gabriel's hard set features struggled with a smile, but ended with an interrogative look of uncertainty. 'Legally it is bound to become mine in the end,' he finished lamely. He set about pouring coffee for Claude and himself, more or less recovering the air of proprietor.

Claude took his time, relaxing, sipping and preparing to speak. 'I can tell you that your wife has survived entry into the cave system, a traumatic experience that can easily cause death in itself. My source of information relies upon two individuals who have independently found ways of making an escape. They are now devoted to making life in the caves easier, and because of their presence in the world outside, I do not believe that you can completely rule Julia out as a person, able to escape. Assuming she does survive then you must be prepared to find her smaller but still very fit in mind and body. I would suggest that you don't hurry to sell up at once; for if she doesn't survive my informants will soon tell me.'

'How did she come to get mixed up in a police operation in the first place?' Gabriel sounded potentially aggressive in his casual question, even though he was already refolding his papers.

'The pilot said the two women were looking for the Commissar. I can but deduce from what I have heard that they were looking for you yourself, sir; with the joyous news that Julia was pregnant. The pilot directed them from the aircraft, but it is easy to lose your way in that place and I guess they took a wrong turning.'

Gabriel exhaled noisily, bordering on exasperation, put down his cup and sank back into the firm embrace of armchair leather. 'That puts us back right where we were.' The words came more as a prolonged gasp.

'Well not quite the same, for to continue I think you will need someone else to mind this property for you. My sister was married to a successful policeman in a respectable private enterprise, and since his company knows of my ability they have recently offered me a position as Chief Executive. You see, sir, when I was made Acting Commissar to enable you to become a high flier, I did expect it to be no more than trial period for me, after which you would relinquish the local job; but that never happened. Ever since then I have been at a disadvantage with fellow officers of the same rank and more recently with the local council. Even my recent success in solving a mystery that has baffled all police efforts for years has not received the recognition due. Is it surprising then that I begin to look elsewhere?'

Fingers drummed upon the leather upholstery as a Chief of Police listened. 'Tell me how things might have changed had you got your wish? You have always appeared so pleased to be chasing our criminal element, that mundane things like staff salaries suited you to come from somewhere else. When I last visited your commissariat you had retired into your shell and staff came to me with their problems, so I did think that my background work was still necessary and a help to you.' He summoned up an almost hurt expression chiselled deep into his florid face.

'As Commissar I should be able to afford this place whenever it becomes available, I like it here. In the interim my sister could join me here and live in this property, and as she is pleased to spend her life polishing and other domestic pursuits thus the home will hold its value as at present. Assuming there is a rent that takes account of the agreement's transitory nature, I would sell my house and she hers.'

Gabriel smiled, admiring the man's effrontery, it was the next best thing to selling it in its entirety, and the way that property values were increasing this could be a profitable deal. 'I will think it over,' he said slowly.

As Gabriel left, Claude made a point of saying that personnel matters would surely happen in his new job as well, and if there were no ambiguity about his status he would expect to take it in his stride. But whether he stayed, or acted for him privately via his new business, he would personally keep a check on Julia Masse, that was a promise.

For him there was the small matter of cleaning and putting away the tray and crockery. He retraced his steps into the library where there was a bottle of cognac, and mused over the possible future of this delightful place. Of course it was true that any reappearance of Julia would not be without significance for him as well as Gabriel. Yes there would be complications arising from that, but those were the sorts of complications that he always enjoyed most. And as if to put icing upon the cake it was the very next day that he heard of an official upgrade in his status.

46

Brussels

It was Monday of the working week that Marc had targeted to arrive at his own front door. Anxiously he knocked repeatedly and waited with his spirits rising as the interval lengthened suggesting that no one was home. With relief he turned to go, leading Hazel to the floor below and the apartment occupied by Blanche. She was delighted to see them, but here Marc had the dreaded experience of meeting someone he knew well, and experiencing a reaction to his new diminutive state that would have to be relived each time he met a friend.

Blanche took his explanation without embarrassing him too much, adding what she knew of Greta whilst expending most of her curiosity upon Hazel. 'Greta has gone back to Lutz-St-Saveur to meet you,' she said cautiously. 'I know because she rang from Lutz a good three days ago.'

'Did anyone go with her?'

The reply was again cautious, almost calculating. 'I didn't see anybody.'

Blanche had the key, so it was but a short while later that Marc was opening his own front door. On the surface things were moving much as he had expected, and the fact that Blanche had been reticent to speak about her close friend being accompanied, did even more to confirm the matter.

Greta might have only recently moved away, but she had left a formidable stack of unpaid bills behind her, and it was evident his creditors were now well into the threat stage. Marc thrust the bills aside. They all must at least wait another day for payment. Despite all this the electricity was still on, and bills declined in importance as they prepared for an immediate meal. The homecoming was celebrated with wine, but they toasted nothing beyond this, for it would be some time before they knew whether Marc's ruse had borne fruit. There was no sign of the video in the flat but its introductory note was in with the kitchen waste, suggesting the message had been received, much as envisaged.

The following day was all set to be a busy one in which Hazel would be left to her own devices. This they both knew meant shops; particularly as she had never been to Brussels before – a grey-looking place, but who knows what shopping delights existed there.

For Marc it was the familiar journey to his place of work. He was deliberately late, knowingly missing a crush of familiar faces. This however singled him out to the man on the gate, who was immediately all set to stop him. Quickly he asked to talk with his secretary, talking as if he were a representative of one supplier from the many he knew, rather than announcing himself and entailing further complications. On being handed the telephone receiver he gained entry through the gate in a place always strictly controlled.

Stella didn't immediately recognize him, remaining nervy and unsure of the little man with the familiar name who spoke virtually as Marc did and whose features looked the part. It was a big step having to accept that her boss had changed that much. 'If I were not seeing this, I would not believe it,' she said, summing up her conflicting feelings.

Marc handed her the newspaper with headlines concerned with Terry's death, and then she began to comprehend. Marc let her read it, before he added more. 'That fellow was as tall as me when he started out, so you see there are extra reasons why I shall never return properly as your boss. The same sort of reasoning tells me that if he's gone to the same location you probably will never see your present boss either.'

'That will hardly distress me I can assure you Monsieur Casserta,' said Stella emphatically but still avoiding calling him Marc as she had before. It was clear from the expression that accompanied her words that Jan was not one of Stella's favourite people.

'Now I am going to be here for a while, so for a start perhaps you will arrange for me to see these people as soon as you can.' Marc passed her a list of people he wanted to see individually and then entered his own office. Within a very short time, going over his affairs he was aware of the mess Jan had made of things, and began rectifying them in a series of memos.

Stella had worked quickly and he was soon seeing his immediate superior, the director who had previously promised help. His boss came to him, part alarmed after talking to Stella. There was the usual run-in over his size, although behind the desk and perched upon an adjustable stool he couldn't have looked all that bad, especially in respect of his director's first words.

'You can have your old job back, but you may need an assistant to do some of the running about – that is, if you take up the offer.'

Marc was flattered by this tribute, but no, he had no intention of saddling his old firm with an employee's incapacity. No indeed, he had other ideas and produced a video tape he had brought to back up his ideas, one intended for a comprehensive presentation to the directors. The tape was a copy of the one given to the jeweller, and it showed the full extent of the Green Nun treasure. Marc left his boss excited after the viewing and found him full of encouragement when he explained, his ideas. 'I want to be the company agent who sells goods to these people. They need the electrics and trust me enough for me to be sure of the trade. And because I shall relocate in that vicinity, you will not feel the need to help me with a job.'

Marc was given his grandstand late morning and put his plan to sell the Hades cave-dwellers many kinds of heavy plant in exchange for the gold treasure, pointing out that there was in reserve nothing less than a gold mine that was all ready to be exploited. From its very nature the underground complex would make a continuing demand on them for electrical plant, probably well in excess of five years. Those who were there around the boardroom table already knew of Marc's ability in the production manager role and could see no reason why he would not do this job equally well. His words and the video were soon over, and having caused quite a stir he left the boardroom, whilst his letter from a jeweller in St-Sauveur was there on the table being studied. The subsequent interest in his proposition caused much interaction among the board, and its members produced a thumping great 'yes' for his proposal. But their decision wasn't known until mid-afternoon, and that was when Stella received all the affirmative paperwork from the Managing Director's office. Accompanying this, there was now the need to see a company doctor, to support the extra insurance cover necessary in respect of his higher-paid post.

There were several gaps in his first day at work and this enabled

Marc to depart and sort out his finances about the locality. First he sold his Mini and later moved on to the rent office with ready money. There Marc discovered that the rent arrears were no problem as the flat's rent had been paid once from his bank account and then again quite recently; so intent on leaving shortly he gave notice of termination. This he followed up by paying the overdue electricity bill. Overall the outgoings had not consumed his small fortune as he expected they might and that was welcome. He arrived back to hear news of his new position in the company and also of an early doctor's appointment the next day. The new appointment had then to be celebrated with his boss, and feeling somewhat worse for wear Marc found himself a taxi home.

Marc's appointment with the insurance doctor took him across town to a private address. He satisfied the doctor's initial tests, giving normal values in respect to life-threatening conditions, so apart from his intractable size problem it was apparent that he was healthy. Then it was that the doctor got round to reflexes, and the lightweight circular spheres in Marc's scrotum that he did not relish coming to light. The man seemed puzzled that neither testicle seemed to possess the expected qualities of flesh, nor give the expected reflexes; it was something that had the doctor stroking his beard in a puzzled manner. Together they transferred to a nearby clinic containing much up to date diagnostic gadgetry. An ultrasound detected the abnormalities; Marc heard the technician say excitedly to his doctor, 'This man appears to have two undescended testicles – and a further two that have!' Marc found himself in two minds about this, whether to tell them what he thought likely or have them properly investigate what had happened to him.

It was a small bombshell to the medics, who feverishly transferred him to a radiology department and the X-ray technicians took over. He was soon finished with and returned to the perplexed doctor, who still had the duty of assessing him. In all his experience hitherto the man had never heard of anything like it before, and he was soon framing difficult questions.

Marc began a tortuous explanation of how the accident that was also responsible for his small size had rendered him insensible, and he remained that way until rescued by members of a female religious sect who had nursed him back to life. It would seem that they carried out primitive surgery as routine, which may be responsible for the oddity.

Novel to the medics, his scrotum held two spherical non-metallic objects, which were both very roughly the right size; it would seem the proper organs had simply been driven back along the way they arrived initially, and were resting against the large intestine.

'It could be a way of stopping spermatozoa formation,' said his doctor, trying to see in it some unusual kind of contraception; further explaining that without the relative cool of the scrotum, sperm would not be made.

Marc shook his head; the women believed they were infertile so this was unlikely.

'Wrestlers are said to have a similar trick to avoid injury, could that be it?

Marc knew instinctively that this could be so, as he had indeed met some rough handling. His mind moved on from there and asked, 'What about the hormones normally produced in the glands, wouldn't they be affected too?'

'Oh, I should think that they would be normal, but that would be dependent upon how the testes came to rest physically,' the doctor replied.

Marc was astonished when he realized that all those white soups were intended to enhance his masculinity, rather than replace something he lacked. Thinking beyond that he began to be aware of a deception arising from perhaps ages ago in which the rest of the men would pity the concubine instead of the reverse; he remembered early on how he was the butt of Arthur's derisory coarse humour. This smacked not only of a public relations move, but also a detrimental effect upon the man concerned and how he would regard himself, something he already knew. Did Hazel know of this? He suspected that she did know, all of the women must have known. He became preoccupied and angry at the thought, but the doctor was addressing him, and he began to attend.

'You need to have this seen to, and as I understand the position, you are ready to travel very shortly. Suppose I arrange with my local surgery to do a small operation and rectify matters at once, would you be prepared to stay in the ward overnight?'

Marc had no hesitation at all in accepting the arrangement. Hazel was out when he rang, and it was necessary to leave a message with Blanche, the briefest possible message. His new understanding had increased doubts about Hazel, but gone would be the days when she knew more of his personal plumbing than he did. Marc was determined that Hazel would be the last person he would confide in, however curious she might be. With several disagreements existing between them at the moment there was no reason why he should tell her at all. Fortuitously the remote possibility of Greta returning to the flat had given them reason to sleep apart.

The clinic did not keep him waiting for long, and in the early afternoon the operation was progressing under a local anesthetic. 'Shoehorn surgery,' the surgeon called it. He was talkative during the operation and was soon marvelling at the odd smooth yet hard properties of what Marc identified as ancient seedpods. These so-called pods were deferentially put into a specimen jar, which was locked among bizarre specimens in a cupboard to avoid the cleaners discarding them. It should be said in conclusion that the specimens were later moved to a more honoured position in the local hospital museum. Knowing nothing of the brainteaser he had set for future eyes, nor yet of the botanists who would struggle to identify the peculiar pod, Marc rejoiced in being restored as a normal male. There was of course the need to weather the effects of soporific injection, followed by the necessary painkilling tablets, given to take the edge off sometimes excruciating twinges.

Free of cares, and like the conquering hero returned, he called in at the garage where he'd sold the Mini, as he returned home. There he'd seen a number of 'homes on wheels' from which he was all set to choose the best, a new four-wheel-drive caravan. It would be fully paid for by his employer who would own it as their new representative's residence, but he alone had the choice. Among the models immediately available there was one heavy vehicle with power steering and a four-wheel drive, which suited his ideas admirably. The pedals would need redesigning, as would the driving seat before he could manage it; but the conversion would take time and that was something he must hurry along. Not that he helped over the coming week, returning repeatedly with radio equipment and parts of a hi fidelity system that mostly he fitted himself.

Hazel was back to the shopping she loved, but with dwindling resources in a country that tended to be expensive, which meant

444

that her first purchases were mainly chocolate. She had enjoyed shopping enormously in Toulouse, but did so even more here – the experience was sheer bliss. Crowds were a problem as they always would be for her, ensuring she had a poor view of everything at the height of most shoulders. Her parasol might keep a pavement space all right, but that was no help whatsoever inside popular shops, where people behind her invariably tried to trade with counter staff over her head.

Blanche came in during the early evening to deliver Marc's message, but then her curiosity encouraged her to hang around hoping to determine the relationship between the two. Her evening finished late, telling Hazel about other shopping haunts. 'Why not go together,' and on that she found agreement. But however well they got on, there was a married man at the centre of it all, and so the conversations stayed relatively near the surface.

It was a relief for Hazel to see Marc next day whilst she was having lunch with Blanche at home, a person she was now addicted to on account of the large sums that the woman spread so liberally among the shops. Marc detached her to view the caravan in the showroom workshop – much too huge and heavy Hazel thought, not that there was any chance of her sitting at the wheel. There was a beautiful streamlined caravan standing nearby, bearing her favourite colours in a two-tone splash. 'What about this one, wouldn't it be marvellous?' she enthused, only to be squashed by Marc pointing out it had to be a house on wheels intended for a company's representative and that demanded a separate bedroom upstairs. The colouring might be brash but she couldn't choose to live in anything else, the fact remained that it was going to be their house, and all costs borne by Marc's employer.

There were more days of shopping for Hazel and she was better matched for Blanche once Marc had improved their common finances. So she continued to shop with Blanche who knew all of the best places, and protected her from the worst aspects of crowd. Her shopping spree was soon curtailed, as Marc preferred to eat in the flat, and in addition to housewifely duties, he was expecting her to provision the caravan. She saw very little of Marc for he was frequently conferring with the directors of his firm and coming home a little tipsy, because social niceties seemed to take place concurrently. He split the rest of his time with the caravan, fitting the equipment that he had bought in quite separate bouts of shopping to hers. Their hectic week culminated in clearing the flat, as it was time for the road. Some of its contents were already on wheels; the rest either went to charity shops or to Blanche.

47

Upon Stony Ground

The huge luxury caravan trundled along the motorway at a steady pace. 'We have to run in the new engine,' Marc said in an off-hand sort of way when Hazel complained. Complaint came frequently to her lips these days, with him taking no notice at all. He had been beastly ever since meeting her family, and she was aware that he was unimpressed with them; but on the other hand she mused at such times they had been totally unimpressed by him. The caravan had supplanted her in his affection, a lumbering beast that he doted upon, and spent every available moment of the day with; even their meals needed to be snatched to keep driving that ugly hulk. After another day of slow motion they began to move faster, and it was evident to Hazel that they were 'run in'. Not that it made much difference to Marc for he continued to put in just as many hours at the wheel as before. The new caravan had gone to his head; he nursed it, conserved it, drooled over it, and frustratingly played recorded classical music in it.

Hazel took out the map and reasoned with him that the route taken was poor and so was his timing. 'We must stop for provisions,' she directed. 'How about the next town? You cannot go on like this, it is ridiculous.'

Marc ignored her argument, and pointed out that it was she who was charged with the provisioning of a journey that was not unreasonably long. 'You failed us and if we are short of something you will have to wait until I stop.' He ignored her further pleas just like he ignored the complaints she uttered, but did find it in himself to stop long enough for the buying of provisions. He bought in sizeable quantities, asserting his own ideas and prising Hazel off even the smallest of decision about what to buy.

These stops further fuelled Hazel's discontent, for now she felt

447

relegated to second place in even the housekeeping – yes, she was feeling decidedly bitter.

In the evenings sometimes they discussed a long term influence they might bring to bear on the society in Hades, but after agreeing that their efforts could bring about change, they disagreed about any they might make. One evening their argument was particularly upsetting to Hazel, despite being in full agreement.

'I am glad Freda didn't want your burglar alarm,' said Hazel, wanting him to forget it since his initiative seemed wasted on a woman suspicious of his help. 'For you do know, don't you, whichever man she chooses and knows its secret has signed his own death warrant.'

'You didn't use your influence to avoid her inflicting it on me or Terry though,' Marc accused her.

Hazel felt affronted, he should be grateful. 'She didn't ask me, and you wouldn't stop, even when I advised you to go.'

Marc conjured up an incredulous look. 'But I thought it was safe, as you even gave permission for Terry's involvement in the electrics of this alarm, despite knowing all of the consequences for that. You remember him, the one who was so stupefied with love for you that he just stood by like a puppy whilst the farmers besieged the village.'

'And what was so great about your exploits then?' Hazel turned on him, eyes flaming.

'I left him bothered for you by the village arch, and took a raiding party round the back, to the pool gatehouse.'

'Traitor,' choked Hazel, ready to burst into tears.

'Not a bit of it,' said Marc emphatically. 'The women chucked us right into the middle of their enemies. What were we supposed to do?'

'Why bother with their perishing burglars then?'

Marc was at once circumspect. He still retained an ulterior motive. 'I think there is someone possibly in there who given the job would richly deserve to take his chances.'

Hazel screwed a face. 'You surely don't mean Jan.'

'You are forgetting that I was teed up for execution on three different counts, if you include Patricia's intention to cut my throat. His is only a single death sentence; or a double one if they choose to make him concubine.'

448

There was a sharp intake of breath from Hazel. She did not say anything, but realized only then that one of those virile, handsome German climbers would already be being considered for execution; one more consequence of Marc's cave extras.

Marc continued on hearing her reaction, 'If we are improving their lot by our efforts, then he will also benefit; my suggestion will merely redress the balance.'

Hazel knew well that Jan deserved it; but of course Jan must look out for himself, it could be that everybody would be suited if he died in isolation. She quickly changed the subject. 'However much we do, the inhabitants of that place will remain pretty miserable, even Jan will not see sunshine unless moves are made to open it up. How everybody manages to live through life in there without sun mystifies me.'

Marc took some pleasure in correcting the errors contained within her supposition. 'They never were without the sun; for the sun causes their waterfall to work, allowing them to reconstruct its light as electricity. It also provides food for bats which fly in, so if you add their meat to the light produced, and then the droppings that crops grow on; you could say it is a very concentrated dollop of sunlight in there.' He laughed an irritating kind of laugh.

Hazel saw this as a new habit of Marc's. She was hearing too many laughs like that lately, and they always came to inflame her many discomfitures. 'You are beginning to sound just like Freda in her most boring and annoying kind of talk,' she said angrily.

'I am sure that Freda would see it just as easily. Apart from an odd stone or two, there's nothing too remote or impossible about Hades.'

'It's a weird name to choose. I wonder why they called it Hades in the first place, mused Hazel, taking up his final word principally to blunt the attacking style of speech.

'I think all cavers habitually do that,' said Marc affably. 'If it is underground, then it is in the province of "Old Nick",' and must be named as such.'

Marc turned on his new equipment, and put on the CD with which he was slowly driving her mad. The last night in Brussels they had celebrated by visiting the Opera House and enjoyed Mozart's 'The abduction from the Seraglio'. Marc thought it so appropriate, coming after the cave situation, that he not only bought it but also extended the Turkish element with Beethoven's piano variations. It had ceased to be enjoyment for Hazel, for now the music that belted out was being used as a brake on discussion.

Hazel gripped her necklace; it did always seem to come naturally into her hand at times of stress. Each time that it happened she was reminded of her gifts unthinkingly directed to Freda and Bernadette. Annita's present, arriving as it had in the reverse direction, niggled her; an omission that was causing regrets. She found a silence between outbursts of music, and voiced her thoughts loudly, making him turn down the volume. 'Do you think it would be a good idea to buy a proper saddle for Annita?'

Marc regarded her with a calculating look that was almost disapproval. 'There are a few market towns ahead, you could be lucky – but first you have to agree to my deciding where we keep it.' Marc was flexing his muscles; a proviso that he was later to enforce with Victorian severity. But having given way in just a small thing, he followed it up with one of his nastier comments. 'You can overdo putting materials into the caves you know. We don't know yet whether all that soap you sent in will come through in the spa waters that everybody drinks.' He spoke as if it were the most natural of consequences, whilst reaching out to turn the volume up.

Hazel sat there open-mouthed and horrified. 'You didn't say anything to stop me at the time,' she cried out, rocked to the foundations of her being.

Again the racket quieted as Marc replied savagely, 'At no time did you ask my opinion, so you didn't have it. Your unaccompanied knickers may not have done the spa much harm with your first volley; but second time around you personally may have succeeded in putting them out of business altogether.' The volume returned to its former level; moments later Hazel brushed by in tearful state heading for the bedroom.

To Hazel the saddle did seem big when she bought it; but it was a child's saddle, and a very good fit for her, which probably meant it actually was quite small.

Marc did not appreciate the logic of that, nor yet her statement that the expensive leather ought to accompany them into prime living space. 'It must be stowed away,' he said.

All attempts to make him see sense failed, and a frustrated Hazel ended up sobbing upon the bed. Not that he ever came up to pacify her these days, all love and desire seemed to have vanished from him. Why he even stayed firmly to his side of the bed every night. He was a creep after all, and his reference to her lost clothing not damaging the spa much was proof. For in knowing about that, he must have been listening at the door when that nice policeman Commissar Brie interviewed her. He was sneaky, devious and a traitor, pity that she had not seen him in his true colours before. Freda had him to rights when she refused to talk to him. This thought appealed to her and she vowed to be less cooperative.

They stopped at a heliport on route, and Marc sought out contractors keen to airlift his motors; then having practically clinched a deal, he added one further stipulation to facilitate the meeting of his commitments. Emerging from the offices, he spent a while lashing that bulky saddle to the roof of the caravan, and soon there it gleamed with sunlight bouncing off transparent plastic wrappings. The whole thing now securely held in place with spare rope gleaned from the friendly airport business. And back on the road they were making good progress, even appearing to have time in hand; in fact later the same day they were meeting intermittent rain on the road to the Cirque de Gravanie.

They swept past the Lutz turn-off, despite Hazel sitting there with her map hollering, 'Turn right – turn right!' Hazel could hardly believe it as she watched both the cave turn-off and the town turn-off disappear in quick succession. She knew Marc had taken the wrong road, but infuriatingly he just laughed at her and drove on regardless. Several more miles of hill road elapsed before Marc took to a side road, and having passed by a busy quarry continued on for several hundred yards over a row of decidedly large stones embedded in the road before he stopped. Such a row of permanent bumps were particularly relished by Marc who had purchased the caravan with that sort of rough track in mind; and having passed his test strip by he stopped filled with appreciation, able now to conclude that the caravan's suspension worked very well.

'Admit that you were wrong,' Hazel stormed. 'Now you will have to go all the way back again.'

Marc laughed his annoying laugh. 'You can if you like; but if you are coming with me, then on we go. It is a question of whether you see your future on your own, or with me. The alternative is fine by me – just take your bags and go!'

Hazel looked at him as if he were crazy. A flurry of rain spattered the side window in the silence that followed. He meant every word; she could see it written in the way his face was set. 'You are despicable! The last thing I want is a life with you,' she jerked the words out angrily, threw back the driving partition door and flounced out. 'You must be out of your tiny mind!' The words receded as she pounded her way up the stairs, and arriving there commenced banging doors and fittings.

Marc grinned as he sat there, backing up the caravan to where the quarry wheel tracks ground deeply. Hearing the continuing sound of drawers being slammed in the bedroom compartment, he could be sure she was packing. Grabbing a plastic sack as protection from the worst of the rain, he reached up from the cab and released the near end of the saddle. Dismounting he climbed the footholds at the back end after which, the saddle complete with wet wrapping struck the stones and lay gleaming in the dusk. Marc returned to face a wrathful Hazel, humping down her cases. Picking them up Marc stacked them neatly for her close to the saddle, and waved a hand to the side and back. 'There is a quarry over there, and drivers galore must pass here. It is a good place for you to be conveyed anywhere that your desire might take you.' He climbed back into the cab, slammed the door with a flourish and shouted through the window. 'I wish you every success with your mission.' The caravan travelled forwards, and stopped right where it had originally stopped: Marc was all set to camp overnight.

Hazel turned into the wind, which currently threatened her umbrella, pulled it low over her head and sat upon the cases tight in to the saddle. She was keen to protect her legs from the patter of rain. A feeling of despair hit her as the huge, ugly vehicle pulled away. Emotions settled uneasily because it stopped again, quite near really. 'Pig,' she shouted repeatedly, with the open-air draughts swirling about her. He was staying to gloat, well let him, for she had no intention of moving until there was some let-up in the rain. Surely it was more to do with his business they were going, the saddle was an afterthought, in fact she didn't need to go at all. Did the track just double round in a D shape and put him back on the road to Lutz? Was he just dumping her? She tried vainly to see ahead through the gloom and then sat there pondering in the gathering dusk, trying to work it out.

Marc looked through the bedroom rear window – yes, she was

weathering the rain well, much as he thought she would, despite it coming down a lot heavier now. The fact was underlined by the rain starting to pelt down with increased vigour on the roof and making a thunder with its drumming. He had an inevitable stray thought, that he would not sleep so well tonight without something soft on the roof to dampen it, or her warmth in the bed. He watched Hazel; at least she was not walking back the way they had come. Marc felt a longing for the lone figure outside and a lump came into his throat. He put on his Beethoven to cover the drumming, for he didn't want to be reminded of how wet she must be – through to the skin by now probably. Turn the mind to something more pleasurable like food, for after a long day's drive he really ought to consider a meal. Marc moved towards the stove.

He was mad, she had been right to label him so from the start. Hazel fumed to herself as the rain hit her in gusts like she was adrift on a raft at sea. The fanatical piano noise sounded through the gathering dusk, causing her to eye the shadowy hulk of the caravan, spilling vapours into a grey evening sky through its chimney. Interrupting her gaze the rumble of a heavy truck crunching the stones met her ear, and she turned to face it, waving her free arm with considerable vigour. The truck pulled over, and she waited whilst the driver wound down his window. She shouted the local names she knew, and received an unintelligible babble of Spanish in reply, but noted the fellow was pointing quite the opposite way. She waved him on with the wind turning her umbrella inside out, and by the time she righted it the truck was gone. As though to underline the nonsense of this procedure, torrential water was running from hair into the eyes and then trickling down the side of her nose.

Surely Marc had motors left in the caves, and he must meet his deadline or not sell them at all. That aspect hadn't properly hit her before; more she had seen it as her need to continue helping her friends in the caves. By comparison his was a whole livelihood at stake, and this opposed to her earnest desire to get there for more personal reasons. He would have to be there for sure. Hazel's head jerked in the direction of the inelegant mismatch of colours splashed upon the ugly vehicle steaming nearby, checking it over once again. No it had not moved, and what's more was spewing out that manic piano music again. It was turning the sound she had enjoyed in the theatre into something twisted, and so very like him. The smell of frying bacon had her nose turned into the wind. The sod, he was doing it deliberately; duplicating a mouth-watering experience that she had once admitted to him when they were friends.

There came a knocking on the side of the caravan. Marc hurried to the door and there beheld the face of his soaking wet damsel.

'If you are having tea before you leave, I wouldn't mind joining you.' Hazel made her intention to come up out of the wet clear, because in the course of her trying experience outside she had decided there must be better moments to part from Marc.

'There's plenty here, I should be delighted if you would join me.' Marc sounded very formal, his voice just clearing the music as he invited her in.

Bedraggled and dripping with water, Hazel changed into Marc's dressing gown, noting that the sound volume subsided before she reached the table. 'I could tell, even back there, that you were a bad judge of portions, and came in to save you getting over fat,' she said, tucking into the several piles of best bacon, stacked on a central plate.

Having eaten, Marc backed the van towards the suitcase heap, and flung plastic sacks down; her belongings would keep for the morrow, he personally had no intention of getting wet.

Hazel was soon pointing out that it was his deadline at the caves, not hers, so if he were merely using this as a campsite, then she would stay awhile.

'I decided to take a look at the collapsed side first,' he said gently.

'We needed to see Monsieur Zoub tomorrow,' Hazel reminded.

'Oh that! I sent him a letter; we are to talk on the radio at 4 pm tomorrow.'

Hazel shook her fist at him as the inevitable laugh hit the air, but it was not as aggravating as others she had weathered. Appreciating the softening of his attitude, she eyed an extra pile of fried bacon still on the cooker, and obviously used to tempt her. Hazel was undecided whether he had been playing cat and mouse games, or had simply taken pity on her. The ensuing conversation did not help either. 'I think that the bacon was overdone,' she disdainfully remarked, covering both the cooking and the amount under one head.

'It's not bad as bait though,' was his cheerful rejoinder and that had her realize he was not in the least put out about how she saw it.

Marc realized his remark was a mite inconsiderate, and wanted to ease the atmosphere a little, so he told her more of the story. 'Freda wanted me to correct the cave system maps leading to Hades, and that I did; but to my surprise they also contained shorter routes leading to the Spanish side, that is the main reason for going.'

'Aren't you taking a bit of a risk? There are only three days left.'

'Oh, I do like a good gamble,' said Marc and laughed his infuriating laugh.

The incident had not changed much at all, and Marc was treated to all of the concentrated ire that it is woman's natural ability to impart. Hazel knew that he was having her on, there had to be a catch in it somewhere, or there was something he was not telling her. If she had to spend time with a madman and his abduction music – it was only to be justified, for as long as there was a deluge going on outside. After that where he went would be no concern of hers. The double bed in the roof of the caravan saw Hazel the hedgehog resurrected, despite the fact she lacked a nightie, her back made clear her present opinion of him.

Marc let her sulk, what he had in mind was entirely reasonable, as Hazel might find out in good time. He was following up something specific even though it must be over twenty years old, something that hopefully had not altered with time. Marc remembered Maria more tenderly now for she had been one of his more considerate loves. There were many things she had been quite ready to tell him in the secluded closeness of their evenings together. She had told him much of her life before the caves, not knowing that his interest was sparked off from curiosity, following seeing the women's map and realizing that the additions to the map – the ones suggesting a Spanish route – were hers.

455

48

Shangri-La

Marc rose at first light to collect Hazel's things, and left handfuls of waste cooked bacon in their place, an act which brought down two huge carnivorous birds that inhabited the air spaces of this mountainous region, the ones that spend their day wheeling about the sky. He checked over the saddle's waterproof envelope, and finding it intact, hauled the lot with his ropes; tied so as to move the big package quietly over the roof. And well before Hazel had managed to put a sleepy head out of the bed covers, the van was jolting on its way.

The sense of motion soon had her peeping round the upper curtains. All chance of dismounting had gone, for they were climbing steadily, and she could now say for sure that the track did not swing round in the D shape envisaged last night – another forlorn hope demolished. She saw it as a virtual kidnapping, for she had not said she was going with him, and must now consider herself consigned to go with him – a prisoner in a box on wheels rattling through the mountains. No point in complaining, for the act was both deliberate and premeditated. Any complaint, she reasoned, could very likely result in her being set down even more remotely than yesterday. To hold on, and await an opportunity to escape still appealed to her as the most sensible course.

She ate a meagre breakfast before joining Marc in the driving compartment, their conversation virtually non-existent. The caravan was set on a dwindling track that was elevating all the time, and before midday they were in Spain. No customs post, just a sign that displayed the information on a board to one side of the bumpy stone track. Vegetation here was interspersed with rubble, the foliage being far too sparse to cover it; but in fact there was so much loose rubble and stones around that the track was presenting a surface perfectly suited to the kind of vehicle they possessed.

456

Sitting there Hazel had time to appreciate the robust and highly damped nature of their mobile home, as the many out of line stones punished the tyres, leaving some smaller ones to pop out noisily as from a gun. Such easy progress was not to last, and later that morning the stony road gave way to a higher proportion of dirt track, one that was heavily scored through by water running off the mountain. Ruts, part full of yesterday's rain, punctuated their way forward.

Soon Marc was preoccupied in crossing even deeper furrows, using various lengths of wood taken from the rubbish at the side of the track to smooth their path. Before long he had a collection of timbers dragging behind the van for sorting the bigger ruts out. Occasionally they passed a faded notice 'Privato', sometimes with wreckage suggesting past habitations owned this as a service road. But such notices were always in bad condition and Marc doubted that they still meant anything, especially as the road must be impassable to an ordinary motorcar. It was arid, little grew from a poor soil, just tiny shrubs or the occasional badly nourished bush. Low gear now and climbing steadily; a process he had to interrupt for his radio contact.

During the broadcast exchange, Marc entered the value of each piece on a duplicate of the photograph he had posted to Monsieur Zoub from Brussels. He hardly needed to add the sums together for it was evident that the total was well beyond a hundred million euros, a finding that left him feeling triumphant; the promises to his employer had been justified. He pulled the plugs, and leaving the vehicle still at an awkward angle on the up slope he broke into a large bottle of Chablis, which Hazel steadfastly refused to drink. Swigging the best wine they had on board, Marc continued celebrating until carefree and part inebriated he decided to reach a spot with less tilt.

Hazel had begun making the bed, but the jerk as they started, and the horizon tilting about the windows soon had her feeling unsafe – downstairs her drunken madman drove. She rushed to a lower level convinced she should have left much sooner. 'The road will sooner or later level itself out more,' Marc said in an overloud voice, his eye keeping a good watch on the mountains ahead for something beyond mere road furrows. The dirt track did level out and widened at the same time, although in the evening light it was difficult to tell exactly where the track was.

It was getting dark when Marc excitedly pointed ahead and above, he could see red brown stains on the rock face. 'See that landmark Hazel? It shows that we are in the right area. I think that we can stop for the night here.'

Hazel looked at the rocky landscape quite unimpressed; this was just another dusty stop, amid dreary grey rock with its crystalline content glinting in the fading sun. Their vehicle had been catching the sun for some time now, trapping the heat and causing the air conditioning to function. Despite fully appreciating the kitchen's stable atmosphere, Hazel felt miserable. She was tired from a long day's travel in low gear, worsened considerably by the knowledge that each successive mile took her further away from her intended destination. The unappetizing meal she roused herself to prepare came and went in silence, after which a lacklustre Hazel moped. Marc found alternative music to serenade her on his new radio, but Hazel still did not thaw out and there came another hedgehog night, be it a more comfortable one in a nightdress.

Next morning the rains came, and a sudden mountain storm flushed so much water over the windscreen that Marc couldn't move. Hazel was in bed and remained there, what point was there in getting up to this? She weathered his energetic opening of all the curtains without so much as a movement, relieved only when his footsteps retreated. Rain lashed her brilliantly lit cube, with her reclining deeply relaxed upon feathery softness, able now to snuggle down and drift dreamily into the light grey void of a totally uncharted world.

Freda looked down from a long way off, calling her by name; it was a stern face and a most authoritative voice, repeatedly calling 'Hazel.' Then she came close before shearing away again; perhaps repelled by her chosen recipient's involuntary shudder as she heard the mere fragment that followed her name. 'Hazel – remember your duty as a Queen.' Turning her head, she thrust her face deep into pillow, burrowing to be away from a vision that filled her with such chill apprehension. There were now several bright jellyfish floating in front of her eyes. Which way were they up? She couldn't tell or even which way up she was herself. The pattern faded as she struggled to stay with it, all of the time losing her battle to conjure up Freda's face again; feeling she needed to be more receptive and wanting to see her again in friendly guise. The sky lit all those background windows so brightly now she was stretching her imagination to search it, and coming perilously near to wakefulness as she failed to conjure up anything. Now it seemed the glass was unaffected by her fancy and displayed a wide stretch of puffy clouds without hint of face or fish.

She lay in contemplation, the mind still fuzzy and unsure. She realized she was more awake now after the shock of repelling the Freda vision, knowing the next words to come must contain the word 'manning'. The execution of her man was still wanted, even if she had resisted hearing it. But what now, was she still one of them, much as the 'green nun' had stayed committed? If she was still inclined to do battle for the colony she must view the man as a subversive, who could so easily slip guns through to the men. The man came from top management; a fact she had since learned and the thought left her in doubtful about engaging in a battle of wits with someone deemed intelligent. She was now thoroughly disillusioned with Marc, and the memory of his traitorous con-fession on the way here drove her into glorious flights of revol-utionary thought. Ideas of taking the caravan by force stormed through her mind in one heroic stampede. That she could so easily do; but then reversing a caravan on the mountainside or finding her way through the tunnels was not something she would be very good at.

No, she was fully awake now, and realizing the Freda dream was no more than a summing up of her own uncertainties; it was they that had to be sorted out. Even though Marc had clearly declared his opposition to the women, he still had brought her along with him knowing full well that she might counter any tricks; so perhaps he wasn't that committed. On the other hand it had not passed Hazel's notice that he was attempting to promote Red from the outside, the one man Freda distrusted most of all. Even taking that consideration seriously, anything underhand was severely limited because Red spoke in a local English dialect, and from this she concluded he was too primitive to have any other tongue. If that were so any plotting could be overheard; and even beyond that, anything passed in must first pass her eyes. As Marc's bigger, stronger companion she was easily the more able fighter of the two, and because of her superiority in this she was confident the man would remain non-partisan whilst under her eye.

Why should she feel just like she'd been kidnapped, when all of

459

the time it was she who was able to dictate exactly what was done; it was only in recent days that she had taken a back seat. But that was so easily reversed, she could remain that way until such a time that he began to jeopardize her friends' safety and then she should act. Spiritually she was part of the women's world, be they savages or not, she was still one. Assuming execution became a necessity, she would need to live up to her words, but until that time she could act just as civilized as any other lady. The Commissar had thought she needed to adjust and he was quite right, she was proud still to be one of them; the fact that her dress had adjusted was simply surface self-preservation. Visions of her rounder face set in one of those lovely new dresses occupied her mind, remembering how everyone said she looked a beauty; men were swayed by that and without doubt even tallish men had looked her way very wickedly. Marc was by comparison too small for normal life, he had only her, and she had never knowingly dressed up for him.

Purposefully she pressed her face back into the pillow, keeping it there, though by now she was long awake. Just as she had rejected the grey dresses, maybe Marc had rejected her because he wanted to erase any thought of being a concubine. Surely that was the point of all his horrid music; for however unpalatable her presence was, he could not function very well without the assistance of someone. She rose and dressed in one of her more appealing outfits.

Rain had lashed the caravan for nearly six hours, after which the sun shone brightly, as if intending to erase every drop. Marc having eaten looked at his watch, could they still make it? He debated whether or not he was likely to reach a wide enough space to put reserve plans into operation, because a lot depended upon those furrows he could see brimming with water.

Hazel was entering the cab, a splash of colour in the background and seemingly a refreshed one. She sounded more interested in what he was attempting to do, and pressed him to tell what he had in mind. Marc put the vehicle into gear. 'There is a fault in the rock somewhere along here, one that we shouldn't be able to miss. According to Maria, it looks like a temple, with big columns like cats' paws at the door.'

Hazel decided to watch out for it, but there were so many rusty marks in the rocks above her that she felt there was a host of cartoon characters up there. The best course was to ignore them altogether and leave it for Marc to sort out. She relaxed in the seat, having sorted out her own priorities with the help of a little dreaming, she felt supremely at ease now as his passenger.

But rounding a bend they both saw an unmistakable rock formation and neither had any doubts about those paw-like appendages on lower parts of the pillars where they narrowed to claws. Whatever it was, was still distant and the track had started to climb with the ruts widening appreciably; part-filled narrow ruts had been relatively easy, but now the uncertain depth of each one often meant getting down to look before continuing. It slowed them for two hours, and only then did they reach a line of derelict buildings that marked a deserted village. Many of the dwellings stood on mounds, the worst of which had crumbled to be mere outlines on a base, even the best exposed a wealth of lime mortar at anything above window height. The going became easier, benefiting from having entered a village and getting a choice of way, but on the debit side the road was strewn with building debris. Aside from the buildings the area looked to be on a wide and fertile strip of land, a sight which delighted Marc, who saw his back-up plan now as feasible. To Hazel it spelt desolation, and that they were on their own, for certainly no one had been up here for years.

Marc stopped the engine and put the brake on. 'Are you ready to go?' he asked, picking up a pair of heavy duty plastic sacks – so useful for popping out into showers.

'Is that it, up there?' Hazel asked, angling for more explanation.

Marc was ready to explain, and did so as they climbed the steep slope carrying in addition some empty water containers. They approached from below the lion paw shapes, which lost all characteristic by simply becoming too high to see properly. 'Maria came in this way,' he said. 'Her villa is only just up the road. Together she and her husband collected unusual mushrooms in these caves, for she was cooking like a fanatic even then. The caves she told me were nothing as caves go; but they contained fresh spring water as well as choice fungi that made their visits an essential routine. That's what she said; and apart from our own need for fresh water, I still need to check that nothing has changed.'

They arrived at the mouth of the cave, which had already lost any appeal it presented from a distance. Weathered basalt columns towered above their heads. It was rock that stood out from the mountain cave on either side, and looked more robust than the rocks all around. Underfoot felt wet; a clear stream of water created a wide puddle less than a centimetre deep across their path, exiting the cave and flowing swiftly down hill. As they entered a dark pool lay at their feet, and evidently the puddle's source, because the flow seemed to have wetted everything from that corner to the left of the cave entrance.

Handing his wet-weather protection to Hazel, Marc became engrossed in filling all of their containers with fresh water. Then he turned his attention to her and led onwards to the depths of the cave where they were confronted by a maze of blank walls. His torch flashed here and there but although Hazel looked attentively she failed to see a hole big enough to lead elsewhere. Nevertheless Marc seemed satisfied, nodding his head as he peered closely at the earthy rocks; all with the same wet appearance and sporting a rich harvest of unattractive gnarled brown fungi. Distinctive they might be, but appetizing they were not, Hazel wanted nothing to do with them as she was definitely off that kind of food. Besides that it was a thoroughly unpleasant place, and reminiscent of the old bat cave except for a smaller size. Tugging at his hand she was surprised that he came away so easily. Marc might have seen what he wanted, but was not letting on to Hazel despite some small interrogation. Soon they were carrying the fresh spring water down to their home. Marc told her mostly about the recommendation that it would make very good tea.

The caravan had travelled just half a mile before a clump of trees appeared, heralding a splash of more greenery that partially hid the way ahead. 'This is it,' shouted Marc. 'Maria and her husband planted them. Let's park under the trees.' The trees, which looked less healthy close up, proved just too low for such a vehicle and Marc soon gave up the attempt in disgust. He was raring to go and too full of excitement to park tidily, so he turned off the engine and leapt down. He was soon calling words of encouragement to rouse his less than enthusiastic partner who appeared stuck to her seat.

'Come on, we have got to find Maria's villa!'

He was just as sure as Hazel was doubtful, and in the event neither one was wholly right. At road level, and just beyond some spindly trees, stood an arch with barely enough room behind it for even a garden shed. The light filtering through the trees made it clear that there was no such thing as a building behind. Marc's face took on an anguished look as cautiously he passed the arch, but to his instant relief he discovered a spiral stairwell of decorative ironwork descending behind it. There was a black metal nameplate raised above the arch; Hazel read out a house name – Shangri-La. After this her curiosity was fully engaged. But then Marc insisted she wait whilst he went right down the stairs, and he took his time about it, examining all of the support structures as he went.

She came when called, and found him waltzing about in the nearest room; it was a very extensive one, with a kitchen off to one side and a bedroom upon the other. The bedroom was a wreck, and still dripping with water from this morning's downpour; water trickled off a roof gaped open to show branches and an expanse of sky. Plaster had fallen down onto the bed; a place where brown, shredded linen suggested rodents had chewed, and beyond even that the remnants had been subject to either insect or mould attack. 'That's one of their trees that did not last the course,' Marc laughed.

Large windows covered in cobwebs were duly wiped in the main living room, giving a most stupendous view of a wide if featureless landscape stretching across the living room's entire width like some huge panoramic picture. But not only that, if you looked downwards there was a Spanish garden immediately below with terraces packed in a multitude of wild flowers. Standing proud was an ornate fountain without water; the customary sounds or splash had obviously departed from it long ago. The sight of so much blossom so delighted Hazel that she tore about the house looking for a way down to the lower level. Marc was not far behind, but with a more sedate movement critically scanning the ironwork steps as he did so. Hazel met him in the largely self-set flowering wreck of a garden and threw her arms about him. 'Thank you, darling, I don't know how I came to deserve all this, for I have been horrid to you. You must really love me, to put up with my moods. But I can promise you better ones, if you still think me worth the effort?'

'Do you think you could live in sin with a cable firm rep?' queried Marc. This he followed up with another one of his annoying laughs, which did much to decrease any romantic impact that it might have carried.

'I could give it a try. I like the bloke, but not the laugh – it will have to go.'

'Try convincing me tonight – how about that?' Marc set her a target.

Hazel looked radiant, and as flushed with excitement as ever he'd seen her. 'That's one date I can promise you, sweetheart. There will be the most magnificent meal you ever had, and then there's me as aphrodisiac afterwards, for I'd like to be the relish that tops the lot.' The soft tender love in her eyes matched the warmth in her voice; but the moment was soon evaporating in her present mood for she was re-focusing over his shoulder on those attention-grabbing self-set flowers. The root cause of her outburst and source of this emotion couldn't remain under wraps for much longer. 'Do you think we could mind this plot for Maria? It would stop deteriorating if we lived here,' she murmured in his ear.

'The mortar is barely holding on in places,' he rejoined, looking critically in the direction of cracks in both brickwork and mortar bordering the bottom ironwork steps. Ever wary of womanly wiles and their temporary abstractions, he was not easily going to be bounced into reconstructing the place on mere promises.

'Isn't it all right then darling?' Hazel said it with an obvious note of mock concern in her voice, but pitched seductively low, instantly transferring his attention from mere bricks and mortar. Her strong arms wrapped round him, intentionally causing him to collapse on to the bottom step under the greater weight of her body. The step promptly snapped as it suddenly took their combined impact. She hung on exerting her extra height and weight, exhilarated to feel its full extent, cuddling and kissing without let-up. Knowingly and sensuously she initiated love, which spread through him like a fire. It was now his turn to set her pulses racing, and temper her mind into more physical acts of love – that was, until the step began to sink further into mud and meet some very fresh and watery soft mud below.

'It can stay missing until I do some cement work.' Marc broke free to rise and look at the extent of his challenge, and to the otherwise intact staircase. 'It's not bad at all, this building, considering Maria must have been away for over twenty years. If I decide to work on it, then we could live here. Forget the garden: what do you think of the house?'

'Oh yes please Marc. I'd love to live here.' She was bubbling over now with enthusiasm. 'Can we go to Toulouse for curtains? There are lovely materials there.'

'Hold your horses,' laughed Marc. 'We are caravan dwellers for the moment, this job will take time.' He led the way towards a much safer construction, inadequately tested so far, but which he knew to be a superior kind of bed mounted on four wheels. Hazel's newly exhibited depths of emotion had to be plumbed and now needed some urgent attention.

As evening supervened, a more extravagant aroma of cooking wafted on the breeze, delicate and subtle, in fact nothing at odds with their re-discovered bliss – all vestiges of bacon thoroughly erased. Soft music barely impinged upon the locality, and the lights continued unabated into the night as loving soporific humans neglected them.

The sun shone brightly as they prepared for a full day's expedition, although Marc did not believe that today's limited process of agreement over trading plant for gold need take too long. As he went to change Hazel raked over the collection of torches he had assembled all with new batteries, there were far too many; he's overestimating again, she decided and finally chose the combination Marc had stolen from her bedroom. Males tended to be bad judges of everyday requirements so she would prompt him with good advice. 'Put plenty on, it will be chill in there,' Hazel called out to him, laughing as she remembered giving the same advice to Terry, and the lack of substance that finally materialized. Nothing of hers need be stinted this time, for she had shopped in Brussels with caves in mind, and the bulky absorbent linings that she now wore left not even an ankle uncovered. A smart leather jacket and slacks completed the outfit, all of which was soon in place and being studied in a handy mirror. She nodded approvingly, just the thing for caves. By comparison Marc was dressing down and very sparingly. She smiled, for it was just as pointless telling him as it was telling Terry, amazing how advising men was always a waste of breath.

Marc took the wheel and drove to a point directly below the caves; soon they were struggling uphill encumbered in the main by Hazel's saddle.

Marc stopped just inside the cave mouth, and began to strip, putting all of his clothes into one of the plastic bags. 'As I was telling you, Maria and her husband collected fungi, carrying away spring water from this pool. But in a year of drought they found the level of this pool had fallen by over a metre. Reaching for the water had her husband realize the water hole was more complicated than they had thought. Entering it he was able to bob his head up out of another hole – ahead there were more passages.' Marc talked on, ignoring Hazel's gasp of dismay. 'Inside they found an interesting lot of caves, and these they could not resist exploring. This they continued to do even after the water rose again, so it was inevitable then that they would arrive in Hades at some stage of the exploration.'

Hazel looked into its black expanse and swore. What she had planned as a nicely comfortable and warm expedition did not include a naked entry into caves through ice-cold water; but there facing her was the reality, black and distinctly cold. 'I must get my towel. You didn't tell me I'd have to swim in that,' she said angrily.

'It is in the other plastic bag,' he answered, stripping off his clothes and putting everything in his favourite plastic sack that normally functioned as an umbrella. Flattening and tying its end to be ready he slipped into the water, and found his feet did not bottom in the deep stream, which surged past him. He part hung on to the nearby rocks and part trod water, as he swept the torch over the space ahead, discovering a dark space nearby beyond the sill slab his head currently rested against. His free hand reached towards it and broke the surface, warily his head followed it until with relief his face met the still air of a cave system; the flat rock over his head had given way to a wide opening that could now be probed with the torch. He breathed further deep gasps of relief.

An arm became visible to Hazel, who watched it anxiously crooking over the edge and back into view. Marc was but a moment away, and his head followed quickly bobbing up in the pool. 'The space back there echoes, so it has to be the right place. Be careful not to get swept along when you come in.' He then instructed her to pass the bag of torches to him and set down one that blinked every few seconds on a slab near the pool. 'I suppose you could pass that saddle to me.'

Hazel had a struggle to submerge it because the saddle shape itself made hard work of exhausting the package; but after a while she saw it lodged under the rock and being dragged forwards by

Marc. Hazel swore and swore again as she dragged off all her felted linings, stuffing them into the plastic sack with her towel, they would be difficult to put on again the other side, even given the fact he had provided a small towel. Entering the icy cold water provoked even more unladylike language.

Marc shivered inside, and seeking a small towel rolled up in one of his plastic bags, he quickly dressed and was ready for Hazel's arrival. There was already a torch directed at the water surface to help Hazel find it, but it was an angry woman that joined him he could tell; even so she was keeping her grievances to herself. He congratulated himself on the fact that her attitude appeared more compliant, even if she did make him wait unduly whilst she got ready. A sparse selection of clothes now covered her body, donned in a light that flickered intermittently, as it would for the rest of the day.

Whilst she dressed Marc explained that they had until midday to succeed, after which he had arranged back-up with the heliport, assuming they might want picking up. Feelings of rage welled up in Hazel, but again she suppressed them. Recollecting the wealth of suspicions she had about him not being utterly dependent upon finding a Spanish way, it ought not to have been a surprise. But shock it was, for there had been no sign of this in their preparations on the way here – if she had known this fact then it would have put an entirely different complexion on nearly everything.

His voice droned on about the few minutes' lift it would take to put them down near the beehive cave, but she wasn't listening. Should she forgive him? To forgive him, she felt, could take much serious bribing; but if she let the matter go he would escape punishment altogether and make it more difficult to put all of her resolutions into practice. Hazel was becoming rather attracted to the former alternative, and resolved to maintain her huff, at least until the message got through.

They walked for over an hour carrying the saddle between them, before Marc entered caves that were at all familiar, putting down flashing lights to point their direction at every intersection. Arriving in the cavern, he sought out his hiding place for the camcorder, it was a tunnel Claude would have labelled simply 'enquiries desk'. The playback revealed images that were sufficiently close for identification, as two figures busily hauled plant –

the video record ceased when they had rounded the bend of the tunnel dead ahead. The fact that those figures did not come back again indicated to Marc that his plot had been successful.

Well before the agreed time, Hazel and Marc combined forces to drag away the generator on its canvas sheet, which still protruded from the sentry bend. It was fortunate that the rear ropes had been left tied on the canvas, helping both retrieval then and the loading task later on – their careful planning had paid off.

From various hiding places in their previous base tunnel, Marc retrieved the gold-plated trolley and then the telephone handset. The trolley was set upon its inward course and passed through the sentry at precisely 4 pm.

Very shortly after this, the telephone vibrated into life and Jackie's voice came over loud and clear.

'Do not send any more reject people. Hades is full!'

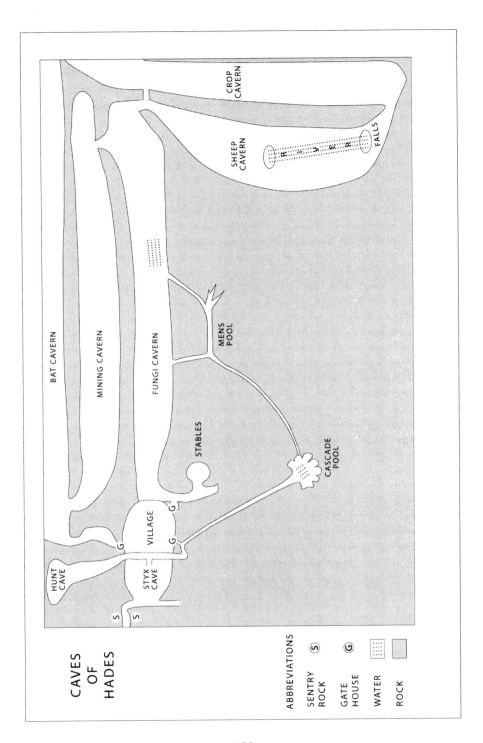

CAVES
OF
HADES

BAT CAVERN

MINING CAVERN

FUNGI CAVERN

CROP
CAVERN

SHEEP
CAVERN

RIVER

FALLS

MENS
POOL

STABLES

CASCADE
POOL

VILLAGE

HUNT
CAVE

STYX
CAVE

ABBREVIATIONS

SENTRY
ROCK   (S)

GATE
HOUSE   (G)

WATER

ROCK

469